MY DEMON HUNTER

Praise for

ⅢY FUNNY DEⅢON VALENTINE

"A spicy supernatural good time. With endearing characters and humor baked into a fun and unique love story. I'm so excited for the next one!"

—Hannah Nicole Maehrer, #1 *New York Times* bestselling author of *Assistant to the Villain*

"Holy hot grand piano keys! This one hooked me from the first chapter and didn't let go until the very end. Ash was so sweet and lovable but still had the vibe of a man who would bring you the head of your enemies! So perfect, basically. Eva was strong and held her own. Combined, these two make for a deliciously devilish romance."

—Kimberly Lemming, *USA Today* bestselling author of *That Time I Got Drunk and Saved a Demon*

BY AURORA ASCHER

The Hell Bent Series

Hell Bent

MY DEMON HUNTER

Aurora Ascher

KENSINGTON
PUBLISHING CORP.

kensingtonbooks.com

To my own hunter from the sky . . .
Thank you for encouraging me to reach for the stars.

PROLOGUE

Two months ago . . .

THE DEMON HOWLED IN TERROR AS IT WAS DRAGGED BY crumpled wings down the dark passage. Its claws scratched futilely at the cold floor, seeking purchase on the cracks between stones. Occasionally, it would succeed, finding something to grasp, but its strength was no match for the one who held it.

Mishetsumephtai gritted his teeth and tightened his claws around the leathery appendages as he stalked steadily onward. He felt no sympathy for his prey. This was what happened when the rules were broken. This was the consequence of insubordination. If the demon had wished to avoid this fate, then it shouldn't have disobeyed.

A memory surfaced. *He perched atop a wind-beaten tree, the briny ocean scent stinging his nose, and peered through a window into the house below. A demon entered the kitchen and wrapped his arms around a small human female—*

With a jerk of his head, Mist shoved the image away and returned his focus to the shrieking traitor on his way to face punishment. *This is what happens when the rules are broken*, he repeated like a mantra. *This is the consequence of insubordination.*

He had learned this lesson the hard way, many times over.

The tall double doors swung open as he approached the throne room, indicating that his mistress was already aware of his arrival. But of course she was. Nothing went on in her lair without her knowledge.

Paimon, Queen of Hell, lounged upon her throne in all her dark glory, great wings draped over the sides, clawed hands linked atop her leather-clad knee. Beside her, legs tucked neatly under its sand-colored body, her camel steed, Shaheen, surveyed the room with a glowing red gaze. The skeletal, cadaverous beast was her constant companion and often spat at or bit anyone who showed the slightest disrespect to his mistress.

Approaching her throne, Mist tossed his blubbering prey at Paimon's feet and then melted back against the stone wall to await orders. She showed no surprise at his successful return, not that he expected her to. He was the Hunter. He was always successful.

Except for one time. But he would never tell a soul about that.

"So you thought to escape me," Paimon said to the demon at her feet. When her thin lips parted, four fangs were visible on her upper jaw, another four on the lower. Neither feminine nor masculine, Paimon's features were striking, but she had never been famed for her looks. She was known instead for her viciousness and unswerving loyalty to Lucifer.

"N-never, Mistress, I was o-only—"

"*Silence.*"

Instant quiet fell upon the hall at the word uttered with the Queen of Hell's great power.

"We had a deal."

The trapped demon trembled beneath her stare. Her voice was so devoid of warmth, icicles formed on the cavernous roof and the edges of the throne and pillars. The only light in the black stone castle came from the flickering candles of the chandelier high above, suspended by thick chains.

"You swore to serve me."

Despite his diligent self-reminders of the futility of rule breaking, Mist couldn't blame the wretch for trying to escape. "Serving" Paimon was not something he would wish on his worst enemy. Even he, as her most esteemed and powerful servant, lived a pitiful existence in a dank cave when he was not out hunting.

Consequently, he lived to hunt. It consumed him. He practically salivated at the chance to leave his cave and stalk and corner his prey. It mattered not to him who they were or what they had done. He only wanted the opportunity to be untethered for a while, for the mad dog to be unleashed, tasting the only form of freedom he had ever known.

"And I m-meant it, of course, Mistress," the demon whimpered. "I w-was only—"

Paimon talked over him as if he hadn't spoken. "And yet you thought to run from me? You thought you could lie to me? Trick me?"

"N-never, Mistress—"

"Silence!"

This time, the silence that fell was accompanied by the soft whimpering of the damned, now prostrated at the Queen's feet.

"I had such plans for you." Paimon shook her head.

Her braided hair was adorned by a black jeweled crown that fit between her two sets of horns. The front set curved down, framing her face, the sharp points angled forward. The second jutted straight back from her head like lethal spikes.

"But now that you've betrayed me, you're useless for anything except gorath meat."

Mist winced inwardly. Unfortunately for the miscreant, being eaten by a gorath would not actually kill him. A demon could only be killed by a ritualistic beheading and total inciner-ation of the remains via hellfire. If even one piece survived, he would regenerate. Slowly and painfully.

This traitor would be eaten by the monsters, only to regen-erate inside their stomachs or in their feces and, as soon as the beasts scented his regrown flesh, be consumed once more. It would be a never-ending cycle of agonizing death, for as long as it kept Paimon entertained. And he shuddered to think what she'd come up with when she got bored of that.

"Mistress, I b-beg of you—"

She flicked her clawed fingers in dismissal. "Throw him in the Pit, Mishetsu."

Mist pushed off the wall and approached the groveling demon. He told himself he felt nothing as he grabbed the crea-ture by his shredded wings once more and dragged him kicking and screaming out of the hall. He was numb, encased in meta-phorical ice that was his only way to remain sane.

And yet, deep within, a part of him that shouldn't exist felt things no demon should feel. In order to survive, he worked hard to bury it where no one, not even he, could find it. The battle grew more difficult every day.

And he had already failed once.

Against his will, the memory resurfaced again. *A radiant smile adorned the woman's face, her hands busy chopping vegetables while the demon rested his chin atop her head and smiled with contentment. She leaned back and said something that Mist couldn't hear over the roar of the ocean. Whatever it was caused the demon to throw back his head and laugh. He scooped up his tiny human and spun her around while she shrieked with delight.*

It was the first time Mist had ever heard such a scream. A scream of happiness, not of pain or terror. What could such intense joy feel like? How was it possible to be so consumed by happiness as to want to shout from it?

His steps faltered, and he stumbled slightly on the uneven floor, drawing him back to the present. He shook his head to dislodge the memory and realized he had reached the end of the long, dark tunnel. The shadows flickered from the torches on the wall. Ahead of him was an iron gate.

Through those interlocking bars, the goraths waited. Their eerie screeches and the squelching sounds they made when moving filled the air as they caught the scent of approaching meat. Crushing the demon's wings in a vise grip with one hand, Mist turned the crank on the wall to raise the barrier with the other.

Without pause, without allowing himself to feel anything, he hurled the demon inside, hearing his screams increase in volume as he caught sight of the monsters. More shrieking came from the goraths as their plethora of eyes latched onto their prey.

Mist lowered the gate and turned away, walking back to the throne room without waiting to hear more.

Paimon turned a satisfied smile on him as he entered. "Always so loyal, my Hunter."

"Mistress." He bowed to her as he had been trained to do. Deep within, that broken part of him filled with loathing, but he kept it buried. There was no space for regret in his life. Obedience meant everything.

"I have another job for you," she said when he straightened. "An important one. Possibly the most important you have ever been sent on. Lucifer himself has ordered this mission."

Mist gave no outward reaction, but he was immediately wary. Anything regarding Lucifer was something to be concerned about. To survive in Hell, it was best to stay far away from its High King.

"Four powerful demons have gone rogue."

Again? he thought, immediately recalling Eligos once more. This time, he slammed the door on the memory before it could arise. Even thinking of his failure in front of Paimon was too great a risk.

"You are to track them down on Earth. Take whatever measures are necessary to subdue them. It is understood there might be collateral damage."

"Should I destroy them if they refuse to cooperate?"

Paimon shook her head. "Lucifer wants them alive. He plans to make a spectacle of their punishment. A reminder of the consequences of insubordination, if you will. If they are together and you risk being overpowered, return to me to report their location. Legions will be sent to secure them instead."

Legions? Just who were these demons? Mist frowned slightly, the only outward display he allowed of his apprehension. He could not allow anyone to realize the turmoil that spiraled within.

He . . . felt things. And it terrified him.

"Who are they?" he asked in his flattest voice.

"Asmodeus, Raum, Mephistopheles, and . . ." Paimon's lip curled off her fangs. "Belial."

CHOCOLATE THERAPY
Present Day

MISHETSUMEPHTAI SELECTED A PIECE OF POPCORN from the bowl with careful claws. Setting the buttery morsel upon his tongue, his head tilted as he chewed. The flavor was bland, the texture crunchy and chewy at the same time. He could tell it held little nutritional value. And yet, something had him reaching for a second piece as soon as he finished the first.

"See?" the human beside him said. "It's good, right?"

Technically, Eva was actually half human, but she had only recently discovered that.

"I don't know that I care for it," Mist replied, selecting a third piece.

"And yet you keep eating it."

"I can't seem to stop myself."

Eva chuckled and then winced, shifting atop her pile of couch pillows with a hand over her abdomen. A movie played on the TV that neither of them were paying much attention to. "I think that means you like it."

His eyes narrowed as he chewed his fourth piece. "I remain unconvinced."

Eva shifted again with a muffled groan. "These cramps are a bitch."

As far as Mist was concerned, she was clearly a human—angel blood or not, she still suffered from the agonies of the human female race.

"And this movie's terrible, isn't it?"

"It is difficult to grasp the appeal of watching humans that don't exist struggle with problems that aren't real." He watched the on-screen couple regard each other warily from across a crowded room, both erroneously believing the other had said terrible things about them. "I have observed many real humans with real problems. I don't see the need to invent new ones for entertainment."

"Maybe it's so we can dissociate from our own for a while." Eva grabbed a handful of popcorn and consumed it with relish.

"Their issues could be solved in one conversation. Why are they incapable of basic communication?"

She laughed, though it ended with another wince. "Because then it wouldn't be dramatic, and they would have trouble stretching out the storyline over an hour and a half. The writers would've actually had to create some sort of plot, and that's apparently too much to ask in this case."

Mist watched her grimace as she held her abdomen. "You appear to be in pain."

She cocked a brow. "Ya think?"

"Where is your electrical blanket? Have you taken a numbing pill?"

She burst out laughing. "You crack me up, Mist."

He frowned.

"I have my blanket here, but I'm sweating already in this heat, and I don't want to be any hotter. And I already took a painkiller. But . . . there is something I want."

"What?"

She closed her eyes, and a wistful smile overtook her face. "Ice cream."

"Ice cream?"

"Chocolate ice cream. With chunks of chocolate. And swirls of chocolate. And sprinkles of chocolate."

"That sounds like a lot of chocolate."

"The more the merrier."

"Perhaps you can arrange for Asmodeus to procure this for you."

"It's Thursday night, remember? He's at Bootleg, and there's no way I'm calling him back." The jazz club Eva worked at had a weekly jam she and Asmodeus often attended. "I'm still amazed he went without me. I'm so proud of him for coming out of his shell."

Mist tilted his head as he considered this. "Asmodeus is lucky to have you."

"He is, isn't he? I'm quite a catch."

"Catch?" He frowned. "But you told me you were with him willingly. How can that be if he had to catch you?"

"No, that's not—" She dragged a hand down her face. "It's a figure of speech. Nobody caught anybody. That's not how real relationships work. Everything is mutual and consensual."

He supposed he did recognize the expression—demons could intuitively speak all languages and adapt current speech patterns to better blend on Earth—but he was inexperienced at human interaction. For all his many millennia of hunting, he had never conversed with humans until now and had much to learn.

Finding Belial and the other rogues had been easy, but instead of returning to Paimon as instructed, Mist had broken the rules again. Eager to experience for himself the freedoms the rogues enjoyed, he had offered them a deal. In return for sheltering him and teaching him about humans and how to interact with them, he would not reveal their whereabouts, nor Eva's forbidden existence.

Angel-human hybrids, called Nephilim, were considered an abomination. Angels would exterminate them on sight, and demons would capture them for the magical properties of their blood. Once Mist had realized what Eva was, he had used that information to secure his alliance.

A month and a half had passed since the commencement of his temporary vacation, and, thanks to Eva's instruction, he'd since discovered humans were not as simple as he'd always believed. For example, if he wanted a human friend—they were called "friends," not pets—it wasn't as easy as picking one out from a crowd, though he still thought it ought to be. He was a powerful, immortal being. Humans were small and weak, with short lifespans.

But Eva had told him he had to see them as equals and learn to appreciate the nuances of their differing personalities. He had to learn to tell them apart.

"I have an idea," she said, smiling mischievously. "You go."

"Go where?"

"To the dep. For ice cream."

"What is a dep?"

"Depanneur. Corner store, Quebec style. Ice cream supplier extraordinaire."

He sat upright. "You want me to go to the store?"

She nodded.

"But—" He looked down at himself.

His skin was ash gray, his fingers tipped with claws, every tooth in his mouth a razor-sharp point. His eyes were an eerie bright yellow, his pupils thin and slitted like a snake's. His leathery wings draped off the end of the couch, and his tail curled in his lap, long and smooth like a coiled whip.

He looked nothing like a human, and, as a result, he would

be invisible to them, thanks to the glamor that disguised the supernatural world from unsuspecting mortals.

Until he'd met Eva, he had never taken human form in all his long existence. He hadn't needed or wanted to. His job was much better suited to a stealthy, invisible demon than a soft human with fleshy fingertips.

But something had shifted in him since the day he'd broken the rules for the first time, and try as he might, he couldn't put it right. He was curious and restless and in search of something, though he didn't quite know what. He just hoped he found it before he inevitably had to return to Hell.

"There's a dep at the end of the block," Eva said. "All you have to do is go there and get the chocolatiest ice cream you can find. The only person you have to talk to is the cashier."

Mist twisted his claws together. "I would have to hold human form for the duration."

"You've been practicing and you're getting good. You're ready for this." When he still hesitated, she added with a smirk, "I think you're scared."

His spine stiffened. "I am the Hunter. I am not scared."

"Tell that to yourself. I know you can hold on to your human form now, yet you always choose to stay behind when we go out. I thought you wanted to interact with humans."

"I do," he grumbled.

"Then challenge yourself. Go get me ice cream. Plus, hello, I have my period right now, and it's your duty as a man to bring me anything I want."

She was right, he realized. He was ready. He could do this.

He rose from the sofa and stretched his wings, stiff from sitting on them for so long. "I require a shirt." He rarely wore them. For a winged demon, they were inconvenient, to say the least.

"You can borrow one of Ash's if you don't want to go upstairs."

He was currently staying with Asmodeus's brothers in an apartment on the floor above. He slept on a mattress instead of a cold stone floor, and in the morning, sunlight entered through his very own window. Belial often prepared him human food dishes to sample, and if he chose, he could do nothing but relax for an entire day. He had never experienced such things before, but he reminded himself constantly not to become complacent.

All of this was only a temporary reprieve.

Five minutes later, he was in human form, wingless and wearing a borrowed black T-shirt, and he and Eva had rehearsed his future transaction. She'd explained several times why he had to *pay* for the ice cream instead of just taking it, and he was beginning to understand. If nothing else, he would abstain from thievery to avoid attracting attention.

"You look great," Eva said, smiling from her pillow pile. "You make a very handsome human."

Though considerably shorter than his full demonic height, he was still taller than most humans, standing a few inches over six feet. His skin was bronze, and the brands hidden on his gray skin now looked like bold tattoos.

It was the thing he disliked most about this form. As a demon, it was easy to pretend the markings weren't there. As a human, he had no choice but to be reminded of their existence every time he caught his reflection.

"Take one of my reusable bags from the basket by the door," Eva said as he readied himself to depart. "And my keys so I don't have to buzz you in. You can't do your mist trick to get in since you're supposed to be practicing being human, and that's cheating."

Agreeing to play mortal, Mist rode the lift down and stepped onto the sidewalk. There he paused, taking a deep inhalation of the humid summer air and double-checking that he still held on to his human form.

He ran his tongue over his teeth. *Still flat.* He checked the skin of his arm. *Still light brown.*

The darkness was illuminated by overhead lamps and light from the storefronts. Across the street, people were spilling out of a restaurant and lounging on the terrasse of a pub. Somewhere down the block, the sound of live music wafted on the hot breeze.

Someone walked past Mist, and their eyes traveled over him. They saw him. They were looking right at him and seeing nothing but a regular man. He headed down the street in the direction Eva had told him to go, confidence building with every step.

At the end of the block, right where she'd said it would be, there was a small convenience store with faded cardboard adverts in the windows for beer and ice cream. Steel bars intersected over the panes of glass, and an array of cigarette butts littered the ground outside. Overhead, a neon sign read "Dépanneur Au Coin," though the lower half of all the letters had burnt out.

It was beautiful. A shining example of current human consciousness. Paradise, compared to anything in Hell.

Taking a breath, he entered the store, all his hunter instincts fixed on locating the ice cream freezer.

Lily Donovan stared at the row of dreadful, delicious chocolate bars and questioned her life choices.

How the hell had she come to be standing in a dep at ten thirty on a Thursday night, debating which sugary monstrosity to consume alone in her apartment?

Well, she wasn't quite alone. She was babysitting her sister's grumpy cat, and she had his charming company to look forward to. *Grand. Just grand.*

After finishing university last year, Lily had searched high and low for a job in her field of environmental engineering, but nothing had seemed to fit, and no one had been particularly interested in what she had to offer. Or maybe she was just terrible at job interviews.

Whatever the case, a year later, she was still making all her income selling her clothing designs online, and she was beginning to wonder why she'd bothered torturing herself with four years of university and student debt in the first place.

She shook her head at her negative thoughts. She tried hard never to fall into the mire of self-pity, but sometimes it was hard not to. Some days—like today—no matter how hard she tried to be strong, her mind seemed determined to self-destruct.

She had friends, but she'd refused all offers of socializing in favor of staying home with Grimalkin and her sewing machine. She'd accidentally-on-purpose missed her yoga class today, only to end up in this dep perusing the chocolate bar selection. And she could already tell that later, after indulging herself, she was going to have a hard time silencing that stupid whispering voice in her head that made her feel guilty about it.

She was healthy; she knew she was. She ate well, she exercised, and most of the time, she liked her appearance. Her body type just wasn't what society had deemed ideal, and she was constantly bombarded by subconscious messaging that told her she wasn't worthy unless she looked a certain way.

Her sister said she was "curvy" or "thick." Lily didn't care what she called it. At the end of the day, she still ended up sewing all her own clothes because the ones she liked never came in her size. The heroines in her favorite movies never looked like her, and any product designed for a woman of her build was for the purpose of weight loss or "slimming."

Annoyed with her spiraling thoughts, she snatched a chocolate bar off the shelf, going for the only fair-trade option this depanneur sold. She may have been in a mood, but that didn't mean she couldn't make ethical purchases when possible.

She grabbed two for good measure.

And then decided to get a bottle of wine while she was at it.

Heading down the aisle to the alcohol section, Lily stopped in her tracks when she saw a man at the end staring determinedly at the Ben & Jerry's freezer.

He was tall. Very tall. Taller than most tall people, and she definitely wasn't one of those. And he was broad, his muscular back and shoulders stretching his black T-shirt in all the right places.

As she watched, he dragged a hand through his mop of messy black hair, the ends brushing his shoulders.

Normally, she would have been attracted to a man like that, but right now, she was mostly just intimidated. It was a healthy response for a woman alone at night with no badass self-defense skills.

Unfortunately, the wine selection was right beside him.

It was either brave proximity to the muscled giant or forgo the wine. And she wasn't that cowardly, nor did she actually expect him to have any ill intent toward her. In all likelihood, she was just paranoid, and he was a perfectly nice man who happened to have won the genetic lottery for height and enjoyed going to the gym.

Plus, she really wanted wine.

Taking a breath, she headed down the aisle, stopping beside him. She tried to study the selection but couldn't focus on anything except the looming presence beside her. All she felt was this burning intensity that made her heart pound and her palms sweat.

Deep inside, long-buried instincts suddenly flared to life for the first time in years, warning her that she was in the presence of something dangerous. All her assurances to herself about him being harmless were drowned out by her suddenly pounding heart. The labels and prices before her eyes blurred together in a stew of brewing panic.

Screw it, it's all wine in the end. Snatching up a random bottle, she was seconds away from escaping when the stranger spoke.

"Excuse me."

Oh god. He wasn't talking to her, was he? No, he was probably on the phone. She hadn't seen a phone in his hand, though. Maybe he had earbuds in, and she couldn't see them. Bottle clutched tightly in her fist, she turned—

And stopped dead.

He was looking right at her, and he'd definitely been speaking to her.

This time, she felt the glimmer of attraction shine through all the trepidation. His eyes were incredibly beautiful. A warm amber, like glittering gemstones, and so bright they were mesmerizing.

His face was masculine yet elegant, his clean-shaven jaw square while his mouth was soft. His skin was tanned, and his hair was black. Somewhat more intimidating was the thick, black geometric tattoo encircling his neck like a collar.

She stared at him, though she knew it was embarrassing as hell.

"Excuse me," he said again.

"Y-yes?"

This was the city. People didn't make small talk with strangers in the city, and they certainly didn't converse in depanneurs.

There was an unwritten rule that deps were safe zones. No matter what weird stuff you were in the middle of doing, nobody would bother you as long as you didn't break any laws. You kept your eyes down, paid for your stuff, and got out of there unscathed.

Lily had been counting on that. She never would've braved a trip here if she'd imagined she would be forced to converse with a strange, gorgeous man.

"You are female," he stated.

Her eyes widened. Okay, that was weird. And creepy. How did she extract herself from this?

At least he'd spoken English. Montreal was a bilingual city, but she hadn't become fluent in French in the nine years she'd lived here. She'd been too busy trying to adopt a North American accent, and her disjointed French made her feel self-conscious, so she didn't practice as often as she should.

"Um . . ." Was he going to proposition her? Try to assault her? Oh god, why didn't she carry pepper spray? If she survived this, she would buy some first thing tomorrow. And why hadn't she spent her entire life in rigorous martial arts training? In fact, why had she thought it was a good idea to leave her house at all? She should have—

"Which of these flavors has more chocolate?"

He held out two cartons of Ben & Jerry's.

She stared at them, confusion overriding every other thought in her brain. "What?"

"I'm purchasing ice cream for a menstruating female. She demanded chocolate. But these both have the word 'chocolate' in the title, and I don't know which she would prefer."

Her eyes wandered from the ice cream back up to his striking face, which she stared at with amazement. He was completely sincere. This utterly gorgeous, tall, muscular man with neck tattoos was buying ice cream for his "menstruating" girlfriend.

Forget being afraid, she was in love.

Where can I get myself a man like that?

"Buy them both," she said immediately. "That way she can choose one now and have more for later."

His eyes widened. "That's good advice."

She found herself smiling, her earlier fear dissipating. "Well, I'm an expert in all things chocolate."

"You enjoy it too?"

She nodded and held up her chocolate bars with a sheepish smile.

"You should buy ice cream as well."

"Oh no, I can't. That stuff goes straight to my hips, which are big enough already, thank you."

His gaze slid down her body. "You're very small. I don't see a problem."

She wanted to melt into a puddle and ooze through the cracks in the faded linoleum. "Small in height, sure, but not in width."

He blinked, gaze returning to her face. "I don't see a problem," he repeated.

She stared at his puzzled look. Did he genuinely not understand why she would care about her size? Her gaze flicked to a faded advertisement on the wall beside them of an ultra-thin, bikini-clad model licking an ice cream cone suggestively. There were images everywhere of what their culture thought the ideal female body should look like, even here in this crummy old dep. How could he have failed to notice any of that?

He turned from her then, opening the freezer and grabbing another carton of ice cream. She expected him to try to give it to her, but he didn't. It seemed he wanted to be certain he got the right one for his girlfriend.

Whoever this girl was, Lily hoped she appreciated what she had, because *damn*. A man who looked like that, buying a girl ice cream on her period? It sounded like something out of a romance novel.

There was an awkward moment of shuffling as they determined who would walk down the aisle first to reach the cash register. Or maybe it was just awkward for her. Mr. Tall, Dark, and Handsome just watched her with those hypnotic eyes as he stood back and waited for her to go first.

Cheeks flaming, she did, feeling his gaze on her back and hoping he wasn't staring at her ass. Or maybe she hoped he was. No, she didn't. But it wouldn't be terrible if he was. Oh god, was he?

She paid for her Single Girl's Night Alone supplies—all that was missing was batteries for her vibrator—cast a farewell smile to the hot stranger, and stepped back outside. The air was humid, the temperature barely any lower than during the day. Another summer heat wave.

She made it only a few steps before she heard, "Wait," called out from behind her. Glancing back, she saw the mystery man standing outside, a reusable cloth bag in one hand.

He had gone to the dep prepared with his own shopping bag. Who was this guy?

Maybe it was foolish, but she stood and waited while his long strides ate up the distance between them. "Is it safe for you to walk alone?" he asked.

She stared at him. "Um, yeah, I do it all the time. Montreal's a pretty safe city."

He frowned, tilting his head in a way that she had never seen a person do before. A reptile, maybe. But not a person. "I would like to escort you for protection."

She hesitated. Hot or not, there was no way she was letting some rando walk her home and find out where she lived.

His eyes widened suddenly. "But you should refuse because it's not wise to allow a stranger to discover your lair."

Her *lair*? She almost burst out laughing. Wow, he spoke strangely, especially because he had no trace of an accent.

"Um . . ." She didn't want to offend him, but he was bang on the money.

"You're very smart," he said, and this time she did laugh. "Thanks. I hope your girlfriend likes the ice cream."

"She is a friend that is a girl, a girl friend, but not a girlfriend." His face scrunched up. "I find this term confusing."

Another startled laugh escaped her. He really did say the weirdest stuff.

"That's really nice of you to take care of your friend," she said with a smile, utterly charmed by this strange, strange man. "Have a nice night."

"This is for you." He dug into the shopping bag and held out a carton of Ben & Jerry's.

Her heart melted faster than the ice cream in this heat. He *had* picked the extra one up for her.

"It's good to have things you enjoy. Human lives are short. It's better to leave your mark on the world by being full of contentment than full of longing."

Lily stared at him, tilting her head back to look into those beautiful eyes. Slowly, she stretched out a hand and accepted the ice cream.

The flavor was "Chocolate Therapy."

She stared down at the silly little cow beneath the title and felt her stubborn bad mood finally melting away. He was right. She didn't want to be the kind of person who spent her whole life second-guessing herself.

"Thank you," she said softly, looking back up at him. He was a good six inches taller than her.

"I'm glad we met this evening."

"Me too," she replied, and she meant it.

With a single nod in farewell, he turned to go.

He made it halfway down the street before spontaneity seized her and she called out, "Wait!" just as he had to her.

He turned back, brows lifting in question.

"Maybe . . . I would like you to walk me home after all."

2

A MIST OPPORTUNITY

THE FEMALE SMELLED INTOXICATING.

As the Hunter, Mist relied heavily upon his sense of smell—both a blessing and a curse. A curse because foul smells were that much fouler to him, and for a creature from Hell, there were those in abundance. But it was a blessing too because when he smelled something delicious . . .

His eyes briefly shut with his next inhalation. There were no words to describe the pleasure.

She smelled sweet and fresh, like a field of flowers, but there was a dark undercurrent to her scent that stirred something primal inside of him. It was sharp and spicy, and so subtle he had to keep inhaling deeply just to get the faintest whiff of it.

He would have preferred to pin the small woman against the wall so she could not escape and bury his nose against her neck to breathe that aroma freely. Perhaps he would sink his teeth into that soft flesh to taste her, further increasing the sensory experience, and hold her still beneath him as a hunter preferred his prey to be.

He curbed the instinct, however. Eva's "How to Human" lessons were fresh in his mind, but even without them, he knew that his urges would be considered inappropriate to the average human.

Instead, he attempted to seek a conversational topic to fill the silence growing between them as they walked. He knew humans liked to talk about the weather, but Eva told him to avoid bringing that up because it was "lame." He also knew humans liked to complain about their jobs or their physical health, but Eva had told him not to do that either because it was "even lamer." While he scrambled to remember something he *could* talk about, his companion saved him by speaking up first.

"So, do you live around here?"

He looked down at her. She was short, even for a human, and spoke with a subtle accent that suggested origins outside of North America. Her blond hair was piled in a messy bun atop her head, her eyes a pale green, and her features were delicate, with soft lips framed by round cheeks.

Most enticing of all, however, was her bountiful figure. The sight of her was like gazing upon a decadent feast. If ice cream would actually make her hips wider, he thought she should be making a determined effort to consume as much as possible.

"Yes," he said before he made her uncomfortable by his prolonged silence. "My current dwelling is one block from the store in the opposite direction."

"Oh." She looked ahead. "Have you lived there long?"

"One and a half months."

He sensed her wanting to ask where he'd lived before that, but in the end, she remained silent. He was glad. He wasn't sure how to answer that question.

He wanted to ask *her* questions—he wanted to know everything about her—but he didn't know if the things he wanted to know were normal topics or strange ones that Eva might deem inappropriate.

His goal was to appear as human as possible, and for that reason, he might have chosen to simply remain silent had he not sensed her discomfort.

She kept glancing up at him, and he could tell the silence was making her nervous. He supposed he hadn't given her reason enough to trust him, and he worried that if he didn't speak soon she might start to regret allowing him to accompany her to lair.

Her *home*, he mentally corrected. Humans lived in homes. Demons lived in lairs. He knew this.

He searched desperately for a safe topic of conversation. "You speak differently from others," he finally said, deciding it was a harmless enough observation. "Do you originate from outside this city?"

She made a face. "Yes, actually. I'm surprised you picked up on it so fast. Most people tell me my accent isn't that noticeable."

"It isn't."

"I'm from Ireland. I moved here with my sister nine years ago."

"Why did you move?"

There was a pause, long enough that he feared his question might have been too personal. "We wanted a fresh start," she said finally.

He knew better than to ask her why that was, though he was very curious to learn. "I understand," he said instead, because he did. He too would have liked a fresh start if that was an option available to him. He supposed his coming here was as close to that as he could get. A temporary fresh start. A pretend fresh start.

"What about you?" she asked. "How long have you been in Montreal?"

"One and a half months," he replied, tensing in anticipation of her next question. He'd hoped he dodged this line of inquiry when she hadn't probed further about his living situation, but alas.

"Oh, so you just got here then. Where did you live before?"

He debated how to reply. He didn't want to lie to her, but he was also well aware he couldn't tell her he'd been either hunting for rule breakers or hiding out in a dismal, dark cave in Paimon's lair.

"I traveled often," he eventually said. "For my . . . work." He nodded to himself, satisfied at his response. Hunting was like a human's job, wasn't it?

But then she had to ask further questions. "Oh really? What kind of work?"

He glanced down at her. She was gazing up at him with an open, guileless expression, a soft smile on her face. She was genuinely curious about him. She truly had no idea what he was, not the slightest inkling that he was a soulless creature of Hell.

He found himself feeling guilty for the deception, though it wasn't an emotion he was familiar with. He didn't like the idea of lying to her, and simply avoiding the truth was, by default, a lie.

Still, he knew better than to reveal himself. He had no choice but to dig himself deeper into his pit of deceit. But how to explain his duty?

"I . . . retrieve things," he said. "Lost things."

Her features scrunched into a frown, and she opened her mouth. She was going to inquire further, he realized with some panic. His answer had confused her and now she would ask for clarification, and he would have to lie even more.

"Is your home on this block?" he asked quickly before she could respond, hoping against all hope that it would be enough to distract her.

"Oh!" She blinked, looking around at their surroundings. It was dark, but the glow of the streetlamp above illuminated her just enough for him to see a flush rise to her cheeks. "We actually walked past my house already." She pressed a palm to her face. "I got caught up in the conversation and didn't even notice. How embarrassing."

She spun around and began retracing their steps, and he followed dutifully. He wanted to keep speaking with her, but he was afraid of her probing. She seemed very perceptive, and he hadn't expected that. He needed to consult with Eva about how normal humans avoided personal questions.

She stopped again before they reached the end of the block, pointing up at a spiral staircase leading to a balcony with doors for the upper floor apartment entrances.

"This is me." She smiled but avoided his eyes. He thought she might still be embarrassed about walking past her house, though he hoped she wasn't. It seemed an honest enough mistake, and if anything, he was pleased that she had been so invested in his stilted speech that she'd forgotten her surroundings.

He studied her closely, analyzing her behavior. He sensed that she was somewhat shy and unsure of herself, but he couldn't understand why. She appeared strong and capable, appealing in every way. Her scent, her bountiful figure, the rare shade of her eyes . . . In his opinion, she had more reason than most to be self-assured.

Perhaps it was him making her nervous? After all, he was just standing there staring at her. He chastised himself for his awkwardness. He really was inept at humans. Perhaps she was still afraid of him and was hoping for him to leave as soon as possible.

"I guess I'd better go up before my ice cream melts," she said, lending credibility to his hypothesis.

He nodded, fighting to hide his disappointment. He may have bungled this endeavor thus far, but perhaps there was still some way for her to leave their interaction with a positive impression.

"You should eat as much of it as you want," he said.

"What?"

"You should eat as much ice cream as you want."

A surprised laugh burst out of her. "And why would I do that?"

"Because you like it. And because you are very small, and it wouldn't be bad if it made you bigger."

Her laughter died instantly, and she stared at him with a slightly open mouth.

He groaned inwardly. He'd made it worse again. He wanted to disappear. No, he wanted to fling himself off the edge of the Pit into the hungry mouths of the monsters below. He wished Eva was here to help him figure out what was and wasn't appropriate to say.

"I will go," he said in case she feared or detested him now, though it was the last thing he wanted to do. There were still so many things he wanted to know about her. She was by far the most interesting human he had encountered, and he couldn't seem to stop breathing in her tantalizing scent. "Thank you for allowing me to escort you. I enjoyed the experience."

He gave her a small bow and instantly regretted it. Humans didn't bow anymore, did they? He didn't think so; at least, not in this culture. Not to mention, bowing was a habit he had acquired over millennia of servitude, and he resented the symbol of his bondage.

He spun, ready to make a swift retreat to lick his wounds and reflect upon his spectacular failure.

"Wait," she said before he could.

He turned back around.

"What's your name?"

Did this mean she wasn't afraid of him? "I am called Mist."

"I— Oh. That's an unusual name."

"It's a nickname." He wasn't going to offer his real name. If anything would give him away as not human, it was that.

Unlike Asmodeus and his brothers, he would derive no pleasure from confusing her. "And you?"

"Lily."

"Like the flower."

She shrugged. "It's a pretty common name."

He inhaled another lungful of that heady aroma. "It suits you. Your scent is like flowers."

Her eyes widened again, and he cursed inwardly. Perhaps that was also insulting? He ground his teeth. This was too difficult.

"Do you have a phone?" she blurted, and her cheeks turned scarlet once more.

He frowned. "No. Why? Do you need to call someone? Are you in danger?" He glared into the suddenly suspicious darkness, fighting back an instinctive growl.

"No, no. Nothing like that." Her cheeks were flushed so deeply red, it almost didn't appear natural. "Never mind. Have a good night, Mist. Thanks for walking me home."

He sighed inwardly, feeling the sting of disappointment. He wanted to make her stay or create some opportunity to meet with her a second time, but she had clearly dismissed him. The interaction was over. He had lost his chance.

She offered another smile and headed up the staircase. He didn't try to stop himself from watching the luscious mounds of roundness that comprised her ass. The flesh jiggled slightly with every step, and it was the most decadent sight he'd ever beheld. His mouth actually watered.

At the top of the stairs, she unlocked the third door on the left and disappeared inside, so Mist headed for his own place of residence. As he walked, he fought back a sense of regret at the thought that he might never breathe that scent or look into those light green eyes again.

When he reached his own building, he let himself into Eva

and Asmodeus's apartment and found things exactly as he'd left them. Eva lounged on the sofa watching a movie, and the rest of the house was quiet.

She looked over when he entered. "You're back! With ice cream!"

"I purchased two flavors so you might choose which you prefer now and have more for later."

He set the shopping bag on the couch and proceeded to remove his shirt so he could shift back into demon form. Stretching out his wings with a sigh of gratification, he flexed his claws and whipped his tail back and forth. How any demon could stand being in human form for prolonged periods was beyond him.

"You're a genius!" Eva, used to his demon form by now, was too busy selecting her ice cream flavor to notice. She chose "Chocolate Therapy" and then held out the bag for him. "Thanks, Mist. You're the best."

"I will bring you a utensil." He took the bag and put the extra carton in the freezer, returning with a spoon and sinking into the sofa beside her.

She immediately dug in. "So what took you so long? Not that I'm complaining."

"I encountered a female."

"Really?" Her silvery eyes lit up. "What happened?"

"I asked her which flavor you would prefer, and she told me to buy both."

"I like the sound of this girl."

"Then I got a third one for her because she said she liked chocolate."

"That was nice of you."

"I then offered to escort her home for safety, and she accepted."

"Mist, you sweetheart, I didn't know you had it in you." Eva lowered her spoon and beamed at him. "I doubt Ash or his brothers would ever have thought to do something so nice. You're really good at this human stuff."

His mouth twisted. "I don't know. She kept asking me questions I didn't know how to answer, and I think she was afraid of me. It was all very confusing."

"Why do you think she was afraid of you?"

"She seemed somewhat unsure of herself, and she kept staring at me with wide eyes."

Eva snorted. "I don't think that was fear, honey."

"I don't understand."

"Have you seen yourself? You're hot. She was probably attracted to you."

Mist stared at her incredulously. Surely he wasn't so ignorant of humans that he would have missed that? He narrowed his eyes, his mind quickly running over their entire interaction.

She hadn't wanted him to walk her home, but then she'd changed her mind and decided to trust him with the knowledge of where she lived. She had told him her name when he asked. She had thanked him for buying her the ice cream. She had smiled at him and seemed curious about his life.

Was she attracted to him?

"I thought I frightened her," he said weakly.

She reached over and patted him on the arm consolingly. "You'll learn." After scooping another spoonful of ice cream into her mouth and sighing with pleasure, she asked, "So I'm guessing you didn't you get her number."

"What number?"

"Her phone number. To call her?"

"No. Should I have?"

"Well, you can't make plans to see her again if you don't get her number, now can you?"

He stiffened. "She said goodbye. I didn't realize that was an option."

Eva consumed another spoonful of ice cream and shrugged. "Damn. A missed opportunity, I guess, but it's probably for the best. It sounds like you need a bit more practice in public first before you think about going on an actual date with a girl. And we need to get you a phone."

His shoulders slumped slightly, but he knew she was right. He hadn't been prepared for Lily's questions about his "work" and he still had no idea how he would have answered her if his attempted distraction hadn't been successful.

"What is the importance of phones?" he asked. "Lily asked if I had one, and now you—"

"Wait. Lily is the girl you just met?"

He nodded.

"She asked if you had a phone? What did you say?"

"I said no. Because I don't."

Eva slapped a palm to her forehead. "Damn it, Mist! She was asking for your number! She wanted you to ask her out."

His eyes widened. *No.* He refused to believe he had made such a colossal blunder as to misunderstand that interaction. He'd thought she was in danger. He'd been ready to kill whoever wanted to harm her. But she'd been trying to get him to ask her on a date.

He revisited his earlier urge to launch himself into the gaping maws of the gorath in Paimon's Pit.

"Why wouldn't she have just said that?" he said with a groan. "Humans are confounding. How is asking if I have a phone equivalent to planning a date?"

"We have more work to do than I thought. I can't believe you let her get away."

He growled, his tail snapping with frustration.

Eva's expression turned sympathetic. "Don't worry. I doubt we'll have trouble finding other girls who are interested in you. We can get you another date."

"But what if I want that particular human?"

She just shook her head. "Then you shouldn't have blown her off when she asked for your number."

Lily slumped on the sofa with her glass of wine and Ben & Jerry's. Thankfully, the dep only sold the mini size, so she didn't feel too gross eating right out of the carton.

Setting her laptop on the coffee table, she hit play on *Hocus Pocus*. She'd seen it a thousand times, of course, but it was her favorite movie. God help her if her sister ever found out how often she watched this particular film.

As if summoned by thoughts of Iris, Grimalkin jumped onto the sofa and curled into a ball on the cushion beside Lily as if he approved of her entertainment choices.

She glared at the black cat. "You would like this movie."

He glared back, unimpressed. He was a jerk, but she'd always loved the lemon-yellow shade of his eyes against his pitch-black fur. Unfortunately, now it reminded her of another pair of eyes she had looked into tonight.

"Instead of asking for his number, I asked him if he *had* a phone. What kind of question is that? Everyone has a phone!" She snorted. "Well, everyone except him, apparently."

Grimalkin looked offended by the tone of her voice.

"The worst part is, he had no clue what I was talking about. And did I explain myself? No, I just let him walk away. But seriously, who can't take a hint that big? I feel like he would have figured it out if he was interested."

She sighed and turned back to the movie without actually watching it. "It's probably for the best, anyway. The dep is hardly the place to meet guys. I don't know anything about him except that he's gorgeous and nice enough to walk random girls home and buy ice cream for friends on their periods." She groaned. "Who am I kidding? He's perfect."

Her phone rang, and she groaned again when she saw the

call display. Pausing the movie, she shot a glare at Grimalkin. "Somehow this is your fault."

She swiped to answer the call. "Iris. Hey."

"Lil, are you coming? We're getting started right away—"

"You know I'm not. I told you to stop inviting me."

Iris huffed. "You should be here. It's in our blood. It's who we are."

"It's not who I am. I am who I choose to be, and that's not what I choose."

"I don't see why you're so against it. It's our heritage, our—"

"We've had this argument a hundred times, Ris, and I'm not changing my mind. Just give it up already."

Thank god her sister didn't know she was watching *Hocus Pocus* while sitting beside a black cat. Then she'd never hear the end of it.

Iris sighed. "Fine, but I miss having you here, Lil."

She hadn't been to a coven meeting since they'd left Ireland nine years ago, but Iris always acted like she'd stopped going yesterday. "Sorry, but it's not for me. I want a different life."

"Just because Mam and Dad are g—"

"Please don't bring that up right now."

"Fine, I won't. But I just don't want you to throw this big part of yourself away because of the past. Mam wouldn't want that for you. She'd want us to b—"

"I'm hanging up now."

"All right, all right. Before you go, how's Grimmie-poo?"

Lily glanced at her silently disapproving companion. "As grumpy as ever. When are you coming to get him?"

"In a couple of days. I need some time away from my house right now."

Lily sighed. "Why don't you just break up already?" Iris's boyfriend was an asshole. While Lily tended to avoid social interactions of all kinds, her sister sought them out and often latched onto the worst type of people—especially men.

"That's the thing. We did."

She sat up straighter. "You did?"

"Yeah, and this time, I mean it. I'm done. I gave him three days to pack up his shit and move out. I'm staying with Suyin in the meantime. I wouldn't put it past the bugger to steal Grim, which is why I asked you to take him."

"Oh my god, Ris, that's—" The best news she had heard in months. Hell, years. "Why didn't you tell me sooner?"

"Because I knew what your reaction would be. I'm impressed you're still holding it in."

"Can I do it now?"

"Fine." Iris blew out a breath. "Let me have it."

"Good riddance!" She tried not to shout, but it was hard. "I never got what you saw in him. He was a bastard to me and all your friends, and you can do so much better. I never liked him from the day I met him. Sure, he was fit, but honestly, his personality was so crap it ruined anything appealing about him. Every time I saw him, I just wanted to kick him right between the legs. You have no idea how long I've been dying for you guys to break up."

"You done?"

"I can keep going if you want."

"I think you've made your point."

"Are you . . . okay? And stuff?"

"I'm fine. It's been over for a while, you know?"

Lily scoffed. "It was over before it began. He was never close to good enough for y—"

"Okay, Lil, I get it. We're starting now, so I gotta go. Sure you don't want to be here? Not even to support your poor, brokenhearted big sis?"

She rolled her eyes yet again. "I'll never tell you what a bastard Antoine is again if you never ask me to come to another coven meeting again."

"Touché."

"And you're not my *big* sis. You're an hour older than me."

"Hey, a lot can happen in an hour."

"Not that much. Now go to your meeting. I have to get back to—" She stared at the movie, paused on Winifred Sanderson's buck-toothed sneer. "Work."

Iris snorted. "Yeah, okay. Have fun at 'work.' Make sure you get lots of 'work' done."

"Thank you, I will," she replied haughtily and hung up.

3

A MARKED MAN

THE BRAND ON HIS NECK STARTED TO BURN THE NEXT morning.

Mist sat up in his soft bed and touched the mark gingerly. He'd known this was a temporary reprieve. He'd known he would eventually be summoned and have to return to his duties. He'd just been hoping he would have longer.

Evidently, he'd been a fool.

Rolling out of bed, he dragged his claws through his tangled hair. Strands hung in his face and stuck up every which way, but it didn't bother him. He'd never cared much for his appearance the way other demons did. He spent a great deal of time invisibly stalking prey or moving as particles of vapor. It didn't matter what he looked like.

Yet, for reasons unknown, this morning he found himself stopping in front of the mirror on his way past and regarding his reflection. Familiar yellow eyes stared back at him, but it felt like he was looking at a stranger. The neck brand blended against his dark gray skin, though by the way it burned, he half expected it to be red and swollen.

He shifted into human form. As he stared at this weaker, more vulnerable version of himself, for the first time, he felt something other than mild revulsion.

He looked like someone else. Someone who wasn't the Hunter. Someone whose existence wasn't controlled by another and who had a choice in their future.

This was why he had begun this experience living on Earth. He had sought an escape, however temporary, because he wanted a break from being what he was.

But, judging by that brand on his neck, that respite was at its end. Not for the first time, he wondered if death was preferable to an eternity of servitude. And not for the first time, he couldn't decide.

Belial's booming voice thundered from the kitchen. "Come eat breakfast while it's hot or I'll bash your skulls in with this frying pan!"

Mist snapped to attention, shifting back to demon form as soon as his focus lapsed. One did not disobey a command from Belial. Especially when that command contained the promise of his cooking.

Stalking into the kitchen, he perched on one of the barstools at the island where they gathered for meals.

"You're the first one here," Belial said, "so you get a reward." A steaming espresso shot was deposited in front of him. "First coffee of the day. And"—he piled the contents of the frying pan onto Mist's plate—"extra food."

Mist stared at the coffee and food and felt a warm sensation he couldn't name. He glanced at Belial, who met his gaze briefly before turning back to the stove.

Meph and Raum breezed into the kitchen a moment later. "Ooh, coffee." Meph stretched out a tattooed hand to steal his espresso shot.

Mist didn't have a lot of things that belonged to him, so when he acquired something, he became extremely possessive of it. He snatched the shot away and hissed in Meph's face with bared teeth.

Meph just laughed. "Come on, be a nice demon and share."

"Touch his coffee, I'll rip your fingers off," Belial snapped. "Sit your ass down and eat."

It was hardly a difficult command to obey. The four of them dug into their meals with gusto.

When they finished, Mist stayed to help clean up after Meph and Raum disappeared. He enjoyed having something to do with his hands that didn't result in violence, even indirectly. Washing dishes was about as harmless a task as there was, and he found it soothing.

He was just hanging the dish towel off the stove handle when Belial spoke.

"Were you planning to say anything about that brand on your neck?"

Mist's head swung around. Belial was leaning against the island counter with arms crossed. Even in human form, he was enormous, as tall as Mist's demon form, with shoulders twice the width of a normal man's.

"She's summoning you, isn't she?"

Mist glanced away. "How did you know?"

"I just know."

Mist supposed there wasn't a lot Belial didn't know, considering he was a fallen angel and one of the greatest powers in Hell.

"So?"

Mist glanced back at him in question.

"Are you going back?"

"I have to."

"What happens if you ignore the brand?"

He plucked at the fraying edge of the dish towel with his foreclaw. Everything in him rebelled at responding—his brands were his greatest weakness, and a smart demon knew never to reveal such information. But there was no denying Belial when he wanted something, and Mist didn't view him as an enemy anyway.

Which was yet another thing wrong with him. A proper demon viewed everyone as an enemy.

"It acts as a compulsion. The urge to return will get stronger every day, and the burning will increase."

"And if you don't go?"

"You would have to restrain me. It becomes overwhelming."

"Okay, say I trap you in prison wards. Then what?"

"The burning eventually becomes hellfire. It will first burn through my neck and will not stop until my remains are incinerated." Decapitation followed by a total incineration of the remains by hellfire—the only way to kill a demon without an angel's consecrated blade. He would be dead. Permanently, irrevocably eliminated.

Not necessarily the worst option.

Bel breathed a low curse. "And what happens if we kill Paimon?"

"The brand would activate, and I would die too. My life force is tied to hers."

"Of course it couldn't be that easy."

He frowned. "Why would you want to help me? When I am gone, you will no longer have to worry about my presence endangering your secrecy, and—"

"Shut up." Belial waved a hand. "You sound like a martyr, and I've always thought martyrs were fucking idiots. Answer me this: Do you want to belong to Paimon forever?"

Mist slowly shook his head. He couldn't even speak aloud how much he despised belonging to Paimon, lest he lose his mind in his hatred of her.

"That's what I thought."

He stared into those piercing blue eyes, waiting for Belial to speak.

"Look." The former King of Hell dragged a hand through

his pale blond hair. It was short and had been for a while. His hair instantaneously grew every time he flew into one of his infamous rages, but he hadn't had one in nearly a month, something that was apparently unprecedented.

That wasn't saying he seemed calm and relaxed, however. Rather, it was the opposite, as if holding back his rage was taking its toll. Shadows lurked under his eyes, and his hands were clenched into fists more often than not.

"I'm going to say some shit to you, and I'm only going to say it once, so pay attention. And if you ever repeat it, I'll kill you, and all the work we're doing to help you will go to waste. Got it?"

Mist nodded.

"Okay." He seemed to be building himself up. "The truth is . . . I like having you around. You appreciate my food, and you help me clean up, unlike my idiot brothers. You're Eva's friend and you make her happy, which in turn makes Ash happy. Which makes me happy. So we're all happy motherfuckers, thanks to your creepy gray ass.

"So . . . you want to stay here, you're welcome as long as you want. You want my help getting free from Paimon, you got it. So don't give me shit about how I'll be glad to see you go because I don't want to hear it. Have I made myself clear?"

Mist nodded again. While he almost couldn't believe what Belial was saying, he did know he valued it in a way he didn't quite understand.

"Now that I've said my piece, you're not going to question me or make stupid martyr comments anymore, right?"

"Okay."

"Good. The first thing I have to do is some research. I've seen those brands before, but it was a long time ago, and I don't know if I remember where. You tell me everything you know, and then I'll do some digging. I'll probably have to consult fucking Dan." His lip curled.

Eva's father was one of the Grigori, warrior angels that had fallen from Heaven long ago to mate with humans. Belial and his brothers had formed an uneasy truce with him due to Ash's relationship with Eva.

Though Dan hadn't been happy about that, he'd accepted the logic of having a Prince of Hell guarding his Nephilim daughter and knew Eva would be angry if he killed her boyfriend. And Ash had accepted that Eva wouldn't appreciate it if he killed her father.

Thus, an alliance was born.

"In the meantime . . ." Belial tilted his head and stared at him.

Mist stared back. The silence stretched on.

"Go out with my brothers. Get drunk, get laid, party—whatever you want to do. You came here for a vacation, isn't that what you said? So go out for once and stop lurking around the apartment."

Mist had been trying to get rid of his brands without success for a very long time. Certainly, he'd never had Belial's help before, but he wasn't without his own resources. His hopes weren't high, and he knew from experience he had less than two weeks before he couldn't fight the compulsion to return to Paimon any longer.

Maybe it was time to push himself out of his comfort zone. The first time he had, he'd met Lily. Maybe he'd lost his chance to see her again, but perhaps there were other human females as enticing as her, and he could find another.

The following Thursday, He Who Does Not Shut Up, aka Mephistopheles, aka Meph, sprawled in the bench seat beside his brother and partner in crime, Raum. At the back of the club beneath colorful lights, Ash and Eva were onstage. There were other musicians too, but the two of them stole the show.

Since the first night Eva had talked Ash into going up to jam, he'd been hooked like a regular heroin junkie. Now, broody, sullen Asmodeus was smiling up at his woman like the sun shone out her ass as she flew over a crazy solo on her flute. He filled the spaces between her notes with fancy shit on the piano, the music flowing effortlessly from his fingertips like it was second nature. He wasn't even looking at his hands, yet every note he played sounded like perfection.

Meph didn't know anything about music, but he still understood that what he was witnessing was epic. Ash was in his element, and so was Eva, and the two of them combined were like a force of nature. The entire club was transfixed.

In that moment, Meph hated himself a little bit. He wanted to enjoy it like everyone else. He wanted to be happy for his brother. But instead, he was feeling sorry for himself.

And then disgusted at himself for feeling sorry for himself.

And then more sorry for himself for feeling disgusted at himself for feeling sorry for himself.

And so on and so forth.

He knew he was a train wreck. He was a demon with a serious dark side—and he didn't mean "dark side" like a human with a weird kink or something. His dark side was a psychopathic, sociopathic alter ego that was not something he could ever let out of its cage unless he wanted people to die horribly. His attempts at being good—whatever that even meant—were a recent endeavor that in no way made up for the centuries he'd spent as an evil, nefarious bastard.

Selfishness was second nature. Hell, it was his only nature. He was self-destructive and impulsive. He broke everything he touched, and he loved touching things. He was constantly getting into trouble and seemed to be incapable of getting out of it. How his brothers put up with him would forever remain a mystery, because he couldn't even put up with himself most of the time. And that wasn't even starting on—

"Meph, snap out of it."

He blinked and found Raum watching him with those too-perceptive gold eyes. They peered at him from a perma-scowling, dark-skinned face, mostly hidden beneath the hood of a baggy sweatshirt.

"Wherever you were in your head isn't a place you wanna be."

Fucking Raum. He was always at it with this wise-guy shit when, really, he was just as screwed up as the rest of them and spent just as much time falling into dark places in his head.

Raum was a kleptomaniac with a three-hundred-year gap in his memory, and he had no clue what depravity he'd committed to earn that heavenly punishment. And he always had to hover around Meph like he needed babysitting—

Which he kinda did. But damn it, he didn't *want* to need it.

"Just concentrate on keeping an eye on Mist," Raum grunted. His face was fixed in its usual scowl—the only expression it ever seemed to make—as his striking golden eyes scanned the packed bar.

Since the day they'd met, Meph and Raum had been inseparable. It didn't make sense, really. Raum never smiled; Meph had a perpetual shit-eating grin plastered across his face. Raum was quiet and stoic, and when he spoke, he generally had something meaningful to say; Meph couldn't be serious to save his life, and any opportunity to make a sex joke was seized with gusto. They were different in every way, but maybe that was precisely why their dynamic worked.

Following his brother's request, Meph scanned the club for their other companion. Mist wasn't hard to spot. He was big even in human form, and since Belial had stayed home tonight, there was no one else around close to his size.

"He really is clueless about humans," Meph said, watching Mist stoop to sniff the hair of a woman in front of him. He recoiled, scrunching his nose like her scent offended him, and moved on to the next. "What's he doing in such a rush any-way? He looks like he's on a hunting mission."

"I dunno," Raum said idly.

But something about his tone had Meph glancing back at him with narrowed eyes. Raum could lie with the best of them, but not to him. They knew each other too well.

"What is it? You know something."

Raum downed the second half of his beer. "Nope."

"Don't give me that 'protect baby Meph from the truth that will hurt him' shit. I'm sick of everyone tiptoeing around me like I'm a fucking infant. Tell me what or I'll make a scene right here, right now."

Raum lifted a dark eyebrow. "And that would be acting like an infant."

"Tell me, damn it."

"Fine. You know how Bel let it slip that his tattoos are brands?"

Meph clenched his hands into fists. He wasn't about to for-get that any time soon. "Yeah."

"You know he's bound to Paimon, and she can control him through the brands. Well, apparently, she's summoning him now, and he has to go back."

Meph's eyes widened, and he felt vaguely nauseous. He knew well how it felt to be controlled and used by a powerful demon. It was a pretty sensitive topic that his brothers were generally careful to steer clear of, and he understood why Raum had tried to avoid talking about this, even if it pissed him off.

He swallowed, trying to keep his cool. "How long does he have?"

"Not long, I don't think. The summoning started last week, but I only just found out today."

"How?"

"Overheard Bel talking to him about it. They're planning

to meet with Dan and see if they can figure out how to get rid of them."

"Fucking fuck the motherfucker."

The whole fist-clenching thing wasn't working, so Meph planted his elbows on the table and dragged his fingers through his hair a few times. Then, he sat up abruptly and stared at Raum. "We have to do something. He's fucking branded!"

"Keep your voice down, idiot. Bel's looking into it with Dan, like I said. There's nothing else we can do, so chill."

"I can't be chill about this."

"Which is why I didn't want to tell you."

Because this shit hit a little too close to home for anyone's liking.

Meph sought out the broad figure of Mist in the club. He was still sniffing random women and appearing repulsed by them. He didn't look remotely human. His head was cocking this way and that, his hair wild, his eyes too bright, and though he was missing the sharp teeth and gray skin, he still managed to just look *creepy*.

"We should help him get a woman." If Meph couldn't help with the brands, he could at least make sure Mist enjoyed whatever time he had left on Earth. "That's what he's on a mission to find right now, right? A human *pet?*"

They both snickered.

"It'll be a challenge if he keeps acting like that," Raum said.

"Eva told me about that chick he met last week. He must have some game. And there are plenty more women around."

"I don't think he likes anyone here."

They watched Mist recoil from another female and then growl at a human who accidentally bumped into him. The guy backed away with palms up.

Meph flicked his tongue piercing against his teeth. "I have an idea."

"Uh-oh."

"Shut up." He slid around the table and stood up. "I'm gonna see if he wants to leave."

He wound his way through the crowd of bodies, ignoring the cautious glances of the dudes and covetous looks of the chicks.

Yep, he ignored the chicks.

He had never ignored chicks. He loved female attention. He loved sex. He loved lots of it with lots of different women, separately or together, consecutively or simultaneously, he wasn't fussed.

Except . . . ever since Eva's dad had tossed that consecrated blade into his chest, he hadn't felt like himself. He wondered if the Empyrean magic had crossed some wires in his brain because lately, he wasn't in the mood.

It wasn't that he'd lost his sex drive; he just didn't want anyone touching him. He felt nauseated by physical contact, like every touch was dragging something ugly to the surface where he would have no choice but to—

A pair of amber eyes blinked, snapping him out of it.

Oh, look, he'd crossed the bar and was standing right in front of Mist. He'd gone to that dark place in his head Raum had told him to avoid again.

"You wanna get out of here?"

"Yes. Humans keep touching me, and I want to bite them. And I scented all the females, and none are appealing."

Meph signaled to Raum over the heads of the crowd, and the three of them made their way toward the exit. "But I heard you already found one you liked."

"Yes, but she isn't here."

They stepped onto the street, leaving Eva and Ash behind, lost in their bubble of musical bliss onstage. The pair probably wouldn't notice they were gone for another hour, but Meph shot a quick text to Ash anyway, just in case. His stick-in-the-mud brother was likely to worry if they didn't let him know where they were.

Damn, when had they become so bloody domesticated?

"Shall we return to the lair?" Mist asked. "I'm weary of my human form. My shoulders ache without my wings. I don't know how you maintain it constantly."

Meph wasn't about to explain why he never shifted. He also wondered how Mist was going to find himself a woman if he couldn't handle ditching the wings for more than an hour. Guess it would have to be a casual relationship.

Meh. Those are the best kind anyway.

"I've got a better idea. Tell me where your human lives, and let's go there."

Mist shot him a narrow-eyed look. "No."

"Why not?"

"I will not reveal her location. She's mine."

"She's not yours if you didn't even get her number."

The Hunter growled.

Meph held his hands up. "Not trying to steal your girl, dude. Only trying to help you out. Here's my plan. You write her a note with your new number on it and put it in her mailbox. When she checks the mail, she'll find it, and if she wants to see you again, she'll call. Easy as pie."

"That's actually not a bad idea." Raum sounded surprised, the jackass.

"It's a fucking fantastic idea."

Mist scrutinized him for so long, a lesser demon might have lost his nerve. But Meph lacked the ability to feel insecure, so he just stared back at him, customary grin plastered across his face.

He knew he looked like an idiot most of the time, smiling like that, but he didn't care. Raum wore a scowl like a mask, and Meph did the same with a smile. His grin was his armor.

Finally, the Hunter nodded. "I agree to this plan. But she is mine." The word "mine" came out like a growl. "We'll go now." He strode off into the darkness, newfound purpose in his step.

GLOW UP

"ILY, YOU HAVE TO HELP US," HER MOTHER WHISPERED
from the darkness.

Lily spun around, seeking the source of the voice.

"We need you," her father pleaded from somewhere else.
She spun that direction, finding only blackness.

"It was your fault," Iris whispered. "Our fault."

"Where are you?" Lily asked the dark, spinning around and
around.

"It's our fault they're gone."

"Why? What did we do?"

"They're dead because of us."

"No, that can't be!"

"They're dead and gone, and it's *all your fault*—"

"No!"

She jolted upright in bed, panting.

A soft glow permeated the dark room. The luminous,
pale light wavered gently in the darkness, like the sun shining
through water. She looked down.

The origin of the light was her own body.

"Shit!" She looked like the ugly troll night-light she'd had as a kid.

Not again. "Shit, shit, shit . . ." She scrambled out of bed and stumbled into the kitchen, fighting back the panic. It had been so long since this happened, she'd started to think it wasn't coming back.

Yanking open the freezer, she peered through the condensation clouds until she found what she was looking for: the bottle of whiskey. She despised the taste of hard alcohol and drinking it straight was the last thing she wanted to do.

And yet, she stood there in her kitchen, freezer door wide open, and chugged the burning liquor right out of the bottle like it was water.

Okay, not like it was water.

After two swallows, she choked and staggered to the counter, bent over the sink, and tried not to gag. Then she forced herself to drink more. Eventually, the alcohol hit and, mercifully, the glowing subsided.

The bottle was returned to the freezer, and a now decently drunk Lily staggered into the living room and collapsed on the sofa. The clock on the wall told her it was nearly two a.m. The room spun, and she hated it.

But at least she wasn't glowing anymore.

There were two types of witches in the world: blood-borns and practitioners. By far the most common, practitioners were regular humans that, for whatever absurd reason, chose to study the supernatural. They trained to develop the Sight and studied Temporal magic, learning the art of sigil drawing and performing power-enhancing rituals.

Blood-born witches, on the other hand, were a rare, mostly extinct line of supernaturally gifted women, descended from bloodlines spanning back centuries. Longer than anyone could trace.

Lily and Iris were two such witches. Twins, actually, which

was supposedly a wildly auspicious phenomenon that meant they were destined for greatness, blah, blah, blah.

Their mother had been a powerful blood-born and coven leader: beautiful, charismatic, a force to be reckoned with. She'd been young and yet so gifted that Lily had no doubt she could have extended her lifespan by centuries if she'd wanted. But she'd never gotten the chance before she'd been killed in a fire with Lily's father, along with their entire coven.

All the power and ancient blood flowing in her veins hadn't saved her. She and her husband and their coven had been trapped in the building and perished within.

The End.

As a result, Lily questioned the point of practicing witchcraft when life was still just as fleeting as it was for regular people. Knowledge of the supernatural world hadn't saved her mother's life, so why should Lily waste her time with it?

Thus, she'd chosen to turn her back on it and live as a regular person. She and Iris had left Ireland and moved to Canada shortly after the funerals, and she hadn't practiced magic since. In fact, she'd done everything she could to leave that part of herself behind.

They had both worked hard to adopt Canadian accents, though they still slipped occasionally, and tried to blend in. She called her winter hats "tuques," and she owned a parka fit for Arctic exploration, which was what it felt like was happening when she walked to the metro station in winter.

She'd gone to university and gotten a "normal" degree. She didn't use that degree and designed clothes for a living instead. She bought groceries and took walks in the park. And maybe one day, she would find a man to start a family with, and her children would be boys so she wouldn't pass on her curse to them.

The End.

Except . . . here she was, awake in the middle of the night because she was glowing. Again. Her repressed powers didn't give a damn what she wanted, and she worried the suppression of her abilities was turning her into some kind of magic battery.

She did not want to find out what that battery powered. She just wanted it to go away.

Worst of all, she hadn't told a soul. Not even Iris knew of her mysterious affliction, and her head-in-the-sand policy of determined ignorance prevented her from researching her condition. She had no idea what was happening or why. She only knew that if she chugged hard liquor, it went away. It probably had something to do with alcohol being a neurotoxin, murdering her precious witchy brain cells and keeping them from—

The familiar screech of her rusty mailbox opening made her jump.

She went stiff as a board on the sofa, heart pounding. Was someone delivering mail at two in the morning? That would be ridiculous. But then who was opening the mailbox? Was someone trying to steal her mail? Or searching for a spare house key?

Oh god, was someone trying to rob her? She almost regretted giving Grimalkin back to Iris the other day. Toss him at an intruder, and they'd run screaming as their face was clawed off.

The mailbox screeched again as it was closed.

Before she had time to consider whether it was smart or not, she was off the couch and throwing the door open. She blamed her recklessness on the whiskey, since Sober Lily would be more likely to sneak out the back door.

Sexy Depanneur Guy was standing outside.

He looked like he wanted to flee but someone had hit pause on the world. He stared at her with amber eyes she'd forgotten were so gorgeous, his arms lifted midstride. Even one of his feet was in the air.

A long, awkward silence ensued.

She felt like she should say something, but she didn't. Part of her was ecstatic to see the hot stranger again. She had thought about him all week, no matter how hard she'd tried not to. He'd become the monkey of her monkey mind that leapt determinedly into her thoughts whenever she tried to push him out.

She had gone over their conversation so many times, she could write a transcript of it. She'd rehearsed the multitudinous ways she could have not been an awkward recluse who asked a man if he possessed a phone rather than explicitly stating that she wanted a way to contact him so they could see each other again.

The other part of her was wary and even a little afraid of him. He was a big, muscular man, and he was lurking outside her flat at two in the morning with no explanation.

"Say something, idiot," someone called out from the street below.

She leaned over, craning to see who it was, and saw two more equally large men waiting at the base of the stairs. It was too dark to see much, but . . . were those tattoos on the one guy's face? Her gaze shot back to Mist. Just who had she let walk her home that night?

His friend's words seemed to unfreeze him, and he slowly turned to face her, assuming a more relaxed position. She was instantly lost in his eyes.

"I wrote you a letter."

"Pardon?" She could hardly focus when he looked at her like that.

He pointed at the mailbox. "It's there."

"You had to deliver me a letter at two in the morning?"

"I expected you to be asleep."

"Why aren't *you* asleep?"

"My sleeping schedule fluctuates, and I am often nocturnal."

She blinked. Was that supposed to be a joke? His poker face was inscrutable.

"It was not my intention to wake you." He shifted on his feet and looked away.

His obvious discomfort relaxed her. He was aware of how weird it was to be on her balcony at two a.m., which made it easier to accept him being there.

"You didn't wake me, actually. I was having trouble sleeping, so . . ."

"Are you okay?" he asked, frowning. His eyes flicked back to hers, and the intensity of his stare somehow deepened, though she wouldn't have previously thought that possible. "Are you in danger?"

"No, I'm not in danger. I'm perfectly fine." What was with this guy and danger? That was the second time he'd asked her that. "I just . . . had a bad dream."

As soon as she said it, she regretted it. She had no idea how she would answer if he asked her about the dream.

Thankfully, he didn't. He was still frowning, and she could see the question in his gaze, but something held his tongue. Despite the natural poise he exuded, she got the impression that he was as awkward and unsure as she was in their interactions, and she found it oddly reassuring.

Instead of speaking, he continued to stare at her. She stared right back at him, transfixed.

God, his eyes were beautiful. Everything about him was so damn appealing. His looming height. Those broad shoulders. The messy black hair half falling in his face.

She'd wondered all week what had given her the nerve to ask for his number, clumsy as her attempt may have been. It was so unlike her, Iris probably wouldn't believe it if she told her. But now that she was looking at him again, she understood. A guy like him probably had women asking him out everywhere he went.

Which made it even stranger that he had turned up on *her* doorstep.

"Can I read your letter?" she asked, just to break the stretching silence.

He nodded. "It's for you."

She took a tentative step out from behind the safety of the door. She expected him to step back, to give her space, but he didn't. He stayed right where he was.

She wished she was wearing more than her short, slinky nightie, but it was that or be naked in this heat. She was self-conscious of her thighs and generally avoided wearing clothes that showed them, but her curiosity about the letter overrode her hesitancy.

The minute she pulled the door the rest of the way open, his entire demeanor shifted. His posture stiffened, and he suddenly looked like a hungry predator who had chosen her for his next meal. His gaze traveled down her form like he was trying to devour her with his eyes.

He didn't even try to hide that he was checking her out. There was no subtle flick of the gaze followed by a quirk of the mouth. He simply stared at her. All of her.

And she . . . let him. Being insecure about her thighs suddenly felt entirely irrelevant in light of this man looking at her the way he was. She liked that he wasn't subtle. If he'd tried to be, she probably wouldn't have had a clue what he was thinking. But when he stared at her like that, it left absolutely no question as to what he was thinking.

He wanted her. He really wanted her, and she'd be damned if it wasn't incredibly flattering to be desired that way. To be the recipient of such a hungry, dark look, like he was barely holding himself back from pouncing.

That didn't mean she didn't race to the mailbox, grab the letter, and dart back behind the door like a startled rabbit, however. Because she totally did. Maybe she enjoyed the intensity of his focus, but old habits died hard, and she wasn't used to receiving that kind of attention.

She started to open the letter but stopped and glanced up when she heard Mist clear his throat. "Shall I . . . go?" he asked.

He was back to looking unsure again. He obviously didn't want her to read it with him standing there, which was fair.

"Oh. Um, okay." Disappointment coursed through her. But two a.m. was hardly the time to plan a date. This whole situation was so bizarre, she didn't quite know what to make of it.

She did know, however, that if she let him get away a second time, she would never forgive herself.

"Can I . . ." She swallowed and gathered her courage. "Will I see you again?"

He smiled. It was devastating. It nearly knocked her flat.

"You should read my note," he said.

"Okay." She offered a smile back. "I will."

"Goodnight, Lily."

"Goodnight."

He turned with a final nod and descended the stairs to the street below, where his friends were waiting. She watched him go—or rather, she watched his firm, muscular butt go—while unconsciously fanning herself with the letter.

Gathering her wits, she stepped back inside and locked the door. The second she was inside, she flicked on the hall light and unfolded the paper, heart racing in anticipation.

> *Lily,*
>
> *Thank you again for allowing me the honor of escorting you home. I realized my error in not getting your phone number, and I would like to rectify that now. I regret my misunderstanding when you asked me. I've been thinking about you all week, and I would very much like to see you*

*again if you are amenable. I hope you will con-
tact me.*
   Mist

A smitten smile spread across her face, and her heart began to race. *He thought about me all week!* And he'd come with his friends in the middle of the night to give her his letter. She clutched it to her chest like the treasure it was.

It was so formally worded, it felt like a courtship request from the 1700s, but she adored it. He *was* awkward, but in a very suave, completely non-awkward sort of way. He seemed rigidly controlled and barely leashed at the same time. As if he was putting up a sort of façade to contain some wild, feral creature living inside of him.

The idea was utterly ridiculous and completely outlandish, yet it thrilled her all the same.

She didn't have a lot of experience with men. In her teens, she'd been too shy to date much, and then after immigrating to Canada, there had been too much grief and stress for her to take interest. Things were better now, but old insecurities still lingered, and she was a generally introverted, quiet person. She knew she was too emotionally open, too empathetic, and it sometimes got her into trouble.

If Iris had been there, she would have told Lily to play it cool, to not give away her interest lest she scare him off or worse, open herself up to being easily hurt. But Iris wasn't there, and Lily was far too excited by Mist's romantic gesture to restrain herself.

She ran to the kitchen where she'd left her phone, opened a new text message, and punched in the number he'd written at the bottom of the letter. She wrote, *Hi, it's Lily*, with a smiley face and hit send.

Immediately, doubt crept in. Maybe she should have waited until morning. Would he think she was desperate for texting him so fast? Was the alcohol clouding her judgment and making her think something foolish was a good idea? Oh god, what if she blew it—

Her phone buzzed. Her stomach backflipped when she saw he'd answered.

Hi, Lily.

Her smile returned with a vengeance, and she spent a moment doing a rather undignified happy dance around her kitchen. While she did, the phone buzzed again.

I apologize for scaring you. I expected you to be asleep.

It's okay, she replied quickly, thumbs flying over the on-screen keyboard with record speed. *You only scared me for a minute, until I knew it was you.*

The three little dots appeared at the bottom of the chat, showing he was in the process of messaging her back. She waited with bated breath. It felt like forever passed. She even glanced at the clock.

It was nice to see you again, he finally replied.

That was it? Either he'd been debating on his response for a while, or he was a very slow typer indeed.

You too, she wrote back. *I'm glad you reached out.*

Again, an ice age passed before his response came through.

I felt very foolish for misunderstanding you when you asked about my phone. My friend explained it to me afterward.

She laughed. *Don't feel bad. I felt stupid for asking in such a terrible, confusing way.*

The three little dots appeared, and she waited (im)patiently for his reply, smiling so wide her face hurt. Eyes glued to the phone screen, she went into her bedroom and dropped into the pillows. She might as well have been kicking her feet with how besotted she was acting, but she didn't care.

You shouldn't feel stupid, he replied. The dots appeared again. God, he really did type slowly. This was painful. *If I was better at human conversations, I would have understood.*

The dots appeared again. *I didn't mean to say human*, he added. *I wish there was a delete option for these messages.*

She laughed aloud. God, he was so weird, but it was incredibly charming. *Don't worry, I'm not very good at human conversations either*, she replied. *And I think you're really good at them. It was very sweet of you to buy me ice cream and walk me home that night.*

I wanted to. I was looking for any excuse to spend more time in your presence.

Oh dear god, if he kept this up, she was going to melt.

Well, it's a good thing you wised up and gave me your number then, she texted back. *Now we can text whenever you want.*

Just when she started to fear she'd been a little too forward, he replied, *I would like that very much.*

Me too.

Can I see you again in person as well?

She hesitated, thumbs hovering over the screen. Obviously, the answer was yes, but she was trying to find a way to communicate it that wasn't shouting "YES PLEASE" in all capital letters and looking completely desperate. As she deliberated, he sent another message.

If you would prefer to only communicate by text message, I would understand.

No, I would like to see you, she replied quickly.

When?

She hesitated again. If she suggested tomorrow, that would definitely look desperate. Iris would tell her to wait at least a week, but she didn't want to wait that long. Maybe she ought to ask him what days worked for him? If she said, "Any time, my schedule's completely open!" that would make her look like she had no life, and she didn't want—

Tomorrow?

She stared at the screen. He actually wanted to see her tomorrow? Was this real?

Another text came through, confirming she was not, in fact, hallucinating. *Or rather, tonight? Since it's already well after midnight.*

Maybe she'd fallen asleep and was dreaming because this kind of stuff did not happen to her. Gorgeous men she met in depanneurs didn't leave romantic notes in her mailbox. Gorgeous men didn't even go to depanneurs.

Suddenly, she didn't care. So what if he wanted to see her tomorrow? Was she going to waste time questioning everything? She didn't want to push away what seemed like a perfectly nice man solely because of her stupid insecurities.

So, swallowing her self-doubt, she typed, *Tomorrow/tonight sounds perfect. :) How about you come over for dinner?*

I would like that, he replied.

Is 7 okay?

Yes. I can't wait to see you.

She was almost ready to scream with glee. Her cheeks burned and her heart was positively racing with excitement. She scoffed at herself, but she couldn't help it.

I'll make sure to not be wearing pajamas when I answer the door this time, she texted back with a laughing-face emoji.

The dots appeared.

You looked beautiful, he said.

She was pretty sure her heart either stopped completely or burst out of her chest and flew away to live happily ever after in the clouds. Tomorrow couldn't come fast enough.

DINNER AND A DEMON

THE DOORBELL RANG AT TWO MINUTES AFTER SEVEN.

"Crap, he's here already! I have to go."

"Okay, just don't hyperventilate."

Lily tried to laugh, but it was hard because she was doing just that. Her twin knew her too well.

"And remember to check in every hour or I'll show up, guns blazing, to save you."

Iris had scolded her for inviting a stranger over to her house for their first date instead of choosing a public location. Her paranoid sister had insisted on waiting in the park at the end of the block and had given Lily strict instructions to text her immediately if anything seemed off.

While Lily had agreed that it would have been wiser to plan a public date, she was far too awkward to suggest a change in venue after Mist had already confirmed. So she agreed to Iris's protective measures.

At the same time, Lily was certain she had nothing to fear from Mist. Her instincts told her he was safe. Well, actually, her instincts told her he was very dangerous, but not to her. Somehow, she just knew he would never hurt her.

Besides, he'd known where she lived for a week. If he'd had nefarious intent, he could have acted on it already—particularly the moment when he'd shown up at her house and caught her in her nightdress.

"Holster your weapons," she teased her twin. "I'll be perfectly fine."

"You'd better. If anything seems off—"

"I'll let you know immediately. Yes, I know. I'm not a child, Iris. In fact, I'm only several minutes younger than you."

Iris's protectiveness, while often overbearing, was her way of expressing affection, since she wasn't usually comfortable with it in other forms. The things they'd been through had changed them both, and Lily couldn't fault her for that.

"All right, all right," Iris said. "I just want you to be careful."

"I know, and I will be. Now, I have to go!"

Lily hung up, heart in her throat as she hurried down the hall to answer the door. She paused briefly in front of the mirror on the way to fiddle with her hair and check her teeth for the tenth time. She'd taken a risk and worn a low-cut summer dress that showed a little extra cleavage and fell to just above her knees. It was one of her new designs and she was proud of it.

Stomach somersaulting, she soldiered on from the mirror, flipped the lock, and opened the door.

Mist stood outside with a bottle of wine in his hand. He was twice as gorgeous as she remembered, which should have been impossible because every time she saw him, she swore he got better looking.

He wore a black T-shirt that accentuated his eyes and matched his messy hair, the upper half tamed in an unruly knot while the lower fell onto his shoulders. It also drew attention to the intricate geometric tattoo collaring his neck, standing out against his deeply tanned skin.

"Hi," she said, blushing down to her toes just looking at him.

And feeling him look at her. Because he was really looking. He was doing the same shameless, intense staring thing he'd done last night, positively burning her up with his intensity. It half made her want to rip her clothes off and parade around naked, half made her want to do the melt-through-the-floor thing again.

"Hello." His deep voice sent shivers down her spine.

She smoothed her hands down her dress.

"I was told it was customary to bring an offering." He held up the wine, and her eyes got momentarily stuck on the veins tracing his forearm.

She laughed despite her nervousness. He had such a strange way of speaking. "Thank you. Please come in." Taking the proffered bottle, she stepped back and gestured for him to enter.

The minute he did, it felt like her flat shrank by half. The already crowded entrance was like a broom closet, and the way he towered over her made it seem like the ceiling was coming down on their heads.

She moved into the hallway, but it didn't help. A tiny voice whispered that Iris was right, and she shouldn't have invited him over on their first date. It was too intimate, and her flat was too small and not impressive at all, and besides, nothing magical or romantic ever happened to her, so why would she think—

Shut up. She shoved Negative Lily back into her box and slammed the lid. It was the voice of her insecurities, and she refused to let it ruin her enjoyment of tonight. She was going to be Confident Lily and no one else.

As Mist stepped into the hall behind her and she turned

to face him, her eyes traveled by chance to the wall above the door. Perhaps it was a fluke, or perhaps they were led there by the sudden change she may have been imagining.

A year ago, when she'd first moved into this apartment, Iris had drawn some type of protection ward above the front exit, a sigil about a foot in diameter. Lily had scoffed, writing it off as her twin being her usual paranoid self, and ignored it. When it came to reminders of her heritage, she was good at ignoring things.

She frowned at the ward now.

It was dark bloodred. But she could have sworn it had always been black.

With a shrug, she looked away and met Mist's gaze. The directness of his stare would have been extremely unnerving if she wasn't so attracted to him. He didn't appear to have noticed the ward, thankfully.

She lifted the wine bottle and smiled. "Let me just put this in the kitchen, and then I'll give you a tour. Dinner's ready, so we can eat whenever."

In the kitchen, she shot a quick text to Iris. *He's here and everything's fine. You don't have to wait around if you don't want to.*

After deliberating for a moment, she typed a second text on a whim. *Btw, what's that ward you put above my door supposed to do?*

Tucking her phone in her pocket—all her dresses had them, and it was one of their best-selling features—she hurried back down the hall to find Mist already exploring the front room.

The long, open space was bisected by an archway. The front half contained her living room—a sofa, a big window, a bookshelf, and a collection of plants. The back half contained her workspace—her sewing machine, mannequins, rolls of fabric, and a desk and computer where she drew her designs and managed her online store.

It was a mess. She was actually quite a tidy worker and made sure to sweep up the fabric scraps and stray threads every time she finished working. But there was simply no way to tidy the stacks of fabric and unfinished projects.

"This is the living room," she said unnecessarily as Mist stepped closer to peer at the bookshelf.

She felt her cheeks heat as his gaze traveled over her extensive collection of romance novels and all the witch-related texts from Iris on her many futile quests to get Lily to embrace her heritage. There were biographies of famous blood-borns, grimoires of common sigils, and guidebooks of medicinal herbs and their uses. Lily had barely glanced at any of them. The romance novels, on the other hand, were well used.

Mist frowned at the shelf, spending an extra moment perusing the witchy texts, but said nothing, thankfully.

"And my workspace is back there," she said, stepping back toward the hallway and hoping he would follow and forget to question her about her book collection.

Her distraction attempt was a success. Straightening, he bypassed the shelf and stalked into her workspace. There, he looked carefully around, studying each item in the room with an unreadable expression on his face.

She squirmed uncomfortably, not sure what to make of his thorough perusal. Through a stranger's eyes, she saw the table covered in uncut fabric and the half-finished pieces pinned to the mannequins, and she wished she'd done a more thorough job of tidying up.

Mist had frozen in front of the row of mannequins, his head cocked to one side. She waited for him to say something, but he didn't. Instead, he turned, stalked over to the sewing machine, bent down, and sniffed it.

He actually *sniffed* it. Like an animal. A tingle of wariness rose, and she recognized it as the same gut feeling she'd had when she first saw him in the depanneur. There was something so . . . otherworldly about him. Inhuman, almost.

But that was just silly.

He straightened and looked back at her. "What is this device?"

Her phone buzzed in her pocket at that moment, but she ignored it. "It's a sewing machine." How could he not know that?

With narrowed eyes, he glanced at the row of mannequins. "Why do you have statues of headless females?"

A startled laugh burst from her. "They're mannequins. I use them for designing clothes. Haven't you seen them in store windows before?"

His expression cleared as comprehension dawned. "I have. I understand. You're a clothing maker."

"Exactly." She was still surprised he hadn't put it together with one look at the room. "That's what the sewing machine is for. And all the fabric." She was half teasing him; it seemed so obvious, it hardly warranted explanation.

Yet apparently, it did. "You're an artist," he said, and if she wasn't very much mistaken, he looked almost reverent.

"Well, yes, I guess you could say that."

"What sort of clothing items do you make?"

"I design clothes for plus-size women. I always had a hard time finding stuff I liked in my size, so I decided to make it myself."

His eyes trailed down her body, and the heated look in them made her cheeks burn and her stomach flutter. "I like your size very much." Her heart skipped a beat at his growly voice.

"Oh, um. Thank you." Her cheeks were burning again.

Negative Lily was trying to claw her way back out of the box to whisper hateful things. *He might say that now, but just you wait. Give him a couple months, and he'll start telling you to go on a diet like the last guy you dated.*

Mist was still staring at her, but her attraction and arousal were being diminished by the stupid self-conscious whispers, and she needed a moment to collect herself.

"I'll go pour us some wine!" She spun around and fled the room.

Her phone buzzed again when she reached the kitchen, so she pulled it out and read the texts from Iris. *It's a signal ward that warns you if you're in the presence of supernatural beings. Why are you asking that right now?*

The second message told her she'd better not delay replying any longer. *Did something happen? Are you okay? Answer me right now or I'm coming over.*

That tiny whisper of wariness flared again, but she pushed it away. Instead, she rolled her eyes at Iris's paranoia and fired back, *No, don't come! I asked because the ward is dark red, but I thought it was black before. I'm obviously imagining things. Please don't panic because everything is fine. Gotta go!*

Deciding she was done catering to her sister's overprotectiveness, she put her phone on silent and tossed it on the counter. Then, she opened the cupboard with the glasses and rose onto her tiptoes to reach for the top shelf—

She froze, feeling a presence behind her.

Mist. She hadn't heard him move. She couldn't even hear him breathing, and yet there was no question that he was there.

Her heart slammed against her ribcage as she slowly lowered to her flat feet, quest for wine glasses forgotten.

"You scared me," she whispered without turning around.

She felt him step up behind her. They didn't touch, yet she knew that if she were to shift slightly back, their bodies would press together. Rough fingertips swept the hair off one side of her neck, and she nearly fainted.

"You should never run from me."

His voice was a low murmur, yet it never lost its husky

growl. It came from right behind her ear. The hairs on the back of her neck and arms stood up.

"It is difficult to fight my instincts with you," he said.

"W-what instincts?" Her breathing was uneven, and her eyelids fluttered.

"To hunt." His fingertips brushed her hair back again. "To capture and subdue."

She swallowed. She felt his warm breath against her skin moments before he pressed his nose to her neck. This time, she could hear the deep inhale he took.

He was *smelling* her.

It was animalistic, inhuman, bizarre, and yet . . . the muscles in her lower abdomen clenched with a sudden wave of arousal.

"I find your scent . . . intoxicating."

Her hands shot out, and she gripped the edge of the counter and squeezed to keep from falling over. Oh god, this was complete madness, but she wanted him to kiss her. She wanted to spin around and press against him and be kissed senseless.

And why shouldn't she? A sexy, slightly feral man was in her kitchen sniffing her and telling her she was "intoxicating." She was not foolish enough to ruin a moment like this.

Gathering her courage, she started to turn . . .

Only for him to fix his teeth on the exposed skin of her neck and growl. *Growl.*

He only touched her there, where his canines dug into her tender skin. She froze, understanding it was a warning for her not to run. What human man did stuff like that? Certainly not one she'd ever heard of. If another man had done this to her, she would have laughed in his face. Or slapped him. But something about Mist was so very different from any other man. For him, it seemed instinctive.

His strangeness didn't curb her desire in the least. Rather, it inflamed it.

"I'm not going anywhere," she whispered. "Promise."

The teeth lifted from her skin. Intuitively, she sensed he was making a concession, and she wanted to prove it was the right choice. *That makes no bloody sense, Lily.*

I don't care in the least, she told herself.

Still holding on to that courage, she turned until she was facing him.

She craned her head up to look at him, and her heart skipped a beat. *His eyes.* They were definitely otherworldly, the amber glow just a little too bright. In fact, all of him was otherworldly. The tilt of his head, his fluid movements that belied his impressive size . . .

As if to prove her point, his nostrils flared as he drew in another breath, and she knew he was smelling her again. And judging by the heat in his gaze, he still found her intoxicating.

She swayed into him, thoroughly seduced by his strangeness. At the first brush of her breasts against his hard body, the breath gusted out of her, and she heard him growl again.

For the first time, she began to wonder just what sort of man she had invited into her home. And whether he was a man at all, or something else entirely.

Right now, she didn't particularly care what he was. Perhaps she would later, when she returned to her senses, but for now those seemed very far away indeed. She craned her head back, and her heart pounded as he stooped to her level.

He was so gorgeous it took her breath away, and he was going to kiss her. Somewhere in her head, there was a version of herself running in circles, ringing bells and shouting into a loudspeaker, *He's going to kiss me, he's going to kiss me, he's going to kiss*—

And then he did. Their lips brushed briefly, and her erratic thoughts ground to a halt. It wasn't quite a kiss—more like a caress. It made her head spin, but she definitely wanted a proper kiss. She wanted to be snogged within an inch of her life.

She pressed a little closer, tempting him to take what she was offering, and that deep growl rumbled in his chest again. She couldn't breathe and was lightheaded from an overintake of oxygen at the same time.

When he leaned down to caress her a second time, she pushed into the kiss until their lips pressed fully together. His were surprisingly soft, full and warm and so indescribably delectable. Time had frozen for her to experience every little nuance of this perfect moment. Just for a moment, he kissed her back, tilting his head to fit them better together.

But then he pulled back.

"Your taste . . ." His gaze flicked between her eyes and mouth several times. He looked *hungry*. There was no other way to describe it. "I want more."

"Kiss me again." Was that her voice? Was she the bold, sensual woman who'd just said that out loud?

A wild look came into his eyes—which suddenly seemed more yellow than amber and were even brighter than they'd been before—and he leaned down and captured her lips again. This time there was no softness or hesitation. This time felt like a claim. Long fingers threaded into her hair, the tips digging into her scalp.

The *sharp* tips. Almost like . . . claws?

Didn't matter. She was lost to the kiss, to the feel of his big body surrounding her and the dark, spicy scent of him. Yes, his scent. Maybe he was making her feral too, because suddenly, she understood the urge to bury her nose in his neck and take a whiff.

He stepped into her, and she stumbled back until she hit the counter. He pressed her into it, stooping down to kiss her deeper, angling her head so he could better reach her lips.

Her neck strained, but she had nowhere to escape with his

grip so tight on her hair. She didn't want to escape anyway. His hold demanded her surrender, and she gave it to him readily.

He broke the kiss again, and she sucked in a desperate gasp, head spinning, her gaze still locked on his mouth, which she wanted pressed against hers again immediately.

"I wanted to do this from the moment I saw you," he said in a low growl.

Any other time she might have taken those words and replayed them over and over with increasing delight. As it was, right now her brain wasn't quite functioning properly. She was still staring at his mouth, and the only word she could seem to formulate was, *"Yes."* Panted and gasped and entirely too wanton.

He apparently enjoyed it, because his eyes darkened and he granted her unspoken wish, kissing her again. This time, their lips parted, and his tongue flicked into her mouth.

She sucked in a breath. The sensation shot straight between her legs, and her hands reached up to grip his delectably firm biceps lest she topple over right then. He flicked his tongue again, and this time, she was bold enough to meet it with her own. They brushed together. More sensation. Hot and bright and centralized between her trembling thighs.

He growled again.

God, that sound. It would be her undoing. Boldness increasing, she slid her hands up to his firm, sculpted shoulders and then wrapped her arms as far around his neck as she could reach. She tightened her grip, hauling him down to her level as their tongues began a luscious dance between their fused lips.

She hadn't breathed in far too long, but right now, she didn't need oxygen. She needed his tongue in her mouth, and she would rather faint than relinquish it.

He pressed harder into her, until her spine dug somewhat painfully into the counter, but she didn't mind in the least. The angle was somewhat awkward due to their height difference, and he seemed to understand this. His big hands slid down the curve of her waist, and then he boldly palmed her ass.

She moaned just as he hefted her, lifting her effortlessly and setting her on the counter. Apparently, things were escalating. She was fully on board with this, so she wrapped her thighs around his hips and tugged him into her.

Their bodies collided, which meant she felt the long, hard bulge in his pants right between her legs. She nearly fainted. No, she nearly had an orgasm. Both, perhaps. A fainting orgasm.

He was growling again, and she threw her head back as his mouth traveled down her throat, licking, sucking, biting. *Biting.* He definitely liked to bite, fixing his teeth around her soft neck and growling against her skin. It was positively feral and by far the sexiest thing that had ever happened to her.

She wanted him to bite her breasts. She wanted him to leave marks all over her. She wanted him to tear her dress off and throw her down on the ground and take her right there and then.

Screw dinner. Screw exchanging pleasantries and taking it slow and playing it safe. She wanted to be claimed like an earthy goddess on the forest floor beneath the full moon in the most wild, animalistic way possible.

His teeth fixed around the top of her shoulder while his palms slid up her bare thighs under her dress, and she moaned at his touch on her skin. Her own hands had slid inside the neck of his T-shirt, reaching as far down as she could to dig her nails into the muscles of his back.

His hips were still pressed into hers, and she rolled her own, far past caring if she was being too forward or presumptuous. Judging by the deep groan that rumbled out of him, he did not think so in the least.

His hands were on her ass now, inside her dress, and he pulled her to him, pressing so hard into her, it sent shockwaves of heat to her blooming core. She rolled her hips again, suddenly certain that she might actually be able to orgasm like this.

"Mist," she moaned as his hungry mouth consumed the skin just below her right ear.

He growled at the sound of his name and lifted his head, seeking her mouth. They clashed together again, and she rolled her hips with abandon while their tongues tangled.

Again: the sexiest thing to ever happen to her.

"Lily," he groaned, and his deep, breathless gasp made her moan again. "You are mi—"

He broke off suddenly.

His head jerked up, turning sharply to one side, and he appeared to be staring down the hallway. His entire demeanor changed in a split second. All that intensity that had been focused on her was suddenly fixed at whatever he was looking at. His grip on her tightened, all but wrapping her in his embrace.

"Someone is here," he growled in a low, deadly tone.

She clutched at his strong shoulders, her head spinning from the pleasure and the sudden shift in the atmosphere. "I don't hear anything."

"I smell them." He pulled her even closer, like he was shielding her from some perceived threat.

He smelled them? Surely his sense of smell wasn't that good. "I don't think there's—"

Banging sounded on the front door.

She glanced sharply up at Mist. Another growl rumbled in his chest, this one scary instead of seductive. How had he known that? And who was knocking—?

"It's me! Open up!" Iris's muffled voice faintly carried down the hall.

No. No way. She closed her eyes and groaned. "It's my sister." A sister who was about to get yelled at.

Some of the tension bled from Mist's body, but not all. "Your blood relation is here?"

"Yes, and I'm going to kill her." She'd told Iris not to bother her again, and she knew it hadn't been an hour since her last text, so she couldn't use that as an excuse either. "Let me just go deal with her, and then I'll be right back."

Instead of releasing her, however, he seemed to freeze as if at war with himself. His grip on her tightened again, and he seemed to be trying to shield her from the outside world by covering her completely with his own body.

Was this about his "instincts" again? Could he not let her go because it would feel like she was running and trigger his need to chase her?

She ought to have laughed at such an absurd notion, but instead, she felt the need to reassure him.

"I'll be right back," she repeated softly. "I promise."

She looked up into his narrowed eyes, seeing the conflict there. Seeking to appease him, she relaxed every muscle in her body so he would know she had no intention of trying to escape his hold. Having her pliant in his arms seemed to lessen his tension, and after a long moment, he finally released her.

She smiled, pleased with his acquiescence even though it made no damn sense. None of this did. He wasn't some alpha wolf in a mating ritual. He was just a man, and human men didn't have feral instincts. The idea was ludicrous.

Still, she couldn't shake the feeling, and she wanted him to trust her. Stepping over to the table she'd set for dinner, she tugged one of the lilies out of the bouquet in the center.

"I'll be right back," she said, holding out the blossom to him. A token of her promise.

His expression was intense as he accepted her gift. He stared down at the flower. And then his fingers wrapped around the stem, and he held it to his chest possessively. Much like he had done with her moments ago.

She had no idea what she was doing, why he was acting the way he was, or why it was so important to her that he didn't misunderstand her, but none of that mattered. She waited until she found what she was looking for in his gaze—a look of acceptance instead of distrust—and then hurried down the hall to answer the door.

KNOW YOUR ENEMY

*H*E'S HERE AND EVERYTHING'S FINE. YOU DON'T HAVE TO *wait around if you don't want to.*

Iris Donovan wasn't going anywhere. She'd insisted on staying close by during her sister's date, and she wasn't changing her mind. Lily called her paranoid, but she had a damn good reason to be—even if her twin didn't know it.

Since the day they'd left Ireland, she'd made it her mission to continue her parents' work and keep herself and her sister safe. The guilt of lying ate her up inside, but she didn't see a way out. She was in too deep to go back now.

So, she sat her arse down on a swing in the park at the end of Lily's block, slapped her headphones over her ears, and got busy getting fired up to the best band of all time: Rage Against the Machine. Hood up, head down, she loitered in the park like a regular juvenile delinquent.

She was a chick with blue hair and tattoos who liked angry music.

Call her cliché—she didn't give a fuck.

All she knew was that Rage made her feel invincible. Listening to them made her feel like she could launch fire from her fingertips and chop the heads off demons. She would be forever grateful to that band for giving her the strength to get through some pretty dark times in her life.

Her phone buzzed in her hand with another text from Lily.

Btw, what's that ward you put above my door supposed to do?

Immediately, Iris's heart started pounding, and her anxieties went spiraling. Why would Lily be asking that right now? She tensed to leap from the swing and rush to her sister's rescue but stopped and forced herself to think rationally.

She needed to chill. She was riding a fine line with her overprotectiveness, and if she pushed too hard, at some point her twin would start pushing back. And maybe Lily was just asking out of curiosity. Her sister's instincts were good. If she was concerned, she would have said something.

It's a signal ward that warns you if you're in the presence of supernatural beings, Iris texted back. *Why are you asking that right now?*

Pleased with her reasonable response, she decided to give Lily five minutes to reply before she freaked out. So she cranked up Rage again and tried to relax.

A moment later, the sharp scent of cigarette smoke snagged her attention. She was always on her guard, so, without changing her position on the swing, she paused the music to listen to her surroundings.

Peeking around the edge of her hood, she saw a guy making his way across the park toward her. Clad in a baggy tank top and high-top Nikes, a backward hat on his head, he looked as much a delinquent as she did. Somewhere in her mind, the part of her that dwelled on deep shit wondered how much of it was an act for him too.

He stopped under the glow of a streetlamp, and she got her first proper look at him in the light. Her eyes widened in appreciation.

Damn, he was built. And he was covered in tattoos. Not just his arms, or even the odd bold one on his neck or hand. *Covered.* Every available inch of his skin. Even half of his face. It was fucking hot.

The sound of a tinny phone speaker exploding with angry hip-hop suddenly filled the night, and she smiled to herself. A man of fine taste, evidently. He balanced his cigarette between sexy lips—made sexier by the snake-bite piercings on the lower—and pulled his phone out of his pocket.

She pretended to be busy on her own phone so the stranger wouldn't think she was eavesdropping if he looked over. For some reason, it was important that she overheard what he said on the phone. Or maybe it was just because the guy was fine as hell and she didn't get out enough.

She wasn't going to approach him or anything—she wasn't looking to date or even hook up. Lord knew she needed a break from men after finally cutting Antoine out of her life. She'd only just gotten her flat back, and poor Grimalkin was still traumatized from their break-up fight.

"Where the fuck are you?" the stranger said into the phone, and Iris fought the urge to fan herself.

What could she say? Foul-mouthed, tattooed jerks were her kryptonite.

"I don't give a fuck. Get your ass over here. I'm bored shitless."

God, she was getting turned on just listening to him swear like a trucker.

"I know it's stupid, but I told Mist I'd hang out nearby while he was on his date in case he started sniffing her or something and I needed to do damage control." He dragged on the cigarette. "Fuck you, I'm not being *nice.* I'm just being . . . helpful. Shut up."

Iris stiffened. Mist happened to be the unusual name of Lily's date, and the very reason she was hanging out in this park alone in the first place. So was he friends with this guy then? She didn't like the idea of Lily dating a guy whose friends had face tats.

And why would Face Tats think he'd need to do damage control? Her eyes narrowed. This Mist bloke better not mess with her sister or she was going to make him regret it.

She sent another text to Lily, starting to lose the battle against her need to panic. She still hadn't found out why she was suddenly asking about the wards, after all. *Did something happen? Are you okay? Answer me right now or I'm coming over.*

Lily's response came almost immediately. *No, don't come! I asked because the ward is dark red, but I thought it was black before. I'm obviously imagining things. Please don't panic because everything is fine. Gotta go!*

Meanwhile, Face Tats was still talking on the phone. "That shit about Paimon fucked me up. I know this doesn't help him in the grand scheme of things, but I had to do something, you know?"

The world ground to a sudden halt as several things sunk in at once. The bastard had just name-dropped Paimon. And Lily's signal ward had turned red.

Paimon = demon. Red = demon.

Motherfucking *demons.*

There was a demon in her sister's apartment, and, in all likelihood, another standing right in front of her.

They'd been found. After all these years of hiding and all the precautions she'd taken, the wards, the bindings, the rituals . . . they'd been found.

She was out of the swing and running toward Lily's place before her next breath.

Lily marched down the hall, pissed at her sister and more turned on than she'd ever been in her life. Her heart was racing, her body temperature at a thousand degrees, and the hottest man she had ever seen was standing in her kitchen.

So what if he was a little feral. The whole sniffing and biting thing was really doing it for her.

She threw open the door. "Why are you here? I told you I was fine!"

Iris pushed back her hood, and Lily did a double take at the genuine fear in her eyes. "The ward is red? Are you sure?"

"It was more burgundy than red, but yeah. Why does that matter right— Hey!"

Iris grabbed her arm and yanked her outside, slamming the front door behind her.

Before Lily had a chance to react, Iris dabbed the tip of her already bloody finger onto the center of a new ward on the front door.

"What the hell?" The mad witch must have been lurking outside drawing the sigil before she'd knocked. "What on earth are you doing?"

"If the signal ward turned red, it means there's a demon in your house."

Lily scoffed even as part of her went cold. "That's ridiculous. Mist is—"

"A bloody *demon*, Lil. There was another one with face tats in the park too. I overheard him talking on the phone. He mentioned Paimon, who is a crazy powerful—"

"You're unbelievable!" Lily threw up her hands. "I can't believe you would show up here and interrupt my first date in years with your paranoid delusions! It's like you want me to be miserable and alone forever."

"I'm not delusional, Lil! He's a demon. The ward doesn't lie. If it's red, there's a demon in your house. Period. And I just trapped it." She pointed to the sigil on the door.

"You . . . what?"

"I trapped it."

"You *trapped* it?"

Iris nodded, a malicious glint in her eye. "It's only a single-level prison ward, since I didn't have time to run around the block to get the back door, but it should be strong enough. As soon as you came out, I activated it with my blood. The demon is trapped inside."

Lily stared at her sister with her mouth open.

"Do you know what this means, Lil?" Her eyes flared with perverted excitement. "I've caught a real live demon. And I'm going to find a way to kill it."

No. This was too much. Iris had gone too far. Even if Mist was a demon, which Lily highly doubted, there was no way she was letting her twin kill him in cold blood.

They had good cause to be fearful, however. Humans were under the protection of Heaven unless they chose to dabble in the supernatural, like practitioners. Blood-born witches, on the other hand, were considered supernatural beings and were therefore ineligible for heavenly protection from birth, thanks to whatever was in their blood that gave them their abilities.

It didn't help that there was an old myth that stated the original blood-borns came from the offspring of a human and a demon—an impossibility, since demons weren't capable of procreation.

Whatever the case, demons could kill witches without breaking rules, and Heaven would not intervene.

If Mist was a demon, it meant he'd come into her life with some ulterior motive to lie and trick her. And if he discovered what she was, he could kill her simply because it entertained him. The thought froze her blood and broke her heart at the same time.

But she still didn't wish him dead, and she didn't condone murder of any kind. Of any creature. Call her weak, spineless, whatever. She wasn't a killer, and she wasn't letting Iris travel down that path.

"Iris, listen to me," she began, head spinning. "You can't just—"

She trailed off as the front door opened.

Mist stood there, looking between them, the lily she'd given him still in his hand.

She and Iris froze. How much had he overheard? Was he really a demon? Would he try to attack them?

But he couldn't because of the prison ward. He was trapped, which she wasn't sure was a good thing. If there was any way to piss off a demon, that was it.

He lifted a hand, and she flinched. Except he stopped with his palm flat and almost seemed to be miming an invisible wall—

The barrier. As his palm connected, the energy warped around it. Green light flashed where he made contact—the color of Temporal magic. Though indiscernible to the un-trained eye, both Lily and Iris could see the shimmering of the ward's force field.

Oh god, he really was a demon.

He pushed against the barrier. They both tensed as it flexed outward, but it held.

"You're trapped." Iris's voice was hard, but the slightest tremor betrayed her nerves. "If you want to make it out of this alive, you'd better tell me who the fuck you are and what you want with my sister."

Mist said nothing, gaze fixed on Iris with a penetrating stare, head cocked slightly. He dropped his hand and stepped forward.

Leaning one shoulder against the barrier, he pushed again. Green light traveled down his arm—the ward was electrocuting him. The pain must have been excruciating, but a muscle tick-ing in his jaw was the only indication of discomfort he allowed.

"You won't be able to break it," Iris said. "So you might as well give u—"

He pushed through.

His shoulder gave way first, and he stumbled a little. Then, steadying himself, he stepped over the threshold and stopped on the welcome mat, staring them down.

Iris made a choking sound. "H-how . . . ?"

Amber eyes that were far too bright fixed on Iris's stunned face. Lily's heart pounded so loudly it was hard to hear anything else.

"It would take far stronger wards than that to trap me, witch."

His eyes flashed, and for a second, yellow bled into the rest of them, filling the white completely. Then he looked at Lily, who stood rooted in place, speechless and terrified.

Except, his expression . . . There was something so tormented in his eyes, it made tears spring into the corners of hers.

Which was absurd. A demon had kissed her, and this was her reaction? To want to cry because he looked sad? But she couldn't help it, couldn't stifle the ache that sprang up in her chest.

They looked at each other, and for a moment, everything was forgotten, and they were right back in her kitchen, tangled up in each other.

Then he turned away, and the spell was broken. He descended the stairs to the street below. He didn't attack. He didn't threaten them. He just left.

When he reached the ground, he tugged his shirt over his head, revealing a broad back ribbed with strength. One she had been running her hands over only moments ago. He looked over his shoulder to where she watched from the balcony.

Before her eyes, he shifted.

First his skin darkened, becoming an ashy gray that matched the shadows cast by the streetlights on the pavement. He grew nearly a foot taller, making him absolutely enormous. His eyes turned back to the glimpse she'd seen of glowing yellow. Claws elongated from his fingers. Claws she hadn't imagined feeling after all.

And finally . . . wings.

Black wings burst from his back and spread wide. Like a bat's, fine bones delineated the segments of leather-like membrane stretched between them. The top, reminiscent of the shape of a hand, was tipped with a long, curved talon where the thumb would be.

Lily gasped, and Iris cursed. All the while, Mist stared at her.

At this point, the natural glamor hiding the supernatural would have made him invisible to anyone else nearby. But Lily wasn't a regular human, and Mist knew that now. He knew she could see him. He was showing her exactly what he was, giving up his charade.

But why?

She didn't have time to wonder. The next moment, he finally turned away. Crouching deeply, he sprang, pumping those great wings, and launched into the air, that lily still clutched in his claws.

And then he dissolved into a black cloud and disappeared completely.

He dissolved into . . . mist.

MIST VERSUS REALITY

THE BLACK MIST CIRCLED THE APARTMENT BUILDING BE-
fore finally slipping through the crack in an open
window.

Mist solidified in his bedroom. Through the closed door,
he could hear Belial banging around the kitchen and talking to
someone—probably Raum, since he knew Meph would still be
waiting in the park. Meph had offered to wait there during the
date in case of emergency, though he surely hadn't imagined
anything like this happening.

Mist surveyed his surroundings and finalized his plan. He
had to move quickly and quietly. There was a greater chance
of someone realizing he was missing the longer he delayed,
and he wanted to be long gone before anyone thought to look
for him.

It was for the best.

The brand on his neck burned fiercer than ever, and he had
only a few days left before he could no longer fight the compulsion. He'd known he couldn't ignore Paimon forever, but he'd
been in denial. Excitement at playing human and hunting Lily

had distracted him from contemplating the futility of his entire sojourn on Earth.

He felt a pang of regret at the thought of leaving. He would miss his . . . friends. Yes, he supposed that was what they were. Eva had explained the concept of friendship, and he felt certain he had formed such bonds with her and the other demons.

And Lily.

He'd wanted to pretend he could live like Asmodeus and Eligos with a human female that looked upon him with acceptance instead of horror. But he had seen Lily's face tonight when confronted with his true form, and it was nothing like the way Eligos's female regarded him.

Lily's eyes had been wide, her mouth open, her expression one of revulsion.

Something inside Mist had withered at that look, and he realized he no longer cared to find a human female if he had to pretend to be something he wasn't.

And if he couldn't have Lily, he didn't want another anyway. He had scented every female he'd come across and none appealed to him as she did. He wanted her or no one.

In the end, however, it didn't matter what he wanted.

The truth was that he was the Hunter and nothing more. He did not have a choice in his future. He was not free. He served a purpose, and it was not to form bonds or indulge his desires. He was bound to his role for eternity by the brands on his body.

After carefully setting down Lily's flower, he stripped off his human pants—a little tight now that he was back in demon form, but not much. Ash had explained how they always bought their clothes slightly too big so there was room to shift. Unfortunately, human pants in any size did not have space for a tail, so it was only after he'd removed them that Mist allowed his to reappear.

Folding the human garment and setting it on the bed, he extracted his wyrm-leather pants from the dresser drawer and donned them. If a demon shifted into a drastically different form—like his mist form or Raum's crow form—the magic would shift the clothing with them. But a minor shift, like the transformation from human to demon, was not enough to affect most materials, and it would stretch or tear.

Wyrm leather, however, could grow and shrink along with a shifting demon, and it was a hot commodity in Hell, selling for exorbitant rates on the Blood Market. Mist's two pairs of pants, custom-made for a demon with a tail, were the only thing of value he owned.

After dressing, he cleared floor space by moving the dresser and then retrieved the chalk he'd hidden in the drawer for this purpose. He traced the hellgate on the floor, adding a lock sigil so it could not be reactivated once he passed through.

Finished, he stood back and surveyed his bedroom one final time. He'd never had possessions before, besides a few meager trinkets to hide in the corner of his cave. It would be a shame to leave them behind now.

He hoped his friends wouldn't be angry he had left without saying goodbye—especially Meph, who would be waiting in the park for a very long time. Just in case, he removed his cell phone from the pants he'd discarded and typed a text message.

I have returned to my hunting duties. The blood contract remains binding, and I will not reveal your whereabouts or Eva's existence.

He paused, struggling to find words to express his feelings. In the end, he couldn't think of anything, or perhaps just wasn't comfortable exploring it, so he simply added, *Thank you*, to the end of the message.

As he sent it, he told himself he was expelling such sentimentalities from his mind forever. Taking a breath, he banished all thoughts of Lily and his friends and stuffed his newfound emotions in a cage deep within. He locked them up tight and mentally discarded the key.

They were gone, and he was the Hunter once more.

And yet, at the last moment, he reached over and grabbed the lily he'd placed on the dresser. It was *his* flower, and he was keeping it.

Then he stepped into the hellgate and disappeared.

Lily and Iris didn't move for at least two minutes after Mist vanished into the night.

"Bloody hell," Iris said finally.

They went together into the house after rubbing out the ward on the front door to hide the evidence from the neighbors. Lily collapsed at the kitchen table. The aroma of her uneaten dinner permeated the kitchen, but her appetite was long gone.

How could Mist be a demon? But he was. Undeniably. And yet she couldn't get the look in his eyes before he'd shifted and flown away out of her head. And she couldn't stop thinking about the way he'd kissed her and held her against him so possessively. And the way he'd fixed his teeth on her neck and growled when he thought she was trying to escape.

Against her will, her stomach fluttered.

In truth, he'd been pretty terrible at acting human, and she was a little embarrassed that she hadn't figured it out sooner. But his desire for her hadn't seemed faked, and she couldn't reconcile what her instincts were telling her with what she knew about demons.

"I can't believe it," Iris was mumbling, pacing across the kitchen so fast it was making Lily dizzy. "I can't believe you had a demon in your flat. And he just broke through my ward like it was nothing. *Damn* it!"

Lily flinched at her shout.

"You know how long I've practiced to master that ward? Who the hell is this guy? Mist . . . It's short for something, but

I don't know what. What I can't figure out is how he found you."

"What do you mean, found me? You make it sound like he was looking for me in particular."

Mist was obviously powerful, but she had nothing that would be enticing to a demon. No money, power, or influence. She could have believed she was a target because of her bloodline, but she wasn't even a practicing witch while Iris so obviously was. It didn't make sense.

"What did you guys talk about?" Iris asked, ignoring her question. "Did he ask you about anything?"

"He just— He bought me ice cream the night we met. And he asked about my designs, and he just seemed interested in . . . me."

She couldn't talk about this. All it was doing was reminding her of the sweet things he'd done. And the way he'd kissed her . . . If it was all an act to lure her in, he had done a perfect job. So perfect, she was still affected by it even after learning it was a lie.

"He didn't ask about Mam and Dad or anything to do with the coven?"

Lily shook her head. "I never told him I was a witch." He hadn't even asked about her bookshelf.

"Did he know about me? That we're twins?"

"I told him I had a sister, but I don't think I mentioned we were twins. Why would that matter?"

A banging on the front door cut off Iris's reply, and they froze.

"Who is that?" Iris whispered. "He didn't come back, did he?"

When neither of them moved, the banging sounded again. "Open up or I'll kick it in!" a male voice shouted. Not Mist.

Lily stared at her sister. "What should we do?"

Iris shook her head, her eyes wide.

"Let me in, that's what you should do!"

How had he heard them? They were whispering all the way across the flat.

"Not joking about kicking in the fucking door!"

"Oh my god," Iris whispered, recognition flaring in her eyes. "I think it's . . ."

"Yeah, it's the scary guy from the park. Boo. Now open the damn door."

"Let's slip out the back." Iris whipped open the utensil drawer and dug out Lily's biggest knife, clutching it like a lifeline.

"You do that, I'll just follow you, and we'll still end up having this conversation. Or you can open the door and save yourself the trouble of replacing it later."

"We should talk to him," Lily whispered, unsure why she felt so strongly about it.

"He'll kill us!"

"He won't hurt us." Again, she had no idea why she was so certain about that.

Brandishing the cleaver, Iris looked dubious.

Unwilling to ignore her instincts, Lily jumped up and raced down the hall before her sister could stop her. Iris called out, "Damn it, Lil!" but Lily didn't stop until she was at the front door, unlocking and throwing it open.

Iris reached the end of the hall right as Mist's tattooed friend walked in like he owned the place, closing the door behind him and staring down Lily like he was a pissed off parent and she was the naughty kid.

The loose tank top he wore bagged under his arms and showcased the tattoos covering his torso. On his face, an illegible gothic script ran above his pierced left eyebrow, and the strange symbols beneath his eye looked like something out of a grimoire. More writing ran in vertical lines down the left side of his face. He had a ring in the center of his nose and two on either side of his lower lip. A backward hat held down short black hair, and his eyes were red.

Not reddish brown. Red.

"Where the fuck is he?" He glared at Lily, who had frozen like a deer in headlights.

"Where the fuck is who?" Iris snapped.

"Mist!" He hadn't stopped looking at Lily. "He was here, and now he's not, and I got this weird text from him, and now he's not answering his . . ." He trailed off as his gaze finally landed on Iris. "Phone."

His eyes flared in blatant appreciation as they ran up and down her body. He started to smile. "You have blue hair."

Iris gaped at him. "Yeah, I have blue freaking hair. So what?"

"So, it's cool. I like it."

"Brilliant!" She threw up her hands, including the one still clutching the meat cleaver. Both Lily and the newcomer flinched as the blade passed inches from their faces. "And if you're looking for your friend, he shifted into a fucking demon and flew off!"

"Shit. You're witches, then?"

"Powerful ones," Iris said haughtily, chin up and hands planted on her hips.

He started to grin again. "I'll bet you are, sweetness. So what'd you do to Mist to make him run away?"

"What did we *do* to him? He's a demon!"

"Yeah, a demon who was trying to have a nice, roman-tic dinner date with his girl." He gestured to Lily and shot a glare at Iris. "Don't tell me you scared him off. I recognized the remainder of a prison ward on the front door, not that that measly thing would keep him in."

"*Scared* him off? He was here to hurt my sister! I would have killed him if he hadn't fled!"

He scoffed. "Yeah. Okay. Good luck with that. And he

wasn't here to hurt her, unless it hurt when he— Never mind. So, Mist was having a good ol' time before you started painting prison wards and threatening him. Then what happened? Where'd he go?"

"I didn't threaten him! He threatened her!"

"Answer the fucking question!" he snapped with a sudden ferocity. Until that moment, he had retained his cool. Something flared in his eyes then that was dark and deadly.

"You're a demon too," Lily breathed, shrinking back.

"Uh, yeah." He looked at her like she had slugs for brains.

"B-but—"

He rolled his eyes, chill demeanor firmly back in place. "But what? You're expecting me to call on the fires of Hell and threaten to steal your soul?"

She winced. "Well . . . maybe."

"Nobody wants your soul, okay? You're too . . . good, or whatever, to be useful to Hell. Trust me, the humans we deal with are scum. Real lowlifes, backstabbers and liars and rapists; the kind of people you'll probably never come across in your life." He shot a warning look at Iris. "Unless you go looking for trouble."

"But . . ." Lily couldn't find the words.

"But what was Mist doing here? Told you, doll. Try to keep up."

"Don't call her that," Iris snapped.

The demon grinned at her. "You this fierce for everyone, doll, or am I special?"

"Tell me what you want with us, or I swear to god I will find a way to kill you."

His grin widened. "Chop off the head and burn the body to ashes with hellfire—that's how you kill a demon. Has to be legit hellfire, and you have to incinerate it completely. Otherwise we'll just regenerate and come back really pissed off."

They both gaped at him.

"What? You're witches. I hope you knew that already. And if you ever got close enough to succeed, the demon would deserve to die for being an idiot." Abruptly, his expression darkened. "Now tell me where Mishetsu is."

"Mishetsu?"

"Mist."

"Told you," Iris said, "he sprouted wings and flew off."

"He didn't say anything about where he was going?"

Lily shook her head.

He yanked his hat off and dragged a hand through his hair before jamming it back on. "He's probably done something stupid."

Pulling his phone out, he made a call right there while the two of them were staring at him. Part of Lily wondered if she was asleep having a vivid dream because every minute of this night kept getting stranger. She'd barely been able to believe it when Mist had kissed her, and now this?

"Yo. Is Mist at home? Tell me he's there." A pause. Then, "Fuck the motherfucking fucker."

Well, he certainly knew how to express himself.

"I'm at Lily's. That's his girl. Yeah. Apparently, she's a witch. No, he didn't know. Crazy, right? But it gets worse. Her sister's a crazy-ass bitch"—he grinned shamelessly at Iris when she pointed the cleaver in his face—"and she crashed their date, drew a prison ward, and threatened to kill him. Lily said he shifted in front of her and took off."

He paused, nodding in agreement with whatever the person on the other line was saying. Oh god, it was probably another demon.

"I know. It's messed up. And he's not answering his phone. Do you think . . . ? He wouldn't be that stupid, would he? Shit. All right, I'll be back in a few."

He hung up and looked at them.

"Well, ladies, it's been a slice"—he gestured to the cleaver with a wink—"but I'm out. Gotta go save a demon, if you know what I mean. We were trying to help Mist get out of a bad situation, but it seems he's gone right back to the lion's den by choice. Idiot."

Undaunted by the knife still in his face, he shot Iris a heated look, goofy grin back like it had never left. "It's a shame we had to meet like this, sweetness. Any other time, I'd have loved to take you out." He looked at Lily. "Sorry you had to find out your date was a demon, but he's really not a bad guy."

Turning toward the door, he glanced over his shoulder. "Oh, and if you're going to practice witchcraft, stay away from summoning, yeah? Easiest way to get dead, guaranteed." He waggled his fingers. "Toodles."

The door slammed, and he was gone.

8

DENIAL AIN'T JUST A RIVER IN EGYPT

Lily HAD NOT RECOVERED FROM HER SHOCK BY THE next morning, nor had Iris stopped fuming. They loitered in the kitchen with iced coffees and bagels, Iris pacing and mumbling, Lily sitting and staring at the wall. Just like last night.

After Mist's friend left, Iris had spent a good hour trying to convince Lily to stay at her place. Lily had obstinately refused. If the demons had wanted to hurt her, they'd had ample opportunity. And if they wanted to find her again, they would, whether she was in her home or running scared.

Of course, Iris had then declared that if Lily was staying, so was she. After making a series of mysterious, hushed phone calls and drawing wards over all the walls, her sister ended up crashing on her sofa. Lily had tried to sleep but just stared at the ceiling all night instead, trying to process everything that had happened.

Now, morning had arrived, and she didn't feel better. She didn't have closure. If anything, she felt worse.

"We need to double the strength of the cloaking," Iris was muttering as she paced. "We'll need to bring in outside manpower. Maybe I'll call the Toronto coven for support."

"What are you talking about?"

"What I can't figure out is why he was stalling. Why play human and bother with the fake date charade? Why not just snatch you up the minute he got close? Why walk off when he had us both within his grasp? It's not like he would've needed reinforcements to overpower us."

"What if he wasn't after anything at all?" Lily dared to ask, though she knew better than to reason with her stubborn sister.

"What?"

"What if his friend was telling the truth? What if he really just wanted to go on a date with me?" *Why are you even trying to get through to her?*

"Lil . . ." Iris got that pitying-the-sad-sister look on her face that Lily hated. "He's a demon."

"Yeah, but what do we really know about demons? I mean, who says they can't go on dates?"

"I know a lot about them. And believe me, they are just as evil and soulless as the legends say. There is no such thing as a good demon."

"But how do you know for sure? I mean, they're conscious beings with thoughts and emotions, so they must have some free will like humans. Therefore, it's theoretically possible that they could choose *not* to be evil."

"Listen to yourself." Iris shook her head. "Demons are demons. They're evil. They tempt you to do evil to claim your soul for Hell. That is their one purpose, their only reason for existence. There is no gray area. There are no good demons."

"But how do you know for sure?"

"Because I've seen it with my own eyes! I've seen what those monsters are capable of."

"What are you talking about?" Lily frowned at the anguish suddenly flashing in her twin's eyes. "What have you seen?"

A shadow passed over Iris's face before she turned to face the window. "Nothing."

"Ris, what aren't you telling me?"

"It's nothing, seriously. Just trust me when I say they're evil. All of them."

"Hmph." Lily slumped back in her chair. She knew her sister well enough to know when she wasn't going to say more. "Something's not adding up."

"You could say that again."

Except they were saying it for different reasons.

Iris thought it wasn't adding up because she couldn't pinpoint the demon's evil motives. Lily wasn't convinced Mist had an evil motive at all.

What if the tattooed demon hadn't been lying? *We were trying to help Mist get out of a bad situation, but it seems he's gone right back to the lion's den.* What bad situation? And what did he mean by the "lion's den?" Was he referring to Hell?

She was more confused than ever. Worst of all, her annoying witchy instincts were screaming at her again, so much it was making it hard to breathe.

Sorry you had to find out your date was a demon, but he's really not a bad guy.

Her heart squeezed. She couldn't shake the feeling that Mist was in trouble and needed help. It was absurd, but she felt it nonetheless.

"Iris," she said suddenly, sitting upright again. Her sister was mid-rant about the evilness of demons, but Lily hadn't heard a word.

"What?"

"Do you ever feel certain . . . instincts? Like a really strong urge to do something you might not have done otherwise?"

To her surprise, Iris flopped into the chair opposite her. "Honestly? No, I don't."

"Oh. Never mind, I'm probably just—"

"You're not imagining it. Mam told me about it. She said it's a manifestation of our gift. She said all the greatest witches in history have written about having a guiding instinct along with an individual manifestation of their abilities. Like a special power, kind of. She told me that if I ever felt the instinct, I should listen to it unfailingly." She breathed a bitter laugh. "She never told me how to feel it in the first place, though."

"So you don't . . . feel anything ever?"

She shook her head. "I think I used to. Before they died. But I was young, and I didn't pay enough attention to it, and now it's gone. Probably a stress response to the trauma or whatever. But I can't figure out how to get it back." She shrugged. "Maybe I'll never get it back."

Lily stared at her sister. Though they were close, it was rare for Iris to open up this much.

"I think that's partly why I study and practice so hard. I don't have any of the abilities that the greatest of our kind have, so I guess I'm hoping if I work hard enough, I'll make up for it with book knowledge. Which is stupid, I know. But I don't know what else to do."

Shame crept up the back of Lily's neck. While Self-Doubt Lily ran rampant in her thoughts, she'd been busy pushing aside those empowering instincts. She'd spent years ignoring them, while Iris had spent years wishing she had them.

Iris looked up suddenly. "Why? Are you feeling something now?"

She hesitated. Iris was hotheaded and opinionated, and she'd made up her mind about demons. Would it make a difference? "Yes. At least, I think so."

"What are you feeling?"

"Last night, I should have been afraid, but I wasn't. Because I knew I wasn't in danger somehow. And now, with everything, I just . . . I can't shake the feeling that he's in trouble. And that I need to help him."

"That who's in trouble? The demon?" Iris looked incredulous. "He's a bloody *demon*, Lil. When are you going to get that? If he's in trouble, good. He probably deserves it for all the terrible stuff he's done. That creature belongs in Hell, and you need to get any ideas of him being some wounded puppy out of your head right now."

"Yeah." Lily sighed. "Okay."

Except hadn't Iris just told her of their mother's counsel? To listen to her instincts?

If she abandoned this right now, she would never get another full night's sleep because that damn intuition would keep her up, urging her to act. She'd probably spend the rest of her life chugging whiskey to keep her night-light magic battery from reaching full charge.

Or . . . it might finally go away like it had for her sister.

A day ago, she would've been glad. Now, something had shifted, something she wasn't sure how to name yet. But she wasn't ready to let go of that part of herself anymore.

What she needed was more information.

An hour later, after triple-checking the wards all over the apartment, Iris left for work at the occult shop that was a front for her coven's meeting place. She spent most of that hour trying to convince Lily to go with her, but again, Lily refused.

She wasn't in danger. She knew that because when she tuned in with those instincts, they told her everything she needed to know.

As soon as Iris left, she snatched her phone up and made a call. Did she feel bad going behind her sister's back? Absolutely. Was that going to stop her from doing it? Apparently not.

Unsurprisingly, the phone rang through to voicemail. She hung up and called again. The second call did the same, so she made a third. And a fourth. And a fifth. She made so many calls, she ate breakfast, finished her coffee, and washed all the dishes with it ringing on speaker the entire time.

Finally, she gave up. Either Mist really had gone back to Hell, or he just really didn't want to talk to her. Whatever the reason, it was time to move on to plan B: taking matters into her own hands.

The air was thick with tension.

Belial ground his teeth and glared at the Grigori standing across the room. The Grigori glared right back at him.

The last time he'd seen the guy, he'd tried to murder his brother, so Bel had flown into a rage and nearly burned down the building he'd been trapped in by angelic prison wards.

He still hadn't quite let that go.

Nor had he forgotten how he'd been so busy having a tantrum that he'd nearly gotten Meph killed. Raum had melted his hands off trying to pull the consecrated blade out of Meph's chest, but Belial hadn't even noticed, too busy tossing fireballs to help. Too lost in the rage to be aware of anything else.

Worse, he could have pulled it out with no ill effect. Since he was technically a fallen angel—a very fallen angel—he could withstand the Empyrean magic of a consecrated weapon. As far as he knew, he and Lucifer were the only demons who could.

Nearly two months later, his stomach still churned whenever he thought about it. His guilt was partly responsible for why he hadn't gone into a rage in weeks, but he wasn't sure it was an improvement.

He was so strung out from repressing his temper, he couldn't think straight. He drank obscene amounts of coffee and alcohol, and he rarely slept. The only thing that kept him from killing people was avoiding them.

Meph hadn't gotten over the whole fiasco either. He'd started disappearing for hours without telling anyone where he was going, even Raum. He'd been jumpy and even more unstable than he normally was.

For that reason, Bel had sent him and Raum on a bullshit grocery mission with the most convoluted shopping list he could think of. The last thing he needed was Meph deciding he wanted revenge on Eva's dad and starting shit. Not that Bel would blame him.

To call the truce they had formed with Dan "uneasy" was an understatement. There was only one thing holding that flimsy alliance together. Or one person, rather.

"Dad!" Eva burst through the front door, and Bel exhaled in relief.

The Grigori scooped his daughter up into a tight hug, joy suffusing his face. Two months ago, his wife had kicked him out for lying about what he was for twenty-seven years, and he clearly wasn't coping well. There were shadows under his eyes, his face was drawn and tired, and his hair was a mess.

Bel had overheard Eva and Ash talking about how Jacqui still refused to see him or talk to him, but that was all he knew. He made a point to stay out of other people's drama. He had enough of his own.

While father and daughter reunited with cringe-worthy sentiment, Bel dropped into the sofa and tried not to puke. Then he snorted as Asmodeus slipped in through the front door and slunk around Eva and Dan to sit beside Bel.

Ash slumped into the cushions and crossed his arms, long hair all in his face as he watched Dan through narrowed eyes like he expected him to attack at any moment.

Bel elbowed his sullen brother. "Aren't you gonna greet your father-in-law with a hug?"

Ash transferred the glare to him. "He's not my father-in-law."

"He could be."

He probably would be at some point. Bel could totally see Eva convincing Ash to enter into holy matrimony, which would be infinitely hilarious.

Asmodeus, former Prince of Hell, former Prince of Lust, a married man. Bel was liable to bust a gut laughing at the thought.

The saccharine greetings eventually concluded, and Dan sat on the sofa opposite the demons, Eva beside him. No one spoke for several moments.

"Asmodeus," Dan finally said. He didn't even bother greeting Belial.

Ash grunted.

"I hope you've been treating my daughter well."

"Really, Dad?" Eva groaned. "Can we not do this?"

"I just want to make sure you're safe."

Ash huffed indignantly as if he'd been dealt the highest of insults. "Our apartment is heavily warded, and I protect her with my life every moment of every day. A fact you would know if you visited more often."

"Ash," Eva warned.

Dan blinked. "You . . . want me to visit more often?"

Ash's lip curled. "Obviously *I* don't. But Eva does."

"Ash!"

"She's remarked that since she knows about your teleportation ability, you should be able to come to more of her gigs. But you don't."

"Ash, stop it."

Dan looked stricken. "I didn't know you felt that way, Eva."

"It's fine, Dad, really. Ash is just—"

"I stayed away because I thought you didn't want me around, not because I didn't want to be here."

"Why wouldn't I want you around?"

"Well, because of . . . everything that happened. And because you're dating *him*, and we're not exactly friendly, and your mom always said I have a tendency to smother you, so . . ."

Eva chuckled. "You guys will learn to get along—"

All three of them scoffed.

"You will! So don't stay away because of that, okay?"

"All right, I won't." Dan smiled at his daughter. "I'll be at your next gig for sure, honey."

She smiled back. "Thanks, Da—"

Bel coughed loudly. "Now that that's done, can we get to the matter at hand?"

"Mishetsumephtai's brands." Dan looked around. "Where is he?"

Eva had filled him in on the purpose of Belial wanting to meet, but obviously hadn't mentioned Mishetsu's disappearance. "He went back to Hell."

Or so they had concluded last night after receiving his vague text message. Meph had returned shortly after and filled them in on the unfortunate coincidence that Mishetsu's date was a witch. Poor bastard couldn't catch a break.

Dan frowned. "So he's where he wants to be. What's the problem?"

"He didn't go voluntarily. He's controlled by the brands, and he wants them gone. I want to help him."

Dan narrowed his eyes. "Why? What's in it for you?"

Bel said nothing. He'd already explained his reasons to Mishetsu, and they were for him alone. He wasn't justifying himself to some angelic prick.

"Mist is my friend too," Eva cut in, interrupting the staring contest. "We've been hanging out a lot the last month, and he's really sweet. I want to help him."

"Of course you do." Dan shook his head. "When you were

a kid, you always rooted for the monster in the story. I should have known you'd be trouble."

"What can I say? I love a good antihero." She smiled at Ash.

Bel rolled his eyes.

She turned to Dan. "Mist is a good guy. He deserves a chance. Please help us?"

"All this 'good demon' stuff is new to me, so I'm choosing to trust your judgment. Tell me about the brands."

Belial explained everything he knew about how they worked. Thankfully, he'd forced Mishetsu to let him snap a few pictures after their conversation, and he passed his phone over to Dan now to let him study them.

"Hmm." The Grigori stared at the pictures for a time. "It looks familiar. I must have read about it at some point, possibly in something on Sheolic magic in the Empyrean library, but it's hard to remember now."

"What do you remember?" Belial asked.

Dan studied him. "What do *you* remember? I think you'd have more knowledge on this than I do."

"I remember something," Bel admitted, "but it was from a very long time ago. I wanted to hear your thoughts to verify if my memory was accurate or not."

Dan nodded. "The memories tend to blur together over the ages, don't they?"

"Often to be lost completely."

A moment of understanding passed between them.

They both grimaced and looked away. Belial was not getting friendly with an angel. He'd rather have Dan's knife stuck in his chest.

"My best guess?" Dan said. "The design of the brands looks like something from the Shehanva."

Belial cursed.

"You thought that too?"

He nodded.

"What's the Shehanva?" Eva asked.

"The Shehanva were a race of nomadic demons," Bel explained. "Savage little shits. They were skilled with magic and big on magical branding. They were wiped out of existence ages ago. They pissed off one too many territory rulers in their many attempts to take more land, and it was one of the rare instances where demons banded together to defeat a common enemy."

"So how were they responsible for Mist's brands if they're extinct?"

"Mishetsu has been around a long time. He would have gotten them before then. Paimon probably hired someone to perform the magic for her."

"Either way, it's a dead end," Asmodeus said. "The Shehanva are gone, and so is all knowledge of their magic practices."

"So there's no way to help Mist?" Eva looked devastated. "He's doomed forever to serve a horrible demon queen?"

"There has to be something." Bel stroked his chin and tried to remember.

It was hard to dig up memories from thousands of years ago, however. His mind had once been a very dark place, and after a certain point, he'd just deleted some of what was in there so he didn't go crazy from all the disturbing shit lurking around.

"There is someone I could ask," Dan said, though he didn't look happy about it. "But it's against the rules, and I don't feel right asking her to break them on behalf of a demon."

"Please, Dad?" Eva made doe eyes, and he caved instantly.

"Fine, fine. I have a friend. Well, more of an acquaintance. We were friends before I fell, and we've kept in touch over the ages. I could ask Sunshine to have a look in the Empyrean library for me."

"Her name is Sunshine? That doesn't sound like your typical angelic name."

"Her real name is Shamsiel, but she goes by Sunshine now. Long story. There's bound to be something there, but it'll take time since I'll be asking her to go behind her superiors' backs. She's not technically allowed to associate with the likes of me."

"But she'll do it?"

"Like I said, we've known each other a long time. But it could take a week or more."

"You could reach out to your sources too, Bel," Ash suggested. "You've always gotten what we need through all the idiots who owe you favors. Remember how quickly you got that Nephilim blood?"

Bel scowled. "It's not happening."

Because the source Ash was referring to was Naiamah, whom he hated with a burning passion. She was his best, most well-connected contact, and thanks to his negotiation skills and Naiamah's desperation at the time, he'd bound her with a contract owing him one thousand unspecified favors.

He'd used up most of them over the years and was down to his last hundred, but as a succubus, Naiamah would often make an exception to do the job in exchange for sex. Belial was an ancient, powerful demon, and the sexual energy she got from him was potent, to say the least.

Except he was sick of whoring himself out for favors, and he was sick of how easily Naiamah could convince him to give her what she wanted. Every time he saw her, he caved, and he hated himself for it.

One month and eighteen days ago—but who was counting, really—he'd made a pact with Eva's friend to remain celibate for six months. It would be the longest he'd ever gone without fornication since he'd fallen from Heaven at the dawn of creation. So, basically, since forever.

He'd already made it this far, damn it. He wasn't going to break now.

"We need to get Mishetsu back before we do anything else," he decided. "Who knows what Paimon will do to him for disappearing."

"But he's in Hell," Eva said. "How do we get him back?"

"We'll summon him."

"You can do that?"

"Demons can't summon other demons. But a human can."

"Who? Me?"

"No. You don't know the first thing about Temporal magic, and you're not technically human either."

"Then who?"

"A witch."

Eva's eyes widened. "But—"

"Well." Dan jumped up. "On that note, I'm out of here."

"What? Why?"

"Hon, it's already so against the rules for me to even be in the presence of rogue demons without trying to kill them. I can't knowingly sit around and listen to you plotting to summon one, and I certainly can't participate in it. Call me later, and we'll have dinner, okay? In the meantime, I'll talk to Sunshine and see if she can help us out."

As Eva bid her father farewell, Ash turned to Belial. "Meph said the witches were terrified of Mist and wanted to kill him. How are you going to convince them to help us summon him?"

"Easy." Bel smiled like the devil he was. "I won't give them a choice."

LE REPAIRE DES SORCIÈRES

THE DOOR SCREECHED LOUDLY AS LILY PULLED IT OPEN, and she froze, checking over her shoulder that she was alone. She shook her head. The alley was empty, and she already knew no one was inside—the shop had closed hours ago, and Iris had already texted to confirm she was home after her shift.

Lily even had a key. It wasn't like she was pulling a B&E.

Slamming the fire door behind her, she felt around in the pitch black for a switch. A moment later, the room flooded with light. She found herself in the back of a little Mile End shop that had been there longer than she'd been alive. Everyone in the area had heard of Le Repaire des Sorcières—The Witches' Lair—but most had no idea the name was so literal.

The back room of Le Repaire looked like any old store's. Paint chipped off the walls, the floors were slanted, and the gaps in the hardwood were big enough to lose a pen in. A tiny table and chair were positioned opposite a cracked sink with a vintage microwave on a shelf above that had to be in violation of a hundred safety codes. Every other inch of the room was packed with shelves, boxes, and racks of stock.

Parting a rack of flowing floral skirts, Lily pushed and shoved her way to the expertly buried far wall. There, a small gap between piles of boxes revealed an intricate sigil.

Realizing what she needed to do, she grimaced. Why did magic have to be so obsessed with blood?

Iris always had a knife or something sharp on her, but the only thing Lily had was her emergency sewing kit, and she refused to stab herself with a sewing needle on purpose.

Luckily, this was the witches' lair, and she didn't have to look far to find a tool. Resting atop the box pile beside her, the knife had obviously been used for this purpose in the past. A lighter on the tray beside it served as the only form of disinfectant. *So, so gross.*

Gritting her teeth and blocking thoughts of proper sanitary practices, she singed the blade and pricked the pad of her finger with the sharpened tip. Most witches had done this so many times, they'd lost all nerve sensation. Lily, not so much.

Wincing at the pain, she pressed her finger into the center of the sigil. Instantly, the protection spell shimmered and disappeared, revealing a tiny door in the wall. She unlatched the rusty bolt and pulled it open, using her phone flashlight to illuminate a narrow staircase to the underground cellar.

Despite knowing this room was frequented by witches, even her own sister, it didn't quell the creepy sensation of descending a staircase into blackness by herself at night. She kept expecting the door to slam or a monster to growl from the dark.

At the bottom of the stairs, she felt around for the switch, and the lights flickered on.

The sight before her was not what one would expect after the spooky staircase. The stone walls and floor of the surprisingly spacious, low-ceilinged cellar suggested the building's construction dated back at least a hundred years.

Rows of bookshelves were surrounded by several large worktables. A chalkboard hung on the opposite wall. Piles of stacked chairs were arranged by the entrance, and casting materials were stored in organized bins beside them. For a basement coven lair, it was all very . . . conventional.

Except for one thing.

Painted on the floor at the far end of the room was a large, complex sigil with piles of melted candle wax and dusty crystals positioned around it, suggesting it had been there for a while. In the center circle, set in a velvet-lined box, were two vials of blood (gross) and two locks of blond hair that looked eerily similar to Lily's own shade (also gross).

A chill crept down her spine at the sight, but she didn't allow her attention to be diverted for long. She was here for a reason and learning the purpose of that sigil wasn't it.

Feeling like the intruder she sort of was, she tiptoed across the room to the bookshelves. Everything was scanned and organized on the computer database, but she didn't want to turn one on in case it was somehow traceable.

She scanned the shelves of ancient, decaying grimoires in the "D" section. It didn't help that half the books were in Latin or other dead languages. Her Latin was terrible, but at least "demon" was a fairly universal word.

Finally, she found what she sought. A book as thick as the length of her forearm, likely older than the building it was being stored in.

Daemonium Compendium. She snorted. They couldn't come up with a more creative name?

Tugging the hefty volume off the shelf, she dropped it on the nearest desk, where it landed with a thud and shot out a cloud of dust. Coughing, she waved a hand to clear the air.

Then she started flipping pages.

Thankfully, despite its unimaginative Latin title, this compendium was written in English. She carefully maneuvered the frail pages until she found the letter "M." She knew Mist was a nickname, but his friend had also called him Mishetsu, and she was hoping it would be enough to go by.

And it was.

Breath catching, she carefully read the entry that was shorter than all the others.

"Mishet— Whoa." She squinted and sounded out the complicated name. "Mish-et-su-meph-tai. Mishetsumephtai. The Hunter. The legendary tracker of Hell. Greater demon of unknown power and status, a creature of mist and shadows. Ancient, deadly, rarely glimpsed. Little is known of this elusive demon."

And that was it, all the information there was. Some of the entries had pages full of information, but Mist barely got four sentences. Below the short write-up was a sketched image of what was supposed to be his demon form.

She peered closer and laughed. The image was of a gargoyle-like monster with a curved spine and hideous snout. His hands looked like eagle talons and his arms like spider legs. Evidently, the artist had never actually seen Mist in the flesh because the drawing looked nothing like him. At least they hadn't lied about him being rarely glimpsed.

But that wasn't the information she was after.

Below the write-up and drawing was a miniature rendition, no larger than a teacup saucer, of his summoning seal.

She reached over and flicked on the desk spot lamp, peering so closely at the intensely detailed drawing that her nose nearly touched the page. She straightened abruptly and blew out a breath.

It had to be the most complicated seal she'd ever seen. The circular design was full of hundreds of smaller sigils, intersected by intricate lines. Each one required a precise audible syllable to be chanted during the process of drawing and activating it. One mistake and the whole thing would fail.

Lily had never even considered dabbling in demonology before, but even if she had, she would never have attempted such a difficult summoning. In fact, successful summonings of a demon this powerful were so rare, the last one she'd heard of had to be nearly a century ago.

And didn't that just give her a big ol' boost of confidence.

Rather, she was already breaking into a cold sweat just considering it. But she did have one advantage—hopefully. She was pretty sure.

She was banking on Mist realizing who was summoning him and therefore not fighting it. It was the demon's resistance that made it such a risky venture. The more powerful the demon, the stronger they resisted the seal's pull. She'd never read about a demon that *wanted* to be summoned before, but she could only assume it would make the job easier.

Mist had to want to come, right? Even if he was angry with her, wherever he was in Hell couldn't be preferable to her company, could it? And even if he didn't want to come, if she screwed up or wasn't strong enough to trap him—a distinct possibility—he wouldn't want to harm her, right?

How much did she really know about him? Basically nothing. She hadn't even known his full name until she'd found it in this book.

Everything she knew about demons said they loathed being bound into service and would fight with everything they had to escape. And if they did, best believe you were going to wind up dead. Humans that dabbled in the supernatural were exempt from heavenly protection, and a demon would never miss an opportunity to kill without consequence, especially if the human he was killing had tried to entrap him.

Little though she knew about Mist, however, she just couldn't believe he would harm her.

But was she willing to stake her life on it? Because that was precisely what she would be doing. And for what purpose? To help someone she'd met twice, who'd lied about who he was? Was it really worth the risk?

Logically, no. Not even close.

But there went that instinct again telling her that yes, it *was* worth it. That she had to do it. And damn it, she was tired of being afraid of everything.

She wanted to be fearless and strong. She wanted to look in the mirror and think, *That is one badass lady.* Not, *I really shouldn't have had that cake last night.*

Mist was right. Life was too short to spend it full of longing, and she was done being a coward.

All fired up from her mental pep talk, she used her phone to snap a few pictures of Mishetsumephtai's seal. After returning the dusty tome to the shelf, she dug through the organized containers and gathered all the casting supplies she could possibly need and then some.

Chalk. Lots of chalk. And candles, crystals and other semiprecious stones, feathers, some incense and herb concoctions—all the typical witchy stuff. All she really needed was the seal and the chalk, but the other stuff helped focus the energies, and she'd take any boost she could get.

Supplies gathered, she loaded everything into her oversized purse, flicked off the lights, and headed upstairs. Closing the door and reactivating the wards, she rearranged the ugly robes and flicked off the back-room lights.

Her phone rang the moment she stepped outside.

Cursing, she slammed the fire door shut and dropped her giant bag to dig for her phone at the bottom. She debated ignoring it, but what if Iris was freaking out again? It had taken a lot of effort to convince her to go home after work and not back to Lily's place, and she needed her sister to stay away for a while.

When she finally found it, she gasped when she saw the call display. "Mist? Is that you? Where did you go? Your friend said y—"

"It's not Mist."

The deep voice had an undertone of something scary, and the hairs on the back of her neck stood up.

Slinging her heavy bag over one shoulder, she hurried toward the street. "Who is this? And why do you have Mist's phone?"

"Are you Lily?"

"Yes . . ."

"Judging by the thirty-five missed calls from you on Mishetsu's phone, I'm guessing you wanted to speak with him."

"Yes, and?"

"He's gone back to Hell and is currently unreachable. That's why he hasn't returned your calls."

Her steps faltered as she turned onto the sidewalk. "He's actually in Hell?"

"Not because he wants to be. Because he had no choice but to go or die."

"I'm sorry, what? Die?"

"Meph told me you tried to trap him with your sad little prison wards. So why would you want to talk to him now?"

"I didn't trap him in the wards. My sister did. And I want to talk to him because . . ."

She trailed off and winced. If she was actually attempting this insane venture, shouldn't she at least have a clear response to that question?

"Because I want to give him a chance to explain himself. Because my gut is telling me there's more to this, and I want to understand."

As she continued toward home, she kept checking over her shoulder, expecting her sister to leap out at any moment.

"All right, human. So you want to speak to Mishetsu. I know how to make it happen."

"Well, actually, I was going to try summoning him myself."

"What?"

"I was going to try summoning Mist myself."

There was long silence, and then the man—demon—barked a laugh. "Here I was thinking I was going to be dragging you here kicking and screaming, and now you're telling me you were going to try summoning Mishetsumephtai by *yourself*?"

"Well, yeah . . ." He laughed again, and Lily glared at the empty sidewalk ahead of her. "Why don't you think I can do it?"

"I don't think you can't do it. I know you can't do it. No simple witch could."

She gritted her teeth. "Who says I won't be the first?"

"You won't. I'd say you're welcome to try anyway, but I need you alive for now."

How reassuring. "Why?"

"I don't explain myself to humans, and certainly not witches. I'll make you a deal. I won't kill you if you do what I say."

Her heart skipped a beat. "I thought you wanted me alive."

"Yeah. If you do what I say. Otherwise, I'm not fussed."

"W-what do you want me to do?"

"Come here and summon Mishetsu under my surveillance. I'll channel power into you so you're capable of it, since you won't be otherwise. Afterward, you're free to go."

She swallowed. Sure, she'd been planning on summoning Mist anyway, but she wanted nothing to do with whoever was on the phone right now. It was obvious by the tone of his voice that he wasn't making idle threats.

"You either come here of your own volition now, or I'll track you down and bring you here myself. Don't try to run because I will find you, and it will be ugly."

She took a breath and gathered her courage. "I'm sorry," she said in a wavery voice, "but I don't trust you. Thanks for the offer, but I respectfully decline."

There was a pause.

"Don't even *think* about hanging up on—"

Lily ended the call.

Heart pounding, she stared at the empty street ahead of her. She couldn't believe she'd just done that. He'd threatened to kill her, for god's sake. Was she insane? Stupid?

Possibly. Probably.

A moment later, she started running.

10

HELL HOLE

THE GATE SIGIL HAD TAKEN MIST TO THE SAFETY OF HIS cave, where he'd hunkered down to wait as long as possible before making an audience with Paimon. She would've been aware the second he arrived, but his delay was a small act of defiance.

He had never bothered to be defiant before. What was the point? Pain and torture followed disobedience. Rule breakers were punished, and he was far too clever to be one of those.

But now . . . he had lost his simple conviction, and nothing seemed so black and white anymore.

Finally, he could ignore the summons no longer. He double-checked the flower he'd stowed in the crevice with his other possessions, making sure it was safely hidden. The blossom had already died—within minutes of arriving in Hell—but it didn't matter.

It was his, and he would keep it safe until it disintegrated to dust.

Dissolving to mist, he ghosted through the passages of

Paimon's lair until he was outside the throne room. There, he reformed his body, taking a moment to listen through the door.

The hall was known to play host to any number of nefarious activities, from torture parties, orgies, and fighting rings, to decadent feasts and drugged-out EDM raves. Unfortunately, now he heard only silence.

He'd hoped to arrive while Paimon was too busy to question him on his disappearance, but it appeared luck was not on his side. Upon entering through the towering doors—without banging the gargoyle-head knockers, since they were made of actual severed gargoyle heads—he found the hall mostly empty.

Except for Paimon, of course.

The Queen of Hell sat in all her demonic glory, clad in leather armor and gauntlets with deadly spikes protruding from the shoulders. At her side, Shaheen rested on the floor, red eyes gleaming beneath his long lashes. The camel's spindly legs were folded beneath his skeletal body.

Paimon's double horns and dark wings completed the forbidding picture, and her hair was wound into a braid and pulled over one shoulder, falling past breasts that were hidden by her armor.

She was not a succubus, and there was no other use for feminine softness in Hell. As a result, she did such a good job disguising any female attributes that most human records listed her as a "male with a beautiful face."

Ignoring his heart's nervous pounding, Mist approached the throne like he was making his usual report and nothing was out of the ordinary. Paimon was a volatile beast; there was no telling how she'd react. At least his brand had stopped burning now that he'd returned.

"Mishetsu, what a surprise," she drawled as he halted before her.

Several of her minions hovered around, fanning her with some poor wretch's amputated wings and balancing trays of dark red drinks that were probably blood, complete with straws and tiny umbrellas.

Mist bowed at the waist.

Paimon raised a brow at his failure to greet her as "Mistress" as he normally did. But he couldn't bring himself to be subservient and willingly play the role of her dutiful Hunter as he had for millennia.

"Care to tell me why you've been out of touch for two months?"

"I was hunting my targets," he replied, straightening.

Every ounce of control he possessed was channeled into maintaining a blank expression and even heart rate. If he so much as breathed unevenly, Paimon could discover his lies, and there would be hell to pay.

"And you couldn't check in with a progress report in that time?"

"I have no progress to report. Thus far, I have been unsuccessful."

Her brows climbed her forehead. "I find that hard to believe."

With good reason. There had never been a target he hadn't apprehended within a month or two, and the times it had taken that long were few and far between.

The truth was that he'd found Asmodeus only one week after his escape from Hell, shadowed him for another, and then located the others as well. If he'd reported his success to Paimon then, he would likely be out on his next assignment by now.

But he had lied.

Just as he had lied about the fate of Eligos.

"Belial is unlike my usual targets." That much, at least, was true. "It's probable he has discovered a way of masking his scent. I have not sensed his presence anywhere."

"Hm." Paimon steepled her claws. "And the other three?"

"I believe they remain together."

She scoffed. "I never understood what they were doing, opening the borders between their territories like they didn't *want* war. Perhaps they escaped to Earth to live peacefully like the humans they obviously adore." She gave a bark of chilling laughter, but she had no idea how close to the truth she was.

As abruptly as it had come, the humor vanished, and she pinned him with a hard stare. "So, you're telling me in two months, you haven't found a single trace of them."

"Correct." His tail flicked.

"And you think that is because Belial has found a way to mask his scent. Nephilim blood, perhaps?"

"Perhaps."

"Hm."

She leaned forward and studied him through narrowed eyes. Leaning an elbow on the throne's armrest, she propped her chin on one hand and said nothing. Neither did he.

Finally, she leaned back, shaking her head. "You're lying."

His blood went cold.

"Which is funny because, in all your time of service to me, I don't think I've ever felt that certainty before."

He thought of Eligos. At least he'd gotten away with it once.

Her head tilted, shifting the shadows on her face. "You've always been so obedient. What changed? What are you hiding from me?"

He lifted his chin though his blood was ice. "I am hiding nothing." Yet he couldn't bear to confirm her first statement and claim to be obedient. Even thinking the word made his stomach churn.

"Hm." Her head tilted the other way, those great horns tilting with it. "No, I don't think I believe you. I think you've been lying from the moment you stepped in here."

"I have not lied, Mistress." He had to grit his teeth to get the word out.

Where was his control? In the past, he would say or do anything to escape these meetings unscathed. Pride was for the foolish. The cleverest hunters waited in silence and stillness to conserve energy.

She flicked her claws, dismissing his efforts. "Let's try again. This time, before you answer, remember what happens to those who try to betray me. *Try*, because they do not succeed. Now, where have you been, Mishetsu?"

His mouth had gone dry, so he swallowed before forcing his reply. "I was hunting my targets."

"And did you find them?"

"No."

She shook her head and clucked her tongue. "Let's try again. Where have you been?"

"I was hunting my targets."

"And?"

"And"—his tail flicked restlessly—"I have not found them."

Her claws drummed on the carved-bone armrest. Her horizontal pupils burned with warning. "Where. Have. You. Been."

"Hunting my—"

His words cut off as his heart seized in his chest.

Mist dropped to his knees, the pain of his frozen heart unbearable as his lungs sought oxygen and his blood stagnated in his veins. A human would have lost consciousness instantly; a demon was not so lucky. Gasping, he gripped his chest and fought with everything he had not to fall at her feet.

Eyes alight with the thrill of violence, Paimon leaned forward, her power stirring the air as she manipulated him through the brands. Beneath all that leather armor, a mark nearly identical to his graced the center of her chest, giving her complete control over him.

His life, his whereabouts, his liberty—even his heartbeat belonged to her.

Oh, how he loathed her. He hated her so much, it made his stagnant blood boil with rage. But it was a useless emotion because there was nothing he could do against her.

He was weak. He was powerless.

Sometimes he would rather be dead than remain her unwilling servant for even a moment longer. Now was one of those times. After tasting freedom on Earth and breathing Lily's scent, he could not bear to endure another minute of this cursed life.

An involuntary gasp tore from him as Paimon released control of his heart and it lurched back to life. Coughing, lightheaded from the sudden influx of oxygenated blood, he tipped forward onto his hands.

His head hung, his hair falling over his face to hide his murderous expression. His wings draped limply over his back onto the cold stone floor.

"I'll ask again, Mishetsu. Where have you been?"

Was this it, then? Did she plan to torture him until he told her the truth?

Then she will torture me for all eternity.

No matter what horrors she did unto him, he could not betray Belial and the others because of the blood contract that prevented him from revealing their location or Eva's existence.

He was glad he had agreed to it now. It meant he could let go of his sanity to survive the agony without fear of violating the agreement.

No matter what happened, he would not break.

"Hunting . . ." he hissed, his heart still stuttering painfully back to life. "My . . . targets—"

It seized again.

His spine arched from the pain. His lungs fought to work, his blood burned in his brain, his body felt as though it might rupture.

Again, she released him. And again, he swayed, but he used every ounce of strength he possessed to remain on his hands and knees.

He would not lie prostrate before her until he was fully unconscious. This newfound pride had suddenly become the only thing giving his life meaning, and he clung to it.

Paimon's power flared, the dark scent tainting the air as she activated the next set of brands. Manacles formed on his wrists, directly over the tattoo-like bands, a heavy length of chain between them.

The manacles adhered directly to his skin, and there was no way to remove them without her magic. They also bound his ability to turn to mist—there would be no escape that way. He'd tried severing his hands at the forearm before, and though he was freed for a time, as soon as his limbs regenerated, the cuffs reappeared.

The links between the manacles joined a longer chain in the center that led directly to Paimon's outstretched hands. She gave that length a powerful yank, pulling his arms out from under him, dislodging his balance and forcing him to fall forward.

She smiled as he struggled back to his hands and knees, only to be jerked flat to the ground yet again.

"Keep going, Mishetsu. I can do this for days."

She stopped his heart again, his breath rattling out like the wheezes of a dying man, and then restarted it. This time he blacked out, toppling over, only to climb back to his hands and knees as soon as he regained consciousness. His hair hung in his eyes, but he had no strength to brush it aside and welcomed the curtain blocking Paimon from view anyway.

"Tell me where you were, where you *really* were, and this ends now. I'll let you go right back to hunting like nothing ever happened. All you have to do is tell me the truth."

"I'm telling . . . the truth."

"Did you forget who your mistress is? Do you think I can't recognize a lie when I hear it? You'd have better luck fighting off my hungry goraths in the Pit. Which is exactly where you're headed if you don't start talking."

So his fate was to be devoured by monsters before an audience, over and over again until Paimon chose to have mercy on him. Which would likely be never. Because she wasn't capable of it.

"I'll pull your half-digested carcass out when I need you to hunt again." She cocked her head. "Or not."

Some time later, the Hunter finally lost the ability to fight back, and Paimon grew bored. She had won their battle of wills, but she didn't feel satisfied. Mishetsu's stubborn silence kept her from reveling in her victory.

Her Hunter had lied to her. *Her* Hunter and no one else's. The wrath bubbled inside like an active volcano, and she knew she needed more blood, more violence, more screams. More, more, more. *Always more.*

She stood suddenly, stretching her wings. Beside her, Shaheen lifted his head and blinked in question. He too had become bored by the spectacle and craved more exciting violence.

Dropping the chain connected to the Hunter's cuffs, she approached his still form. Halting beside his head, she saw his yellow eyes blink groggily up at her. Not fully unconscious, then. Her lip curled with annoyance.

She lifted a boot and placed it on one of his delicate wing bones. And then she stepped down. The bone's snap echoed through the cavern, and Mishetsu exhaled a low groan of pain.

Still not enough.

With a sigh, she beckoned to a nearby minion who hastily approached. Sensing his mistress was in a volatile mood, the gargoyle bowed deeply, careful not to meet her gaze.

"Yes, my unholy queen?" His bow was so low, his snout scraped the ground. Her servants all had remarkable hamstring flexibility.

"Drag Mishetsu through the castle by his chains. Make sure he is seen by all in this state." She kicked at his side idly. "Perhaps that will take his pride down a notch."

"Yes, Mistress." The gargoyle remained folded at the waist, his wings submissively tucked against his body.

"On your way, spread the word that he'll be thrown in the Pit. Wait until he's healed enough to put up a good fight and the crowd has gathered, and then do it."

She didn't miss the stiffening of the gargoyle's spine. Yes, anyone in the room had heard her make the threat when Mishetsu refused to talk, but she supposed they doubted she would actually dispose of her most valued servant.

"Yes, Mistress."

"I want everyone there, do you understand?"

"Yes, Mistress. Your will be done, Mistress."

She narrowed her eyes at the creature's back a moment, disgusted by his meek subservience. This was why she had always favored Mishetsu. He was compliant and loyal, but he had a brain and could think for himself. Why had he felt the need to use that brain to betray her? He'd ruined everything.

She remembered a time after the branding ritual was completed that he'd tried to defy her, but she had eventually broken him. She'd drilled into him over and over that disobedience was punished and rebellion was never worth the consequences. He existed to serve, and he had always known it.

Until now.

She kicked him again. "Get him out of my sight."

The gargoyle hurried forward to collect the length of chain and then heaved with all the might in his stubby body. Mishetsu barely budged. Eyes bulging with panic, the gargoyle heaved again, and this time, the Hunter slid forward . . . several inches.

Paimon's nostrils flared with irritation. Now sweating profusely, nervous gaze flicking between her and Mishetsu, the gargoyle yanked again, gaining but a few more inches.

"What is taking so long!"

The demon lurched, trembling. "He's h-h-heavy—"

"I didn't ask for excuses, imbecile!"

"Y-y-yes—" The gargoyle set about his task and again proved himself useless. Dispensable. Disposable. Was there no one left to serve her who wasn't just wasting air?

With a shriek, she snatched up the demon and buried her fangs in his squat neck. She drained the creature into a withered husk and then ripped his body into several pieces, tossing them across the room to hit the walls with a hollow thud since there was no blood left to squelch or spray.

Boring.

"You'll have to do it, Shaheen, since you're the only one without a rock where your brain should be."

Shaheen rose gracefully and approached, picking up the chain in his teeth and striding toward the exit, the Hunter dragging behind him.

"You lot"—she pointed to the remaining servants cowering against the wall—"go with him and assist in spreading the word. Do not anger me or you'll join Mishetsu in the Pit." They began to bow customarily, and she snapped, "Now! Get out of my sight!"

Alone at last, she slumped back into her throne and drummed her claws on the armrest.

Mishetsu was up to something with Belial and the other rogues, and she needed to find out what.

Belial's defection had shaken the very foundations of

Hell—literally. He was so powerful that his presence actually played a critical role in upholding the foundations of the underworld. There had been several devastating earthquakes after he'd abandoned his territory, and the entire Screaming Souls mountain range had disappeared into an enormous crack that spontaneously appeared in the ground.

Why would a demon that powerful willingly leave Hell for a meaningless existence among mortals? His great power was dampened on the Earth plane, his indomitable demon form exchanged for a lowly human one, his lairs, legions, and servants all abandoned in favor of . . . what?

What could he possibly seek on Earth that would gratify a demon of his caliber? It was the great mystery, the whispered gossip spreading across Hell like wildfire.

And now this. She was certain her Hunter had found him. Maybe what Belial had left Hell to seek, Mishetsu wanted as well. But what? Riches? Power? It couldn't be, for there were none with more of those than Belial, save Lucifer himself.

Paimon sat up straight in her throne.

The only one with greater power and influence than Belial was Lucifer himself. And Belial knew that.

What if he wanted to shift that imbalance? What if he sought some new power source on Earth because he planned to unseat Lucifer as High King? There had been talk among Belial's legions for ages about him making a play for the throne, but most of the rumors agreed that he wasn't powerful enough to defeat Lucifer head on. Perhaps the entire reason behind his escape to Earth was to secure some secret means to stack the odds in his favor.

And if Mishetsu had found them, Belial could have offered him freedom if he joined his cause. She had always known her Hunter would give anything to be rid of his ties to her. It was why she'd so carefully chosen the ritual that bound him. If there was a means of escape, he would have found it long ago.

But if Belial had convinced him he had the power to remove the brands, Mishetsu could be tempted by the offer.

If this was true . . . the implications were enormous. The search for Belial would need to become more than Mishetsu's job. She would need to go to Lucifer himself.

She winced, quickly backtracking. She wasn't going near Lucifer unless she had solid proof of her theory. Hell's High King was everyone's worst nightmare, and every instance she'd met with him stuck out among her most unpleasant of memories. His Unholiness had complete power over every being in the underworld, and he loved to abuse it.

Before she did anything drastic and risked facing his displeasure, she needed more information. She didn't delude herself into thinking she could find Belial as easily as Mishetsu could—he was called *the* Hunter for a reason.

But perhaps there was another way. Perhaps, if she could find out what power source Belial was seeking . . . it might lead her right to him.

PIT STOP

MIST ALLOWED HIMSELF TO BE DRAGGED TOWARD THE Pit by his chains. He'd drifted in and out of awareness while that cursed camel hauled him through the lair to make a spectacle out of his punishment. He might have been ashamed had he not welcomed the chance to regenerate his brutalized heart and broken wing.

Sometimes the smartest course of action was to swallow one's pride and play dead. Because he had, he was now stronger than he would have been if he'd continued to fight. Now, hopefully, he'd be able to last more than five minutes in the Pit.

He'd still end up as gorath meat in the end, however. Strength or no strength, his future looked bleak.

This is what happens when the rules are broken. This is the consequence of insubordination.

"Oi," the gargoyle lurking next to Shaheen said. "Time to wake up from your nap, boss. Time for playtime in the Pit." He chuckled maliciously.

The gargoyles called him "boss" because he'd often used them on his hunts. But, of course, they wouldn't hesitate to throw him to the dogs at Paimon's command. No demon in his right mind would. A demon in his right mind seized any chance for violence with enthusiasm.

Mist had recently discovered he was not in his right mind.

Somehow he had managed to escape his fate the first time he'd broken the rules, but evidently, he wouldn't manage it a second time. Paimon knew he'd betrayed her, and he doubted he would be free to hunt again now that she didn't trust him.

If he wasn't useful to her, he was useless. If she ever got bored of torturing him, she'd likely petition to have him destroyed. He was too powerful for grunt work and posed too much of a threat for anything else.

This is what happens when the rules are broken. This is the consequence of insubordination.

He knew this. His entire life had been spent learning this lesson. So why had he been foolish enough to try in the first place?

It didn't matter, in the end. Whatever his reasons, he was about to end up in the Pit like every other rule breaker he'd tossed in there at his mistress's command. A fitting end, he supposed.

He was surprised at how little emotion he felt regarding thoughts of his own demise. He had once loved hunting, had lived for the pursuit of prey and reveled in their terror when he caught them, as if they'd actually believed they could elude Hell's Hunter. He hadn't even minded the brands so long as Paimon continued awarding him assignments.

But in recent years, he'd been haunted by his victims' screams and cries for mercy. Knowing they were rule breakers did not lessen his guilt. And his hatred and resentment of his mistress had grown with it, until finally, he could pretend no longer to be something he wasn't.

"Here we are," the gargoyle announced, halting the unceremonious progression. With their pig snouts, underbite fangs, and bat ears, gargoyles were not only ugly, but exceedingly dim-witted. Their skulls were exceptionally thick, which was an added challenge in a fight but meant their brains were barely acorn sized.

They were outside the heavy gate to the Pit. Within, he could hear the characteristic squelching of the slimy go-raths and the dull hum of the excited crowd. There would be a large one for this. Everyone would want to see the fall of Mishetsumephtai.

"Mistress said to take the chains off so you can put up a good fight, but the cuffs stay on."

He'd expected as much. Without them, he'd simply turn to mist. Not much fun for the spectators.

Mist held out his wrists dutifully, and the gargoyle un-locked the chains. It grated his pride that this lowly creature could remove them when he could not. Though only a simple locking bolt connected them, the magic of the brands made it so he couldn't budge it.

The chains disappeared as soon as they were unlinked, and Mist straightened and stretched his wings, discarding the pre-tense of weakness. He considered his options.

He could go into the Pit and fight the goraths tooth and nail. He could hold his own, certainly, but there were half a dozen of them and one of him, and with the grate over the top preventing aerial escapes, he wasn't getting out of there until Paimon let him. Eventually he would tire, and the ghastly feed-ing would commence.

Or he could fight now and escape.

Though he might be free for a time, Paimon would just summon him again. If he ignored it, the brand would eventu-ally kill him.

Not a bad plan, all things considered.

There was a chance Belial might actually be able to find a way to remove the brands. And if not, well, as long as he tied himself down so he couldn't obey the compulsion, he would escape being eaten by a gorath and die on his own terms.

Flexing his fingers, his claws lengthened, and he struck out at the gargoyle, slicing its thick neck open. It fell to the ground gasping and clutching its throat, but the blood flow dried up in seconds and then it lay still.

He looked at Shaheen, who blinked lazily at him. Just as Mist sank into a crouch, prepared to fight the demonic camel he'd always loathed, half a dozen more gargoyles stepped out of the shadows.

"Mistress said you might try somethin'."

"So she sent only six of you?" He was almost offended.

"No," a cool voice said from the darkness. "She came herself."

Paimon stepped out of the shadows. Standing at full height, she had nearly a foot on him, and her wingtips scraped the tunnel ceiling.

"Are you ready to tell the truth, Mishetsu?"

He said nothing, but he felt his stomach hollow with despair. Until this moment, he realized he'd held on to hope that he would fight his way out of this predicament. Besides Paimon herself, there was no one in this lair that could best him.

But here she was.

"I guess not. It pains me to lose my loyal Hunter, but alas. It'll make a good show." She flicked her fingers. "Open the gate!"

Behind him, the metal barrier creaked and groaned as it slowly lifted. The dull hum of the audience increased to a roar of excitement.

"Throw him in the Pit!"

The crowds howled in approval. He was seized around the arms by the gargoyles flanking Paimon and tossed unceremoniously backward. He could have fought, but he was going to end up there either way, and he'd rather do it with his heart beating properly. It had only just regenerated, after all.

He climbed to his feet just as the metal slammed to the ground, never taking his eyes from Paimon, who stood behind the safety of the bars with a cruel smile twisting her lips. Beside her, the camel smiled too.

A low hiss had him spinning around.

And there he was. Face to face with one of the nastiest creatures in all of Hell.

They were like enormous centipedes, with long scaled bodies and hundreds of legs, each a curved scimitar. A circular mouth took the place of any sort of head, complete with countless rows of sharp teeth, spiraling around the death trap.

They caught their prey with retractable tongues that shot forward from their throats and stuck to their victims with a noxious saliva that burned anything it touched. The saliva produced a drugging effect that entered the bloodstream through the acid burns and disoriented the victims.

Most disgusting of all was their eyes. Like a snail, they were on long stalks that extended from the goraths' mucous bodies. Unlike snails, however, they had exceedingly sharp vision. Their eye stalks could rotate rapidly around, making it difficult to keep out of their sight. And there were dozens—each gorath had at least thirty eyes.

Currently, every single eye on every single gorath was fixed on him.

Nearly two hundred eyes, he calculated in some distant part of his mind.

The creature closest gave a horrific shriek, so loud his eardrums distorted. It wiggled its slimy, scaled body and charged, stabbing blade-like legs forward with its rapid approach.

The tentacle eyes were a gorath's one weakness. When severed, they grew back quickly, but without their sight, they were useless hunters, for they possessed no other senses. Mist sank into a crouch, flared his wings, and flexed his claws out as long as they would go.

At the last second, when the monster was nearly upon him, he launched into the air, immensely glad his broken wing was healed enough for flight. The beast's tongue shot out, missing him by inches, so close that several drops of saliva hit him. The sizzling of his skin reached his ears over the monsters' shrieks and the audience's screams, but he tuned it all out, intent upon his task.

As he flew past the gorath's gaping maw, he swiped one hand out with his claws extended, severing a dozen eye stalks in the process. The eyes tumbled to the ground, oozing a grayish slime that was quickly trampled by the next charging gorath.

Flitting through the air, dodging shooting tongues and slurping mouths, he felt like a tiny fly, a mere annoyance to these behemoths. Nothing but a quick snack when they finally caught him.

But if he was a fly, he was a clever one who knew how to fight.

The only way to kill a gorath was by damaging its heart. Oddly fitting after what he had just endured. Unfortunately, there was only one way to get to the heart: from within.

Their outer armor was basically impenetrable. It could withstand all but the most potent hellfire, and Mist couldn't call on hellfire at will anyway. That meant he had to get *inside* the creature to kill it.

That meant he had to let it eat him without chewing him up first.

Swooping as high above the monsters as he could without hitting the grate over the Pit, he studied the writhing mass and picked his first target.

His eyes landed on the biggest. Mist was at his strongest now—after defeating one, he would be weakened. It would be best to take that one out first and save the smaller ones for last.

A wave of despair washed over him as he contemplated the monumental task ahead of him. But fighting was his only option, so he pushed it down, studied his target, and waited for his chance.

And then took it.

The biggest monster stretched its mouth wide, rows of teeth flattening against its dripping gums as its long tongue reached toward him. Mist took a breath, tucked his wings against his sides, and dove straight down its throat.

At the last second, he squeezed his eyes shut and braced for impact.

A slimy esophagus closed around him, and instantly, acidic saliva began to burn through his flesh. Down he slid as the throat muscles flexed.

The pain of his skin melting nearly stole his consciousness, but he fought through it and focused. Gathering strength, he maneuvered his hands so his claws were out.

And then he started shredding.

He stabbed and slashed the creature from the inside out, fighting through layers of leathery tissue toward the heart. At some point, a part of his mind switched off and dissociated from reality. He felt nothing. The numbness was likely a side effect of the drugging saliva, but it was to his advantage in this case. If he'd had the awareness to contemplate what he was doing, he might have passed out from sheer revulsion.

And then he actually succeeded. His claws cut into the pulsing organ, and the creature exploded.

He didn't have to claw back out of the body because when a gorath died, it ruptured like it had swallowed dynamite. Gray blood and gore showered the arena and all its spectators, but that was by far the least disgusting thing he'd experienced in the last several minutes, and he felt nothing but crushing relief as his feet landed solidly on the ground.

His legs immediately crumpled beneath him.

A hush fell over the crowd. No one moved; no one even breathed.

Any other time he would have enjoyed his success, but currently, he was too focused on regrowing his skin. He hadn't lost any critical appendages or facial features, but he was extraordinarily bloody. And weak. His head was spinning, his vision dancing with spots.

And he still had another five goraths to go.

"Attack him while he's down, you useless wretches!" Paimon screamed into the silence, breaking the spell.

Mist had just begun hauling himself up when a long tongue shot out from behind and wrapped around his middle. All that work, and he was about to get eaten before he had a chance to fight again.

Several things happened at once.

He sensed the sudden stirring of magic in the air. It wasn't a familiar magic, nothing he had ever felt in Paimon's lair. Powerful and deep, he felt it tether somewhere inside him like yet another binding. For that reason, he resisted it.

He hadn't much focus to spare, however, considering he was currently hurtling with incredible speed toward the gorath's waiting mouth. And he wasn't positioned to fight back. His back was to his foe, and he was upright, so the beast would have to chew to get him down.

And then everything shifted.

One moment he was rushing toward certain doom, and the next he was whooshing through space, surrounded by green light. *Temporal magic.*

And then he was slamming back into his body, back to the world, into the ground . . .

And landing in the middle of a summoning seal on Earth.

The sigil's magic tried to constrain him, and he instinctively used every drop of his remaining strength to fight it. Somehow, he felt his ability to turn to mist return, and he did so, pushing with all his might against the barrier until he found a weakness. *There.*

He burst through like a cloud of death and rushed to destroy whatever foe had dared try to enslave him yet again.

12

SUMMONING UP
THE COURAGE

A S THE BLACK MIST SPUN LIKE A VORTEX INSIDE THE summoning seal, Lily finally admitted she'd been a little reckless. It was her first time being confident, and she might have gone overboard. She had spent all night and half the morning readying for this, and she realized she was still woefully underprepared. If she could go back now, she would've taken that demon's offer of help in a heartbeat, whether he threatened her life or not.

She'd banked on Mist knowing it was her when he was summoned and not fighting back, but that wasn't happening at all.

The magic in the air was so thick it choked her. Wind blasted through her flat, knocking things off shelves, blowing the coats off the racks and the cushions off the sofa, and oh god, her fabrics were a mess—

She tried to silence her thoughts. Distractions would get her killed, and she already knew she was losing the battle against

the demon because the chaos should have been confined within the sigil. The fact that it was leaking out was not a good sign. *Must . . . keep . . . focused!*

Blinded by the wind, bent nearly in half to keep from falling backward, she lifted an arm to shield her gaze and visualized the seal with all her concentration. She kept chanting the syllables, sweat dripping down her back, limbs shaking with exhaustion. The roaring was so loud, she began shouting, and— Oh no, had she just mispronounced the last—?

The sigil ruptured in a blinding flash. Lily screamed. A furious snarling deafened her, and suddenly, black mist swirled everywhere. Amid the cloud of rage, she caught glimpses of sharp teeth and claws and knew they were coming to kill her.

So she turned and ran.

Racing down the hallway, following a purely instinctual urge to flee, she ran with no thought to where she was going or what she would do when she got there.

She didn't make it far, anyway. The mist crashed into her back, knocking her flat. The air gusted from her lungs and, winded, she couldn't draw another breath. Clawed hands formed from the cloud over her wrists, pinning them to the floor. Sharp teeth opened over the side of her neck from a mouth wide enough to tear out her throat in one bite.

But he didn't.

He froze.

Everything froze, in fact. The snarling, the winds, the mist—all of it, Lily included.

She lay there pinned beneath the demon she should never have underestimated and waited for him to kill her. The teeth were still at her throat. She could feel their sharp tips digging in with a stinging burn, breaking the skin.

Cheek pressed to the floorboard, eyes squeezed shut, she waited. And waited. And still, she wasn't torn apart or beheaded or any terrible thing a demon might do to a witch who failed at a summoning.

Slowly, she cracked an eyelid and saw a dark shape. A wing. Fine boned and leathery, the talon was planted on the floor beside her head. Her gaze shifted, and she saw gray skin—a long, muscled arm was reaching over to pin her wrist down.

"M-Mist?"

A low growl was his response. His teeth still hadn't left her throat, and she didn't dare move an inch.

"It's me. Lily."

Silence was the only response she received, but he seemed to vibrate with tension. She hoped that meant he was battling against the urge to eat her. She hoped he was winning that battle.

"I'm sorry I s-summoned you." Her voice cracked with tremors. "I thought— Well, I didn't think— But I hoped—"

Her babbling was cut short as he suddenly lunged off her. Scrambling away, she rolled over and sat up to find him crouched in the hallway, staring at her with wild eyes.

She took one look at him and gasped. If she'd had more air in her lungs, she would have screamed. And not because he was currently in the form of a huge, gray monster with sharp teeth, glowing yellow eyes, and leathery wings.

And a tail. She hadn't seen that when he'd shifted the first time. Like a supple whip, it snapped in the air behind him.

But all that had become the least of her concerns.

"What happened to you?!"

He was positively bathed in blood. It looked as though he'd taken a swim in a slaughterhouse sewer. His hair hung in wet clumps, and red ran in rivulets over his skin. Skin that was covered in wounds that looked like . . . burns?

His proud wings were full of holes as if they too had been burned, and, somehow worst of all, gray flecks of . . . something were stuck all over him, commingling with the blood.

It looked like brains from a zombie movie. Chunks clung to his mangled skin and dripping hair, and strings of sinew tangled with his claws like spiderwebs. The scent of gore fouled the air and turned Lily's stomach.

Mist stared at her without recognition. If she'd been the prey fleeing the predator, then he'd been lost to the hunt. But as she watched, he blinked several times, eyes coming into focus, and she knew the moment he finally realized where he was.

"Lily?"

His voice was deeper than the Mist she knew but only slightly, and it was more than a little disconcerting hearing it coming from the sight before her.

"H-hi."

He blinked some more, but each blink seemed to get heavier. "Lil . . . y?"

"It's m— Oh my god!"

As she spoke, his eyes rolled back, and he toppled forward to land on the floorboards in a pool of blood.

Mist regained consciousness to a cool sensation against his brow. The wet, soft thing stroked several times, and then he heard the sound of water splashing and fabric being wrung out. The sensation returned, this time along his jaw.

His eyes snapped open with the speed of one who'd learned long ago never to be caught vulnerable. He heard a gasp and a shuffling sound, and his blurred vision showed him a shape lurching back instinctively.

He jolted upright to face the unknown foe, his head spinning and his movements sluggish. Everything shifted as he met a pair of wide green eyes. He saw round cheeks with a red flush and honey-blond hair, and then he finally remembered where he was.

On the floor in Lily's apartment. Because she had *summoned* him.

He swung his head around to stare at the remains of the seal, and then he swung it back to stare at her. In all his long existence, no human had ever achieved what she had.

He became aware of the bucket of red water, the stained, wet cloth in her hand, and the fact that he was significantly less bloody than he had been.

While he'd been unconscious, she had . . . cleaned him.

Now that his vision had focused fully, there was no mistaking the row of tiny punctures along the side of her throat in the shape of a bite mark. *His* bite mark. Because he'd been seconds from tearing out her throat. If he hadn't taken that one instant to inhale before he bit down, causing that heady wildflower scent to flood his senses, he would have killed her.

And yet, he couldn't deny he liked the look of his mark on her skin.

"Lily," he said again because he couldn't seem to find other words.

"Hi." It seemed she couldn't find words either.

A long silence ensued in which they stared at each other from across the hallway.

"What happened?" she finally asked in a small voice.

Where to begin? Despite how they'd parted, he didn't want to upset her any more than he already had, so he opted for an abbreviated version of events. "My mistress was displeased, so she threw me in a pit of goraths as punishment."

"Mistress? Who—? What—?" She squeezed her eyes shut and opened them again. "What is a gorath?"

"A centipede the size of an airplane that consumes flesh."

"An airpla—" Her mouth dropped open. "It tried to eat you?"

He nodded. "I killed one, but there were five more."

It suddenly occurred to him that Lily had summoned him at the exact second he was about to be consumed. He could not have dodged his fate a second time, and yet he had. Because of her.

But perhaps the bigger question was, why had she summoned him? The last he'd seen her, she'd been staring in horror as her sibling made death threats. Did she hope to enslave him?

That would be just his luck. From one cruel mistress to another.

Then again, he thought, inhaling another lungful of her scent, he might not mind belonging to this mistress.

"For what purpose did you summon me?" he asked.

"I was hoping we could talk."

"About the task you want me to perform?"

"I don't want you to do any task. I just want to talk."

His brow furrowed. "You don't wish to enslave me?"

"No!" she said emphatically, and he cocked his head.

He wasn't sure he believed her. Everyone wanted something. There was always a motive. Even Eva, whom he had formed a bond with, likely only tolerated his company because she felt safe within the vow he had sworn into to protect her identity. That was okay. It was something he understood.

"I know it looks bad," Lily continued, glancing at the sigil in the other room, "but I swear, it's not. I really just wanted to talk, and I didn't know another way to get you to come back, especially after your friend told me you returned to Hell."

"Which friend?"

"The one with the tattoos. And another with a scary voice." She shifted until she was sitting on one hip with her feet tucked under her. She was so round and soft, and her scent was so tantalizing. Even now, it teased his senses and made it hard to concentrate.

Want to chase her again. Want to bite her again. Not to hurt her. Just to mark her.

"I made him mad," she said, "and I think he might show up here looking for me."

She must have been speaking about Meph and Belial. He wasn't concerned about either of them. "What do you wish to talk about?"

She finally looked at him and then blanched, as if she had forgotten whom she was talking to. "It can wait. Maybe we should treat your wounds first."

He was a powerful demon, and he healed quickly. Though his senses felt dulled and his mind sluggish, he could tell he was already much improved.

"Talk now."

"But your skin—"

He looked down. His skin was already regrowing, but he could see how it might be upsetting to a human. The easiest solution would be to wash. By the time he finished, his wounds would be mostly closed and would not bleed more.

"I will use your shower," he decided, climbing to his feet. His head swam, his legs felt rubbery, and he immediately swayed.

Lily dropped the bloody cloth and raced to help, only to freeze with her hands out as if reluctant to touch him. While he was sure the blood was part of it, it was obvious she was repulsed by his demon form.

He had seen the look on her face when he shifted. It was not one he would soon forget.

"I am fine." It came out as a growl, and he swiped his claws for her to stay back.

Using the wall for balance, he maneuvered down the hall, his wings dragging on the floor, leaving bloody handprints on the walls and a trail in his wake.

To his surprise, Lily slipped past him and rushed ahead into the bathroom, and he heard the water turn on before he made it to the door. Once inside the cramped space, he found her bent at the waist, testing the temperature from the tap before pulling the lever to activate the shower. He couldn't stop his

growl at the sight of her on display for him. *Want to chase.*
Want to bite.

She jumped up and spun around, her cheeks' flush deepening, reminding him that she was not actually offering herself in
that way. At least not when he looked like a demon.

She wrung her hands. "I made it warm but not too hot. I
figured hot might hurt your wounds, but nobody likes a cold
shower, so I thought somewhere in between would be better. Is
that okay?"

The temperature mattered little. One did not serve Paimon
for millennia without developing a high tolerance for discomfort. He stepped further into the bathroom, and Lily flattened
herself to the wall to avoid him.

Part of him wanted to shift to human form because he
missed the way she responded to him, and he wanted to experience it again. But another part, the darker, wounded part,
wanted to force her to see this form. If she didn't like him as he
was, why should he change for her?

He stepped into the tub wearing his pants because they
were as filthy as the rest of him. Wyrm leather cleaned easily
and would dry in seconds, faster even than skin.

He'd never been inside a small human shower before as
Belial had specifically outfitted the one in their apartment for
a being of his size. The ceiling was too low for a creature with
wings, and he was forced to wrap them awkwardly around
himself to fit in the narrow stall. Worse, the shower nozzle was
below his head height, and even when he ducked, he couldn't
fit beneath it.

Lily stared at him, muttering, "A demon is in my shower.
A very large, very bloody demon. Is in my shower. That's fine.
Demons take showers. Of course they do. This is perfectly
normal."

Mist gripped the curtain bar to aid his balance as he tried
again to duck beneath the spray. Unfortunately, the moment he

put the slightest amount of weight on it, it ripped from the wall in a cloud of dust and tile chunks. Without the plastic barrier, water sprayed everywhere.

Growling, he dropped the bar and curtain. He reached up to the nozzle, intent on tearing it from the wall to change the position of the spray.

Just as his claws fixed around the attachment, Lily suddenly leapt into action.

"Let me help!" She reached out and grabbed his arm. "I'll do it. I'll hold it for you."

He looked down at her. "You can't reach."

"Just . . . sit in the tub. And I'll stand here and wash you."

She would? He almost didn't believe it, but he was curious enough to try. Dutifully, he sank into a crouch, angling his wings overhead so they wouldn't crumple beneath him. Then he looked up at her expectantly. He didn't have to look up very far. Crouching brought him nearly to her eye level.

She swallowed. "Okay. Time to wash the demon in my shower. Totally normal. Let's do this."

She rose on her tiptoes, slipped the nozzle out of the slot it rested in, and then aimed it in his direction.

Lily was washing a demon. Had she said that aloud enough times already? It didn't seem to help it sink in.

She watched him sort through her body wash collection on the side of the tub, his nose wrinkling as he sniffed each bottle until he finally found the unscented one. He squirted half the contents into his large palm and then got busy washing himself.

First, she angled to spray over his thick hair and winced as he scrubbed it vigorously with those wickedly sharp claws. His poor hair. It was so tangled, he hadn't a hope of getting his fingers through it, and he didn't try. Then, he moved straight to his body, running his big hands over the planes of muscle stretched under that dark gray skin.

The water ran red as it rinsed down the drain, and the chunks of awful flesh that had been stuck to him went with it. That should have been the detail she fixated on. Not his strong hands sliding over his wet skin. Not the way the strength in his arms and back shifted as he moved, the tight muscle rippling with each motion.

He was *gray*. He was also a demon. This was not a normal man in her tub. Nothing about the situation was normal, despite what she kept muttering to herself.

She was further reminded of that when he flexed his wings, opening them up at his sides and angling them under the spray. She helped by moving the showerhead so the gore would rinse off while he continued using those big hands to rub them clean.

He struggled to reach the back side of his wings, and before she knew what she was doing, she was reaching forward and taking over the task. Showerhead in one hand, she used the other to sweep down the back of one leathery expanse.

As soon as she touched him, he stilled, and so did she.

"It's so soft," she whispered. Somehow, she hadn't expected that.

His head turned, and he pinned her with a glowing yellow stare over his shoulder. Her hand was still out, frozen on his wing. The shower continued spraying everywhere, and she had to wonder if she was flooding her own flat. She'd be enacting her favorite scene from *The Shape of Water* if she kept this up.

She immediately regretted thinking of that because images of Elisa and the Asset embracing in the bathtub immediately sprang to mind. Mist may not have been an amphibian man, but he was certainly strange looking, and he was sitting in her bathtub and staring at her with those reptilian pupils, and she couldn't help but compare—

"Why did you summon me?" he asked, snapping her out of it. Good thing too, because her bathtub fantasizing had shifted to images of her and Mist, and she was not going there with him. That wasn't what this was about.

Iris's words ran through her head. *There are no good demons.* But then so did the tattooed guy's . . . *He's really not a bad guy.*

"I need to understand," she said finally. "Why did you seek me out? What did you want with me?"

"I sought you because of your scent. And other things about you that appeal to me. I wanted . . ." He broke off, turning away to stare at the tile. "It's irrelevant what I wanted. This is what happens when the rules are broken. This is the consequence of insubordination."

She frowned. By the mechanical way he spoke, he seemed to be repeating something memorized. "Did you break the rules? How so?"

As a blood-born, she knew about the rules that governed the actions of supernatural beings on Earth. She knew because those very rules had put a target on her back from birth, and she resented them more than a little.

"I should not be here," Mist said quietly. "I should be facing my punishment."

"How did you break the rules?" It suddenly became essential that she understood.

"That is what happens. That is the consequence of—"

"How did you break the rules, Mist?"

His head swung around again, and she fought to keep from flinching from the intensity of his stare. "I wanted to taste freedom. I wanted to bond with a female. I wanted to be something other than myself. But I cannot. I am the Hunter, and I don't get a choice."

"I don't understand. Why don't you get a choice? Why can't you—"

"Because I am nothing." He lurched suddenly to his feet, causing her to stumble back. The showerhead sprayed everywhere, but she wasn't paying attention to that anymore. She was staring way up at the enormous demon above her, his wings spread across the tub and beyond, his tail whipping furiously against the tile.

"I am nothing, and I have the marks to prove it." He thrust his wrists out. "These cuffs—"

He froze, staring at his arms. "Where are the cuffs?"

She couldn't have been more confused if she'd been dropped into another dimension.

At his wrists were two bands of textured black-ink designs that were almost invisible on his gray skin. She saw no signs of cuffs.

His eyes lifted to hers, and this time she saw shock. Awe, even. "You summoned me."

"I— I tried, I guess."

"You summoned me from Paimon's lair, and you summoned me out of the cuffs."

"What cuffs?"

"The manacles. How did you do it?"

Manacles? "I didn't do anything special," she said weakly, struggling to keep up. "And I didn't do a very good job, considering you escaped—"

His eyes had widened. "You're a very powerful witch."

She scoffed. "No, I'm not—"

"Your magic overrode that of the brands. It should be impossible."

"What brands? And why do you say you're nothing? That's not true. You're—"

"Enslaved," he growled, holding out his wrists again. "Bound here." He placed one hand over the matching circular design on his chest. "Controlled here." He pointed a claw at the tattoo encircling his neck. "Tethered here."

Her blood went cold, and suddenly, everything started to make sense. What the tattooed demon and the one on the phone had said. The way Mist kept referring to a mistress. His mechanical repetitions of the futility of rebellion.

If he was trapped by some kind of magical binding, of course he would have an obsession with rule breaking. It would have been drilled into him, probably with a lot of pain, that he should always obey the one who controlled him or he would be punished.

So why had he disobeyed in the first place?

I wanted to taste freedom. I wanted to bond with a female. I wanted to be something other than myself.

Her heart cracked, her throat constricted, and it was hard to force the words out. But she had to know. "That's why you wanted to spend time with me? Because you—"

"It's irrelevant," he growled, his brow low over his glowing eyes. "It's against the rules, and rules are not to be broken."

He stepped out of the shower and around her. Without thinking, she dropped the showerhead, sending water spraying across the room, and grabbed his arm.

He froze, staring at her hand.

"Where are you going?"

His gaze snapped to hers, his eyes narrowed. "Why do you care?"

She couldn't speak. She honestly didn't know. Years of Iris drilling into her the evilness of demons could not be forgotten so quickly, and yet, she couldn't ignore her own instincts.

He loomed over her, dropping his head to pin her with a fierce glare. His enormous size was never more apparent than it was now. She'd never felt small or delicate a day in her life, but she certainly felt it now. He could crush her in a second if he wanted to.

"Release me now, or I'll give in to the urges I've been fighting since I caught your scent for the first time."

She didn't let go of his arm.

A cruel smile twisted his near-black lips. "I will hunt you and bite you and taste you, *all* of you, and I will do it in this form that repulses you."

Repulsed her? Her head was spinning, but she knew enough to know that wasn't how she'd describe her feelings. She was scared, yes, but not in the way he thought she was.

"I— I don't—" Her useless stuttering silenced when she felt a sleek rope sliding across the backs of her thighs.

His tail. Oh god, he had a tail. Because he was a demon and she was a witch, which meant he could kill her at any time without breaking his precious rules, and no one would come to save her.

The tail went across both her legs and curled around her thigh.

She let out a rather undignified squeak of surprise and dropped his arm, clutching her chest instead. Her heart hammered, though not with fear for her life.

"That's what I thought," he hissed.

He stepped past her without another word and disappeared down the hall, leaving a trail of water behind him.

13

MIST THE MARK

LILY STOOD FROZEN BY FAMILIAR FEAR, HER THOUGHTS whirling. And spiraling. *He said he wants to hunt me. He could kill me as easily as breathing. He could eviscerate me with his claws, strangle me with his tail, or finish the job of tearing my throat out with those sharp teeth.*

He's an honest-to-god demon. Demons can kill witches with no repercussions. Not only should I let him leave, I should run screaming in the other direction. I should learn every anti-demon ward in existence and cover my flat with them. I'll never go outside again, and I'll get my groceries delivered so I don't have to—

"Shut up," Lily hissed at herself, cutting off the anxious thoughts with a firm hand. She was so sick of that cowardly, defeatist voice in her head. The one that made her second-guess and overthink everything she did. The one that made her feel weak and insecure.

From now on, whatever that voice told her to do, she was doing the opposite.

So, after finally switching off the rogue shower, she raced out of the bathroom and down the hall. "Mist!"

The front door was open. She ran outside to the edge of the balcony, leaning out to look down the street. She didn't see him, so she hurried down the steps to the sidewalk and spun around, checking both ways for a glimpse of his looming form. When there was no sign of him, she shouted, "Mist!" as loud as she could for good measure.

Someone passing by on the opposite sidewalk shot her a wary look, but besides them, there was no one else around and no response to her call.

He'd probably changed into mist and disappeared, and she was surprised at the intensity of her crushing disappointment. It hit her so strongly, she trudged over to the steps leading back up to the balcony and sat heavily on the bottom one. She proceeded to bury her face in her hands and sigh tiredly.

She'd gone to all that trouble to summon him, nearly getting herself killed, only for him to walk out the door and be lost again. She couldn't summon him a second time either. Her brain was mush, and she could feel the depletion of her psychic energy. She would need time and rest before performing any more magic.

I will hunt you and bite you and taste you, all of you, and I will do it in this form that repulses you.

She groaned into her palms as her stomach fluttered at the memory. Why couldn't she have just spoken her mind? All she'd had to do was say, *You don't repulse me. I'm just scared because I'd never seen a demon before now, and I'd always been taught to fear them. This is a lot to take in.* Was that so difficult?

Then again, she thought with a sudden scowl, it *was* pretty damn difficult, considering everything. And he'd sure taken off fast. He'd been so sure she was horrified by the sight of him that he hadn't even given her a chance to come to terms with everything he'd just unloaded on her.

I mean, come on. He'd gone from almost killing her to passing out on the floor to destroying her shower to stalking out the door. Was it too much to ask for five minutes to wrap her head around the complete upheaval of her formerly uneventful life?

At least she'd gotten the answers she sought. There'd been no ulterior motive behind their date. He'd broken the rules to be with her, and he was apparently controlled by some other powerful demon. She'd never been in danger, and she wasn't going to be as long as she stayed away from him.

So did she really want him to come back?

She scoffed. *Who am I kidding?* She was bursting with questions, and despite everything, she wanted to understand him better. She wanted to learn everything about him. There was no way she was leaving things like this.

Her instincts had been right. He was in trouble and he needed help, and for some absurd, ludicrous reason . . . she wanted to be the one to give it to him.

How well do you really know him? the little whiny voice whispered from its dark corner. *You don't really know for sure he won't hurt you. How are you supposed to do anything anyway? You're nothing special.*

"I said shut up, damn it!"

"I didn't say anything."

With a yelp, she dropped her hands and leapt to her feet.

The largest man she had ever seen was standing right in front of her. His hair was an incredible platinum blond that gleamed in the sunlight. He was so tall, he had to drop his chin nearly to his chest so he could pin her with his piercing blue glare. And she was certain his broad shoulders were double the width of hers.

He was easily the scariest person she had ever seen, and that was saying a lot considering who had just been in her shower.

She shrank back while inwardly wanting to kick herself. She kept saying how sick she was of being timid, but it appeared old habits did indeed die hard.

"I had to come here and track you down myself," the blond giant said, "and I'm not happy about it. Don't make it worse."

She immediately recognized his voice as that of the demon who'd threatened her on the phone. His jaw was set, and his eyes were narrowed. He looked mad, and it was terrifying.

"Wh-who are y—?"

"Where's Mishetsu? I can feel the magic from here, so I know you summoned him, however the bloody fuck that's possible." He pinched the bridge of his nose, suddenly looking exhausted. "How the bloody fuck is that possible?"

Lily forced her chin up, though its trembling definitely gave her away. "I'm a powerful witch. It was easy." *Yeah, right.*

His brow arched. "Is that why you have a bite mark on your neck?"

She slapped a hand over it. "Who are you?"

"Where's Mishetsu?"

"I— He left."

"Why?"

"Because . . ." *Because he thinks he repulses me.* "He said he's . . . branded, and he broke the rules. He said his mistress found out and threw him in a pit of monsters the size of airplanes to be eaten. He killed one, but there were five more."

The demon cursed in a rumbling growl. His voice was so deep she could feel its vibration in her bones.

"Raum."

Lily blinked. "Huh?"

A large black bird suddenly swooped right over their heads, and she shrieked and jumped back as a man suddenly appeared beside them. He pinned the huge blond with a flat stare, his eyes an unusual bright gold that contrasted with his dark skin. He ignored Lily completely. "Yeah?"

"Go find Mishetsu. He's probably sulking around some-where in mist form."

"If he doesn't want to be found, I won't be able to find him."

"Try."

The two demons glared at each other for a second, and then the newcomer rolled his eyes. "Fine."

Before her very eyes, he transformed into a crow and flew off again.

Her head was going to explode before this day was done. "Wha— Who— He—"

"For a witch who just summoned one of the most pow-erful demons in Hell, you seem pretty shocked by a simple shapeshift."

"I haven't—" *Lily Donovan, I will slap you in the face if you stutter one more bloody time!* "I've never summoned a demon before. Actually, I haven't practiced magic in almost ten years."

"I find that hard to believe."

"That's not my problem." Crap, she'd jumped from startled rabbit to overconfident. Where was the middle ground?

The demon didn't look impressed either. She had the dis-tinct impression he wasn't used to getting attitude, and it was probably because he killed anyone who tried to give it.

A silent staring contest followed. Lily looked into his blue eyes and tried not to cower, and the demon looked blandly back at her. The power he radiated terrified her.

Who *was* he? She was suddenly afraid of finding out.

A moment later, he sighed, and the tension dissolved. "I know you know how easily I could kill you, but I'm not here for that. Just . . . stay out of my way, and don't fuck with me, my brothers, or Mishetsu, and I won't fuck with you, your sis-ter, or your coven. If you tell anyone—anyone at all—that you met us, I will come back here, and I will kill you. It will be slow. It will be painful. You won't escape. Got it?"

Lily swallowed and nodded.

"And don't think you can keep me out with wards or any magic because that will only piss me off. And we've already established that bad things happen when I get pissed off."

She nodded again weakly.

"Good." Without another word, he turned and headed down the street, moving with surprising grace for someone of his size. He made it halfway down the block before she realized it was now or never.

She started running. "Wait!"

He turned back, and as she skidded to a halt in front of him, she saw flames flicker in his eyes. *Hellfire.* She recoiled.

"What?"

"I— I—" *No more stuttering!* "I want to help Mist."

He blinked. "Why?"

"I just . . . feel like he needs help."

"He's got help already. He doesn't need you. And what can a little human like you do anyway?"

She gritted her teeth and planted her hands on her hips. *Screw the middle ground.* "I summoned him out of a pit of monsters and saved him from getting eaten. And I summoned him out of the cuffs." She still didn't quite understand what that meant, but she was hoping the other demon did. "You couldn't have done that without me. Demons can't summon other demons. You need my help."

His eyes narrowed. "Demons can't summon demons, but they can kill witches."

"He won't hurt me." As she said it, a wave of conviction rose, that inner whisper assuring her she was speaking the truth.

His brow lifted. "Won't he?"

"He won't."

They held each other's stares once more, and then out of nowhere, the demon smiled. It was such a change from his terrifying scowl that she blinked in astonishment. Smiling like that made him look oddly . . . angelic.

"Well, well. Seems the Hunter found himself a human after all." He waved a hand, and the smile vanished. "It's not up to me what he does. If he wants to see you, he'll come back."

"Can you just tell him I want to see him if you find him? He won't come otherwise. He thinks I'm scared of him."

"Aren't you?"

"I'm *not*." She said it for her benefit as much as his. "I just needed a bit of time to adjust to seeing his demon form, but I'm over it now. I don't care what he looks like, and if he'd given me five minutes before he took off, he would know that."

The demon looked briefly skyward. "Why am I always in the middle of this soap opera shit? Fine. If I see him, I'll tell him you still love him despite his monstrous appearance, and you're the key to his redemption or whatever."

"I didn't say I—"

"Take it or leave it, witch. I'm not your friend, and this isn't a goddamn fairy tale. Now, goodbye. I hope I never see you again, but something tells me that's too much to ask."

He turned and started walking, muttering, "The shit I put up with. No wonder I can't control my temper, for fuck's sake."

❧

The cloud of mist wedged itself tighter into the corner of the flat roof's ledge, but it didn't make a difference. The crow perched beside him just cocked its head, unimpressed.

With an inward groan, Mist gave up the pretense of hiding and took physical form. His skin and hair were still wet from the shower, but at least his pants were dry.

A moment later, the golden-eyed crow beside him shifted into a golden-eyed man.

Mist crouched on the ledge and picked at the brick with his claws. His companion sat on the ledge and faced the opposite way. Neither of them spoke. Mist was glad for Raum's stoic demeanor. He was not in the mood for jokes and idle conversation.

After a time, the crow demon broke the silence. "Why don't you go talk to her?"

They had both overheard the conversation between Lily and Belial. The only reason Mist hadn't flown down and growled at Belial when he threatened Lily was because he didn't want her to know he was there.

"It's pointless," Mist said. "Already Paimon summons me again."

"The brand is burning?"

He nodded.

"How long do you have?"

"Less than two weeks."

"So that's it? You're just going to give up without even trying?"

"I'm not giving up," Mist growled. He didn't appreciate the insinuation that he was weak.

"Bel's helping you. Lily's helping you. Hell, even Eva's dad is helping you. And you've got a bit of time before you have to go back. A lot can happen in two weeks."

Mist's digging claws managed to break a piece off the brick, and he watched it topple over the balcony rooftop onto the sidewalk below. He didn't correct Raum's assumption that he'd return to Hell when the time came.

He wasn't going back. If it meant his death, so be it.

"And even if we don't find a solution in that time," Raum said, "Lily can just summon you again, right?"

Mist shook his head. "Paimon won't make that mistake again. If she hadn't removed the chains, Lily would not have been able to."

What he didn't mention was that it shouldn't have worked with just the cuffs on either. He didn't know how that had happened, but he presumed it was a fluke that wouldn't work a second time.

"Your human is no regular witch," Raum mused.

"No."

"Blood-born?"

"Must be."

"That's rare."

Mist growled. "She's mine."

"Is she? Because it seems to me you're being creepy on her roof rather than claiming her."

His claws dug back into the brick. "It's for her safety."

"Well, if you don't want her, maybe I'll—"

Mist swung his head around and snarled, simultaneously ripping the entire brick out of the wall and throwing it at Raum.

The demon ducked and then held up his hands with a rare smirk. "Just proving my point." He stood. "If you've only got two weeks, maybe you should spend it with her instead of hiding on a roof. Just a suggestion. The rest of us will keep digging for info on the brands."

Mist's growl died in his throat. He'd done nothing to warrant their help. The contract they'd made only stated they had to provide him a place to live and assistance with understanding humans. There was nothing about helping him be free of Paimon.

It didn't matter whether they succeeded. The fact that they were even trying . . . It meant something profound.

Raum nodded in farewell and then jumped off the side of the building, transforming into a crow as he fell. With a few pumps of sleek wings, he vanished into the afternoon sky.

Mist went back to his gargoyle-like perch on the edge.

It didn't matter what Raum or Lily said. She was better off without him in her life. He was still branded. He was still trapped. He still only had a few days of freedom left.

He told himself to spread his wings and fly away as Raum had, to leave the witch to live her life. He told himself to make the smart choice, the one that would save him the most pain later when things inevitably went south.

And yet, no matter what warnings he gave himself, he couldn't seem to leave.

Meph appeared at Belial's side just as he turned the corner at the end of the block.

Bel groaned. "I thought I told you to stay home."

After Lily hung up on him, Belial had threatened Meph with creative torture until he told him where she lived. Then he'd threatened more torture if he or Raum tried to follow him when he went to pay her a visit.

So, of course, they both had.

He'd seen Raum perched in a tree in the neighbor's yard, but he hadn't noticed Meph until now, and that pissed him off.

"And I told you to be nice," Meph shot back. "Big fail."

Bel made a low noise in his throat. Okay, it was a growl.

Meph didn't take the hint. He never did. "Did you have to be such a dick?"

"Yes, I did."

"Why?"

"Because."

"Because why?"

"Do you ever shut up?"

"Nope. Why?"

He growled again. "Because if she's actually going to be hanging around Mist, she needs to be tough. Things are going to get a lot worse before they get better. *If* they get better. The last thing we need is some shrinking-violet human screaming every time she sees a demon."

"So you wanted to scare her a bit to test her." Meph grinned. Then again, he was always grinning, so maybe his face hadn't changed. "Pretty devious plan, bro."

"Shut up. I told you to stay home. Where were you even lurking?"

"I can be sneaky when I want to be."

A crow swooped out of nowhere and transformed into Raum, who fell into step beside them. He craned his head up to scowl at Belial. "Did you have to be such a dick?"

Bel clenched his fists so hard, his knuckles cracked. "I swear to god if you both don't shut up, I'll rip your tongues out, shove them up your asses, and then strangle you with your own intestines."

"Sounds kinky," Meph said, still grinning.

He groaned. *Just kill me now.*

14

AFTERGLOW

I T'S OUR FAULT," IRIS SAID. "IT WAS ALL BECAUSE OF US."

"Why?" Lily called into the darkness. "How?"

"Everything that happened was because of us."

"I don't understand—"

"It's all our fault. All our—"

"Lily!" It was her mother. Lily spun around, searching for the source of the voice, but again, there was only black.

"Keep digging, Lily. Seek the truth."

"What truth?"

"The truth will make you safe. Don't rest until you understand."

"Understand what?"

"Trust your instincts. Your sister needs you. It's up to you to make this right."

"But how—"

"*Lily.*"

The new voice, deep and male, penetrated the blackness, and suddenly, she was surrounded by swirling mists. They lifted her, and then she became mist too.

"Wake up, Lily."

She groaned, her eyes moving behind eyelids that wouldn't open. She fought against their weight and blinked groggily.

She saw glowing yellow eyes and pointed teeth. She saw huge wings and a large, dark shape.

With a scream, she lurched back, snapping to wakefulness.

Mist was perched on the side of her bed, one clawed hand extended where he'd been shaking her awake. Still half stuck in the dream, she struggled to rejoin reality, but even then, she didn't miss the way he flinched at her recoil.

He shifted to human form a moment later. The wings disappeared, his skin changed to tan, and his eyes became amber. Oddly, his body was lit with an unearthly light that made him glow.

"Mist—" What was he doing here? How had he gotten inside? She'd spent a good hour or two before bed scrubbing away Iris's wards—and cleaning the blood and water in the hall, not to mention the disaster in the bathroom—so she supposed there'd been nothing keeping him out. Not that the wards would have done much good anyway.

"I woke you because I'm concerned about your current state. Is this normal?"

"What . . . ?"

He pointed at her arm, and she lifted it to her face.

She was glowing, not him. He'd only appeared to be because the light from her body was reflecting off him.

"Oh, crap." Her eyes widened and snapped to his. No one had ever seen her like this. No one knew her shameful secret. She couldn't let him see. She had to hide this part of herself.

She leapt out of bed and raced down the hallway to the freezer, pulling out her precious bottle of whiskey and dumping it straight down her throat.

After two big swallows, she gagged, leaning over the sink

as she coughed and gasped for air. She checked her arm. Still glowing.

Grimacing, she lifted the bottle to her lips—

Mist stopped her, pulling the whiskey out of her grip. His eyes were full of alarm. "What are you doing?"

"The alcohol makes it go away. I need it." She reached for it, but he held it away.

"It makes you choke."

"It doesn't matter. It makes it go away. I need it to go away!"

"Why? Are you hurt?"

"No, but—"

"Are you in danger?"

"You don't understand! I have to make it stop!"

"Why?" He searched her gaze almost frantically.

"Because— Because—" To her horror, tears filled her eyes. "Because I hate it. I hate it so much."

"Why?"

She wanted to scream at him to stop asking her that, but she couldn't be mad at his genuine concern. He just wanted to understand.

"Because . . ." She took a breath and let the panic bleed out. "It reminds me of what I am. And what I lost."

"What did you lose?"

She looked away. "My parents."

"Did your parents glow as well?"

She laughed despite herself. "No. At least, I don't think so. But they were witches."

He placed the whiskey bottle on the counter, sliding it carefully out of her reach. "Your mother was a blood-born."

She nodded. "How did you know?"

"You are very powerful."

She snorted again. "I don't know about that. Malfunctioning, is more like it." She looked down at her glowing arm. "I've never heard of a witch who doubles as a night-light."

"Your parents were killed," he guessed, and she nodded. "By demons?"

"No. In a regular old arson fire."

If she was going to tell him this, she needed to sit down. She gripped the counter behind her and lifted herself to sit on its edge, putting them at equal height. Even in human form, he was still so much taller than her, and it was hard not to be distracted by the fact that he wasn't wearing a shirt. The "tattoos" on his chest and neck had taken on a whole new meaning now.

"It happened when I was eighteen. They were going to a coven meeting. They were always going to coven meetings. I didn't want to go, but Iris went. She told me . . ."

She picked at a loose thread on the hem of her nightie. "Mam sent her to the store for supplies. It was late, and she had to drive far to find one that was open. While she was gone, someone set the building on fire. The flames blocked all the exits, and the firefighters couldn't get inside. My parents and everyone in the coven were killed. Iris arrived after it started and couldn't get in. If my mother hadn't sent her away, she would have been killed with them. They never caught the arsonist."

She picked harder at the thread, though she knew it was making it worse. "Afterward, Iris was obsessed with leaving Ireland. I guess she wanted to start over somewhere without any bad memories, and I didn't blame her. We picked Montreal and moved only six months later. We've been here nine years now."

She chanced a glance at Mist to find him watching her intently. She waited for him to say, *I'm sorry for your loss*, or something similar like everyone else did, but he didn't.

She was glad. "Sorry" had never brought anyone back from the dead.

"So you're afraid of glowing because it reminds you of the fire?"

Despite everything, she smiled. His directness made him easy to talk to. In fact, she had never told that story so easily.

"No, it's more like . . . the glowing reminds me of what I am. I stopped practicing after their deaths because I guess I resented that part of myself. My parents spent so much time with the coven when I was growing up. I have all these memories of asking them to go to the park or whatever and them saying they couldn't because they had to go to coven gatherings. I swear half my childhood was spent playing on the floor of the hall while they met.

"All that work, and for what? The person who killed them was just a human. They couldn't save themselves. They couldn't put out the fire."

She swallowed and then admitted what she'd never told another, even Iris. "I guess I just feel like, if they were going to die anyway, their time would have been better spent as normal parents who hung out with their kids. I hate that I resent them for that. They were so passionate. They did what they loved, and now that they're gone, it seems horrible to focus on the negative, but . . . I can't help it."

She looked at Mist. His eyes weren't brimming with sympathy or pity. He wasn't pushing her to embrace her true nature or telling her to confront her past. He was just listening.

And then he said, "I'm glad you're alive."

She managed a smile. "Me too."

And she was. After everything she'd been through, she felt nothing but gratitude to be sitting in her kitchen in the middle of the night with a demon, telling him about the most painful part of her life.

"Thank you for listening."

"I want to listen."

"You're good at it."

"How can one be good at listening? It's simple concentration."

She chuckled. "Yeah, well, most people can't concentrate

worth a damn, and they'd rather talk about themselves than listen to others."

"I like your human stories."

"Even the tragic ones?"

"No." He frowned. "I don't like that you lost your kin. If I could take away your sorrow, I would." He seemed confused about that.

She swallowed the sudden lump in her throat. That, in essence, was what other people meant when they said they were sorry for her loss. But there were varying degrees of conviction. Some were genuine, others just wanted to get away from the uncomfortable emotions as quickly as they could.

But Mist didn't understand platitudes, so when he said that, it was because he meant it. And being what he was, having experienced things she couldn't imagine . . . His words meant everything.

She frowned suddenly. "When did you come back? Your friend made it sound like you were gone."

His amber eyes shifted away. "I never left."

"You didn't?"

"I perched on the roof and told myself to go, but I could not."

"Why not?"

One shoulder lifted slightly. "I wanted to watch over you. You weren't supposed to know I was there, but I saw you through the window, and you had left it open . . ."

And he'd been concerned she was in danger, so he'd woken her. "Mist . . ."

Swallowing her customary lack of courage, she reached out and took his hand, threading their fingers together. He tracked her movements with a sharp gaze. He may have been in human form, but in every other way, he was still the Hunter.

"Thank you for coming back."

"It would be better for us both if I could leave."

"Maybe." She dared to meet his gaze and offered a weak smile. "But I'm glad you're here."

He didn't smile back. He just looked at her.

He was so handsome in this form, with his warm, tanned skin and round, normal pupils. His fingers ended in blunt nails and there was nothing on his back except smooth skin and muscle. No wings, no tail.

It would be so easy to be with him like this, to forget what he really was and where he came from.

But this wasn't truly him. Yes, his human form was part of who he was, but it was only a small part. If he could stand here, holding her hand and listening to her story without batting an eye at the fact that she was glowing like a bioluminescent jellyfish . . . then shouldn't she do the same for him?

She took a breath. "Will you . . . shift for me?"

His eyes narrowed, and she didn't miss the distrust and hurt that flashed in them, though it was quickly masked. She had put that look there, and while she didn't blame herself for freaking out, it was time to get over it.

"Please?"

Slowly, he did. His eyes became yellow instead of amber, and the lemony glow filled the entire orb save for a vertical-slitted pupil in the center. Then, ashy gray bled over his skin, and when it reached his fingertips, claws grew from them.

His wings appeared at his back and unfolded, and she saw his shoulders relax as if he felt more comfortable with their weight. She wondered if it threw his balance off without them. His tail snaked out and wrapped around her ankle, the soft rope sliding up to her calf where it dangled off the counter, but this time it didn't scare her.

Okay, so he scared her a bit. He was just so *big*.

Her flat was old and had high ceilings, but his tall wings made them feel low. His hand was twice the size of hers, and when he curled his fingers around, her palm disappeared completely.

Heart racing, she lifted their joined hands and studied them. Her pale, glowing skin against his dark gray skin made her think of a yin-yang symbol.

"These look really sharp." She tilted their hands so she could see his black claws in the light cast from her body.

He said nothing, watching her with that hunter's gaze.

She glanced up. "Can I see your teeth?" His lips were the same soft, kissable ones he had in human form, only they were nearly black.

He bared his teeth, and her eyes widened. No wonder he'd made that mark on her neck.

"Wow, those look even sharper."

To her surprise, he smiled. It was the first time she'd seen him do it fully. His face still had mostly the same features as his human form, she realized. He was still handsome. He was just also strange and unearthly and gray. With wings and claws and fangs and a tail. But once she got past all that . . . he wasn't so scary.

"A demon takes pride in his teeth and claws," he said. "You've paid me a great compliment."

So basically, judging by the look on his face, it was the demon equivalent of stroking his muscles and calling him manly.

"They're very formidable," she said encouragingly. "I wouldn't mess with you on my best day."

"I won't hurt you." As he spoke, his gaze flicked to where he'd bitten her neck.

Instead of looking regretful, however, his eyes burned.

"I know." At least, she knew he wouldn't intentionally.

"It healed."

"What?"

"The mark." He touched the spot gently with a claw.

She unwound their clasped hands and put her palms there, feeling around for the broken skin and finding nothing. Just hours ago, it had been unmistakable. How . . . ? She shook her head. *Guess it wasn't as deep as it looked.*

She dropped her hands, and he drew her hair back, making her shiver. Stooping, he touched his nose to the skin below her jaw and inhaled.

He was smelling her again. His chest expanded with breath, and when he exhaled, it rumbled with a growl. Her heart pounded until she felt lightheaded.

But when he stepped back, he was frowning. "You're afraid."

"No—"

"I can scent your fear. Do not lie."

"I'm not scared of you."

His eyes narrowed. He obviously didn't believe her.

"Well, I am sort of, but not because— Well, you're very different, and I'm still getting used to it, and I suppose that does scare me a bit. But that doesn't mean I want you to go, and I would have told you that earlier if you hadn't left so fast. The truth is, I'm mostly afraid of . . ." She picked at her nightie seam again. "My reaction to you."

"This form repulses you."

"No!" Her eyes shot up to meet his. "No, it doesn't. And that's partly why I'm afraid."

A crease formed between his brows. "I don't understand."

"It's just, I find you very— You're so big and . . . not human, and I, well, maybe it's not right to— I feel like I shouldn't— It's overwhelming."

She winced at her inarticulateness. *What happened to no more stuttering?*

"I don't understand."

She looked at him. She couldn't not look at him. He was everywhere. The moment she did, her stomach flipped over, and something clenched in her lower abdomen. *His eyes. The way he watches me. The sheer size of him . . .*

His nostrils flared as he inhaled, and his eyes widened.

"You smell like fear and . . ." He inhaled again. "Arousal."

In a flash, his hand shot out and wrapped around her throat. He didn't choke her; he just held her securely so she couldn't escape. Maybe she should have screamed, but that wasn't what happened at all. Her lower abdomen clenched again, but this time it was unmistakably rooted in her core.

He used his grip on her throat to tilt her head, and he pressed his nose to her exposed skin. A growl rumbled in his chest, and her heart pounded faster.

"This scent . . ." He lifted his head suddenly. "But you're still afraid."

How to explain? "I can be scared and . . . other things at the same time. I've never— It's just, you're not human. Isn't it wrong?"

He frowned. "I don't care."

Suddenly, she didn't either. The fear still coursed through her blood, but it was a different kind of fear now. It was fear of the unknown, but it was laced with . . . anticipation. Excitement.

As if he sensed the shift in her emotions—and he probably did—he leaned closer, peering into her eyes. They were in her kitchen, in almost the same place as the first time they'd kissed.

Only this time, his hand collared her throat, and he looked nothing like a human. This time, there were no more secrets between them.

He waited, gauging her reaction, and she felt her cheeks heat at the look in his eyes. No man had ever looked at her like that—half with wonder, half with a near-frightening possessive intensity.

"Mist . . ."

His name was like a trigger. The next instant, his fingers flexed slightly, and he tilted his head and fused their lips together. The air gusted out of her, and she closed her eyes, overwhelmed by sensation.

As he deepened the kiss, she dared to put her hands on his shoulders. Touching him made her feel positively minuscule. Beneath her palms, his skin was so hot it burned, so soft she longed to stroke every inch of it.

He growled as her fingers clenched on the firm muscle, and he released her throat to grip her thighs. She jumped when she felt his tail snaking up her leg like a stray tentacle.

He broke the kiss, searching her gaze as if to see if she looked frightened. She wasn't. His strangeness was quickly becoming something she desired. She briefly thought that with a few kisses, he may have ruined human men for her for life.

Satisfied with what he saw, he leaned down and kissed her again.

The press of his soft lips against hers, his strong body surrounding her, his wild hair brushing the backs of her hands . . . She had never felt anything this consuming. Another moan hummed in her throat as his hands slid up her thighs beneath her nightie.

She'd always felt like her thighs were huge, but his hands wrapped almost all the way around them. When his grip tightened and she felt the prick of his claws, her back arched, her breasts brushing his chest.

Another growl rumbled from him, and he tugged her closer to the edge so their bodies finally aligned. The minute her heated core pressed against him, they both sucked in air from the space between their mouths.

For a moment, they froze like that, just breathing, and time stood still.

And then Lily shocked herself by daring to flick her tongue between the rows of deadly teeth.

When her tongue brushed his, his grip flexed, and he recip-
rocated with a tongue that was decidedly *not* human. It was
long and pointed, and it moved in ways a human tongue could
not. When he wrapped it completely around hers like a lasso,
she nearly had a heart attack.

All of a sudden, she forgot that there was anything unusual
about making out with a giant gray demon. She forgot about
being shy and the fact that she was self-conscious about her body.

She wrapped her legs around his hips, tangled her hands in
his hair, and pressed herself as close to him as she could get.
Their heads tilted opposite directions, tongues twisting between
them.

He pulled her closer and pressed his hips against her, and
she felt the hard outline of a formidably sized erection. She
tightened her legs and tried to squeeze him closer, desperate for
friction at her core.

He dragged his mouth away and pulled back without loos-
ening his grip. Their heavy breathing was the only sound to
disturb the silence.

"Your scent . . ." His voice was nothing but a raspy growl.
"I want it."

She would have been embarrassed he could smell her
arousal so easily if she hadn't already concluded that his hunter
instincts were a turn-on.

"I could follow it anywhere. There is nowhere you could
hide I wouldn't find you."

She imagined him stalking her, led by her scent and her
scent alone, and another wave of desire flooded between her
legs.

"I would want you to find me," she whispered.

Eyes burning, he lifted her off the counter like she weighed
nothing. She'd never had a man carry her before, and the rare
times one had tried even lifting her, watching the poor bloke
struggle had been mortifying.

But Mist tucked her against him like she was a tiny bundle, surrounding her with his arms and holding her so close she could see only him. If there was anything that could make her desire him more, that was it.

By the time he made it to her bedroom, she was squirming. He laid her on the mattress and crawled over her, his looming size and powerful wings blocking out the rest of the world. The light from her skin cast a glow on his features, making him appear even more unearthly. He planted the talons at his wingtips into the mattress above her and his palms on either side of her head.

Their eyes met. Her palms slid over his strong chest, her legs splayed open, and she had no desire to hide from him. In fact, lying there like that, watching his hungry gaze rove over her, made her melt with desire.

His lips peeled back from his teeth, and he growled, "You're mine."

She arched her back and begged him with her eyes to prove it.

15

MINE

THE HEADY SCENT OF HIS FEMALE'S AROUSAL SWAMPED Mist's senses, making him nearly mindless with desire. A dark possessiveness unlike anything he'd felt before filled him, and, had anyone tried to take her in that moment, he knew he'd be capable of a level of violence that transcended anything he'd done in the past.

He gripped Lily's soft flesh and lowered himself until he hovered only inches above her. *Want to taste her. Want to bite her.* He wanted to consume every inch of her. He wanted . . . What he wanted was too dark and intense to put into words, but he knew he needed it.

Without breaking eye contact, he crawled slowly down her body. Then, sitting up, he slid his hands up her hips to her waist, pushing her short nightgown up with them.

She watched him carefully, and though she tensed as he revealed her, she didn't flinch or give any indication she didn't want him to continue.

She wore a tiny scrap of lace for underwear, and the curve of her belly hung slightly over it. He wanted to see the fold of flesh without any fabric in the way, so he hooked his claws on the sides of the fabric and ripped up, effectively tearing it in two pieces.

Lily gasped as he tossed away the shredded fabric. "Mist! Those were my favorite—"

She broke off as he grasped her behind her knees and pushed them up as far as they would go toward her breasts while simultaneously spreading them, baring her to his gaze.

He sat back to survey his prize, nearly mad with need at the sight before him. Her pink flesh glistened with arousal, the delicate folds just begging to be tasted and explored. By him. Only ever by him.

"Mine," he told her.

She nodded with a swallow. Her skin still glowed faintly, but it was beginning to subside. She no longer cast light into the room, and he could now see the red flush in her cheeks that had been hidden before.

She squirmed in his grip. "Mist . . ."

"*Mine.*"

"I know, but . . ." She wiggled again, squeezing her eyes shut and turning her head away.

He released her legs, tilting his head. "What's wrong?"

Her eyes opened as she pressed her bent knees together. "Nothing."

His narrowed, a warning for her not to lie.

She blew out a breath. "Nothing, I swear. I'm just not used to . . . this."

"Good." If she was, that meant he would have to hunt down many humans to kill. No one touched what was his.

She smiled faintly. "I don't want you to stop, I swear. I'm just a little self-conscious, and I'm not used to letting someone look at my body. And since I'm glowing still, I can't exactly ask you to turn out the light, which is what I'd normally do."

His eyes widened slightly. *A light.* What a good idea. He wound his tail around the lamp on the bedside table and flicked the switch with the tip. Soft, orange light flooded the bedroom.

Lily's eyes widened. "No, I meant I wanted it to be darker, not brighter."

"I want to see everything."

She sat up, nightgown slipping back down to cover her, to his dismay. Her arms wrapped around her body, her eyes full of doubt. He didn't like that either. "I don't."

Understanding dawned, and the disappointment was sharp. "I will take human form if you don't want to look at me."

"No! No, that's not what I meant at all!" She slapped a palm to her forehead. "I'm screwing this up with my stupid insecurities like I always do."

He reached out and moved her hand from her face. "You're not screwing up. Tell me what you want and I will do it."

She looked from beneath her lashes and met his gaze. "I want to see you. I like you in this form. A lot."

His eyes narrowed.

"This isn't about you, I swear. You're perfect." She gestured to him. "You're huge and gorgeous and perfect, and I'm just used to hiding my body."

"I'm not perfect. I'm a demon."

She snorted. "I suppose you're right. But you seem pretty perfect to me."

"And you seem perfect to me."

Her eyes flared slightly, and she bit her lip. The sight of her blunt teeth digging into the soft flesh drew his gaze like a magnet.

"Do you really mean that?"

He forced himself to look into her eyes again. "Why would I say something I don't mean?"

She breathed a laugh and reached out to him, gripping his shoulders and pulling him in for a kiss. "Why indeed? You're so straightforward, and I love that about you. Everything seems so much simpler, and I feel silly for worrying in the first place. I want to see you, and you want to see me. Why shouldn't we leave the light on?"

"I think we *should* leave it on," he clarified.

"I know that." She chuckled. "That's what I'm saying."

"But—"

"Just kiss me."

He did, eagerly, still not sure what she meant but really not caring after hearing her request. As she dug her fingers back into his hair, he gathered her nightgown in his claws, intent on tearing it from her body.

"Wait!" She pulled back. "I made this, and I really don't want you to rip it in half."

Dismay filled him at the thought of destroying her creation, and she laughed at the look on his face. "It's fine, Mist. I like that you want to tear the clothes off me like a feral beast. It's sexy." Her cheeks flushed.

He didn't bother trying to reply because the next instant, she tugged the dress over her head and tossed it away. Naked before him, she covered her breasts, and her blush deepened so much, it spread down her neck to her chest.

He wasn't letting her hide anymore. Looming over her, he crawled forward until she was forced to lie back. He grasped her wrists in his hands, drawing her arms up and pinning them to the mattress beside her head. He surveyed his prize a second time, this time fully bared to him.

Her breasts were overflowing with fullness, her nipples hardened into pink points. If that wasn't enough, her belly rounded into a soft mound below, and her hips and thighs were yet another bounty of luscious, biteable flesh. Between them, a tiny wedge of blond curls waited for his exploration.

"Mine," he said yet again because he needed her to understand it. He needed everyone in the realms to hear it. He needed to make it very clear to every single living being that if anyone, *anyone*, tried to take what was his, they would die begging for mercy they would not receive.

He released her wrists only to use his wing talons to pin them back down. His freed hands spread her thighs again, and he groaned as another wave of her scent flooded his senses.

Locking eyes with her, he bent, drawing in deep breaths of her fragrance from its source like it was life-giving perfume. He supposed it was. He'd never felt so alive.

She strained against the wings pinning her down, squirming beneath him as he opened his mouth, extended his tongue, and licked up the center of her core. Her eyes widened at the sight, and they both groaned. Her flavor shocked and soothed his senses at the same time, and something snapped inside of him.

No more waiting. He needed everything, and he needed it now.

He stuck out his tongue as far as it would go and speared her with it, snaking it inside her to flick against her inner walls. Then he dragged his mouth up and fixed his lips around her swollen clitoris and sucked, and her moan was interrupted by a gasp.

"Oh my god, Mist!" She sounded almost shocked at the intensity of her reaction, and it only encouraged him further.

He allowed his tail to trace up the inside of her thigh and probe her entrance, and he lifted his head, still holding her legs open, so she would know exactly what he intended to do.

Head lifting off the mattress, her mouth dropped open as he slid his tail through her wetness and then gently slapped the tip against her clitoris.

She gasped, and her head fell back. "Oh god, that feels good."

He pushed the tip inside before drawing it back up and slapping her lightly again.

She jerked in his hold. "Oh my god!"

Another light slap, and she jerked again, her rapid breathing becoming more audible. She lifted her head and stared at him like she couldn't believe what he was doing to her.

He bent his head and replaced his tail with his tongue, tasting that sweet nectar. The best thing he'd ever tasted. The finest scent to ever fill his nose.

"Mist!"

His fingers clenched around her thighs as they started to tremble. She was close already, and he took great satisfaction knowing he could unravel her so quickly. He wanted to draw it out, but he was too impatient, too desperate to hear her screams and taste her release.

Sucking her clit into his mouth, he plunged his tail inside of her, and she screamed, throwing her head back and yanking her wrists so hard she nearly pulled free of his wing talons. He pressed them down harder and repeated the motion, sucking her again while he worked his tail in and out of her.

"Mist! Don't stop, oh my god—!"

Her bud swelled against his tongue, and a flood of wetness soaked his lips and tail. Her moans turned into cries and her squirms into writhing. But he held her fast with his claws and talons, relentless in his drive to make her shatter.

And then she did.

Her scream pierced his sensitive ears, and it was the purest, most wondrous sound he'd ever heard. Her core muscles convulsed around his tail, and his mouth was filled with the ambrosial taste of her release.

He didn't stop, pushing her further, prolonging her climax until her body shook with great tremors, all that bountiful flesh shaking with it.

He had never seen anything more magnificent. Just tasting her, watching her, hearing her scream his name . . . He would climax himself if he relinquished his control for but a second.

"Mist, oh god, I can't— It's too much—"

He raised his head only when she begged. Then, he lifted his wing talons and released her legs and sat back to enjoy her in the aftermath. She lay sprawled open, no sign of shyness remaining, her chest and belly heaving with gradually slowing breaths.

Eventually, she opened her eyes. Momentary surprise flashed in them when she caught him watching her, but then she smiled.

"That was . . ." Her smile turned secret, indulgent. "Wow."

He smiled back, but his was possessive.

"I didn't expect . . . Your tail—" She covered her mouth with a palm. "I can't believe you did that."

He crawled back over her. "You enjoyed it." It wasn't a question. He was still tasting the proof on his tongue.

He wound his tail around her ankle and up her leg. He couldn't stop touching her. His rigid hunter's control was the only thing keeping him from pouncing on her and relieving the unbearable arousal that was close to making him mindless.

He wasn't entirely sure why he held back. Another demon would not have. But there was something about Lily, something about the way she accepted him though he wasn't human and was supposed to be her enemy.

He wanted her to trust him, he realized. He barely knew what that was, and he knew he wasn't capable of it himself, but he wanted Lily to feel it for him. Maybe that wasn't fair, but he didn't care.

He wanted her to feel protected by him. He wanted her to open herself to him, to hide nothing.

He supposed he'd been feeling that since he'd met her, but he hadn't been able to put it into words before. But now . . . he needed more.

He needed everything.

❦

"Roll over," Lily said, though her heart jumped nervously. This whole Queen of Confidence thing was new, but she was trying it out.

The fact that she'd been given the most intense orgasm of her life by a demon with a pointed tongue and talented tail made her feel like she was in an alternate reality. And in this dream world, who said she couldn't be unashamedly confident?

Mist bent and fixed his teeth around her throat where the bite mark had been, and he growled.

She grinned at the ceiling. She knew what this meant by now.

"I promise I won't try to escape." She stroked her hands up his back. Her heart jumped again when she felt the muscle and bone where his wings joined between his shoulder blades.

It was one thing to see it but another to touch it. She could feel where the skin stretched and became the leathery membrane that would suspend him in flight. It was surreal.

He lifted his head and pinned her with a suspicious look, and she was struck anew by the beauty of his eyes. Strange, yes, but so beautiful.

"Trust me?" She offered a reassuring smile. "I guarantee you'll like what I have in mind."

His eyes narrowed, and she found it sad that he still expected her to run.

It wasn't surprising after what he'd been through—something she still didn't fully know—but she wanted to prove that he could trust her. She made a mental note to watch her words and never promise something she couldn't follow through on. Building trust would take time.

Finally, he relented, rolling onto his back with his wings tucked beneath him. The one closest to her spread again and scooped her up, tugging her against him and wrapping around her like a velvety blanket.

She sat up and petted his chest as a reward for listening to her request. "It's my turn now."

Swallowing her self-consciousness, she swung her leg over and straddled his hips.

He immediately cupped her breasts, a growl rumbling in his chest as they spilled over his big hands. She glanced down, and the sight of her pale, delicate skin against his sharp gray claws sent a thrill coursing through her.

He's definitely ruined me for life.

"Lily . . ."

It was a warning. Not to tease him, perhaps? She had no intention of that, so she scooted down his body, trailing kisses as she went. His skin was so hot he felt like a furnace beneath her.

She stopped when she got to the fastening of his pants. In her mind, she would sexily open them in a practiced motion, and he would be blown away by her seductiveness.

Instead, she climbed off to sit beside him and stare in confusion at the front of the pants, which appeared to have no way to open them at all.

"How do you get these off?"

Great. So much for Lily the Seductress. She was Lily the Inexperienced at the moment.

He lifted his hips and reached beneath him, and the leather waistband came loose with a tug.

"It's for my tail." He used the tip of said tail to flick her hair back as if reminding her what he could do with it. "It laces up in the back."

Her eyes widened. "What a clever design." She wondered what other types of clothing existed in Hell that were designed to accommodate extra demonic appendages. Her mind raced through the possibilities of pants made for tails and shirts made for wings.

Mist blinked.

Shit. Lily the Seamstress had taken over, and that was honestly worse.

"Sorry, it's the designer in me." She blushed furiously and then focused back on her task.

Apparently, Mist didn't have patience for her to remove his pants herself, because he sat up and ripped them off in one rough motion and tossed them away. She quickly forgot about everything in the universe except for the sight before her.

Propped up on his elbows, he stretched out like a naked man buffet solely for her enjoyment.

His cock . . . *Oh my god.* Her eyes bugged. Obviously, she'd been aware of the size difference between them, but she hadn't fully considered the implications. Well, she was damn well considering them now.

His cock was perfectly proportioned to the rest of him, which meant it was huge. Thick and veiny . . . and dark, ashy gray.

A gigantic, vein-wrapped, silky-smooth, *gray* dick.

In fact . . . it looked exactly like the dildo she'd secretly wanted to buy the one time she'd been brave enough to walk into a sex shop. She'd done laps around the store to keep staring at it, but in the end, she'd chickened out and left without buying anything.

Well, now here it was again, attached to a very large, very aroused demon who had just given her an orgasm with his tail.

She was equal parts turned on and nervous. Or maybe she was just turned on because, before she knew what she was doing, she had reached out and wrapped her hands around him.

Both hands. Because one wasn't enough to get a good grip.

His eyes went hooded, and his spine arched as a sharp breath escaped him. She couldn't stop staring, her eyes traveling up and down his body, trying in vain to take in every detail at once.

She stroked up, her fingers getting slicked with the moisture leaking from the tip, and she spread it around the head. He started to growl again.

That sound . . . If she'd been hiking in the jungle she would have started screaming, but knowing it came from him just made her hungrier.

She bent and licked the head over the slit. His chest heaved, and his claws dug into the mattress. Licking her lips, she opened her mouth as far as she could and then popped it over the top.

His head dropped back, and the sexiest moan she'd ever heard rolled out of him like thunder.

She stretched her jaw wider, taking him further into her mouth, feeling like the most powerful being in the universe. He growled deeply, and his legs spread as he flexed his claws, probably tearing holes in her bed sheets. *I'm a bloody goddess.*

Her jaw already ached from his size, but she wasn't stopping for anything. His tail snaked up her back and wrapped around her hair, holding it off her face. She moaned as she remembered it penetrating her, and he made another sexy growl as the sound vibrated around his shaft.

She hummed again, moving her hands in opposition to her lips. She could barely swallow half of him, and she was pretty sure her jaw might have locked open, but she didn't give a damn.

"Lily . . ." It came out like a snarl. His head dropped again and then lifted like he couldn't bear to look away. He sagged into his elbows and then spread them apart and collapsed onto his back.

"Lily—" His abs clenched, rippling with strength as his hips rolled. It seemed to take all his control not to thrust into her mouth, but she was glad he held back because it was going to take some practice to take him any deeper than she currently was.

Practice . . . because she already wanted to do this again.

"Lily, I—" More moans rolled out of him as she increased her pace, her eyes watering now from the painful stretch in her jaw. "You must—" His claws tore up the sheets as he flexed them again and again. "I can't—"

She used her bottom hand to grip his sack, as gray as the rest of him, and massaged gently. His words dissolved into snarls, and he seemed to transform into a mindless beast before her eyes. His tail tightened around her hair, and his whole body tensed, every muscle flexing, every vein standing out.

And then his head tipped back, and with a hoarse shout, he came into her mouth.

The first jet hit her gag reflex, and she choked. Her lips broke the seal, and his release ran down his shaft over her hands. But she didn't pull back. Streams of hot cum filled her mouth, but she was too full of his cock to swallow it all, and she choked again, more spilling around her lips.

Her eyes teared up, and a vague panic sensation told her to gasp for air, but she loved it. She loved every single second of everything.

She felt like she was flying. She felt like the sexiest woman in the universe. There was cum all over her mouth and hands, and she was sucking a demon's dick, and it was the best damn thing that had ever happened to her.

The tension drained out of him with a final, primal growl, and then his tail wrapped around her throat and guided her off his shaft. Again, he didn't choke her, but he held her firmly, and it was perfect. He was careful with her, but he didn't treat her like a breakable doll, and she loved that too.

Smiling, heart racing with the thrill of the moment, she wiped her mouth with her arm since her hands were already covered. She held them out for him to see.

"You made me all wet." She squirmed at the drugged look in his eyes.

"Wipe it on yourself." His voice was deeper and rougher than she'd ever heard it. "I want you covered in my scent."

She did, cupping her breasts and sliding her palms over her stomach like she was getting oiled up for a bikini photoshoot.

She wasn't thinking about her rolls and stretch marks. She was lost in his eyes and feeling this primal fire burning inside at the thought of appeasing his feral instincts.

No, he wasn't an alpha wolf in a mating ritual; he was something way better. He was her demon hunter, a deadly, elusive creature of Hell that had stalked the realms longer than she could fathom.

But mostly, right now . . . he was just hers.

She slid her sticky hands back up to her breasts and cupped them again. Then, she bent down and gave his shaft one final lick. Looking into his eyes while she dragged her tongue up his length, she finished with a flick at the tip and said, "Mine."

16

IN THE PIT OF DESPAIR

MIST DANGLED BY THE MANACLES AT HIS WRISTS, HIS arms stretched painfully from his suspended body weight. He was hanging directly over the Pit, the grate over the top rolled back so if he were to fall, he would drop straight into the open mouths of the goraths below.

In front of him, at the edge of the Pit, stood Paimon, her red-eyed camel by her side. The crown perched between her horns glinted in the torchlight, long shadows cast across her face.

"You can't escape me, you know." She studied her claws. "It's a waste of time to try."

Mist said nothing, but inwardly, he burned with conviction. Giving up was no longer an option. Not now that he had Lily. Not now that she had accepted him for what he was. Not now that he had tasted her sweet release and she had done the same to him.

There was so much he wanted to experience with her. So much he wanted to show her. So much he wanted to give her.

For her, he had to live. He had to believe he could find a way to be free.

"You think you're the only hunter in Hell? The only one who can find wayward rogues?"

"I am the best."

Paimon looked up and smiled. "So confident. I always admired that in you, but right now it's just annoying. Return to me now, and we'll forget this unpleasantness. We'll go back to the way things were."

An obvious lie. There was no "forgive and forget" in Hell.

"So you don't want to cooperate? Fine. Let's try something else." A malicious glint flashed in her eyes. "You were summoned by a human. At the precise moment you were about to be devoured, by freak coincidence, the first successful summoning of Mishetsumephtai in history occurred. You, a demon so unknown, most humans aren't even aware of your existence. Seems odd, don't you think?"

His heart started to pound. This was why he'd tried to leave Lily in the first place. It was like he'd once said to Asmodeus: *If you really cared for her, you would have left her alone.*

He now understood Asmodeus's predicament on a visceral level. Only the cold claws of death could pry him from Lily's side.

But if his witch ended up involved in this somehow . . . if Paimon found out she existed and got even an inkling of what she meant to him . . .

No. He wouldn't allow it to happen.

"Nothing to say?" Paimon reached out and stroked the sandy hide of her camel. "Well, I have plenty. Isn't that right, Shaheen?"

Shaheen blinked his long eyelashes.

Paimon's head swiveled back around. "Since you're being such an obliging listener at the moment, allow me to share. After Belial's defection, I wondered what he could possibly be seeking on Earth when he already had everything in Hell. He was the most powerful King, held one of the largest, most lucrative territories in the underworld, and had legions of desperately loyal followers, waiting at his beck and call to serve him. And yet, he threw all that away to traipse about the Earth like a pathetic mortal, hiding in human form." Her lip curled in revulsion.

"But I have finally discovered his true motives. Belial wants to usurp Lucifer as High King of Hell. Asmodeus, Raum, and Mephistopheles are helping him. Together, they seek a power source on Earth that Belial believes will give him the added strength he needs to defeat Lucifer."

She was so far off, it was almost funny, except it wasn't. Because, deluded though she was, if she was convinced Belial was plotting something, she would respond in kind. And that was no laughing matter.

"Do you want to know what I think? I think you found the rogues right away, as is your wont. I think Belial offered you a taste of power, and you took the bait." She smiled coldly. "Tell me, what did he promise? That he would free you from the brands? That he would gift you with a territory and legions of your own?"

She threw back her head and laughed, the haunting sound echoing around the cavernous chamber.

"You will never have those things. You will never be able to remove those brands. You will never be anything except *my* servant, *my* Hunter, *mine*!" Again, her voice boomed around the darkness. "You will always belong to me."

Mist's hands clenched into fists, his claws digging into his palms until they drew blood. He hung there helplessly while everything inside of him wanted to attack, to rend her limb from limb, to tear her head from her shoulders and paint the walls with her blood.

"Still not in a sharing mood? I'll continue, then. After I made the discovery about Belial's motives, I reached out to my sources, endeavoring to identify this power source he seeks. They returned with an interesting tale.

"Twenty-seven years ago, two witches were born. Twins, from a long line of the most powerful blood-borns the Earth has ever seen. Their coming was prophesied centuries ago and was marked by a rare meteor shower at the precise moment of their births.

"The prophecy stated that the blood-borns would become immortal and so powerful, they would cause the downfall of a King of Hell. No one knows which King, of course, but you can see why that might cause some upset."

Mist forgot about his aching arms and the monsters below as an ice-cold feeling of dread trickled over him.

"The mother of the twins knew of their prophesied power and that supernatural beings would try to steal it or kill them before they could fulfill their destiny. So, she concealed them using powerful blood magic to disguise their potent energies. But nine years ago, at the witching hour on the night of their eighteenth birthdays, the twins came fully into their powers, and the cloaking spell failed. It was only for a brief instant, but it was long enough.

"Duke Valefor—a collector of unique supernatural beings and artifacts, as I'm sure you know—had long been aware of the coming of the twins and had searched high and low for them since their birth. The moment the cloaking failed, Valefor's tracking spells finally provided him with results.

"He discovered the parents and their coven desperately trying to repair the spell. Despite his interference, they were successful, and he could not locate the twins. When he could not breach the coven's perimeter wards, he burned the building to the ground in an attempt to damage the spell and make it fail again. It did not, however, and the twins escaped. Valefor continues to hunt them to this day."

The trickling dread had become an icy wave. Blood-borns with parents that had been killed in a fire. Nine years ago. It was too coincidental that the witch sisters Mist had accidentally encountered were the same ones Valefor hunted . . . but there was no other explanation.

"It is said," Paimon continued, "that the one who harnesses the magic of the twins will be blessed by untold power. Power enough to, say, unseat the High King of Hell." Her brow lifted. "That's what Belial is after, isn't it? That's how he convinced you to betray me."

"I've never heard a more far-fetched story," Mist replied blandly, a cold sweat worming its way down his overextended spine.

Paimon smiled. "You're nervous. I can see it in your eyes." Her smile dropped, and her eyes darkened with wrath. "Serve me or die, Mishetsu. You know how the brands work."

"Then I choose death."

Paimon dismissed him with a wave of her hand. "I already know how to find you, anyway. There are hundreds of prophecies about artifacts, talismans, and destinies. Why do you think I fixated on that one in particular?"

He said nothing because he knew she would tell him anyway.

"I was shocked when you were summoned not only out of my lair, but out of your cuffs, by a human. Did you think I wouldn't be able to analyze the magic responsible? The traces in the air were unmistakable. I sensed the powerful Temporal magic. I *know* who summoned you, Mishetsu. I know you're working with the twins."

His blood froze solid in his veins. He had never known fear like he did right then because, for the first time in his existence, he was afraid for another. Not for himself. For Lily.

"I'm going to find you and them. Since I've had a taste of their magic, it won't be difficult to locate them."

She is lying. She had to be. There was no way to track down Lily based solely on that, especially if she was under a cloaking spell.

But the fact that he didn't know, that there was even the slightest chance she spoke true . . . It felt like having his insides carved out.

"When I do, I will deliver the sisters to Lucifer, and he will use their power to destroy you, Belial, and the three fools allied with him."

Paimon's eyes glittered with triumph as Mist failed to hide his horror. "In the meantime, I'll be summoning you with all my power. I would say you have about two days left before you have to return or— Well, you know the consequences."

Two days? He always had at least a week, if not two. *She lies again.*

She wiggled her claws in a wave, flashing a smile full of sharp teeth.

"I'll be seeing you soon, Mishetsu."

Mist lurched upright in bed. His shoulders burned from dangling over the Pit, the skin at his wrists raw from chafing.

He hadn't actually physically been in Paimon's lair or she would never have let him go, but the Queen of Hell was powerful enough to trap his mind in vivid dreams. Generally only succubi and incubi had this ability, but Paimon was a rare exception. His consciousness had lived the experience, so lingering traces of phantom pain transferred to his physical body as he awoke.

He wasn't immediately aware of his surroundings. Sunlight streamed through the window beside him, so he must have slept through the night. This was . . . unusual. That he'd been able to rest in another's company, vulnerable and unprotected, was a first. But then, that was just what Lily did to him. She made him feel relaxed. Normal. Safe.

Panic filled him briefly when he noticed the empty space beside him, only to dissipate when he heard soft humming from the kitchen and smelled the scents of breakfast. He imagined Lily puttering around, golden hair spilling down her back, and something tightened in his chest so intensely that he gripped it.

Was it possible she and Iris were truly the prophesied twins? Or was it all a ruse Paimon had dreamed up as a way to . . . what?

What would she achieve by lying? He was already branded. He couldn't think of a single thing she stood to gain from making up such an elaborate story, which made him think it was true.

And Lily *was* powerful. No one had ever succeeded in summoning him before, and he wouldn't have thought it possible for him to be drawn out of the cuffs at all, which were supposed to bind him to Paimon's lair.

A sudden searing pain erupted from the brand on his neck.

A low groan escaped him as his skin began to burn. Immediately, he felt a powerful force drawing him downward like a magnet in his chest. It took all his strength not to obey the compulsion right then. He sat there, claws digging into his thighs, breathing through the pain and trying to clear his mind of the urge to return to Hell.

Paimon hadn't been lying.

At the rate his neck was burning, he figured he had only forty-eight hours before the compulsion stole his awareness. And maybe a week before it killed him.

That had been his plan when Lily first summoned him out of the Pit: enjoy his remaining days and then die on his own terms. But after last night . . . he wanted to *live*.

But Lily was in danger, and it wasn't about what he wanted anymore. Now, he had to find a way to keep her safe.

Though he wouldn't have traded last night with her for anything, he wished she'd never summoned him. He would rather be rotting inside a gorath's stomach than know it was his fault she was being hunted.

He should have followed his own advice from the beginning and stayed away from her. He should never have left Hell, never embarked on this fruitless mission to taste freedom and enjoy himself.

This is what happens when the rules are broken. This is the consequence of insubordination.

Every single time. When would he stop this sad attempt to make his life have meaning? His life was worthless. *He* was worthless. He was worse than worthless, because by trying not to be, he had hurt the only thing he cared about.

He climbed out of bed, black spots flaring in his vision from the searing pain in his neck, and pulled on his pants in a daze. He remembered Lily's curious expression as she tried to figure out how to take them off. He remembered watching her bring him to climax, feeling her wet mouth around him, her fingers stroking him, her moans of delight, her taste on his tongue . . .

It was the best thing that had ever happened to him. It was far better than anything he deserved. He would hold on to those memories for the rest of his days . . . however few remained.

BETWEEN TWO FIRES

LILY FLICKED OFF THE STOVE, TURNING WHEN SHE FELT A presence behind her. She smiled at the powerful form of the demon filling the room, still not quite believing he was real. His gray skin was lighter in the morning sun, the brands visible where the light hit them.

Her smile evaporated at the look on his face.

"Mist? What's wrong?"

"You said your parents were killed by an arsonist."

Her fingers tightened around the spatula. It was a heavy topic for morning conversation. "Yes . . ."

"Who can confirm this? Did anyone see the human?"

"Why are you asking me this right now? I'd rather not discuss—"

"Did they?"

"No! Well, I— I don't know for sure." She fidgeted with the utensil's plastic handle. "Iris dealt with the police since she was a witness. She never let me get involved, even when I asked. I guess she wanted to protect me, I don't know. But she told me they confirmed it was an arsonist, and that they never had enough information to find him. That's all I know."

It felt like his stare would burn a hole through her skull.

"Can we please eat breakfast? I don't want to talk about this right now. I just wanted to have a nice morning with you, and—"

"It's my fault, Lily." He dropped into a chair, and his shoulders and wings slumped in the most hopeless posture she'd ever seen.

"What's your fault?" She set the spatula down and approached warily.

"I should never have walked you home that night. I should never have talked to you."

"What are you talking about? You're scaring me."

"Paimon knows about you, and she is hunting you now. Because of me."

"What? Paimon, as in the King of Hell?"

"Queen."

That was news to her. She was pretty sure every book she'd ever seen listed Paimon as a male. "Is that your . . ." She couldn't say the word. The idea of him being someone's possession made her feel sick. "What would she want with me?"

"Your parents weren't killed by a human, Lily. It was a demon."

Her head jerked back. "What? That's crazy. Iris—"

"Either your sibling doesn't know or she lied to you."

"How do you know this?"

"Paimon visited me in a dream. She told me about the prophecy and how Valefor has been hunting you your entire lives. It was he who started the fire that killed them."

"Valef—? Why would he be after me? And what prophecy?"

"There's a prophecy about immortal blood-born twins with great power. There are demons who want it for themselves.

Valefor is one. And now, because of me, Paimon is too. She threatened to hand you to Lucifer if she finds you."

Okay, that sounded scary. *No reason to panic yet.* "There's no way she could find me. And there's no way I'm some prophesied immortal or whatever. You don't have to worry."

"Lily . . ." Mist sat up, pushing his hair off his face. His mouth was pressed into a hard line, and his breathing was shallow as if he was in pain. "That's why you were able to summon me out of the cuffs and why your skin glows. It's a manifestation of your abilities."

She scoffed. "Trust me, I'm not a powerful witch. I haven't practiced in nearly a decade, and I can't even remember how to draw basic wards. When I did your seal, it took me all day, and I still nearly got myself killed."

He flinched, probably at the reminder of how close he'd come to tearing out her throat. It wasn't a memory she wanted to relive either.

"But you *did* succeed. Don't you see? Summoning a demon is not so simple. Most would not dare attempt it. In all my life, no one has ever successfully summoned me."

"That's because you're not very well known—"

"Others have tried. Not many, you are correct. But there have been others. I put in a fraction of the effort I did with you to escape them and killed them all within seconds."

It was her turn to flinch. She knew that was what demons did to witches. She knew Mist was a demon. It didn't make it any easier to hear about him killing people, however.

"You have more power than you believe," he said. "But it's irrelevant whether the prophecy is true. Paimon thinks it is, and she is hunting you. And she believes Belial is hunting you too because he wants to use your power to usurp Lucifer. She is convinced all of us are plotting against him."

Lily stared at him with her mouth hanging open. This was

too much. Belial and Paimon were after her? It was ludicrous. It was insane. It was horrifying—

Need to keep a cool head. Demons lied, and while she trusted Mist, she didn't put it past Paimon to lie to manipulate him. What Paimon said had obviously upset him, which was probably exactly her plan.

The first thing Lily needed was to get information. "I should call my sister and ask about the fire."

Mist climbed to his feet, and she was momentarily struck by his size. She wasn't sure she'd ever get used to the way he towered over her. "You can do it from within the safety of the wards over Belial's apartment. We will go now. It's not safe here."

"Belial? But I thought he was— Wait. I'm not going to hide behind wards, Mist. I'm sure everything is perfectly fine—"

"Nothing is fine!" he suddenly shouted, and she flinched. It was the first time she'd ever heard him raise his voice. "Nothing is fine, and it is my fault!"

"Mist! It's not your fault." She approached with her palms up. "None of this is your fault."

He looked away. "You are in danger because of me. This is what happens when the rules are broken. This is the consequences—"

"That's bullshit. Those are stupid rules, and stupid rules are meant to be broken."

"No." He pinned her with a furious look. "The rules exist for a reason. The rules are safe, and they protect—"

"They protect the people that made the rules. The people who have the most to gain by you following them. Think, Mist. Who made the rule that said you can't come here to Earth and spend time with me?"

"Angels of the highest Sphere. The same ones who made rules that say I cannot slaughter humans at my leisure."

She winced. "Okay, so, some rules are definitely worth

following. But that doesn't mean all of them are. And it's smart to look objectively and decide for yourself which ones are beneficial and which aren't. I don't see how us being together is hurting anyone. I don't see how it can be your fault that I'm in danger. *If* I'm in danger. I still think that's—"

"It is my fault because Paimon summoned me, and I ignored her. And when I finally returned, I lied about where I'd been. I broke the rules and lied about it. And then, when I was to be punished, I escaped and broke the rules again. And now you're in danger. But if I hadn't left—"

"You'd be in some pit of monsters getting eaten!" She threw up her hands. "That's ridiculous! Why would you ever subject yourself to that?"

"Because the alternative is much worse," he growled, his tail whipping furiously. "And what does it matter if I am eaten? Who is there really to care? So Hell has one less soulless monster. It's no great loss."

Her mouth fell open. "How can you talk about yourself like that? That's—" Her eyes stung. "*I* would care if you were gone. I would miss you. I would—"

"You would be happier if you had never met me."

"That's not true."

"You cannot convince me otherwise. Even now, the summoning marks burn." He scraped his claws against the mark on his neck as if trying to tear it from his skin. "There's little time remaining before I'm compelled to return. If I do not, I will lose my mind from it. If I do not respond even then, the hellfire will start. Gone forever." His lips twisted. "I had planned to let it happen before. Now, I don't know what to do."

"Mist." Her palm covered her mouth. The brand would *kill* him if he didn't respond? And he had planned to let it? "How long?"

He looked away. "Days."

"How many days?"

His gaze shifted away, and his wings flexed outward and then folded again. "Maybe one week."

Only *one* week? Her heart started to pound. "Mist, that's . . ."

He glanced at her and growled. "Don't look at me with pity."

"It's not pity. It's—" She struggled to find a way to describe her emotions. "Mist, I care about you. When you talk about dying or about being worthless, it hurts me. You have so much worth to me, and I— I already know what it's like to lose people I care about, and I don't want to lose anyone else."

"You shouldn't care."

"You don't get to decide that for me."

"I am not free." His voice was quieter, the snarl gone. "I never was. This was always just . . . temporary."

"It doesn't have to be."

"Yes, it does. I always knew I would have to return to Hell or die. I tried to convince myself that I could escape, but in truth, I always knew my time was short."

Her chest burned, and her throat felt tight. "So you just thought you'd bring me along for the ride and drop me when it was time to go back? Or worse, get involved with me, come into my life, and then force me to watch you die?"

He looked away. "I would leave. You wouldn't have known."

She hadn't expected hearing that could hurt so badly, but it did. It hurt so much, it was hard to breathe. "So I was just something to be discarded when you were ready to throw in the towel and give up on life."

He stared pointedly at the wall, saying nothing, but a muscle flexed in his temple.

"Well, that's great!" she snapped. "Thanks a bloody lot. I wish you'd told me that before I went to all the trouble of falling—"

"What else can I offer you?" His head swung back around. "There is no way to remove the brands. I have no choice."

"Have you even tried? You're so ready to give up—"

"I've been trying for thousands of years!" His voice boomed around the kitchen. "If I hadn't, I would have let myself die millennia ago! Hoping for freedom is the only thing that has given my life purpose. That and hunting." His lip curled. "Hunting demons and damned souls and dragging them back to Hell. Watching them beg for mercy as I throw them at my mistress's feet. Knowing they will receive none. Knowing I am responsible for their agony."

Her breaths shook. Her heart pounded.

"They broke the rules. That is the consequence. Convincing myself of that was the only consolation I had. And now that I've broken the rules myself, now that I am seeing things from the other side . . . I cannot return to my old life. I would rather die."

"Mist. Stop." She went to him then, grasping his arm, beseeching him to look at her. To connect instead of getting lost in that dark place he was falling into. "We'll find a way to get rid of the brands. We won't stop trying."

"There's no time."

That haunted, hopeless look in his eyes as he finally met her gaze gutted her. Tears sprang into hers, and her throat constricted, but she fought back the urge to cry. She had to stay strong for him.

"We'll use whatever we have looking for a solution. We won't waste a second. Just don't tell me you're giving up, okay? Please, just . . . I need to know you have hope."

He studied her for a long time, and she stared right back, silently begging him to give her what she asked for.

When he spoke, it was quiet. "I will have hope for your sake. If I'm gone, there will be no one to protect you. That is worth fighting for."

There was no way he understood his selflessness. He was just speaking his mind, and that made it so much more meaningful.

"Because I'm yours, right?" Maybe, if she could get him to go all growly and possessive like last night, he would keep his hope. If he had her, then he wouldn't feel alone.

But truthfully, she needed to find some hope of her own. She had no clue how to get rid of demon enslavement brands. She hadn't even known such a thing existed.

"So I'm not yours?" she said when he didn't respond. If he wasn't jumping at the chance to growl, "Mine," at her again, then her work wasn't done yet.

Still, he said nothing.

"Is it because you're leaving?" She refused to mention death because that simply wasn't an option. "I'm not yours because this is just temporary?"

His eyes narrowed to angry yellow slits.

Okay, so maybe she was pushing him a little, but she couldn't help it. She needed a reaction.

"So if I'm not yours, and you're leaving, I guess that means I'm free to find another demon to cl— Eep!"

One second she was provoking him, and the next, he had scooped her up and slammed her back against the wall.

"Mine!" he snarled. "You're mine, and if you try to escape, I will hunt you, and I will kill anyone who touches you."

His mouth descended on hers with merciless determination, and she melted. His possessive words set her blood on fire. Iris would have lost her mind if a man said something like that to her, but Lily . . . she wanted to be claimed by him. She wanted to surrender. She wanted to be his.

His long tongue slid into her mouth. Moaning, her hips rolled, seeking his, her core suddenly so empty it ached.

Last night, she'd felt it was too soon to go all the way, but suddenly, there wasn't time to wait. The future was uncertain.

Everything seemed so fragile. At any moment their perfect peace could shatter, and everything would fall apart. She wasn't wasting a second.

She reached around, fumbling with the laces on his pants. "Mist . . ." She could feel his thick erection through the fabric, and it was distracting, to say the least. "Want you."

He growled, balancing her weight with one arm—*one arm!*—and sliding her nightie up with the other. She hadn't bothered to put on underwear, and thank god for that.

She got the waistband of his pants loose and yanked them down. As she stroked him, he moaned against her lips, and a wave of arousal flooded between her thighs at the sound.

She squirmed impatiently as he carefully maneuvered her nightie up. "Just rip it." Since telling him she'd sewed it, he was treating it like glass. She'd changed her mind about preserving it, however. Being naked was her new top priority.

"Rip it off with your claws." Did she pant a little when she said that? She couldn't help it. It had been sexy when he'd done that to her underwear.

He didn't, sadly. He set her on her feet, and she protested loudly. He ignored her groaning, pulling the nightie over her head. She lifted her arms to aid him, still grumbling, until suddenly she was naked and back in his arms. Her complaints died quickly when he kissed her again and she felt his hard shaft sliding against her drenched core. But he didn't penetrate her.

She wiggled, trying to get in the right position to take him inside. Somewhere in her mind, she remembered they didn't need to worry about protection since demons couldn't procreate or carry infections—a good thing, because she didn't think she could stop for anything.

Screw foreplay. Need him now. She couldn't wait another second. "Want you inside."

"Lily . . ." It was a pained growl, and she wasn't sure what he was waiting for.

"Want you— Yes!" They aligned, and he pushed inside the tiniest bit.

Her moan of satisfaction quickly turned to a gasp of pain.

He froze. She froze.

Okay, so maybe not "screw foreplay" because that *hurt.*

No! She couldn't wait. "More, more, it's fine—" But she gasped again when he tried to thrust.

Damn, he was big. Really big. She loved that. She loved everything about him. She'd loved the obscene stretch of her lips trying to take him into her mouth last night, and now . . .

And now she couldn't have sex with him because he was *too* big.

He growled with frustration, and she agreed. No, they could do this. She just had to relax. Human women could birth babies, and okay, yes, that wasn't exactly pleasurable, but she refused to believe she couldn't have enjoyable sex with him. They just needed to go slow.

Damn it, why hadn't she bought that giant gray dildo and been training with it every day of her life? She'd always had a secret thing for size, but she'd never been with a guy even close to as big as him, and she'd never explored her fantasies either. They'd just lived hidden away in her head like shameful secrets. Her vibrator time was more of a taking-care-of-business inconvenience than anything innovative.

His knees seemed to give out, and they slid slowly down the wall. Then he pulled out suddenly, and she wanted to cry at the loss. Yes, it hurt, but she wanted it so badly.

He picked her up and laid her on the floor. The tile was cold at her back, but it was a nice contrast from the summer humidity and the heat that always radiated from his skin. Before she could beg him not to stop, his mouth was between her thighs, his long tongue dipping inside of her, spreading her wetness around.

Moaning, her eyes fell shut as he licked up to her clit, spiraling around it. Her core clenched with emptiness, and the desire to be filled was so strong, it pushed her faster toward orgasm. The emptiness made her inner muscles ripple with need, and she pictured his thick cock sinking into her as he continued to lick her. The image, the sensation . . . she tumbled into climax, heightened by the growls vibrating down his long tongue.

When she couldn't take any more, he crawled back up her body, and she gripped his shoulders with anticipation. Now he would be able to sink inside her easily. She was so wet for him, it was almost embarrassing.

She wrapped her hips around his and tried to pull him into her. The head of his cock aligned, and she nearly passed out from anticipation. This was it, this was—

She gasped at the pain as he pushed inside only slightly further than before. Her heart lurched as she looked into his eyes. Every muscle in his body radiated tension, like he was using every drop of control to keep from thrusting into her.

Gotta work up to it. It's fine. We can do this. She reached down and rubbed her clit furiously, trying to loosen up and get back to the frame of mine where she was so horny, she didn't care about pain. Beside her head, Mist's claws dug into the tile so hard, she was pretty sure he was leaving scratches in the ceramic.

His tail snaked out and wrapped around her wrist, pulling her hand away. He slid the tip down to tease her clit. *Oh, that tail.* It was her new best friend. Her head tipped back as a wave of pleasure washed over her.

"Should I take human form?" He bent to lick at her neck.

"Mmm, no." Already, tingles were spreading through her body, relaxing her muscles, and the stretch of him inside her was starting to feel erotic instead of terrifying. "Want to be with you . . . like this."

"But we don't fit."

"Yes, we do." Her eyes opened, and she met his gaze when he lifted his head. Reaching up, she smoothed a palm over his cheek and into his hair, her fingers getting caught in the tangles. "I'm yours and you're mine, and we're made for each other."

Yellow eyes darkened to a warm amber. "Mine." His tail tip slapped her clit lightly, and she gasped.

"Oh, yes. It's so good when you do that."

He pushed in a tiny bit more, and this time, she moaned with pleasure. The stretch . . . *yes*. It was scary being impaled with such a huge thing, but god, it felt good.

He continued working her clit, and there was something so sexy about seeing his hands braced beside her head, the muscles in his arms flexing, and knowing it wasn't his fingers teasing her.

She relaxed further and her legs fell wider open, and when he thrust again, she felt nothing but pleasure. Intense, all-consuming pleasure that bordered on overwhelming . . . but pleasure.

With his next thrust, he finally filled her completely. She felt *everything*. She swore she felt every vein and the rounded shape of the head. There was pain too, but the singing nerves in her clit only made it feel good. Better than good. Amazing. Mind-blowing. Life-changing.

"Yes! Oh my god—"

He pulled out with a slow slide and pushed back in again. As deep as he could go. Her muscles screamed and resisted him still, but everything felt euphoric, and she didn't give a damn. He dropped his head next to her ear, and all she could hear was his rumbling growls.

"Lily . . ." His body shook with tension.

She clutched his shoulders. "That feels so good. I love you inside me."

"Not . . . hurt?"

"No." *Yes*. But she liked it now. Who cared if she couldn't walk later? Walking was overrated. "Feels amazing."

One big hand slid down her side, gripping all her fat bits. "So small. So perfect. So mine."

Two could play at that game. She dragged her palms down his pecs. "Mine."

Their eyes met with his next deep thrust, but hers closed immediately at the wave of sensation.

"Open. Look at me."

She did, though all her habits told her not to expose herself. But she fought them for him. His tail continued to stimulate her, and she could feel the pressure building again. Just thinking about what was happening—her demon was taking her with his big demon cock on her kitchen floor—was enough to make her come. But with him doing that, feeling him move inside, stretching her so wide . . .

Her orgasm came like a gentle wave that built into a tsunami. The tremors started in her thighs and spread over her body. Her moans turned into cries and then screams. Her efforts to look at him dissolved as she threw her head back, squeezed her eyes shut, and tried to survive her brain exploding.

She felt him swell inside her as his climax built, and she nearly died from that too. His thrusts became harder, faster, deeper, and *oh god*, it was too much, too much, way too much—

His body locked up, and he buried his face in her neck, fixing his teeth against her and biting down. She felt them break the skin again. She felt him coming inside her, felt him shoot hot jets against her inner walls, and she swore it would have made her orgasm again if she wasn't still riding the waves of the last one.

She wrapped her arms around him and just held on as he rode it out. His wings were spread as wide as they could go in her tiny kitchen, and he was gripping her hips so tightly, his claws would leave marks. Not that she cared.

The only thing she cared about was him. Especially when his head finally lifted, and he looked into her eyes.

There was no shadow in his gaze, no layer to peel back, no barrier to hide behind. When he looked at her, she saw his soul. Screw whoever said demons were soulless because she could see his plain as day.

"Mist . . ."

He lifted a hand, and his foreclaw teased the hair off her face. "Lily."

Then, his gaze caught on where he'd bitten her neck, and horror suffused his features. "I hurt you."

She touched the area. It stung a little now that the adrenaline was fading, and when she lifted her hand, she saw a tiny smear of blood. "It's okay."

He looked devastated. "I wanted to mark you. I wanted to— Why would I want that?"

"It's okay, Mist." She sucked the blood off her finger and then cupped his cheek. "I don't mind a little love bite now and again. I liked it. You didn't bite that deep."

"But I could have. And—"

"But you wouldn't. I trust you not to."

He stilled. "You trust me?"

"Mhm."

"But . . ." He looked almost afraid. "What if I'm not worthy?"

"You *are* worthy. Otherwise I wouldn't trust you."

He frowned as if trying to wrap his head around the concept. Finally, his features settled into a look of fierce determination. "I will be. I'll make sure of it."

"Okay, then. Good." She lifted her hands and threaded them into all that thick black hair. It was coarse and full of tangles. Wild and raw, just like him. His eyes closed as she dug her fingertips into his scalp, so she massaged gently to relax him. He nuzzled her neck, licking at the bite mark.

A minute later, he gathered her in his arms, rolled, and sat up, wrapping his wings around them. Leaning against the fridge with knees bent, he curled Lily into a cozy ball in his lap.

She had never been so happy. She had never felt so treasured and precious. She had never fallen in love so deep or fast.

In fact, she was pretty sure she had never been in love at all . . . until now.

18

MAD HOUSE

AFTER FINALLY EATING BREAKFAST TOGETHER, LILY AL-
lowed Mist to talk her into going to his apartment,
mostly because she was curious to see where he'd been
living. While she didn't fully believe she was in grave danger,
and definitely not that she was part of a prophesied witch
power duo, Mist was genuinely concerned, so she agreed for
his peace of mind.

Should she have been worried about walking into a flat full
of powerful demons? Maybe. But she was with Mist, and she
hadn't lied when she told him she trusted him.

Iris would have sworn this was all part of some elaborate
ruse, but Lily had always trusted her gut. And when she looked
into his eyes, she saw their connection. She felt it in her bones.
She knew it was real, and she was going to fight for it. She was
going to do whatever it took to help him.

It was another reason she'd agreed to his plan. She was
hoping she could ask the other demons if they knew anything
about the brands. She hadn't forgotten that Mist had said
Belial's apartment, but surely she'd misheard. Still, whoever

the tall blond guy was, he had to be powerful. Maybe he knew a way to get rid of them.

Mist took human form to accompany her on the walk, but he still drew a lot of attention since he had no shirt to wear. But he walked with purpose, as if he had every right to be doing what he was doing, and as a result, people seemed to accept him at face value.

When they finally reached his building—an old, brick warehouse that had been rebuilt into trendy businesses and elegant apartments—he stopped outside the buzzer and stared at it.

"Don't you have a key?" As soon as she asked, she knew the answer. Of course he didn't. He had nothing except a single pair of pants.

"I usually go in the window."

"Well, you can ring the bell, right?"

"Yes." He scratched his chin. "I think it's this one."

Her heart melted a little at his puzzled expression. He pushed the button, and a bell sounded. A moment later, a female voice said, "Hello?"

"Eva?"

"Yes . . . ?"

"I have pushed the wrong apartment number."

There was a pause. "Mist? Is that you?"

He shifted on his feet. "Yes."

"Mist!" The door buzzed as it was unlocked, and the phone disconnected. He hesitated and then opened the door, gesturing for her to go inside. Lily stepped past him, fighting back an irrational surge of jealousy.

The second she heard that female voice, she remembered how she'd met Mist in the first place. He'd been at the dep buying ice cream for his friend on her period. *A friend that is a girl, a girl friend, but not a girlfriend.*

How close was he with this friend? Did she know what he was? Did she have a different definition of their relationship?

"Is that the friend you live with?"

"No. She lives on the floor below."

Yet he remembered her flat number and not his own. Her stomach lurched. *You're being silly*, she told herself. *Yes, I know, but I can't help it.*

"Will we go to her place to ask for the number?"

He shook his head. "I'll know which one when we reach the floor."

They rode up the lift in silence, but it didn't escape Lily's notice that he seemed tense. She reached out and took his hand, and he stared down at it like he'd never seen such a thing before. Their gazes met, and she offered a smile. He didn't smile back, but his fingers tightened around hers.

When the elevator doors opened, he led her down the hall and knocked on a door at the far end. It opened a moment later, revealing the demon with the gratuitous tattoos and piercings. When he saw them, he grinned. His red eyes were slightly unfocused, and it was immediately obvious he was drunk.

"You don't have to knock, bro. You live here."

"I have no key."

"Oh. 'Sup, human? Come in. Bel made martinis. Like, a lot of 'em." He stepped back and then scanned Mist up and down. "Where's your shirt, dude?"

Without releasing her hand or responding, Mist went inside, so Lily followed. Closing the door behind her, she looked around and blinked. The apartment was . . . not what she expected.

Floor-to-ceiling windows framed an open-concept room with a modern kitchen featuring stainless appliances. The center wall of bare brick was adorned with a gorgeous painting of a stormy oceanfront with orca fins rising from the choppy waves. Leather sofas were positioned below it beside the big windows, and a collection of succulents on a shelf against the glass added a splash of green to the monochrome palette. It was all very chic and modern.

Her gaze didn't linger on the apartment furnishings for long, however. The other two demons were standing in the kitchen staring at her, and she stared back.

"H-hi." She attempted a feeble wave when the awkward silence became too much to bear.

The one with the golden eyes that had turned into a crow jerked his chin in greeting.

The blond just stared her down, which made her remember their earlier conversation in which he'd threatened to kill her slowly and painfully.

Mist seemed to remember that too because he stood in front of her and started to growl.

"Told you not to be a dick, Bel," the tattooed guy said, sliding onto one of the bar stools and taking a sip of his cocktail. "You made Mist mad."

The blond glared at him, and she saw flames flicker in his eyes.

Then, he tipped his head back and groaned like the weight of the world rested solely on his shoulders. He straightened and fixed a penetrating stare on Mist. "I wasn't actually going to kill your witch. I just needed to scare her a bit and make sure she was for real. Now stop with the growling before you piss me off."

The first guy twisted around on the stool and held up his palms. His *tattooed* palms. Lily winced. How much had that hurt? "Still not after your girl. You can chill. Now be a nice demon and introduce us."

Mist hesitated, still eyeing them warily.

"Mist." Lily patted his arm. "Thank you for protecting me, but the polite thing to do is to introduce me to your friends."

He stepped to the side and opened his mouth to speak, but the other demon beat him to it.

"Meet my dysfunctional family, Lily." His grin was lop-sided and too wide. "The big, baby-faced bastard is Belial. Grumpy over there's Raum. He likes to scowl, but he's pretty harmless."

"Come over here and I'll show you harmless," Raum said.

"And the pincushion is Mephistopheles," Belial said. "But we call him Meph."

"Or 'idiot,'" Raum added.

"'Dumbass' works too."

"At your service." Meph grinned and bowed his head with a flourish, wobbling on the stool precariously. "My other bro is Asmodeus. He'll be here in a sec with Eva."

Introductions concluded, everyone stared at her again, probably expecting her to speak, which would be the normal, socially acceptable thing to do. But she had frozen.

Raum. Mephistopheles. Asmodeus. *Belial*, for god's sake. She had heard correctly.

She'd deliberately stuck her head in the sand in regard to all things supernatural, yet even she knew who these demons were.

"Okay . . ." Meph said when it became obvious she wasn't going to speak. He looked at the others and shrugged. "She's a little starstruck, I guess."

"Oh my god, you must be Lily!" a female voice exclaimed from the front entrance. "Mist, you can't just ring my bell and not come say hello. I'm so glad you're back!"

Lily spun around, coming face to face with a gorgeous woman with a wild mane of ringlets and unusual pale-gray eyes. Was she a demon too? How many demons were there?

"She's not a demon," Meph said, reading her thoughts.

"Can confirm," the woman added, offering an encouraging smile to Lily. "Not a demon."

She looked at the actual demons with a scowl. "You guys need to give her some space. Remember how freaked out

I was when I learned about all this? And you made it so much worse. Mist showing up with his freaky eyes, and Ash shifting right in front of me and smashing out my apartment window. And then we got back to your place, and Bel lost his temper and burst into flames! It's amazing I didn't die of fright."

He did what? Lily didn't even want to ask.

Meph was grinning again. "Those are good memories."

"How is that a good memory?"

"It was funny!"

"It wasn't funny! I was terrified."

"That's what made it funny!"

"Whatever." She glared at Meph and then smiled brightly at Lily. "I'm Eva, by the way. And this is . . ." She turned around. "Ash?"

"Coming," said a voice from the entranceway.

The apartment door was closed, and a moment later, yet another incredibly attractive man came into the kitchen. This one had a hard, angular face, and the most incredible length of straight black hair Lily had ever seen. It fell like a shimmering curtain of silk to his hips.

"This is Ash," Eva said, reaching out and linking hands with him.

Lily gawked. They were a couple? Guess she didn't need to be jealous after all. It seemed Eva had already found herself a demon boyfriend. *A boyfriend, not a boy friend*, she thought with a smile.

"Can you see him right now?" Eva asked.

"See him?" What kind of question was that?

"Like, does he look like a super-boring nobody or a super gorgeous sex god to you?"

"Um . . ."

Meph snorted. "Now who's making the human uncomfortable?"

"I'm just trying to determine if the curse is active!" Eva looked at Lily. "Ash was cursed to be invisible, but he's mostly broken it now. I was curious to know if you could see him."

"I can see him," she confirmed, head spinning. "He doesn't look like a super-boring nobody."

Ash himself remained silent and seemingly uninterested throughout the entire exchange.

"Oh, good. Mist, I'm so glad you're back." Eva smiled, but her eyes were sad. "I was really worried about you."

The roles reversed as Mist inched behind Lily as if seeking protection.

Eva's smile widened as she looked between them. "Oh my god, you two are adorable. I can't even— I need a picture. Where's my phone?" She felt her pockets, looking for it.

Before Lily could come up with a polite excuse, Mist scooped her up, angled their bodies away, and growled, "No."

She smiled. So he had to work on his manners a little, but at times like these, she found she didn't mind.

"Come on, it would be so cute!"

"No."

"Fine, fine." Eva held up her hands. "No photo."

Mist set Lily back down, and she patted his arm in thanks.

"As fascinating as this is," Belial grunted, obviously not one for small talk, "I'm guessing you came here for an update on the brands, Mishetsu. We met with Dan, who—"

"That's not why I came. Lily is in danger."

"Lily? What's she got to do with this?"

Before she could interrupt and say she was fine, Mist explained the prophecy of the fabled witch twins and how Paimon was now hunting them.

"I need her to be protected," he finished.

Belial looked unconcerned. "She's safe as long as she's with you. I don't deny the possibility of the prophecy. It's unprecedented for an inexperienced witch to be capable of a summoning of that caliber. But she'll be fine."

"I may not always be here," Mist said, giving Belial a pointed look. "I need to know she's safe even if I'm not."

She hated when he spoke about the future like he had no hope. "Mist—"

"We'll find a way out of the brands," Belial said before she could.

Mist's jaw shifted. "I need to plan anyway."

"I told you—"

"Of course we'll help keep Lily safe," Eva interrupted loudly. "No matter what happens, we've got your back. Even though she's a strong woman who can take care of herself, we'll look out for her because we're all friends. Right, guys?"

The demons stared blankly at her. Belial's lip curled.

"Never mind." She rolled her eyes. "This lot can be dumber than a bag of hammers, but when push comes to shove, they'll back you up."

Lily's irrational jealousy had morphed into abject fascination. She decided to befriend the other woman immediately so she could pick her brain.

How had Eva and Ash met? How did Eva navigate the complexities of a relationship with a supernatural being who looked repulsed at the mere mention of friendship? Lily needed all the help she could get, especially if Eva was already friends with Mist.

But first . . .

"Is there somewhere private I could make a call?" Lily asked. "I need to talk to my sister."

First things first, she had to find out if there was any truth to Paimon's story about what happened to her parents. Then she would know how much weight to put behind the whole prophecy thing.

Mist threaded their fingers together. "I will show you my room."

"Thanks." She smiled at Eva. "I'll be right back."

Her new friend waved. "Take your time."

Mist led Lily down the hall to his bedroom and closed the door behind them, muffling the sounds of the others' bickering.

There, he finally allowed himself to shift back into demon form. He was starting to believe this form truly didn't bother Lily, and with the pain from his summoning brand clouding his mind, it was hard to concentrate on holding a human shape.

"This is your room?" Lily asked, looking around. Her only reaction to his shift was a smile. Almost as if she preferred this side of him.

He nodded. "I have my own bed. And a window." It was the most luxurious space he'd ever inhabited, and he was proud of it.

"It's lovely." Lily perched on the edge of the mattress. "Very . . . minimalist."

He supposed she might think that. Compared to her, he had nothing.

There was one mattress and one dresser. He kept the single sheet on the bed folded in a neat square, no pillow or duvet, and there was nothing on the surface of the dresser. In the drawers, he had only the clothes Eva and Meph had helped him acquire and the chalk he'd stolen from Belial for drawing hellgates. The closet doors were closed because there was nothing inside.

"You make me feel like a hoarder," she said with a weak smile.

He looked around the room, seeing the place through her eyes. "I don't have many possessions." Did she find it inadequate?

"Maybe we could hang a picture on the wall. I'm sure there's something at my place you could have."

He nodded, though it didn't really matter to him. He wouldn't be spending much longer here, after all.

Everything had changed. His desire to live had been swept aside by his need to protect.

The burning in his neck had increased to the point that it was taking everything he had to keep his pain masked. Even now as he talked to Lily, he dug his claws into his palms behind his back, stopping just short of drawing blood lest it drip onto the floor and alert her. His thoughts were clouded from the pain, and the magnet in his chest drawing him to Hell pulled with almighty force.

His estimation of two days needed revising. He would give himself another twenty-four hours at most. Time was running out, which meant he needed to put his plans into action as soon as possible.

"I'll leave you to make your call," he said, inching toward the door.

She frowned. "Can you come here first?"

He could deny her nothing, not when she'd given him more than he would ever have dreamed of asking. Reluctantly, he sat on the edge of the bed, flaring one wing out to wrap around her like a human might do with their arm.

She reached out to stroke the leathery membrane. "Are they sensitive?"

"It feels nice when you touch them."

She tilted her head to meet his gaze, and he feared she saw more than he wanted her to. "Are you okay? You've been so quiet since we left my house."

He chose his words carefully. "I've been mentally formulating a plan to keep you safe."

"And? Did you come up with anything?" He could tell she was humoring him and didn't yet believe the danger was real.

Lily had said she trusted him. While he wasn't sure how to trust her back, he did know he wanted to be worthy of it. And since trust meant honesty, he supposed that was why he was reluctant to lie. But if he told her the truth, she would insist he change his plan, and he didn't want that either.

So all he said was, "I need to speak to Belial first."

She still looked doubtful, but she nodded. "And then you'll tell me?"

He nodded back. One way or another, she would find out the truth soon enough. "Will you ask your sister to come here behind the wards where it's safe?"

"I'll try, but she's not going to like it."

"Say whatever you need to get her here."

She studied him. "You're really concerned about this, aren't you?"

"And you don't believe me."

"No, of course I do." She reached out and grasped his hand. His other remained clenched into a fist where she couldn't see it. "I told you I trust you, and I meant it. I just don't know if I believe Paimon. I think she's lying to you to make you return to her."

He had thought so too at first. But the fact remained that Lily was too powerful not to consider it, and he was not foolish enough to risk her by being careless. And he was out of time anyway. He couldn't afford lengthy research into the history of his brands. He needed to act now, and he was out of options.

"Lily . . ." He wanted to put his feelings into words, but he didn't know how. He wanted her to understand what she meant to him, but his throat constricted when he tried to speak, and he was afraid she would guess his plan if he betrayed too much of his emotions.

So he went with the same words he had the first time he'd tried, and failed, to express himself to those he cared about. "Thank you."

She reached up to cup his cheek. "For what?"

He didn't know how to answer that, so he leaned down and kissed her. She melted beneath him with a soft sigh that made his gut clench. She was everything to him. *Everything.* She meant more than life itself, and that was how he knew he was making the right decision.

He broke the kiss and stood. "Call your sister and get her to come here."

"I will. You're sure everything's okay?"

He nodded, though the lie cut deep. Everything was not okay. Not even close.

But it was damn well going to be.

19

A LOSING BATTLE

CLOSING THE DOOR AND LEAVING LILY BEHIND TO CALL her sister, Mist strode purposefully back to the kitchen to find the others. Their conversation fell silent when he approached.

"Did Bel tell you?" Eva said. "My dad has a friend named Sunshine who's a real, live, heavenly angel, and she's going to look in the Empyrean library for him for information on your brands. He's going to call as soon as he hears back."

Mist went still. "How long?"

"A week, maybe. It's a big library, and she has to be sneaky since she's not technically allowed to give information to Grigori."

His momentary elation died swiftly. The escape he had sought . . . he was so close. So close, and yet so far. "Thank you," he said, hating those two words and yet not knowing how else to communicate his feelings.

"Of course. I knew we'd be able to find something."

He dragged his gaze from her hopeful smile and looked at Belial. "Could we speak in private?"

Belial's eyes narrowed, but he nodded.

"But I need another martini," Meph complained.

"Make it your damn self." Bel stalked down the hall toward his bedroom, gesturing for Mist to follow.

They entered the largest bedroom of the apartment with a king-size bed and floor-to-ceiling windows. Sheer curtains billowed in the silent hum of the air-conditioning. Though he had more possessions than Mist, Belial's bedroom was nearly as spotless, save for the rumpled blankets and clothes hanging out of the top dresser drawer.

Belial closed the door, stabbed his fingertip with a claw that grew from his other hand, and then pressed the bloodied tip in the seal on the door to activate it.

No one would be able to break that seal. Just the scent of Belial's powerful blood was enough to make Mist's head spin.

Bel crossed his arms and leaned against the wall. "What?"

"I need you to make me a promise."

"No."

Mist clenched his jaw. "Listen first. Please," he bit out. "It's important."

Belial's brow lifted at the use of "please," and he waved a hand for Mist to continue.

"Paimon has increased the power of the summoning. Already, I can't fight the compulsion to return for much longer."

"So I'll seal you in prison wards, and you won't be going anywhere. You heard Eva. In a week we might have answers."

"I don't have that long."

Belial's eyes narrowed. "What are you saying?"

"I'm going back now."

"Why the fuck would you do that?"

"I don't have a week. I don't think I'd last longer than three days, and I can't risk it anyway. Lily is in danger. If there's even the slightest chance—"

"What are you saying? Spell it out clearly."

"I'm going to try to kill Paimon."

There was a pause.

"Your life force is linked to hers through the brands," Bel said slowly. "She dies, so do you."

"I know that."

"And what happens if you fail? Paimon is a Queen. She won't be easy to take down."

"If I fail, I believe she will still give up hunting Lily. She never cared about the prophecy until she found out Lily summoned me from her lair. This was always about my disobedience. If I fail, she will find something else to focus on."

"Yeah. Turning you into hamburger meat as punishment."

Mist swallowed and nodded.

"So . . . you're going on a goddamn suicide mission. You're going to martyr yourself even though I told you martyrs were fucking idiots."

Mist nodded again.

"No," Bel snapped. "That's the stupidest plan I've ever heard. If you fail, you die worse than if you hung out here and casually burned to death. Hell, I'd take you out myself if it came to that."

"I don't care. I don't want Lily to see me die, weak and mindless, trapped in wards. If I fail, then at least she won't be there. But if I succeed . . . Everything I have endured will be worth something if I can die knowing Paimon dies with me. That is the legacy I want to leave behind."

"Fuck leaving a legacy behind. I told you I would help you, asshole. I told you not to give me shit about sacrificing yourself. I even met with the fucking angel for you, and you're giving up just like that?"

They stared at each other. Mist wasn't changing his mind.

"Just go back to Paimon now if you have to," Bel said. "If Lily can't summon you again, I will personally go there myself and pull you out of the Pit. Lily said you killed one of the go-rath. Kickass. Kill another, and I'll kill the rest. Problem solved."

Mist said nothing. Belial couldn't do that, and he knew it. Unless he was there to surrender, Belial's return to Hell would be considered an act of war, especially if he showed up in Paimon's lair.

Hellfire sparked in his eyes like he knew what Mist was thinking. "Fuck this! I refuse to take part in your suicide mission."

"I am not asking you to."

"Then what are you asking?"

"Once I destroy Paimon, Valefor will still be a problem. That is the reason I'm telling you this. I need you to protect Lily and her sister when I cannot."

"You know I will, though fuck you for putting me in that position. I've already got a bone to pick with Valefor for what he did to Meph, so don't worry about him. But Lily will go right ahead and summon you back as soon as she finds out you're gone, and you know she can do it."

"Tell her not to try. I'll draw a hellseal on myself the second I get back there."

"She's going to be pissed."

"Yes." It was the one thing making him hesitate, knowing Lily would be hurt by his leaving.

You have so much worth to me . . . I already know what it's like to lose people I care about, and I don't want to lose anyone else.

His stomach churned, but he forced the guilt away. He had to do this. He'd been over it again and again, and it was the only way.

"I have one more request."

Bel cocked a brow, hellfire still dancing in his eyes.

"On one of my last missions before I was sent to hunt you . . . I broke the rules. There was another rogue."

"Eligos? I thought he was destroyed." His eyes widened. "You sly dog. He's alive, isn't he? You lied."

Mist nodded. "He's hiding behind wards in the Gaspé region. He thinks I'm still hunting him and that I don't know where he is. I had planned to tell him he was free as long as no one else caught him, but . . ."

"You're going on a suicide mission, so you can't, and you want me to go." Bel did not look impressed. "Why not ask someone else?"

"If I do, then they will ask why I can't go myself."

A vein bulged in his temple. "So you asked me because I'm a soulless bastard who doesn't give a shit if you die."

Mist wouldn't have put it in so many words, but it was close enough. Belial was older than he could fathom, and a certain detachment from everything had always lurked in his eyes. He was the epitome of apathetic—so long as the flames of his temper were not stoked.

Bel's jaw shifted. The hellfire had totally consumed his eyes now. "You know what? Fuck you, Mishetsu. Discard my offer of help. It didn't mean shit anyway. Go on your suicide mission and lie to your witch. You want me to watch out for her, fine. You want me to find Eligos and scare the piss out of him, fine. But just know that I think you're a fucking idiot, and I'd like nothing more than to punch a hole through your skull. And if you don't get out of my sight right now, I will."

He reached over, smudged the edge of the seal, and opened the door. "Go on. Get out of here. Go give up on your life."

Mist's stomach churned. "It's the only way."

"I don't give a fuck. Go."

Belial's eyes burned with wrath as Mist searched them, looking for something. He wasn't sure what he sought. Bel had given him the promises he wanted. There was no reason to feel so conflicted.

Without another word, Mist walked past him out in the

hall. The door slamming behind him made him flinch, but he didn't turn around.

"No damn way am I hanging out in a house full of demons! Have you lost your mind?"

Lily winced at the way the phone speaker distorted her sister's shrill voice. "Mist said there are wards around the apartment, and as long as we stay within them, no one can find us here. He said he has a plan, and he just wants us to hang out here where it's safe for the time being. It's not forever."

"I don't give a damn about the stupid wards. I can make wards myself. I'm not going anywhere near that flat."

"This is serious, Ris. Please."

There was a pause. "Tell me why you actually believe the demon when he says you're in danger. I thought he went back to Hell. For god's sake, Lil, I thought you'd given up on all this 'there are good demons' crap!"

She wasn't going into that right now. "Mist said there's some prophecy about blood-born twins. It sounds silly to me, but he said that regardless of whether it's true, Paimon believes it, and she's hunting us."

She paused, phone pressed to her ear, waiting for Iris's response.

And got nothing but silence.

"Iris? Hellooo? Are you still there?"

"Yeah," she croaked, and Lily instantly knew.

"You've heard of it." Her heart skipped a beat. "Why didn't you ever tell me?"

Iris ignored her questions. "So you're saying some uber-powerful demon is coming after us? How'd he find us, though?"

"Well . . . I summoned Mist."

"You did *what*?"

Lily tipped her face up. "Can we just talk about this from here? When we're safely behind the wards?"

"If you think you can be all like, 'Oh, by the way, I summoned a demon. Okay, byeee!' and then expect me to talk about it later, you've got another thing coming."

"Fine," she snapped. Her sister could be the most infuriating person on the planet. "I summoned Mist out of Hell because he was taken back by Paimon, who controls him by these horrible brands."

"So far precisely zero percent of that makes sense." Iris snorted. "The demon was in trouble, so you just summoned him on the fly? Do you have any idea how absurd that sounds? Lil, you'd have to be crazy powerful to manage that."

"That's what everyone keeps saying, but I'm not. Whatever the case, it's not relevant. The fact of the matter is, I summoned Mist, and Paimon sensed my magic or whatever, since it was within her realm—I still don't really understand how that works—and now she thinks we're these prophesied twins that this demon Valefor has been hunting, and she's after—"

"Valefor?"

"Yeah. That's the part I hadn't got to yet. Apparently, Mist thinks Valefor killed our parents and their coven with the fire. Not arsonists."

Silence.

"Iris?"

More silence.

"Iris? Do you know something about this? Is there something you're not telling me?"

"I'll be there in twenty minutes. Text me the address."

"Iris! What—"

She hung up.

Lily lowered the phone and stared at it, a chill creeping up her spine. Every instinct she possessed told her Iris knew about Valefor and the fire. But if that was the case, why hadn't her sister told her? Surely Iris wouldn't be so cruel as to lie about their parents' deaths for nearly a decade?

The door opened, and Mist's towering form filled the frame.

"Mist." She leapt to her feet. She had so much she wanted to say suddenly, and yet the words stuck in her throat.

It didn't matter, anyway. A moment later, he was across the room, kicking the door shut behind him, and burying his claws in her hair as he took her mouth in a passionate kiss.

"My Lily," he murmured, pushing her back onto the bed. "Mine."

She melted for him instantly. "And you're mine."

They tore at each other's clothing madly until there was nothing but skin on skin. Dark gray skin on pale pink skin. A demon and a witch. The most unlikely of allies, which made what they had all the more precious.

Sprawled on her back, she cried out as he pressed her legs open and thrummed his tail tip against her clit. She saw his hand shift to human form as he reached down and penetrated her with one finger . . . two . . . three . . .

"Mist!" The stretch hurt, especially after their first round of lovemaking only hours ago, but knowing what awaited her made her ache with pleasure instead of pain. Looming above her, his tongue swirled around her mouth while he stimulated her with his tail and spread her with his fingers. When she climaxed, he covered her lips with his and swallowed her cries.

He didn't waste a second. While she was still shaking from release, he aligned their bodies and slowly pushed his hard shaft inside of her. "Oh, god, Mist—"

He stilled at her gasp, body shaking with tension. "Hurts?"

"A little."

He started to pull out.

"No." She gripped his arms. "Hurts a little, but I want you. I don't care."

"Lily . . ."

"Just go slow. We're made for each other, remember?"

Their gazes met, and even then, in the midst of their passion, she could see the tightening around the corners of his eyes and something clouding his focus. He felt miles away from her, when before she'd seen straight to his soul.

The distance gutted her. She needed that closeness back. She needed to know she wasn't losing him.

"More, Mist."

He pushed deeper, slowly enough to give her time to adjust. And she did, though she knew she would hurt later. It didn't matter. This was worth it.

Then his tail teased her clit again, his big hands holding her legs open, and the pain dissolved into liquid pleasure. Her arousal coated his shaft, her muscles relaxed, and he sank deep with ease.

They moaned together as he rocked inside her, and there was nothing but the two of them.

His thrusts deepened amid furious growls, and she could do nothing but hold on for the ride, calling his name over and over. He fixed his teeth over her bite mark from earlier but didn't bite down, though she honestly wouldn't have minded.

With a groan muffled against her neck, he came apart, his wings snapping out as his body locked up. He swelled inside her, and she couldn't hold back her cries at the intensity.

A moment later, he collapsed, rolling onto his back so he didn't crush her. She draped herself across his chest, feeling tiny and cherished as he wrapped his arms and wings around her and held on for dear life.

"My Lily," he murmured.

"Mmm. That was unexpected."

"I saw you and I couldn't help myself."

"I loved it."

He opened his wings, and she sat up to look at his face,

expecting to see the same happy, drugged expression he'd had the first time they were intimate.

Instead, his eyes were haunted. His face was drawn, his eyes tightening in the corners, his mouth pressed into a line.

"What's wrong?" she asked, pushing a lock of hair off his forehead. "What aren't you telling me?"

Yellow eyes shifted away, and that was when she finally saw it.

Pain. He was in so much pain, and he was trying to hide it from her.

20

HURRICANE IRIS

IRIS STOOD OUTSIDE THE APARTMENT WITH HER FIST HOV-
ering in the air, afraid to knock. She couldn't believe she
was doing this. She couldn't believe she was even considering doing this. All her years of lying and secret-keeping were
about to come crashing down on her head, and she wasn't
ready.

Why hadn't she told Suyin and the coven where she was
going? Why hadn't she immediately started planning a rescue
mission for her sister? She didn't actually believe there was
such a thing as good demons, did she? She didn't actually believe Lily had found some kind of fairy-tale romance with a
soulless creature from nightmares, did she?

Iris had always hated fairy tales. Especially romantic ones.

She remembered watching *The Little Mermaid* as a kid. All
her friends were giggling away, dreamily discussing what it
would be like to have their own Prince Eric to fall in love with,
while Iris had been horrified.

Ariel gave up her voice, her family, and her badass mermaid
tail to be with some guy she'd only met once? Who then fell

in love with her when she couldn't speak for herself, voice an opinion, or say anything at all?

It didn't sound remotely romantic. It sounded like her worst nightmare. Kinda similar to standing outside a flat full of demons and contemplating knocking on the door.

It opened before she had a chance to draw her admittedly random thoughts back to the matter at hand. Worse, she found herself looking into the red eyes of the demon with the face tattoos. Trucker Mouth. Snark Fest. Sexy Lip Rings.

"Well, well." A grin split his face. "Look what the cat dragged in."

"Look what washed up dead on the beach, rotting and bloated," she snapped. *The Little Mermaid* had inspired her.

His grin didn't waver. Someone in the house behind him barked a laugh.

"Where's my sister?" *Hide the nerves. Hide the fact that I'm stupidly attracted to his fake human face.*

"Hello to you too, Blue Hair." He didn't move aside. He didn't invite her in. He didn't answer her question.

"My name is *Iris*. My hair is blue, but that is not my name. I-ris. Learn it. Use it."

He leaned way into her personal space and slurred, "I-risss."

She recoiled with a grimace. "You're drunk."

"Bel made martinis. Want one?" Despite the offer, he still didn't get out of the way.

"And join your dirty demon orgy or whatever's going on in there? Hell no. I just want to see my sister."

He threw back his head and laughed. Then he folded forward and laughed some more. He wheezed and fanned the air like he couldn't breathe. "Hear that?" he hollered. "She doesn't want to join our orgy!"

Laughter echoed from the kitchen.

Iris ground her teeth. "Just tell me where my sister is."

"How do you know she's not part of the orgy?"

"Meph, stop being a jerk and let her in!" a female voice called out.

"You ruin all my fun," he said back and then smirked at Iris. "Come on in, sugar."

"My name," she bit out, "is *Iris*."

Pushing past him, she marched into the apartment, only to realize that wasn't the best idea when she ended up in a kitchen full of people staring at her. The first person she noticed was an actual giant with the brightest blue eyes she'd ever seen.

Jerk-Off came up beside her. "Welcome to our evil, demonic orgy."

The giant rolled his eyes. "Meph, shut up." He looked at Iris. "Your sister's in the other room. And before you ask, she's fine."

"Who the hell are you?" Iris snapped.

His brows shot up, and everyone stiffened. The air was suddenly thick with tension.

"You wanna try that again?" He spoke slowly, and something in his voice told her that he was not to be fucked with.

"Bel," the woman said. "Be nice."

He transferred his murderous glare to her but said nothing.

"I'm Eva," the woman said. Her eyes were warm, and there appeared to be nothing evil about her, but that didn't mean anything. "That's Bel. Raum. Meph. And Ash." She linked hands with a guy with epic long hair as she said his name.

Iris had definitely heard of Raum, and she had to assume the others were nicknames. "Bel, as in . . . ?"

"Belial," the giant grunted. He pointed to the other demons. "Mephistopheles. Asmodeus." He pointed to the woman. "Evangeline. Not a demon."

Iris's mouth dropped open. No way. *No fucking way* she was standing in a room with those four demons. It was absurd. Impossible. Otherwise, she'd already be dead, or strung up by her own guts, or bleeding out on the floor, or—

What if that's what happened to Lily? "Where the hell is my sister? Where the fuck is she!"

"Whoa, whoa, Lily's fine." Eva approached with her hands up. "She's just in the other room with Mist."

"She's with the demon right now?" Iris's eyes darted frantically around.

"Yeah, they're just—"

"What did he do to her!"

The woman sighed, and Iris didn't miss her rolling her eyes before she closed them. When they opened again, however, she had carefully schooled her expression into one of patience.

"Your sister's fine. She's with Mist in his room of her own free will, and he's not harming her in any way. I already shot Mist a text to tell him you're here, and she'll come out as soon as she's ready. If you want to sit down, Bel can make you a drink while you wait."

Iris took a second to process this. The giant was Belial, fucking *Belial*, and he was going to make her a cocktail because her sister was locked in a bedroom with a demon.

She nearly screamed and threw up at the same time. Only her lips pressed firmly together kept it in.

"Now you've done it." The demon with the gold eyes—Raum—took a sip of his drink and watched Iris's mental breakdown with mild interest.

Eva's eyes widened as she realized what was about to happen. "No, wait! Don't go back there—"

Iris dodged her and ran down the hallway to rescue her sister.

She was fast, but the damn demons were faster. Before she could blink, Meph was standing in front of her, one obscenely ripped, tattooed arm blocking her passage down the hall.

"Sorry, doll, can't you let you cockblock my guy."

"Get the hell out of my way! What is he doing to her? I'll kill you and him and all of you if he hurts her!"

Meph held up his hands. "Jeez, woman, you've got no chill. Lily's fine. I'm only stopping you from going in there and killing the vibe."

"Killing the vibe? Are you kidding me?"

"Trust me, it's a valid concern. I had a nice buzz going on before you showed up, and now look at me. Sober as a judge."

"Get out of my way."

His red eyes narrowed in challenge as he reached out to block her way again. Only that stupid grin never left his face, like this was all a big game to him.

She wanted to punch him, to wipe that look off his face and show him what it felt like to be truly afraid. Motherfucker like him, who spent his life tormenting other people, had probably never felt what it was to be truly powerless, and she hated him for it.

"Just let her go, Meph."

Iris glanced over her shoulder and saw Raum standing behind her. She hated that he'd snuck up on her without her knowledge. She hated that, at any second, any one of them could kill her, and there wasn't a bloody thing she could do about it.

"Fine." Meph dropped his arm. "But don't come crying to me when you get an eyeful."

The two demons went back to the kitchen while debating what the female equivalent of "cockblocking" was, but Iris barely noticed. Her gaze fixed like a laser beam on the closed door at the end of the hall.

"Lily!" The shouted cry was her only warning before she crashed through it like a battering ram.

"Mist—" Lily swallowed hard. How was he in pain? Why hadn't he told her?

"Lily!"

She had just enough time to glance over her shoulder before the door burst open, revealing her blue-haired twin. Mist sat up with a jolt.

Iris took one look at him and murderous rage filled her eyes. She charged across the room, shouting, "Get away from my sister—"

"What the hell, Iris?" Lily had never loved Mist's wings more than that moment when they snapped out and wrapped around their bodies like a blanket. "Get out of here!"

"He's a demon—"

"I know he's a fucking demon, goddamn it!" Lily never shouted, and she rarely swore. But she was damn well doing it now. "*Obviously* I know that! You are the most pigheaded person I've ever met, I swear to god! Get the hell out!"

Iris froze, arms up as if she was still contemplating attacking, her mouth slightly open. Mist, to his credit, just tightened his arms around Lily and let her handle it.

"What are you still doing in here!" Lily shrieked when her sister didn't move.

Finally, Iris lifted her palms and backed out of the room, closing the door behind her.

Lily slapped her palms to her cheeks. "Oh my god, I can't believe she did that! What did she think was going to happen? I don't know what is up with her, but she'd better start talking or—"

She broke off. The problem was, she feared she *did* know what was up with Iris, but she didn't want to believe it. But she knew she needed to hear it, and that started with having that talk. It was the whole reason she'd told her to come here after all, though she was certainly regretting it now.

"Why didn't the others stop her?" Lily mumbled. "They obviously knew what we were doing." Her palms covered her cheeks again. "Oh my god, they knew what we were doing. I might die of embarrassment."

Mist's head tilted slightly. "Because you were with me?"

"What? No, of course not." She slid her hands around his neck and petted his skin. "I'm proud to be with you. Just because it's so embarrassing to think that everyone knew we were having sex."

"Why?"

"Because . . ." She breathed a laugh. "I honestly don't know. It's a human thing, I guess."

He nodded as if this, at least, he could understand.

Now that she had noticed he was in pain, she couldn't stop seeing it. "I need to go deal with my sister, but . . . are you okay?"

A claw gently traced her collarbone and then drew a circle around her nipple. "When I'm with you, the rest of the world fades away."

His words were sweet and warmed her heart, but she still recognized the deflection. But there wasn't time to discuss it now, damn it. Not with Iris raging around in a house full of demons. Lily needed to get to her before she did something really bad, like piss off Belial.

"Can we talk later? After I calm my sister down and get the truth out of her?"

He nodded but didn't meet her gaze.

She kissed him and then climbed reluctantly off the bed. Even in the summer humidity, her skin pebbled with coolness the moment she separated from Mist's heated body. She dressed quickly, sneaking glances at him as she did, noting the pain in all his movements now.

When he stood, he did it slower than usual and wavered slightly as he straightened to his full height. His wings and tail twitched with constant agitation when they were normally mostly still.

At the door, she stopped and turned back, unable to quash her worry. Her instincts were screaming at her not to go, but she couldn't leave Iris out there, and she needed answers.

"I'll come right back," she promised.

Yet she couldn't help thinking it would be too late.

After a quick trip to the bathroom to wash up, Lily hurried into the kitchen to face the music. Bracing herself for drama, she was surprised to find Eva and the demons sipping their cocktails in silence. There was no sign of Iris.

"Hey." She shifted uncomfortably when everyone looked up. "Um, where's my sister?"

"She went onto the balcony." Eva's lips twisted with a sympathetic smile.

"I don't think she likes us much," Meph added with a smirk.

"Okay, thanks." She started to leave and then stopped. "And sorry. She can be a bit . . . intense."

Ash snorted, and Eva elbowed him. "Don't worry about it." She seemed to be making an extra effort to be nice, and Lily appreciated it. To call the demons intimidating was an understatement, even if they were in human form.

"And sorry about before." Eva cleared her throat. "We tried to stop her, but—"

"Oh, it's fine." Lily was right back to wanting to melt through the floorboards. "Like I said, she can be intense. Um, I'll be back in a bit, then."

As she approached the patio, she could see Iris's blue head through the glass, but she didn't turn around when Lily slid the door shut behind her. Outside, the air was thick with humidity, and leaving the air-con felt like getting hit with a wet heat blanket.

"Can we talk?" Lily asked.

Iris finally turned. "Why did you ask me to come here?"

"Because Mist believes we're in danger, and while I have my doubts, I trust him enough to take him seriously. This apartment is heavily warded, and he says we'll be safe here until he makes a better plan. Actually, I don't think it's warded out here, so it would be better if we—"

"You *trust* him. You actually trust a dem—"

"Yes, I trust him, and can you please stop saying 'he's a demon' repeatedly? You sound like a broken record. I don't know if you noticed, but it's pretty obvious he's a demon. He's the only one who doesn't stay in human form. It's not something I'm going to forget."

"It's just . . ." Iris shook her head. "You don't understand."

"Then make me understand. I get there's a bit of a hurdle to overcome in adapting your perception of demons, but it's not that big. Why are you so violently opposed to the idea?"

"There's history. I— *We* have history."

Lily's stomach felt like a pit inside of her. "You're telling me what Mist said was true. The fire was caused by a demon."

Iris dropped into one of the deck chairs and slumped forward, dragging her fingers through her hair. It reminded Lily of Mist's posture that morning, and the similarity struck her as a terrible sort of irony. It felt like an ill omen.

The urge to rush back and check on Mist seized her, but she forced herself to sit on the chair beside Iris. She needed to hear the truth first.

"I should have told you sooner," Iris finally said. "At first, I kept it from you because I wanted to find the right time. But years passed, and there never was a good time, and then, suddenly, it was too late, and I just— I've been living with this guilt and regret and hatred for almost a decade, and I didn't want that for you."

"You don't get to decide that for me," Lily said in a hollow voice. Her sister, her best friend, had lied to her about the most defining moment of their lives, and it felt like a knife in the back. "They're *our* parents, Ris. How could you keep something so important from me?"

"I'm sorry. I really am. I wanted to tell you, I tried, but . . ."

"There's no excuse you can give to make that okay."

Iris looked away and wiped roughly at her eyes.

Lily took deep breaths, trying to keep the anger at bay. It wouldn't help her learn what she needed to. "So, there could be truth to this prophecy after all, then. Why else would the demon come after us?"

"Because demons kill witches. That's what they do."

"But there has to be more to it than that." She refused to believe her parents were killed for no other purpose than senseless violence.

"There is." Iris heaved a sigh. "Your demon's right. Our births were foretold a long time ago by some great seer."

"Oh my god." She took a breath, blew it out. It didn't help. "Oh my god! But, how—?"

"Mam and Dad and the coven knew about the prophecy, and they also knew there would be demons after us. They knew Valefor would come, and they were prepared. The cloaking only fell for a short time, but it was enough. It was the only reason he found us, and even by then, they had already repaired it. He never even knew I was there."

"You knew about this all along. Even before their deaths— How long have you known?"

"Only a few days before. It was our eighteenth birthday, the night we came fully into our powers. Mam explained everything to me right before so I would be prepared.

Lily swallowed the bile rising up her throat. "And she didn't tell me. Why?"

"She never expected the power shift to be so dramatic it would cause the cloaking to fall. She never thought anything like this would happen. She wanted to give you time and space to come into it on your own."

"So . . . she lied to me."

"She wasn't trying to lie. You just never liked the practice the way I did. You wanted to sew, you wanted to paint and draw. You weren't that interested in the coven. She just wanted to give you the space to be yourself."

"A lie of omission is still a lie."

Finally, it was Lily's turn to assume that grim position. Planting her elbows on her knees, she leaned forward and buried her face in her hands.

"Nine years," she said into her palms. "Nine years you've known about this, and you haven't told me. Nine years, and I've never had closure. Nine years, and I thought there was some murderer out walking the streets facing no repercussions for what he did."

"There *is* a murderer. His name is Valefor, and he's a Duke of Hell instead of a human. And trust me, I have no intention of letting him get away with it."

Lily shook her head. That Iris was dead set on revenge was not what she wanted to hear. "The fact that you could lie to me about this for so long . . . It's like I don't even know you."

"You do know me, Lil. You know me better than anyone."

She pinched the bridge of her nose. She was suddenly exhausted. She wanted to curl up beside Mist and fall asleep for days. "I need time to think. And some space. And—"

She stiffened suddenly, twisting in the chair to look through the glass door inside. "Did you feel that?"

"No, what?"

"It felt like . . ."

She felt it again and leapt to her feet.

Magic.

By the time her instincts rose, she had realized several things. One, she should have obeyed her urge and never left Mist's side for a second. Two, she should have pushed him to talk about what was bothering him and share his plans before she did anything else.

And three, in the time it had taken her to figure that out . . . she was already too late.

As soon as Lily shut the door behind her, Mist sprang into action. Her instincts were sharp, and he knew he didn't have long before she would return to check on him as she promised. And the moment he activated the gate, others would feel it.

For the second time that week, Mist drew the complicated hellgate that would return him to the last place in any of the realms he wanted to be. Once again, he added the extra lock sigil to ensure he could not be followed. His plan was simple. Stupidly simple. But he was out of time and options, and it was the best he could do.

And maybe . . . just maybe . . . he would be successful.

If not, well, he was headed there anyway, so at least he could go out knowing he had tried. Wasn't that what Lily had asked of him? To have hope?

Just before he was ready to activate the gate, he paused. He remembered the look on her face as she tried to figure out what he was planning. He thought about how she would feel when she discovered he was gone, and knowing it would hurt her sent a sharp pain lancing through his chest.

For millennia, he had existed in a state of cold indifference, detached and numb, living only for the hunt. Now, he felt things, and he wasn't sure he liked it.

He hated the idea of causing Lily pain, but he knew he had to. He wanted her to be free. He wanted her to forget about him and his doomed existence and go on with her human life where she was safe and happy.

He growled suddenly, fingers tightening around the chalk in his hand until it snapped in half.

That was a lie. He wanted her to need him and only him. He wanted her to wait for him forever, to tear the worlds apart seeking him, and to hunt him to the ends of the earth for daring to leave her.

But he knew that was selfish. His demonic nature didn't care about that, but that other part of him, the part that felt things . . . that part just wanted what was best for her.

So, he would meet his end on his own terms, knowing he had enjoyed the human experiences he wanted and knowing he was keeping Lily safe in the only way he could. And if he failed, he knew Belial would honor his promise to protect her in his stead.

Fueled by his conviction, Mist broke through his final mental barrier of resistance and activated the gate. Immediately, he heard silence fall over the apartment, the hum of voices in the kitchen stopping as they detected the flare of Sheolic magic.

He heard someone shout, "What the fuck?" and the sound of thundering footsteps approaching rapidly.

Seconds before they arrived, he stepped into the gate and disappeared.

21

ONE-WAY TICKET TO HELL

LILY RAN TOWARD MIST'S BEDROOM, HAVING SENSED EX-actly what the demons had. She burst through the door, nearly colliding with Belial's towering form, only to find the room empty.

"Motherfucker," he growled.

"He's gone," Lily breathed in horror. "Where did he go?" But she already knew.

Belial answered anyway. "Through that damn gate, back to Paimon's lair."

"We have to go after him—"

"We can't. He added a lock to the sigil. This gate can't be reactivated or traced."

"But . . . why?" she asked, her voice hollow. "Why would he do that?"

Belial turned around to look at her. And he really looked at her. While she squirmed under the scrutiny, she heard the others come in behind her, crowding through the doorway and in the hall.

"He went back to Paimon because he's going to try to kill her."

Lily's mouth dropped open.

"But the brands," Eva said. "Can he even do that without . . . ?"

"Killing himself too? No. His life is tied to hers. If she dies, so does he."

Lily gasped. "We have to tell him!"

"Oh, he knows."

Horror. Disbelief. "No . . . he wouldn't . . . He promised he would . . ."

She suddenly remembered his eyes. The pain in them, and the tightening around his mouth. The shallow breaths. *The summoning brand.*

He'd told her he had a week, but he'd lied, hadn't he?

"Mishetsu is old. Older than I can remember. He's been trying to get rid of those brands for thousands of years and has never found a way. Combine that with the threat to your life, he decided he'd rather go out on his terms."

Lily stared blankly at the empty sigil, unable to believe what she was hearing. That was what had been going on in Mist's head this whole time? Someone she cared deeply about, might even love, had been ready to give up, and she hadn't had a clue?

Her horror backflipped into sudden rage. "And you just let him go? You knew this and did nothing?"

Belial glared at her. "It's not my place to decide what he does with his life. He wants to go out fighting, he gets to make that choice."

Someone cursed behind her.

"I thought he was your friend! I thought—"

"Don't make the mistake of confusing me with a human." The demon's voice was cold, but his eyes flashed with fire.

"Immortal beings don't always want to live forever, and since there's no natural death to determine our end, sometimes we have to make a hard choice. You don't get to pretend you understand the mind of someone who has been enslaved for thousands of years."

She swallowed her retort as she realized he was right. She couldn't fathom what Mist had been through or how he felt about his past and future.

But she could try. And she could sure as hell fight for him to live.

"He doesn't get to come into my life, make me fall for him, and then just waltz out on some grand mission to sacrifice himself. I refuse to accept that. I refuse to stand by and do nothing while he's in trouble, even if you won't help me. I summoned him once, and I can do it again. With or without your help."

Belial's intense stare never wavered. "He told me to tell you not to try summoning him because he's going to draw a hellseal on himself the second he gets back there."

"What's a hellseal?"

"It'll bind him to the Hell plane as long as it's active. Doesn't last long, but I reckon it'll be long enough."

"When did he tell you this?" Eva demanded, stepping up beside Lily.

"Just a few minutes ago."

"What the fuck, dude?" Meph said from the doorway. Eva shook her head.

"I don't care for your meaningless judgment," Belial snapped. "Mishetsu wants to die, it's not my problem."

"He's your friend!" Eva said.

"Friendship is a human concept." His voice was cold, blue eyes narrowed to slits. "I exist to serve my own purposes and nothing else."

"If you're so cold and unfeeling, care to explain why you have *brothers*, then?" Eva, it seemed, did not possess the same fear of Belial that Lily did. "What's that if not a form of friendship?"

Bel's expression was murderous. Hellfire danced in his eyes, and the temperature in the room dropped.

"I don't care about any of that right now!" Lily cried suddenly. "I just want to know how we get Mist back!"

"There is no way to get him back!" Belial thundered, and she recoiled. "He went to die, and that's his own goddamn choice."

No, she was not sitting back and letting Mist sacrifice himself. She marched across the room and stood inside the sigil on the floor, studying the intricate lines. "How does this lock work? Can't we bypass it somehow?"

Belial pointed to one of the smaller symbols within the complex sigil. "The lock means the gate can only be activated once. It's been used, so the magic is now defunct. If you wanted to use this gate again, you'd have to wipe the lock away, fix the lines, and activate it yourself. You'd have to know exactly what gate Mist linked it to in order to make the connection again, which none of us do.

"But even if we somehow found a way to figure all that shit out, there'd still be nothing we could do. If I show up in Paimon's lair right now, she's going to want me delivered to Lucifer, which I have a problem with. Fighting will ensue. War will follow. The very war I've been trying to avoid for a long damn time."

"This is Mist's life we're talking about!" Lily snapped. "I'll start ten wars if that's what it takes to save him!"

"You start a war, you have to be prepared to finish it. And the end of that war means either I'm dead or I dethrone Lucifer and end up as High King, which is the last thing I want. Not to mention, it could last forever. The whole point was to escape Hell, not to spend thousands of years fighting to rule it."

"That doesn't mean we can't try to help," Ash said, coming to stand beside Eva. "We don't have to kick down the front door. Maybe we can do it stealthily."

"How do you propose we sneak around Paimon's lair? She knows every single thing that goes on in that shithole."

Lily had stopped listening. She was staring at the gate at her feet, studying the intricate design, and feeling some kind of strange energy washing over her.

It felt like . . . Mist. Like traces of his magic. She could feel remnants of the force that had activated the gate interwoven into the sigil. It called to her like a siren's song, beckoning her . . .

She closed her eyes and focused deeper, trying to follow it to the source. That inner guiding voice was whispering at her to do something. The harder she focused on the magic traces, the louder it whispered.

"Lily!" Iris called from somewhere far away.

She'd forgotten her twin was even there, but now, she was glad of it. She needed Iris's help for this. For what, she didn't know. She just knew she needed her.

"What the hell?" someone said.

"She's glowing!"

"Is that normal?"

"No! Lily!" Iris's voice again.

Warm hands gripped her shoulders and shook her, and with that touch, the connection was made. The missing piece slid into place, and this time, when Lily reached out to the magic, she could grasp it. She could . . . read it.

Was this how Mist felt when he hunted? Because suddenly, she was certain she could track him anywhere in the world. Anywhere in the realms.

No matter where he went, she would find him.

Suddenly, she was surrounded by it. All around her, magic swirled like a whirlpool. Without hesitation she dove in, and the world fell away. Distantly, she heard more panicked shouting and was aware of her sister's hands on her skin.

A tiny warning bell sounded in her mind, but by the time it penetrated, it was too late.

Her eyes flew open, and before she had a second to take in her surroundings, she already knew she was not where she'd been standing moments before.

This time, Mist didn't waste a second in his cave.

He loosened and shoved down his pants and then used his claw to carve the hellseal on his thigh where Paimon wouldn't see it. Righting his clothes, he then dug through his meager possessions in the crevice in the wall and pulled out the only weapon he possessed. The small black dagger in its worn leather sheath was slipped into his pocket and tucked discreetly to the side.

A demon with claws did not often require another weapon, but it was far quicker to decapitate with a blade, and he needed things to move as rapidly as possible. As for the hellfire, he would use her blood to draw the sigil once the first step was complete. He was not as powerful as Belial and could not summon it at will.

Weapon secure, he dissolved into mist and traveled down the length of the tunnel toward the main hall in search of the Queen of Hell.

Paimon, of course, sensed him before he entered the throne room. She would have sensed him the moment he arrived through the gate. She sat on her throne with Shaheen by her side, as usual. The shadows cast across her face flickered in the torchlight.

"Back so soon? I thought you'd last another day at least. You were always a stubborn one when you put your mind to something."

Solidifying his physical form, Mist approached the throne. Whispers from the guards along the wall followed him. The gargoyles seemed to be staring at him with awed expressions, though he wasn't sure why.

Normally they glowered at him, resenting him for his position as Paimon's most favored servant. If anything, now that Mist had lost their Queen's favor, he would have expected them to seem gloating. But instead, they looked almost . . . reverent. How odd.

He ignored them and focused on his objective. Sneaking up on his prey as mist was his favorite tactic, but it wouldn't work with Paimon. She sensed him easily, and the moment she suspected him of treachery, she would materialize the cuffs and stop his heart, and all would be lost.

"I changed my mind." His heart pounded, and his mouth was dry. He forced all thoughts of his plan out of his head lest the slightest tell betray him.

Paimon laughed. "Already tired of Belial's empty promises? How sad of you to fall for them at all."

Mist swallowed his pride and forced himself to play his role. "I would rather serve you, Mistress. You are infinitely more powerful."

"You betrayed me. You killed one of my precious goraths. You cannot expect me to forget that, nor can you expect me to believe you aren't lying now. You've lied before, and now I can't trust a word you say." She turned her face away with an anguished expression, as if she couldn't bear the pain of his dishonesty.

"I have a way to prove my loyalty."

"Do you?" Her gaze snapped back to his, dramatics forgotten.

"I know where Belial is, and I know what he is planning."

Her eyes flared with interest, but she quickly masked the expression. It was too late, however. He could tell she'd taken the bait. "Tell me, then." She flicked her claws. "I haven't got all day."

Mist glanced around the hall with fake suspicion. The room was mostly empty save for the guards and a few of her servants puttering about.

"We must be careful who is listening." He gave her a pointed look. "Belial's reach extends further than you know."

Paimon's nostrils flared, and her horizontal pupils dilated with rage as she looked around, suddenly viewing each of her carefully selected servants as a potential traitor.

She leveled that stare back on Mist. "I will not be toyed with. If this is an attempt to trick me, then beware. You will taste the full extent of my wrath."

"There is no trick, Mistress. I seek only to prove my loyalty. Afterward, you can relay this information to Lucifer and increase your favor in his eyes, and then I will gratefully return to serving as your hunter."

She studied him, and for a time, the only sound in the room came from the servants scurrying about. Then, she stood, her powerful wings spreading.

"Come, then. We'll speak privately."

Without waiting for a response, she spun on a heel and strode away, Shaheen at her side. The servants darted out of her way, fanning her with amputated wings as she passed, though the temperature in the castle was already below freezing. Mist followed, ignoring more awed looks and whispers from the gargoyles.

She led him, unsurprisingly, to her favorite room in the castle.

Her dining hall also served as a torture chamber because she enjoyed such entertainments while she supped. While humans liked music or movies, Paimon preferred her meals with a glass of blood and a side of suffering.

A long table of stone was adorned with cobweb-covered

candelabras and a feast of tentacles and gray meats. At the end of the cavern, the floor opened into a yawning pit—*the* Pit. The spectator platforms were carved into the sides of the cylindrical chasm, but the top was reserved for the queen's use only.

Just like in Mist's dream, the barred grille over the mouth of the Pit was rolled back, leaving it open for anyone to fall or be tossed into. Above, suspended from the ceiling, a series of sinister meat hooks hung from heavy chains, connected to a pulley system on the far wall.

Paimon strode to the end of the table but didn't take a seat. Torchlight glinted off the sharp tips of the hooks dangling ominously behind her. Shaheen loped to the far corner of the room and lay down again on folded legs.

"Well? I'm waiting. Where is Belial? Tell me what you know. Prove your loyalty to your mistress."

They were alone, and the camel was far enough away that it wouldn't reach Paimon before Mist did.

This was his chance.

Heart pounding, blood roaring in his ears, he forced himself to walk with measured steps until he was standing right in front of her.

It was the element of surprise or nothing. Now or never.

He lunged.

The blade in his pocket was revealed in a flash and stabbed into Paimon's neck. Her blood sprayed like a punctured water pipe.

She opened her mouth to roar with the fury of a Queen of Hell, but she only choked as more blood spurted around the blade and poured down her front. Shaheen bellowed, rising to his feet and galloping across the room to intervene.

Seconds. Mist had seconds.

Gripping the knife, he pulled and pushed, fighting to saw the blade through her sinewy neck. If he could remove her head now, he would have time to summon hellfire before she regenerated.

Her claws tore up his arms like tissue paper, leaving shreds of bloody flesh and tendon hanging off the bone. Her wing talons stabbed into his shoulders until he fought them back with his own. But her strength exceeded his, and he felt her overpowering him.

Her claws began carving up his face, his throat, his chest. Anything she could reach, she ravaged. Pain overtook his senses. Still, he didn't cease his efforts, forcing his shredded arms to work the blade through her neck until it was half severed . . . three-quarters severed . . .

So close, he was almost there—

Shaheen barreled into him. His blood-slicked hands slid off the knife handle as he was thrown back with immense force, his spine smacking the stone. One of his wing bones snapped on impact.

Shaheen took his vengeance with unbridled wrath. Cloven feet stamping, teeth gnashing, the camel pummeled Mist with a force that would have pulverized a human in seconds. Mist tore his claws and teeth into the beast, fighting back with everything he had. Escaping as mist wasn't an option, as he couldn't spare the concentration to shift.

Finally, he managed to toss Shaheen aside and scramble to his feet, desperate to get back to Paimon and finish the job of cutting off her head.

He was too late.

She stood before him, her neck pouring blood, her head attached by a mere thread of tissue. Gravity alone kept it in place atop her neck. Mist's knife was clutched in her fist, and the fury on her bloody face was bone-chilling. Somehow, she had retained consciousness, and she was ready for retribution.

So close. He'd been so close.

He tried to dissolve to mist at the exact second the manacles appeared at his wrists, binding his form and preventing his escape. His heart sank, and the last of his hope died a cold and lonely death.

At that moment, he knew he'd made a mistake. He shouldn't have come here. He shouldn't have rejected Belial's offer of help. He should have stayed by Lily's side and fought to survive until the very end.

Maybe he'd been afraid of what would happen if he succeeded. Maybe he'd been afraid to find out what freedom felt like. But now that he faced the end, he realized there was nothing he wanted more.

Lily was right. His life was worth something—it was worth a lot—and if given a second chance, he would never choose to carelessly discard it again.

Unfortunately, the time for second chances had passed.

Paimon couldn't speak with her larynx severed, but he knew what she would've said if she could.

He would pay for this as no one had ever paid before.

The silence in the room was oppressive. Belial felt the stares on him like spiders crawling across his skin, and he wanted to rip them off and crush them into guts and blood underfoot.

Chaos had erupted the moment Lily and Iris disappeared through the hellgate, followed shortly by this tense quiet.

"Well, don't just stand there!" Eva finally shouted. "Do something!"

He was getting sick and goddamn tired of mortals telling him what to do. "What?" he barked, rounding on her. "What do you propose I do, Eva?" He spat her name like a curse.

Asmodeus stepped between them. "Cool it."

He was getting sick and goddamn tired of *anyone* telling him what to do, in fact, his brothers included. "Get out of my face."

Asmodeus didn't budge. Bel leaned over him, using his superior height to his advantage. "Move before I make you."

"Guys, we don't have time for this!" Eva sounded close to tears. "Mist is in trouble, and two humans just accidentally went to Hell. I thought you said it was impossible, Bel!"

"It *is* impossible. It should have been impossible." He dragged his fingers through his hair, his temper hanging by a thread. The rage was so close he could taste it. "I have no idea what the hell they just did."

"Well, we have to do something!"

"And why is it immediately assumed that *I* will be the one doing something?" he snapped. "Why is every single fucking thing my responsibility?"

"'Cause you usually have all the answers," Meph supplied unhelpfully. "Normally, you disappear into your room for a while and put a seal on the door so no one knows what you're doing, and when you come back out, voilà. Our problems are solved."

Bel ground his teeth until his jaw cracked. Meph made it sound so easy, but nothing was ever that goddamn easy. Everything had a price, and sometimes, that price was more than he could afford to pay.

"Please," Eva said. "We don't have much time, and this is an emergency. Their lives are in danger. We have to do something."

"I can't go after him. None of us can. I go to Hell, I start a war. It's not happening."

"There has to be something else you can do. Can't you send someone in your stead? Don't you still have people loyal to you down there?"

Yes, but he couldn't send any of them into Paimon's lair without starting a war either. But . . . there was someone he could ask.

He closed his eyes and groaned inwardly. He'd sworn he wouldn't do it. He'd sworn he wouldn't look at or think of or even breathe the same air as that slithering, heinous harpy. But once again, it seemed his vows to himself didn't mean shit.

He opened his eyes and pinned Asmodeus with a glare. "Get out of my way."

His brother studied him for a second and then slowly stepped aside. Bel stormed out of the room, nearly tossing Meph through the wall when he didn't move fast enough. The door slammed, and he reactivated the seal so he wouldn't have to hear them debating how he was going to save the day or worry about them walking in.

Then he drew a sigil on the floor and summoned Naiamah. Again.

The air swirled and evil filled the air, and it was all so goddamn stupid that it pissed him off. Summoning her like this was only possible because of the debt she owed him, but he wished it wasn't.

Moments later, the succubus Queen of Hell appeared, a combination of every man's biggest fantasy and worst nightmare. Or maybe just Belial's.

Today, she wore a sleeveless leather bodysuit with a neckline so deep it went past her navel. The sides were cut high, accentuating a slender waist and the thickest, most luscious hips known to man—or demon. A see-through, gauzy skirt flowed from the bodysuit's bottom seam in a mockery of modesty. Platform boots rose to her upper thighs.

She flicked her silky hair back behind her shoulder and shot him a glare. "Now is not a good time, Belial. I was in the middle of a very important business deal."

Bel's lip curled at the sight of her. "I don't particularly care."

Her eyes narrowed. "Of course you don't. You don't care that the Blood Market would collapse without my presence. You don't care that I have a life beyond granting your precious favors. You only care about yourself and your 'brothers.'" She made finger quotes around the word with long, bloodred nails, her disdain for his familial bonds evident.

Bel ground his jaw, trying desperately to hold on to his calm. "The sooner you shut up and do what you're told, the sooner you can go back to your unsavory business."

Naiamah crossed her arms. However, this served to push her breasts together, and he couldn't help staring hungrily at them. Frustration, anger, *rage* . . . Dark emotions always made him horny as fuck, and she was the hottest thing he'd ever seen. His hatred of her had no effect on that, unfortunately.

"So what is it this time?" she sneered. "More Nephilim blood? You'll need to find a better solution for acquiring it if you want to preserve your remaining favors. At this rate, you'll run out before the year is up. You only have one hundred left, after all." Her crimson lips curved into a wicked smile. "Unless, of course, you want—"

"*No.* I told you, last time was the last time."

"You say that every time, precious. And yet you can never resist me." Her gaze flicked down his body. "Not that I'm complaining."

The red of her lips stood out against her pale skin and jet-black hair. He wanted to spin her around and bend her over the edge of the mattress, gathering all that hair in his fist and tugging her head back until her spine arched while he sank inch by inch into her hot, tight, wet—

He shook himself. *Not happening.* "Mishetsumephtai is in Paimon's lair with two mortals. I need to get them out."

Naiamah blinked. "Two . . . living mortals?"

He nodded.

"There are two living mortals in Paimon's lair?"

"That's what I just fucking said."

She cocked a hip. "Don't give me that attitude. You might get away with bossing everyone else around, but not me."

"Except when I use the favors you owe me to make you to

do whatever I want." His brow arched. "You would do well to remain on my good side. Remember, I can force you to do *anything*—however . . . humiliating."

He had no intention of wasting his favors on petty revenge, but she didn't need to know that. Her steady glare faltered briefly, and he took dark satisfaction at seeing the crack in her façade, even if it made him a bastard. But if he was a bastard, she was a bitch, and she had made it her life's mission to make him suffer. He was just returning the favor.

All too soon, her mask slipped back in place, no sign of weakness visible. "Oh, honey," she purred, shaking her head. "There's no forcing me to do anything. You'll find that everything I've ever done for you has been entirely of my own volition and to my ultimate gain."

"Really. And what do you stand to gain from doing me favors?"

She cocked her head, and it became obvious she wasn't listening anymore. "You look pale, Belial. And there are bags under your eyes." Her head tilted the other way. "You're strung out and on edge."

He gritted his teeth. "Thanks for the assessment."

Her expression cleared as she came to some conclusion. "That's your big plan, then? Repression?" She scoffed. "It won't work."

"I don't know what you're talking about."

"The rage, Belial. I can sense it in you even now, simmering under your skin. It's delicious. You're trying to repress it with whatever disciplines you're forcing on yourself. An admirable effort, but it won't work. Repression never works."

"I didn't summon you to play psychologist," he snapped, hating how his gut clenched at her words. Hating how easily she read him. "Can you help me with Mishetsumephtai or not?"

She shrugged. "He is Paimon's lackey. Why should you want to rescue him from her lair?"

"Can you do it or not?" His voice thundered around the room, and the burning in his eyes told him hellfire flickered in them.

Naiamah's head came back. "My, my, aren't we feeling testy today?"

"I'm warning you—"

She held up a hand to silence him. He hated, fucking *hated*, that he immediately shut up.

Something about her . . . She'd always known how to set him on edge, how to stoke the rage and make him ride the high until it consumed him. Every memory he had of her was also one of him giving in to the darkest, worst parts of himself. She weakened his composure. She made him more volatile and impulsive.

She was the embodiment of everything he hated about himself, and therefore, the thing he despised most in all creation.

"I'll offer you some free information," she said, "so pay attention. If you're looking for someone ballsy enough to go against Paimon, Murmur is your guy. They've been enemies for a long time."

Belial blinked. It was not what he'd expected to hear. "Why would the Necromancer care about Paimon?"

She wagged a finger. "Nuh-uh. You want anything else, it's going to cost you."

"Fine. For the price of one favor, I want you to find a way to get Mishetsumephtai and the two mortals out of Paimon's lair—*alive*—and that includes answering my questions now."

Her lips pursed. "Answering the questions is pushing it. There's no real reason you need to have all the information for your favor to be completed."

"The information is how you convince me you'll do the job properly."

Her lower lip stuck out. "Or I could say no."

"You don't get to say no," he snapped. "One hundred

unspecified favors remaining, remember? You're lucky I don't make you do something worse."

"Oh, the 'worse' favors I'll do for free." She fluttered her eyelashes.

"Don't push me, Naiamah."

She rolled her eyes. "Fine. But this"—she gestured up and down his body—"self-restraint thing you've got going on? It's not a good look."

A growl was his response.

She pouted. "Okay, okay. With his army of souls, there aren't a lot of places the Necromancer can't go if he wants to, nor are there many wards that can keep him out. I've had plenty of dealings with him in the past, and I know that he never makes false claims. If anything, he is secretive about the extent of his power. I don't know for sure why he hates Paimon, but he's always had a hidden agenda. He's a powerful seer, but as far as I know, he never shares his visions, so no one knows what he's up to. He doesn't make allies, and he doesn't spill secrets, so I have no idea what goes on in his mysterious head. But I do know he wants to take her down."

"And? Can you get him to help?"

"He'll have a price. And he's a shady bastard who is generally not to be trusted. He'll say one thing to your face and then turn around and do the opposite. He has a knack for finding loopholes in bargains. He'll help you up only to kick you down himself. Never turn your back on him because there's a good chance he'll stab you in it."

Lovely. That sounded like exactly what Belial needed right now on top of everything else.

"Whatever he wants, it has to be fast. The mortals are in the lair as we speak, and I don't have time for negotiation."

"That means his price will be high. Your best bet with the time constraint is to offer a favor."

"No. I can't agree to that."

She shrugged. "Negotiations take time. I guess it depends on how badly you want his help."

He clenched his jaw. There wasn't time for negotiations at all. Murmur was a powerful demon, but not more so than Bel. If it came down to it, Bel could take him out.

"Fine. Tell him I'll owe him one unspecified favor, as long as he doesn't ask me for anything that would endanger me or anyone I care about." He'd just kill him later if it turned out he wanted something Bel wasn't willing to give. Problem solved.

Naiamah's slender brows lifted like she knew what he was planning. "Don't make the mistake of underestimating the Necromancer."

"Did I ask for your opinion?"

"He might not like the non-endangerment clause."

"But he'll still take the deal."

Her lips pursed. "Yeah, I think he will."

"Well, get to it, then."

"Yes, sir." She smiled wickedly. "Or should I say, yes, *Daddy*."

"No, you should not."

She just laughed.

She turned around, allowing him to discover that the back of her bodysuit was a thong, and her thick, round ass wasn't even close to hidden by the gauzy skirt. Against his will, his eyes feasted on the sight, and his nostrils flared like a bull as he sucked in a breath. *Damn her.*

"Only ninety-nine favors left, precious."

With a wink and a sassy wave, she was gone.

22

GATE CRASHERS

"WHERE ARE WE? WHAT JUST HAPPENED? WHY ARE you bloody glowing!"

Lily didn't answer. She was in too much shock to speak.

The air was hot and stifling, ripe with the pungent scent of sulfur. They were surrounded by rock, the only sound the distant dripping of water, the only light source her own luminescent skin.

As Iris had pointed out, she was indeed glowing.

Immediately, panic set in. She'd been standing in the hellgate that had taken Mist to Paimon's lair. She'd felt traces of his magic and focused on it, but she'd been unable to complete the connection until Iris was beside her. Together, they must have bypassed the lock and reactivated the gate, though Belial had said it was impossible.

Blood-borns were the only humans that could travel through hellgates without demon blood in their veins—which likely contributed to the myth that they were descended from a demon-human pairing in the first place—but that didn't make this any less miraculous.

Another time, she would've spent hours sputtering with disbelief about how a failed witch who hadn't practiced magic in a decade had managed such a feat, but not right now.

Now, she had other stuff to worry about. Like the fact that they were currently standing in Paimon's lair. In Hell.

"We are in Hell." She tried the words out aloud to see if it helped. It didn't.

"You're shitting me," Iris said. "We can't really be in Hell. No way."

They really were. They were two blood-born witches trapped in real, actual Hell. They were doomed.

Stop it. There's no time to panic. She had to stay calm. Giving in to her fear would be a waste of time and energy. No one was here to help them. If she wanted to get them out alive, she needed to get it together and figure out how.

"How did you reactivate the gate? Damn, Lil, when did you become such a powerful witch? And why aren't you freaking out about the glowing thing?"

"*We* reactivated the gate," Lily amended. "I couldn't do anything until you touched me. And I'm not freaking out because it's happened before."

"What? When? And why didn't you tell me?"

"Like you told me about the fire?" She shook herself. She was still angry, but now was not the time. "It's a long story. We can talk later when we get out of here."

Using the light from her own body, she surveyed the cave. The stone ceiling was low and jagged. A single folded blanket on the ground served as a bed, and there was an unlit torch mounted on the wall above. A small crack in the corner caught her eye, and she crouched in front to explore it.

Holding her arm out, she let the faint glow illuminate the alcove.

Inside was a folded pair of black pants that Lily immediately recognized as the kind Mist always wore. There were a few other random knickknacks—pieces of chalk, a blank journal, a tarnished silver necklace, a Bic lighter. And lastly, propped against the stone, withered and dead . . .

A lily.

Her heart cracked at the sight of that dried-up flower. Here, in this dank pit of despair, literally in the bowels of Hell, Mist had placed the flower she'd given him among his few possessions.

"This is Mist's cave," she told her sister.

"He has a cave?"

"I'd call it his home, but . . ." There was nothing homey about this place. No wonder he'd been so proud of his empty bedroom.

She leapt suddenly to her feet, determination coursing through her veins.

So they had accidentally ended up in Hell. Not ideal, but while she was here, she might as well make herself useful. She was a rare blood-born, and supposedly a powerful one, practicing or not. She wasn't helpless.

She turned to her sister. "I'm going to find Mist. You can stay here or come with me. Your choice."

Iris's eyes bugged. "What? No way!"

"Do you know a way to get us out of here?"

Iris looked at the hellgate drawn on the ground and shook her head. "I've never used a gate before, and I have no idea how to activate it. I deliberately avoided learning any Sheolic magic, which I realize now is stupid." She glanced at Lily. "You're the one who's glowing. Can't you do something?"

"The glowing just happens against my will. I have no idea what I'm doing. And even if I could escape, I don't want to go anywhere without Mist. He's here, and he's in trouble, and I want to rescue him."

Iris's mouth twisted. "You have no idea how crazy that sounds. I get you like the demon, and I'm maybe willing to consider that maybe, possibly, not all demons are evil all the time, but we're literally in Hell, and—"

"I love him."

Her sister's eyes looked like they were going to fall out of her head.

"I love him, and he doesn't know. I never got to tell him."

"You barely know him!"

"I know enough."

"Damn it, Lil, this is insane. Do you have any idea how insane this is? We're completely unequipped to rescue anyone. We're the ones who need bloody rescuing right now!"

"If we can get to Mist, he'll get us out of here. And besides, we have power together. Maybe there's something to that prophecy thing. Belial said it was impossible to reactivate that gate, and yet, here we are."

"Yeah, thanks for that! You could have told me you were planning a one-way trip to Hell!"

"It wasn't like it was intentional!" They were shouting now. A distant part of her recognized that was incredibly stupid, but she was too caught up in the argument to listen.

"I can't believe you're summoning demons and traveling through gates, when for years I couldn't get you to attend a coven meeting! Just because you met some guy!"

"He's not 'some guy'! And I didn't want to attend your stupid coven meetings because you were always shoving the damn things down my throat!"

"It's our heritage!"

"It's what killed Mam and Dad!"

"No, *we're* what killed Mam and Dad!"

Silence echoed around the black cave as the sisters stared at each other.

"They spent their whole lives trying to protect us," Iris said quietly. "Mam worked hard to create a cloaking spell powerful enough to thwart Valefor. She was a genius, Lil. She combined centuries of our ancestors' research and created things no one had before. Valefor couldn't break her wards no matter how hard he tried. Even burning the building down didn't work. If I could have even a fraction of her ability . . ."

Lily swallowed hard. "That's why they were always with the coven? Because they were working on a cloaking spell to hide us?"

She nodded. "Valefor was obsessed with us from the moment we were born. From before, even. That's why they were so busy. Not because they didn't love us, but because they did. I know you wished they were around more growing up, but it was the only way they knew to keep us safe."

Lily's palm covered her mouth. All those years of secret resentment . . . only to learn her parents *had* cared about her more than anything. They had cared so much, they'd dedicated their lives to protecting her.

"That night . . ." Iris's hands curled into fists. "Mam made me leave as soon as the spell failed. She knew what was going to happen. She gave me a list of instructions on how to maintain the cloaking spell and made me promise to leave with a blood vow I couldn't break." Her gaze traveled away. "If I was a stronger witch, I could have overruled her stupid vow. I could have stayed and fought. I could have saved them."

"That's not . . . Iris, you can't think like that."

"It doesn't matter what I think. What matters is that they're gone."

"What happened to the spell? Why hasn't the demon come back?"

"Mam taught me it, like I said. The coven and I have been maintaining it ever since. When we moved to Canada, the remaining coven members kept it going in Ireland until we had a chance to get it set up here. We were the only blood-borns in the city, so Suyin moved up here from the States to help."

Lily stared at her, suddenly remembering the vials of blood and locks of hair she'd seen at Le Repaire. "You've been doing it all this time and you never told me?"

She was furious. She was stricken with grief. She was . . . grateful to her sister for protecting her for so many years without ever getting a word of acknowledgment.

"You wanted to be a regular person, Lil. I just wanted you to be happy." Iris looked away. "I'm so sorry I never told you. I wanted to, you have no idea how badly, but I was so scared you wouldn't forgive me." She wiped quickly at her eyes. "I know there's nothing I can say to make it right."

"I'm so unbelievably pissed at you," Lily whispered, wiping at her own eyes.

"I know what I did is unforgivable, and I don't expect you to—"

"I already forgive you, numbnuts."

Iris blinked. "What?"

"This is so not the time or place for this, but I've learned a lot these last few days, and I understand wanting to keep this messed-up supernatural stuff from someone. I could tell Mist felt the same way with me. I'm sick of being this weak, sad person that people think they have to make sacrifices for to protect. I want to be strong enough that you aren't scared to tell me the truth. I want to be strong enough to save the man I love."

"Bloody hell." Iris wiped at her eyes again. "Damn it, Lil, you *are* strong. You're the strongest person I know. You're a fucking rock."

"More like a boulder."

They both snorted.

"No fat jokes, bitch, or I'll punch you." Iris jabbed a finger at her. "I never want to hear you talking down on yourself. I'm not kidding when I say you're strong. Making a living off your clothing design? Never wasting time with men and partying like your screw-up sister? You even went to university."

"All I got from university was a load of student debt."

"Whatever. The point is, Lil, you're an inspiration. You're the person I want to grow up to be."

"Whatever," Lily echoed, voice wavering.

"You're my sister, and I love you, and I promise I'll do better in the future."

"I love you too, stupid."

Iris's voice wavered too. "Shit, I'm choking up."

"Me too."

Two pairs of matching green eyes met in the darkness of the cave. A tear trickled down Iris's cheek, but she dashed it away and forced a smile. "All right. You win. Let's go rescue your demon and get the bloody hell out of here."

"Thank you." She held out her hand, and her sister took it. *Stronger together.*

Grabbing the lighter from Mist's stash, they lit the torch on the wall. Iris pulled it from the sconce, and they headed down the tunnel away from the safety of the cave, stooping under the low ceiling and brushing cobwebs from each other's hair with matching grimaces.

The tunnel wound around a corner and out of sight, but there was only one route to take, so they took it. As they reached the corner, a sudden premonition rose like a flash flood, and Lily tugged on her sister's hand to pull her back.

Too late.

Iris stepped forward and froze, and Lily had no choice but to follow and see what awaited them.

Her heart jumped into her throat at the sight of a wall of demons blocking their passage, the fangs in their ugly snouts bared in malicious grins.

"Well, well, well," one said, rubbing his claws together, "what do we have here?"

The monsters were short, only coming up to Lily's shoulders, with underbite fangs and thick necks. Their faces were asymmetrical and full of blemishes, making them some of the ugliest things she had ever seen.

Gargoyles, she realized. Years ago, she had read about different classifications of demons, and she remembered that gargoyles were usually the lowest and least powerful, and they tended to be underlings to greater demons. But they were just as hard to kill as any other demon, and in large numbers they were still very dangerous.

"What do we do?" Lily whispered.

"I have no clue," Iris whispered back.

"I'll tell you what you're going to do," the first demon said, the others behind him shuffling excitedly. "You're going to keep quiet while we take a little taste of you, and then you're going to come with us to meet our mistress."

"Yeah, how about 'no' to both those things," Iris spat.

"Let me taste 'em," another hissed. "The shiny one looks delicious."

Lily wasn't sure if they were talking about actually eating them or something else possibly worse, but she didn't care to find out. She looked at Iris, trying to see if her sister had any sort of plan that could be explained through an intense look.

The only escape was down the tunnel, currently blocked by the gargoyle gang. Mist's cave behind them was a dead end. Iris glanced ahead and then back at Lily. Lily's eyes widened, and she shook her head. Iris nodded. Lily shook her head again. Iris nodded more forcefully.

Are we really doing this?

Iris's gaze hardened, and Lily realized that yes, they were doing this.

"Now!" With her shout, Iris charged fearlessly into the mob, brandishing the torch like a weapon. Lily had no choice but to follow.

The element of surprise was their only asset, and that only lasted a split second. Shoving the demons out of their way, they managed to make it halfway through the crowd before their enemies caught on.

They were vastly outnumbered. Hands seized Lily from every direction, on every part of her body. The violation made her panic, and she kicked and fought desperately, but it wasn't enough. Two gargoyles managed to catch her wrists and twist them around her back. Another shoved her from behind, and she fell hard onto her knees without her hands to break her fall.

Armed with the torch and her vicious temper, Iris fought harder and for longer, but eventually, she too succumbed. A minute later, she was beside Lily, the two of them surrounded by a circle of gargoyles. Their wrists were tied securely. Discarded on the ground, the torch cast long shadows across the smug faces of their attackers.

Fear made Lily's insides churn and her stomach hollow. She swallowed the urge to scream, frantically seeking an escape and coming up with nothing.

Iris was right. They weren't strong enough to rescue Mist by themselves.

What had she been thinking? That she could *glow* her way through Paimon's lair to his side? That the power of her love would give her magical strength to defeat a Queen of Hell? Stupid, immature, and ridiculous.

The gargoyle leader shoved his pig-like snout into her face, his fetid breath causing her to recoil. "Paimon knew you were here the second you arrived. You never stood a chance of escaping."

His hand shot out and wrapped around her throat. He squeezed, but strangely, it didn't choke her.

"Right now, she's putting the Hunter in his place. She ain't pleased he killed one of her monsters." The responding murmurs from the other gargoyles sounded almost awed. "She's got him strung up now, letting his blood drip into the Pit to drive the beasts into a frenzy. She won't be letting him kill a second one, that's for sure. It'll be a bloodbath this time, no doubt."

"You know what?" Iris snapped suddenly. "Fuck you and fuck this." She spat in the face of the gargoyle trying to choke Lily. "Fuck all you stumpy little bastards! Talk about overcompensating—you have us on our knees because if I stood up, I could use your head as a step stool. I'm not scared of you little shites."

"You'll pay for that, witch." Releasing Lily, he flexed his claws and stalked forward, snarling. "Hold her still."

Two more gargoyles gripped Iris's arms, and another gripped her blue ponytail and yanked her head back, exposing her throat. Lily struggled to come to her sister's rescue, and Iris never stopped hissing and spitting.

"Do your worst, you shrimpy motherfuckers! I'll curse your pricks to fall off in each other's arses! I'll rip your balls off and stuff 'em in yer eye sockets!"

"I'll tear out your throat and eat it for breakfast!" the gargoyle shot back.

"Mistress wants 'em alive," another supplied helpfully.

"I know that! But she never said they had to be intact." He gripped Iris's chin, jerking her face forward. "I'm going to make you regret your—"

He never got the chance to finish his threat. A whistle of sound accompanied the appearance of a red line at his neck, and his face froze in an expression of surprise.

A moment later, his head toppled from his shoulders into Iris's lap.

She screamed and lurched back. Lily screamed too. The other gargoyles spun around to face the new threat as a looming figure stepped out of the shadows. A long, thin sword with blood coating the blade reflected the torchlight.

Lily caught a brief glimpse of white hair and deathly pale skin before chaos erupted.

That narrow blade whistled again, cutting into the crowd of gargoyles. Blood, gore, and body parts flew in every direction.

Iris threw herself into Lily, knocking them both down and out of the path of carnage. Despite their terror and revulsion, this was their best chance to escape. Together, they started to crawl away amid the sounds of tearing flesh and shrieks of agony. With their hands tied, they were forced to wiggle like awkward worms as they attempted to stay below the sword's path.

Lily swallowed her scream as blood sprayed onto her cheek. A severed arm flew past her ear, and she nearly puked when it landed with a squelch beside her head.

Suddenly, silence fell.

The smart thing to do would have been to get up and start running like hell, but she didn't do that. Maybe it was the shock, or maybe it was curiosity. Whatever the case, she sat up and turned around.

The newcomer wiped his blade with a rag before sheathing it with a practiced movement. The tunnel around him was littered with severed limbs. The carnage was so complete, it was impossible to tell what belonged where, the collection of body parts appearing only as a hodgepodge of bloody tissue heaped in a careless pile.

If she stared too long at that, she'd likely succumb to the urge to vomit. But thankfully, her attention was drawn to their unlikely rescuer.

The demon's waist-length white hair was twisted into a long braid. The color wasn't like an elderly human's white, but rather, as luminous as freshly fallen snow. From his temples, black horns swept proudly along his skull and curved upward to regal points above his head. His skin was a milky light gray that reminded her of a corpse, and his bloodshot eyes were a glassy silver-blue with only the tiniest prick of pupil in the center. They were so surrounded by shadows, it almost looked like dark eye makeup.

He used the rag to wipe the blood from his claws next, which were the same black as his horns and . . . tail. Unlike Mist's, his was topped with a sharp barbed spike like a scorpion. He didn't have wings, but she supposed he could have simply disappeared them to aid movement in the cramped tunnel. He was easily as tall as Mist and had to stoop slightly to keep the tops of his horns from scraping the rocks above.

Most unusual, however, was the dark cloud of what appeared to be smoke winding about his feet. It was too dark to distinguish any detail, but it almost looked as though there were haunted, ghoulish faces forming amid the swirls, but that couldn't be right. She shook her head to dispel the illusion, yet it persisted.

He tucked the rag into his coat pocket and then glanced at Lily as if just noticing her.

"You're the mortals, then?" He looked unimpressed. His eyes flicked to Iris and then back to Lily. "You're glowing, but she's not. Interesting."

Iris climbed to her feet. "Who are you?"

"Your new best friend. Come." He flicked his claws and started past them down the tunnel. When they didn't immediately follow, he looked back with so much exasperation it was almost comical.

"What do you want?" Iris demanded.

He scoffed as if that was the dumbest thing she could have asked. "It's embarrassing Belial wasted a favor on you."

"Belial?" Lily cut in. "Did he send you?"

His head cocked in a similar way to Mist, except his impressive horns and zombie-like complexion made him look even more alien. "Do you always ask stupid questions? Yes, Belial bargained one favor for me to extract two living mortals and Mishetsumephtai from Paimon's lair."

"But—"

"The longer we wait, the less blood the Hunter has. Shall we?"

"Y-yes, let's go." Lily scrambled to her feet. If Belial had been here right now, she would have hugged him, no matter how threatening he was.

She started to hurry down the tunnel after their pale rescuer, but Iris said, "Wait," and they turned back.

"Why should I believe you? I don't trust demons, and I don't even know who you are."

"Iris, we don't have time—"

"I am called Murmur or the Necromancer. Either works." He smiled thinly at Iris's horrified expression. "I see you've heard of me. Yes, the rumors are true."

What rumors? There wasn't time to ask. Lily recognized his name but hadn't studied enough to know anything else about him.

"Ris, we have to go." At this point she'd take any ally she could get, and her guts were telling her to trust this one—at least, for now. If Belial had sent him that meant he was their best hope.

"Can you at least untie us?" Iris asked.

Murmur grabbed Lily's arm, and she flinched at his ice-cold hand. A claw tore through her bonds a second later, and she rubbed the blood back into her hands. "Thank you."

He looked repulsed by her gratitude.

After freeing Iris, he stared down at them with utmost disdain. "Try to keep up, will you? I'm not accustomed to pandering to humans."

He turned his back, long braid swinging, and started walking. He may have looked somewhat zombie-like, but he didn't move like one, his lean form flowing with each graceful stride.

Iris grabbed the discarded torch, and they hurried after him down the passage. Leading them past several forks in the tunnel, he appeared to know exactly where he was going.

Lily's head spun with questions. She was pretty sure Murmur was ranked as a Duke of Hell. So how had he gotten into Paimon's lair without her noticing? Or, if she had noticed, why weren't more guards being sent after him? And what was his plan for rescuing Mist?

He stopped so abruptly, she nearly crashed into his back. She saw for the first time that there were slits in his jacket that would allow his wings to fit through if he chose to materialize them.

Despite everything going on, the seamstress in her was unable not to study the design, and she immediately envisioned creating something similar for Mist. Her demon never wore shirts, and she thought he might appreciate one made to fit his wings.

Murmur's words snapped her out of it.

"Head through there. Take two right turns and a left, and you'll arrive in the chamber where Mishetsumephtai is being held. I will aid my souls in keeping Paimon and her guards busy. Once you retrieve the Hunter, return here. If Mishetsu is unable, I will activate the hellgate."

"Head through . . . where?"

Murmur pointed a claw at what appeared to be the cave wall. On closer inspection, however, she discovered what appeared to be the mouth of a tunnel so small, she wasn't sure her butt would fit.

"Oh, hell, no," Iris said when she saw it. "I'm not going in there."

"The tunnel is a direct route to the Pit. It's either that or walk through the lair." He lifted a brow at Lily's glowing body. "You might stand out."

"Doesn't Paimon know about it?"

"It was created by gorath larvae. They explore but are drawn back by the scent of blood. She has no fear of them escaping, so she hasn't bothered to block the tunnel."

Did that mean they had to worry about running into them? She didn't want to know what gorath larvae looked like. Mist's description of the full-grown ones was enough.

"How do you know all this?" Iris asked, still eyeing Murmur warily.

"My souls told me. And I've been casing this lair for a long time."

"Why?"

He smiled thinly. "Because I want it."

Iris opened her mouth, but he cut her off with a slice of his hand. "Go now before I renege on my bargain with Belial out of sheer vexation."

Iris crouched and thrust the torch further into the tunnel.

"Leave the torch. The flame will suck away what little breathable air you have."

Lily gulped. Her palms were sweaty, and her stomach was still churning from the violence. She was so terrified, she wanted to puke and pass out at the same time.

She had never loved the simplicity of her boring life more, and she swore if she survived this, she would never wallow in dissatisfaction again. She was happy being a shy, introverted seamstress. She didn't need anything else.

Except, of course, a demon boyfriend with yellow eyes and a talented tail.

The thought of him suffering at this very moment gave her the courage she needed to get moving.

"I'll go first," she told Iris. This was her mess, after all.

"Lil . . ."

"It's fine. I'm the light source, remember?" She turned to their rescuer. "Thanks for your help."

He grimaced like she had shoved frog guts in his face. "Just hurry. Even my souls can't hold Paimon back for long."

Later, she would figure out what he meant by "souls"—though with a name like "the Necromancer," she could guess. But right now, she needed to focus.

She took a breath and crawled into the tunnel. Iris extinguished the torch and crawled in after her. Inching forward into the blackness, her glowing arms provided illumination only a foot or so in front. Her stomach lodged in her throat, and she had never wanted to scream more.

"Two rights and a left," Iris murmured behind her.

Claustrophobia had never been an issue for Lily, but she had a feeling that was about to change.

23

A FOOL'S CHANCE
IN HELL

THEY CRAWLED THROUGH THE TUNNEL FOR WHAT FELT like forever. The process was slow and exhausting, and it took great effort not to succumb to irrational terror in the confined space. Only constant reasoning—*the only way out is forward*—kept Lily from falling into a catatonic state.

"If we survive this, I'm going to sleep with a night-light for the rest of my life," Iris whispered. "I'll get one shaped like your arse for good measure."

Lily tried to laugh, but it came out more like a sob.

She tried not to think about what would happen if she reached into the blackness and touched a gorath larva. Instead, she fretted over what condition Mist would be in when they found him, which wasn't really an improvement.

Would they be able to get him back through the tunnel? If he was unconscious, there was no way they could drag him. Would he even fit? There was a strong possibility the tunnel was narrower than his shoulder width if the tight squeeze against her hips was anything to go by.

Neither of them spoke, their heavy breathing the only sound to penetrate the quiet.

It was impossible to say how much time passed. Maybe one hour, maybe five. Maybe less than an hour. But eventually, they came across the first fork in the tunnel, and Iris broke the silence with, "Two rights and a left."

They went right. Not too much further ahead, the tunnel forked again, and again, Iris repeated the mantra. After the final turn, Lily's heart began to race again. Only then did she realize she had somehow overcome her panic instincts.

Unfortunately, they returned with a vengeance as she suddenly spotted light ahead. The reality of what she was about to do hit hard, and just like that, she was terrified again.

Wordlessly, they crawled toward the light that grew steadily brighter. Before long, she came face to face with a large boulder blocking the tunnel entrance. There was a narrow horizontal crack just wide enough for Iris's slim figure to fit through, but Lily's butt was a different story.

"Can you see anything?" Iris whispered.

"I'm not sure I can fit through the crack."

Iris scoffed. "Your butt isn't that big."

She was pretty sure it *was* that big. "Only one way to find out—"

"Wait."

She stopped, staring at the little patch of light, waiting for Iris to speak.

"Before you go out there . . . if everything goes to shit . . . I just have to tell you that I love you, and I'm glad we're in this together. And I'm sorry for everything, and I swear I'll never lie to you again."

Lily was too wound up to care about the past anymore, and in that moment, all she felt was gratitude for her sister's company as well. This would have been so much worse if she was alone.

"I love you too, and I'm glad you're with me even if it wasn't by choice."

"Are you kidding? I'd never miss a chance to do something impulsive and life-threatening, you know that."

This time, she did manage a laugh. A sad, breathy thing that died quickly in the face of what they were about to do.

"I guess I'd better see if I can fit through that."

"I'll shove you through like Winnie the Pooh if you get stuck."

With another feeble chuckle, Lily inched forward through the rock, crushing her boobs painfully and sucking in her belly. As predicted, she got stuck at the hips. Fighting down the panic, she braced herself against the sharp stone and pushed.

When she still didn't budge, two palms landed on her ass cheeks, and despite everything, she felt her face flame with embarrassment. She heard Iris grunt with effort as she shoved forward, so she braced herself against the rock to help out.

Just when she was starting to fear she really was stuck, Lily finally slipped through with a painful scrape across her butt cheek. Pulling herself the rest of the way out, she scrambled over the rock and took in her surroundings, ready to face whatever new terror awaited them.

Distantly, she heard Iris climbing through behind her, but everything else faded into the background as she stared ahead.

The spacious cavern was dimly lit by flickering torches on the walls. A long, rectangular table stretched across the space, laden with a literal feast of horrors, though no one was eating the writhing stews and roasted limbs. There was no one around at all, in fact, save for a lone figure.

At the far end of the room, suspended high above from hooks stabbed through his wings and shoulders . . . was Mist.

Choking back a scream, Lily forgot her fear and ran toward him.

"Look out!" Iris called, and she skidded to a halt, not a second too soon.

Another two steps, and she would have run right off the edge of an enormous hole in the ground. *The Pit.* The bottom was black, but she could just discern something moving below and hear a skin-crawling sound like writhing insects.

Mist was hanging right over it, blood dripping from his wounds into the abyss. *Driving the beasts into a frenzy.*

She choked on the bile rising up her throat. Despite what the gargoyles said, she still hadn't imagined something this horrific.

She was going to get Mist out of here if it killed her, and she would do whatever it took to make sure he never set foot in this terrible place again.

Spurred into action, she craned her head back to study the contraption holding him aloft, following the chains to a pulley system near where they had emerged. She wanted to call out to him, but he appeared to be unconscious, and making unnecessary noise wasn't smart anyway.

"Stay there and make sure he doesn't fall in," Iris whispered from across the room, seeing what Lily had. "I'll lower him."

Iris unhooked the chain, grunting with exertion as her arms strained under the weight. The pulley made a great screeching sound as the chains moved, and Lily's heart began to race faster. Terror consumed her as she imagined Paimon bursting through the door at any second.

The chain ran on a track that guided the hooks from the center of the Pit toward the edge. As Mist's feet hit the ground, his knees immediately collapsed beneath his own weight. Lily caught him before he fell, dragging his immensely heavy body away from the edge as best she could.

He groaned, and his eyes shifted beneath his closed lids.

"Mist, it's me." She could barely speak through her constricted throat as she eased him onto the ground on his side. He wasn't supporting his own weight, and there was no way she was strong enough to hold him up. "It's Lily. I've come to get you out of here."

Iris appeared beside her. "Fuck, what happened to him?"

His arms had been shredded nearly to the bone, and his face was bloody with deep lacerations. There were thick manacles around his wrists with a heavy length of chain between them.

He didn't respond and didn't appear to be aware of much. It was a blessing for now while they removed the hooks, but what about when it was time to leave? There was no way they could carry him.

One thing at a time. The ones through his wings were easy enough to remove, though Lily was twice as panicked as she'd been in the cramped tunnel and was close to losing it. Tears ran unchecked down her cheeks as she gently slid the hooks through the wounds in the soft, leathery tissue.

Soon, all that was left were the two big ones through his shoulders.

"We'll take these out together, okay?" Iris's level head was the only thing keeping Lily from breaking down. "Let's start with this one."

"O-okay."

"You hold him in place while I pull from the back. I'll do it in one go so it hurts him less."

She took a shaky breath and nodded.

With a grunt of exertion, they worked together on Iris's count, and the hook slid free. And Mist finally woke up.

With a snarl, he tackled Lily, pinning her to the cold ground. His claws dug into her shoulders, the chains on his manacles draping over her chest. His yellow eyes were crazed, his sharp teeth bared, the wounds on his face dripping blood.

"Lily!" Iris's panicked voice seemed far away.

"It's okay," she said, keeping a level tone. "He won't hurt me."

At the sound of her voice, Mist blinked groggily. "Lily . . . ?"

"Iris and I came to get you, but we have to go now. We're running out of time."

He inhaled deeply. "My Lily."

Her breath caught. "Yes, it's me."

"You're glowing again."

"Yes. But we really have to go. Paimon could come back at any minute."

He frowned like he was struggling to understand. It must've been an immense effort for him to even remain conscious. Slowly, comprehension dawned, and his eyes shot suddenly wide. He scrambled off her, snarling with pain from the movement of the remaining hook in his shoulder. His gaze caught on Iris, and he froze.

"Hey," she said weakly, lifting a hand.

"We have to pull that hook out," Lily said, sitting up. "Iris and I can—"

Mist reached over his shoulder, and with one rough jerk, he tore it out of himself. Iris actually gagged.

"You shouldn't be here," he said, tossing it away. "Why are you here?"

"To get you."

"Lily . . ."

Their gazes met. There was so much she wanted to say to him, and she could tell he felt the same. Why had he come here? He'd promised to have hope. Why hadn't he told her what he was planning? Why hadn't he confided in her?

But there wasn't time. Later, they would talk. She scrambled to her feet, knees wobbling, and grasped his hand. "We have to go."

He painstakingly rose, holding her tightly. Gratitude filled her heart when Iris came over and grabbed Mist's other arm to help. She wasn't thinking about the chains at his wrists that were supposed to bind him to this place. She'd gotten him free before, and she would do it again. Together, they could do this. Together, they—

The door at the far end of the chamber banged open.

A looming figure stepped into the torchlight. Not clearly male or female, the demon was lean and incredibly tall, easily eight feet or more, with powerful, taloned wings. Four horns framed a cruel face, atop which sat an elaborate crown of black jewels.

Lily had never seen this demon before, but she knew immediately who it was.

Paimon had come for the Hunter.

The Queen of Hell didn't rage or yell when she saw them in the process of liberating her prisoner. She strode calmly across the room, an enormous, red-eyed camel loping at her side.

The tunnel entrance was only about twenty feet away. The smart thing to do might have been to run, but all thought had fled Lily's brain in the face of her fear.

Paimon stopped before them. This close, her looming height was even more obvious. She looked down at them like they were mere insects.

"That's *my* Hunter you're attempting to abscond with."

Lily flinched, though Paimon's voice was level. She expected shouting and wrath, but this cool detachment was somehow worse.

"I knew there was a reason Murmur chose to attack my lair all of a sudden. I'm surprised he chose to ally with mortals, however. Then again, the famed blood-borns are no mere mortals." Her thin lips curved as she surveyed Lily's glowing form. "What a unique phenomenon. I wonder what purpose it serves?"

None at all, unfortunately.

Mist inched closer to her, his grip tightening around her hand. "Run," he hissed. "I will hold her off."

Paimon ignored him. "How convenient of you to visit my lair and save me the trouble of locating you myself. Lucifer will be pleased." She flicked a hand at Mist. "Step aside, my Hunter. Or better yet, why not throw yourself in the Pit and save me that trouble as well."

Despite her paralyzing fear, Lily heard herself say, "He's not yours."

Paimon's brows rose. "No?"

She shook her head mutely, bravery dissipating as quickly as it had come.

The demon queen threw back her head and barked a laugh that echoed around the chamber.

"If he's not mine, then why can I do this?" Her gaze snapped to Mist, and she lifted a hand and flexed her fingers.

The sulfuric burn of Sheolic magic singed the air. Mist shuddered, and a low groan escaped him as he fell to his knees, clutching his chest. With a cry, Lily dropped beside him.

Paimon's hand relaxed, and Mist slumped forward onto his hands, panting. He glanced at Lily through the hair falling in his face, pain clouding his vision. "Run . . . now."

"In every way, he belongs to me," Paimon said. "Even his heart does not beat without my permission."

The brands. It all came back to those cursed, awful brands. Lily shook her head in response to his beseeching gaze. There was no way she was leaving him.

"Unfortunately, I haven't got time for games right now, as much as I enjoy your screams. I need to go take care of Murmur before he decapitates too many of my soldiers. Heads take forever to regenerate." Paimon glanced at her camel. "Throw the Hunter in the Pit, Shaheen. Now that I've got the twins, we have work to do."

Before Lily had a second to react, the enormous, skeletal beast knocked her and Iris aside and closed its jaw around one of Mist's wings.

This is not happening. She leapt at the camel, pummeling its hateful face with her fists.

"Go, Lily!" Mist snarled. He put up no resistance as it dragged him away, the chains at his wrists scraping on the stone floor. What was he doing? Why wouldn't he fight?

Iris was there too, but instead of helping, she was trying to pull Lily off the camel, begging her to listen to Mist and run while they could.

The commotion progressed toward the looming edge. There had to be some way to stop this. Something she could do. *Anything.*

They reached the Pit.

Without hesitation, Shaheen swung his neck and tossed Mist over the edge.

Lily's scream echoed around the cavern.

But then . . . a familiar gray tail snapped over the side, wound around Shaheen's leg, and tugged. The camel tripped and, with a terrible, haunting bellow, went sailing into the abyss.

Paimon's shriek of fury rent the air.

If there had been chaos before, it was nothing compared to what was unleashed now.

With her great scream, the halls began to shake with a rumbling earthquake. The dishes on the table rattled, vibrating off the edge to smash on the ground. Rocks dropped from the high ceiling amid a shower of dust.

Ducking under falling rubble, Lily caught a glimpse of black claws clinging to the edge of the Pit. *Mist.* She ran to him.

Paimon saw too and charged toward them. A boulder fell from the ceiling in her path, and the demon queen swatted it aside as though it were a balloon.

Dropping onto her belly, Lily reached over the edge. Her fingers closed around Mist's chains just as Paimon reached her.

Paimon aimed a kick toward her side, but Iris was there, throwing herself in front of Lily. Her body intercepted the blow, and she went flying back toward the table. Lily shouted her sister's name. Still clinging to the edge, Mist reached one hand out and grabbed Paimon's leg. He yanked. Paimon tripped just like her camel and toppled over the edge.

Just before she disappeared, her hand shot out and seized Lily's glowing arm while she was distracted looking over her shoulder for Iris.

And Paimon and Lily went down together.

24

ONE FELL SWOOP

THERE WAS A WHOOSHING SENSATION IN LILY'S STOMACH as she fell, and she distantly thought, *It's definitely over for me now.* Paimon's tangled wings flapped erratically as she tried in vain to slow their descent. There was no way Lily could survive a fall from this height, no way she could—

They hit the ground, Paimon's body crunching gruesomely beneath her, and Lily was thrown from the impact.

She bounced and rolled several times. Her arm or leg should have been broken. Her ribs. Something.

Instead, she sat up with a jolt. "Mist!"

Had he fallen with them? He'd been right there in the skirmish, but now she saw nothing but—

An unholy shriek split the air. Not Paimon.

Lily looked up, way up, only then noticing what was looming in the dark.

Enormous centipede monsters surrounded her. They had no heads, only gaping mouths full of teeth. Eyes on long stalks protruded from their slimy bodies, and their legs—*so many legs*—looked like sword blades.

Her scream stuck in her throat.

Their sheer size short-circuited her brain. Mist hadn't exaggerated when he compared them to airplanes. If anything, he'd understated it.

"You little fiend!" Paimon hissed from nearby, hauling herself up. Her wings snapped out, one crumpled slightly, and she charged toward Lily with ungodly speed. "How dare you defy me! You're mine. Mishetsu is mine. Everything in this castle *belongs to me*! And I will—"

Seconds before she reached Lily, one of the monsters' huge tongues snapped out and wrapped around Paimon's waist. Momentary surprise flitted across the Queen of Hell's face.

And then she was yanked through the air with incredible speed, right into the gorath's mouth.

The crown toppled from her head with a clatter to roll away on the ground. There was a sickening crunch, and Lily was unable to tear her eyes away from the sight of Paimon's body folding like crumpled paper, her shriek abruptly silenced as blood sprayed—

She gagged. Okay, maybe she was able to look away after all.

Especially when she realized the four other monsters who had missed out on the feast were now turning their sights on her.

She pushed onto her palms, scooting back away from them.

A sudden intense burning on her chest made her gasp. A powerful sensation tugged at her chest, linking her to . . . something. Someone, perhaps? The energy felt familiar, safe, and she welcomed the bond without question. The pain vanished the next instant, and she quickly forgot about it in light of current circumstances.

The goraths' eyes tracked her movement. At any second, one could eat her, and she wouldn't stand a chance.

Frantically, she scanned the darkness for Mist. Was he somewhere, fallen on the ground? There was no sign of him or that horrible camel, whom she assumed had been eaten right before his mistress. Had Mist been swallowed too? Her heart lurched. Terror clogged her throat.

"Mist!" Her hopeless cry seemed only to reach the approaching monsters. "Mist!" He had to be here. He couldn't be gone—

A black cloud coalesced above her.

Wings spread, claws reached forward, and she was scooped into a pair of bloody arms.

A gorath's tongue snapped out, inches from them. Lily screamed as Mist swooped to dodge, dropping so low they nearly hit the ground.

His wings beat furiously, but they were shredded and broken, and his flight was erratic. They crashed into the wall a second later. He held her with one arm and used his claws to find purchase with the other, and then he pushed off the stone.

Another tongue snapped out, and again, they dodged. They hit the side again and then dropped halfway down before Mist could find another handhold.

Again, he pushed off, pumping his mangled wings. Again, another tongue snapped out, and he swooped hard to avoid it.

And then they cleared the mouth of the Pit.

Unable to stop properly, Mist simply curled his body around hers, wings and all, and braced for impact.

They hit the ground and slid across the floor, crashing into the far wall.

Silence fell.

Still tangled in his limbs, Lily rolled off him and turned to assess his condition, unwrapping his limp wings from around them.

"Mist?" He didn't move, and her heart seized in panic. "Mist!" She turned him over, pushing his hair off his face with shaking hands. She relaxed infinitesimally when she felt his warm breath on her skin. The dim glow from her palms illuminated his handsome face, and she wondered how she could ever have seen him as monstrous.

"Lily!" It was Iris's voice, and she twisted to see her sister scrambling toward her. There was blood running down Iris's cheek from a wound at her temple, but she appeared otherwise unharmed.

She pulled Lily into a hug. "Thank fucking god. I was ready to throw myself into that pit after you, but I saw Mist, and I knew you'd be okay."

"H-he— I—" Lily couldn't speak through the tremors suddenly wracking her body.

Iris tightened her grip. "It's okay. You're okay."

She *was* okay. That fall should have killed her, but she didn't have a scratch on her. "Y-you?"

"Fine. Well, I might have a concussion and some bruised ribs, but I'm fine."

"Lily."

She jerked out of Iris's embrace at the sound of Mist's voice. His eyes were open, and she had never seen a more beautiful sight. Wary of his many injuries, she barely held back from throwing herself into his arms.

"You're okay." Tears blurred her sight.

He didn't seem to have the same care for himself, shoving onto his hands and forcing himself upright. His eyes were unfocused, his whole body battered and broken, but with incredible fortitude, he started to stand.

"Have to . . . go now. Not safe."

They rushed to help, taking his arms to pull him upright. It was then she noticed the cuffs were gone from his wrists, and she remembered he had turned to mist right before he rescued her. The cuffs must have disappeared when Paimon was eaten.

"We have to get back to the hellgate in your cave," Iris said, hauling one of Mist's heavy arms over her shoulder. "Murmur said he can activate it if you can't."

Lily did the same, and the three of them shuffled toward the door. She didn't even consider the tunnel. The primary threat was eliminated, and Mist was in no state for spelunking.

"Murmur?" he asked.

"Belial made a bargain with him to help rescue you," she explained. She left out the part where she and Iris had been in dire need of rescue themselves.

"Bel . . . was right. Shouldn't have left."

"Which way?" Iris asked. They had made it to the door and faced a long hall lined with torches.

Mist pointed left, so they steered him that way. Sounds of battle were faintly audible in the distance, along with unholy screams that sent shivers down her spine.

Get to the hellgate. Get home. They were so close.

At the end of the hall, just as they rounded the corner, Murmur stepped out from a hidden door in the wall.

Just like before, black smoke swirled about his feet, writhing like it had a mind of its own, leading Lily to conclude that it wasn't an illusion after all. There were vague outlines of something within it . . . but even that wasn't the most alarming thing about his appearance.

He was absolutely bathed in blood. It coated his pale skin and stained his luminous hair, and it was smeared all around his mouth and down his front like he had gorged upon it.

She grimaced at the sight, but Murmur just looked bored. "What took so long?"

"You were supposed to keep Paimon away, not enjoy a blood buffet!" Iris snapped.

He ignored her and looked at Mist. "Ah, here he is. The gorath killer in the flesh."

Mist grunted.

Murmur pulled out his rag and wiped his sword, but the cloth was already blood-soaked and didn't do much good. He gave up, pocketed it, and propped a shoulder against the wall as if he had all the time in the world. In the distance, another explosion sounded, followed by tortured screams.

"You've earned yourself quite the reputation. Word has spread about your triumph like wildfire. They say you let it swallow you whole and then clawed your way out of its belly, shredding the heart in the process. How delightfully horrific. Is it true you killed the biggest one?"

Mist said nothing.

"No one wants to mess with you now. The gargoyles all speak of you with something akin to hero worship." Murmur smiled sardonically, and the shadows at his feet churned with increased agitation. "If I didn't know better, I might think I have competition for the lair."

"It's yours," Mist growled. "I don't want it."

"Now, how can I trust that if you won't even bargain for it? The gargoyles believed that after your victory in the Pit, it was only a matter of time before the great Mishetsumephtai returned to defeat his mistress and claim her territory for himself. Considering that *I* am the one now trying to claim the territory, you can see how I might find that . . . threatening."

Lily's stomach flipped. Was he going to turn on them? Try to prevent them from leaving?

"I don't want the lair."

"Your word alone means nothing."

"Fine," Mist snarled. "Vow you will let us reach the hell-gate unscathed and will not try to track us on Earth, and I will vow not to challenge you for the territory."

Murmur smiled. "I accept your terms, Hunter." Sheathing his bloody sword, he slashed his palm open with a claw and held it aloft. "On my own blood, I vow it."

Mist repeated the words, though he was so bloody already there was no need to cut himself.

"Then this is where our arrangement ends," Murmur said.

"You're free to go. I hope for your sake we never meet again."

"As do I."

With a dip of his chin, he melted back into the hidden passage and was gone.

"That bloke gives me the creeps," Iris muttered.

"Never trust the Necromancer," Mist said. "Despite his vow, I don't believe he won't try to follow us."

"Let's go then!" Lily didn't like the sound of that at all.

"If I take mist form, I can move faster."

"How will we know where to go?"

"I'll guide you." He bent his head to meet her gaze. "I won't leave you again."

"I believe you."

"I was wrong."

She squeezed his arm still draped over her shoulder. "We can talk once we're home."

He nodded, and then before her eyes, dissolved into mist.

"Damn, that's cool," Iris said.

The black cloud swept around their feet and down the passage, guiding them onward. Lily followed with complete faith in him to get them where they needed to go.

Now that they were together, they were safe.

A short while later, Murmur stood alone in the Hunter's empty cave and dusted his hands off for a job well done. High above on the ground level, he could sense his souls still engaged with Paimon's forces. Souls could not be eliminated, but they could tire, and his were nearing the end of their strength.

He needed to return to the frontline and declare himself the lair's new master before he pushed them much further. Plus, he didn't want to behead *all* his new subjects. Someone was going to have to clean up the mess in his shiny new castle.

But there was one thing left to do first.

The humans and Mishetsumephtai had returned safely through the hellgate, and Murmur's bargain with Belial was complete. On Murmur's end, at least. He was officially owed a favor from the King of Hell, and he intended to collect when the time was right.

The scent of Sheolic magic still tainted the air from the gate's activation. As he'd vowed to the Hunter, he had not tried to track their passage.

He hadn't needed to, to get what he wanted.

Mounting his torch in the sconce on the wall, Murmur crossed the dark cave and retrieved the tiny vial from the nook where he'd hidden it. Carefully, he lifted it before the torchlight and studied the contents. A smile spread across his face.

"Look what we have here," he said to the souls at his feet.

The formerly black liquid was now a rich ruby red, indicating the spell had worked.

He dug out the vial's cork from his pocket and sealed it tightly to ensure not a drop was wasted. What he had in his hands . . . He couldn't begin to guess its worth. It may have been the most valuable item in all the underworld, in fact.

He couldn't simply auction it off to the highest bidder, however. It had to end up in the right hands. It had to be given to someone who would further Murmur's own plans. Someone he could manipulate. Luckily, he knew just who to approach.

"Shall we?" he asked his souls, pocketing the vial. He chuckled. "Of course we shall."

They had no choice. They were bound to him until he chose to release them, which might be never. It certainly wouldn't be now, when things were finally coming to a head, and he had just secured himself one of the most heavily fortified territories in Hell.

As he strode down the tunnel, the smile never left his face.

Having his multitudinous schemes align and come to fruition was the greatest pleasure to be had in all the realms. He would know, for he'd tried them all. None matched the high he felt now.

He had not tried to prevent Paimon from finding the Hunter and the twins, as he'd said he would. In fact, he may have accidentally guided her toward the chamber.

He'd wanted the blood-borns to dispose of her, as he'd known they would. He'd wanted to be the one aiding them so he was strategically positioned to take the castle from the inside out. He'd been secretly weakening Paimon's wards for months so that when he'd breached them tonight, it had taken but a moment.

It was all foreseen—the witches, the fall of the Queen of Hell, all of it.

It was *he* who had foreseen it.

25

BRAND NEW

MIST AWOKE TO THE ABSENCE OF PAIN. FOR THE FIRST time in a while, there was nothing wrong with his body. No broken bones or bleeding lacerations. Not even the brand on his neck was burning.

After all the suffering, the sensation—or lack thereof—felt like bliss. So much so that, even though he was awake, he kept his eyes closed and just breathed for a while.

He felt . . . peace. Deep peace. Contentment.

A lily-flower scent tantalized his nose, adding to the joy of the moment. Lily. His Lily. She was here right now, she was—

In his arms. More awareness of his body returned, and he felt her warm skin against him, her soft hair tickling his chest. He lifted a hand, arm heavy from sleep, and petted those silky tresses, and she hummed softly and snuggled closer. His heart nearly burst in his chest.

As he stroked her, the memories returned.

It had taken all his control to allow Shaheen to drag him toward the Pit amid Lily's screams. He feared she thought he'd given up again, when that was the furthest thing from true.

He'd simply been waiting for his perfect moment. When it had come, he'd taken it.

When the camel had tossed him, he'd hooked his claws on the edge and used his tail to slingshot the beast straight into the mouths of the waiting goraths. Two crunches and the demon camel was gone.

He'd tried to do the same to Paimon, had almost succeeded, but she'd grabbed Lily on her way down. He'd been left clinging to the edge of the Pit, watching his beautiful female, glowing like starlight, fall into the abyss. With wings he wasn't sure would hold him, he'd dived off the ledge after her.

And then he'd seen Paimon get snagged by a gorath tongue and caught in the death trap of teeth.

That moment . . . He couldn't say how long he'd dreamed of her meeting such a fate.

And yet, watching her get eaten hadn't meant a thing in the face of his fear for Lily.

In that way, the brevity of Paimon's somewhat underwhelming defeat was oddly fitting. She meant nothing. She wasn't worth the hatred he felt for her or the burning need he'd felt to destroy her. She wasn't worth anything at all.

Mist's manacles had abruptly disappeared—presumably at the moment of her consumption—and he'd misted past the gorath, snatched up Lily, and carried her out of there as quickly as he could with his ravaged wings. He'd forgotten about Paimon instantly, like she'd never held any power over him to begin with.

After they arrived back on Earth, they'd been greeted by the other demons and Eva, who fussed over them accordingly. Mist had approached Belial, who pinned him with a hard stare, and they'd regarded each other in a weighted silence.

Maybe if they were less proud and more human, Mist might have apologized. He regretted putting Belial in the position he had and rejecting his offer of help. But he knew Belial would hate an apology, and he wasn't sure he was comfortable giving one anyway.

So he went with his usual choice of words for when he struggled to express himself: *Thank you.*

Belial had grunted and glared and muttered something about not wasting his time before storming off to the kitchen, but Mist had felt something lighten in the air between them and knew he was forgiven. He was surprised how much that meant to him.

After that, he'd staggered into the shower—the full-size one his wings could fit in—and that was the last thing he remembered, so he must have fallen asleep immediately afterward.

Through it all, Lily had never left his side.

She stirred in his arms at that moment, rolling off his chest onto her side and opening her eyes. She smiled when she saw him watching her. "Hi."

He traced the curve of her jaw with his foreclaw, watching her as closely as he could to ensure he didn't miss a single detail. Her body had lost its ethereal luster, her skin once again as normal as any human's, but that didn't make her any less bewitching. To him, she was perfect.

Except her soft expression vanished in a blink, and she suddenly sat upright with a gasp. Even stranger, she yanked the bedsheet up to her neck, hiding her body from him.

Stiffening, he glanced around, looking for the source of her alarm, but he saw nothing unusual. They were in his bedroom in Belial's apartment, and everything was just as he had left it.

"Mist . . ."

He frowned, trying to understand her anguished expression. Maneuvering his wings from beneath him, he pushed into a sitting position, taking a moment to appreciate the lack of pain in his body once again.

"What's wrong?"

"I have to tell you something. Something I—" She broke off, swallowing hard.

"What is it?" He was certain whatever it was could not be worse than he was imagining.

"It's about the brands."

He glanced down at his wrists. The skin was healed over, and while the cuffs were gone, the brands were not. But he hadn't expected them to be.

"Paimon can't summon me now," he explained. "There's no need to be concerned."

"No, that's not it. I—" Again, she swallowed and tugged the bedsheet higher. "I swear it was an accident. I had no idea it would happen. I didn't even consider it a possibility or else I would never have—"

"I don't understand, Lily. What happened?"

"Oh, Mist. I'm so sorry." With eyes full of tears, she lowered the sheet. It took him a second to see anything except her full breasts with those big, pink areolae.

But there was no missing the sizable mark in the center of her chest.

The circle was centered between her breasts and made of intricate patterns. To the untrained eye, it would appear to be a complex geometric tattoo. But it was not that. Not at all.

He stared in disbelief, his eyes snapping between hers and the design again and again.

"I don't understand." His voice seemed to come from far away.

"It was an accident, I swear. I would never have intervened if I'd known this could happen. It's the last thing I ever want. I—"

"Lily, please explain," he said slowly. "From the beginning."

She covered herself with the sheet again and nodded. "When Paimon got eaten, there was this moment I felt something burn on my chest and this connection. But it seemed safe to me, or familiar, or . . . I'm not sure. But there was so much happening, so I just welcomed it and forgot about it. And my chest was hidden by my shirt, so I didn't notice.

"But after you fell asleep, I went to shower, and I saw myself in the mirror and, well, I screamed. And when I came out everyone was worried, and I was wearing a towel so they saw the top of it, and Belial knew immediately what it was.

"I guess while we were gone, coincidentally, Eva's dad called. He said that while he still hadn't heard back from his friend with information on removing the brands, he'd suddenly remembered reading somewhere that they were transferable."

"Transferable." Mist's heart pounded. "How?"

She bit her lip, taking a moment to compose herself. "They were designed so that if the person who controls the bonds is defeated, their . . . well, the one bound to them will belong to the one who defeated them But the old master couldn't actually be dead, because that would cause the death of the bound one as well."

His rushing blood was creating a hum in his ears that made it hard to hear. From far away, he heard himself speak. "Like Paimon being eaten by a gorath. Defeated, but not destroyed."

Because to truly kill a demon, all remaining pieces of the body had to be incinerated with hellfire. And though she would not be able to regenerate inside the belly of a gorath, Paimon was not truly dead.

Lily nodded mutely. "And in order to defeat the old master and take the branded servant for themselves, the new master had to be the one to do it, and they had to be powerful enough to harness the brands' magic on their own. No one else could do it for them. And I guess that even though Paimon was technically killed by a gorath, because I was the one fighting her when we fell into the Pit, well . . ."

She trailed off. Their gazes met.

"*You're* my new mistress," Mist said softly.

Lily gulped and then finally lost the fight against her tears.

A sob spilled out of her, and she clutched the sheet like a lifeline. "I'm so sorry! I never wanted this! I swear to you, it's the last thing I want. If I could take it back, I would. I would do anything, give anything."

Mist just stared at her.

"Please say something." She wiped her eyes. "I understand if you can't forgive me, but please just tell me what you're thinking."

"You're saying I no longer belong to Paimon." He spoke slowly. He had to be one hundred percent certain of the truth before he accepted it. There could be mistakes or misunderstandings.

She nodded.

"I no longer belong to Paimon because . . . I belong to you."

Again, she nodded.

"So . . . I'm free."

A crease formed between her brows. "Well, no, because the brand is still there."

"But Paimon doesn't control it anymore. You do."

"Yes."

"So I am free. Because of you."

"But . . ." She searched his gaze. "It's not true freedom. The brands are still there. And it forces you to put trust in me when I know you've never been able to trust anyone before. And of course I would never do anything to hurt you, but it's not fair that you should have to be forced to believe me. It's not fair that you should be branded at all. It's not fair that—"

"But I do trust you."

She pressed her lips together. "Mist . . ."

"I mean it."

And he did. For the first time, he understood what trust was and what it felt like. Because he trusted someone. He trusted Lily.

He knew she would never betray him. She would never use the brands to hurt or control him. There was no proof, no binding promise or irrefutable evidence, but he knew it nonetheless. He knew it because everything about Lily assured him of this.

She was the kindest, most empathetic and loving person he'd ever encountered. She'd taught him the meaning of those qualities in the first place, because before her, they'd only been vague, theoretical notions.

He understood them because she had demonstrated them. Because she had given him her love.

"Mist . . ." Her palm covered her mouth, and she blinked rapidly. "I swear I'll never give you reason to doubt me. And I'll never stop looking for how to get rid of the brands, not even for one day. I promise I'll—"

He reached out, pulling her hand away and drawing her into him. "I don't care."

"No, I have to do this. I can't just—"

"I want to belong to you."

"Mist." A few tears spilled over.

"I want to be bonded to you. That way, if you're ever in danger, you can use the brand to summon me."

"But the cuffs. And the heart brand. And—"

"I don't care."

"How can you say that?"

"You freed me from Paimon. Lily, I—"

To his surprise, his throat tightened, and he found it impossible to utter another word. He swallowed, trying to relax the constricted muscles. Simultaneously, he felt an intense sensation in his chest. Urgent yet comforting. Frightening yet addictive.

His face scrunched up. He didn't understand what was wrong with him.

"You saved me," he finally managed.

Something in one eye blurred his vision, and he felt wetness, so he released Lily's wrist to swipe it away. Holding his hand up, he stared in disbelief at the single drop of water perched on his fingertip at the base of his claw.

It was a tear.

"Lily . . ." He looked at her and then back at the tear.

She took his hand and tilted it so she could see. She stared at it for a second, and then she surprised him by throwing herself into his arms with enough force that he nearly tipped backward. Only his wing talons braced at his sides kept him upright.

"I love you, I love you," she said over and over, her voice muffled against his chest. His skin immediately became wet with her tears, which were much less rare than his own. Yet each one was no less precious.

He wrapped his arms around her and held her close. He wanted to say the words back because he'd seen in the human movies he watched with Eva that it was important.

One partner took the risk to say the words and then waited expectantly for the other to reciprocate. If it was the beginning of the movie, they would not, and drama would follow. If it was the end, they would, and the credits would roll shortly after.

But he wasn't sure he understood what it meant, even now after everything he'd learned about humans and experienced with Lily. He might have said them anyway just to appease her, but his newfound understanding of trust made him want to be honest with her in all things.

So he chose to explain himself with words he did understand, and he hoped they would be enough.

"When I left to go after Paimon, I had convinced myself it was the only way. But I was wrong. After so long of having nothing, suddenly, I had everything, and I could not believe in it. Maybe I didn't feel I deserved it. I felt certain everything would be taken from me, and so, to prevent my despair, I decided to end it myself rather than fight."

Lily lifted her head and met his gaze with sorrowful eyes.

"I thought you would be happier without me, though I hated it. I wanted you to hunt me to the ends of the earth, as I would do to you if you tried to escape me, but I never believed you actually would."

Her expression turned fierce. "Of course I would. I would never be happier without you, and I wouldn't let you escape me either."

How had he found such a strong and loyal female? How was he worthy of such a gift?

He didn't care how. He was done questioning his good fortune.

"You are everything good in my world, Lily. You are my freedom. There is nothing I value more, and I no longer have the desire to hunt because I know I have already found the most precious treasure in existence."

"Mist . . ."

"Maybe those aren't the words you want to hear, but I wish to be honest, and I don't know that I understand how to love. I don't know that I'm capable."

She lifted her palms and framed his face. "You are capable, and you just proved it by what you said. It was the most meaningful thing anyone's ever said to me, and it doesn't matter that you didn't use the word 'love.'"

"But Eva said human women want love."

"And this human woman"—she placed a hand on her heart, over the brand—"has found it, and she's never been happier."

"But—"

"No buts. Kiss me?"

He was sure she meant to state it like a demand, but it came out as a question, and her cheeks flushed. It didn't matter. He was more than happy to oblige, and he leaned in and pressed their lips together.

But he jerked back suddenly as something occurred to him.

"Are you hurt?" He would never forget the sight of her falling into the Pit.

"No, I'm perfectly fine. No injuries at all." She reached for him.

"But how—"

"Kiss now, talk later? I promise I'm fine."

He could not ignore that request. Lifting her, he laid her on her back and kissed her hungrily, his tail winding up her thigh. She wrapped her arms around his neck and tangled her tongue furiously with his. So furiously, he had to pull back to ensure she didn't cut it on his teeth.

She wore nothing but a pair of underwear, and though he didn't think she had sewed them, he wasn't going to risk it. Pushing into his wing talons, he sat back and slid the fabric down her legs like it was made of glass. He set the underwear carefully aside and then shot her a glare when she dissolved in a fit of giggles.

He would teach her to giggle at him. Gripping her calves, he pressed her legs up and open and then bent forward and slid his tongue along her sex. *Ambrosia.* The taste of her . . . He had not exaggerated when he called her the most precious treasure in existence.

She writhed under him as he speared her with his tongue, extending it as far as it would go inside of her and rubbing the tip against the bundle of nerves at the front of her vaginal wall. Her head tipped back, and her spine arched off the mattress as she cried out, so he did it again. And again.

Her inner muscles contracted and more of that tantalizing flavor spilled onto his tongue as she hovered on the brink of climax, but she didn't quite go over. He let her ride the edge until her next cry was one of anguish, and then he wrapped his tail around her hip and slid it down past her navel. He lightly slapped the tip against her clitoris while he continued to work her with his mouth. Once, twice—

She cried out, loudly enough to be heard throughout the apartment, but neither of them cared about that. Her inner walls rippled with contractions so intense, they squeezed his tongue, and her thighs shook hard enough to jiggle her bountiful flesh.

It was the most decadent thing he had ever witnessed, and he was nearly ready to climax himself just from watching it.

But he held off. He wasn't finished with her yet.

He lifted her again and maneuvered them so she was sitting in his lap, his legs bent to create a cradle for her hips, her knees spread on either side of him. Her eyes were drugged from her release, and she looked like a goddess as she smiled lazily at him, leaning in for a kiss.

Tilting his hips, his shaft slid along her slickness, stimulating her sensitive clit and making her shudder against him. He repeated the motion, stopping to push just the tip inside her before sliding back up. She draped her arms over his shoulders and stroked his wings where they connected to his back.

"Take me inside," he rumbled, shuddering from the sensation. Being touched with gentleness and care was still new to him, and it sometimes felt overwhelming, but in a good way.

She lifted her hips to line his erection up with her entrance. Gazes locked, he forced his body to be still as she slowly sank down onto him. One inch, and she stopped with a gasp. She pushed a little deeper between sliding back up, coating his shaft in her arousal.

"Take more," he growled, unable to stem his impatience. He didn't want to hurt her, but he couldn't help himself.

She sank down on him again, sliding a little lower this time before lifting back up. She gripped his shoulders now, her fingers digging into his flesh like little claws.

"Again."

She obeyed, and this time, as she lifted up again, she didn't move all the way off him, and began riding the top half of his cock with slow, careful movements. Her nostrils were flared, her eyes slightly wide, her grip on his shoulders vise-like.

But her moans were full of desire. And the more she rode him, the lower her eyelids sank, and the more the tension bled from her body.

"More, Lily." He had to have more.

His hands tightened around her hips as she finally sank the rest of the way down, filling herself with him completely. She froze, gasping, her muscles rigid again.

"Is it too much?" Reason penetrated the haze of lust and reminded him not to hurt her.

"It's just . . . intense."

"Feels good?"

"So good."

His eyes narrowed in challenge, and when he saw acceptance in her gaze, he tightened his grip on her hips and lifted her slightly off him before lowering her back down.

Her eyes fell shut. "Oh god."

"More?"

"*Yes.*"

He gave her more, lifting her a little higher and sinking a little deeper each time he dropped her back down. His muscles strained from the effort of holding back, the urge to give in to release building with each thrust.

"More, Mist. Give me more. I can take it."

He changed tactics, holding her still while he thrust into her from below. She cried out and dropped her head back, and he finally lost control.

He powered into her with deep thrusts, the friction a powerful drug he had no choice but be consumed by. Hovering on the brink of release, the pressure unbearable, the pleasure incomparable, he felt something come apart inside of him.

His world narrowed down to nothing but her. His Lily.

His beautiful Lily whom he would do anything for and whom he . . . loved.

Yes, that is it. This was love, and it was the greatest feeling in the world. In all the worlds. In all creation.

His climax speared through him like a javelin, and he couldn't have held it back if he tried. Waves of rapture blacked out his vision, save for colorful spots that burst in the dark like fireworks. Lust and deep satisfaction filled him, but it commingled with happiness, a sense of belonging, and *love.*

Lily collapsed against him, her body soft and pliant in his arms. So trusting. So precious. So . . .

"Mine," he said, resting his chin on top of her head and wrapping her up in his arms, wings, and even his tail.

He squeezed her as tightly as he could without hurting her, and she made a pleasured hum and hugged him back, her arms snaking around his lower back. He felt his release trickling out of her body where they were joined, and it made him want to growl ferociously at the thought of her full of him, marked inside her body with his scent.

"Love you," he whispered.

She tried to pull back, probably to stare at him in surprise, but he tightened his arms around her, refusing to let go. He didn't want distance between them, and he wasn't sure he wanted her looking into his eyes just yet. His admission made him feel vulnerable, and the sensation was somewhat unnerving.

She seemed to understand this, because she relaxed against him again and squeezed him right back. "I love you too. So much. I couldn't stop if I tried."

"Don't try," he growled, and she snorted.

"I won't. I don't want to. I couldn't, as I said."

"Good."

She laughed again and then purred like a kitten as she snuggled closer. "You know I meant what I said, right? I promise

I won't stop searching until I find a way to get rid of the brands."

"I don't care."

"It's still a symbol of the past. You must want to be rid of it."

He considered this, remembering his former aversion to his human form, not only because of its inferiority but because the brands were more visible.

"I think it would have bothered me at one time," he admitted. "But I feel differently now."

"How so?"

"I like that you are marked with something that ties you to me." The thought did indeed fill him with satisfaction.

"Well, we could go get matching tattoos then! We don't need horrible, cursed brands."

He smiled briefly. "If you one day discover a way to remove them, we'll get matching tattoos. Until then, I like knowing you are marked by me. Maybe it will make it easier not to bite you."

She chuckled. "Okay, well, I guess if you can accept it, then I can too. But I'm not going to stop looking."

He shrugged. He really didn't care if she forgot about it tomorrow. He liked the idea of her being able to summon him if she was ever in trouble.

They held each other in comfortable silence for a time, and then it struck him anew that he was free. Paimon was rotting inside a gorath, and when it finally eliminated her, another would eat her soon after. His days of dragging screaming creatures back to Hell to be punished were done.

The Hunter was retired. Mishetsumephtai had gone rogue. To hell with the rules. He would obey no one but himself from this day forward. No one could hunt as he could, so he would make sure he was never found.

He frowned suddenly as a familiar memory surfaced.

He perched atop a wind-beaten tree and peered through a window into the house below. A demon entered the kitchen and wrapped his arms around a small human female. A radiant smile adorned the woman's face, her hands busy chopping vegetables while the demon rested his chin atop her head and smiled with contentment.

He had once resented Eligos and Asmodeus for the love they'd found because he wanted it for himself, though he'd refused to admit it in so many words.

Now, he had it, and he couldn't help but feel regret at the thought of Eligos spending untold years hiding behind wards, believing the Hunter was searching high and low for him. Mist had asked Belial to communicate with the former Duke of Hell on his behalf, but now that he was free—truly free—he could do it himself. He wanted to do it himself.

"Would you like to take a trip with me?" he asked Lily.

She lifted her head, and he finally loosened his grip enough that she could meet his gaze. "Where?"

"We would go to the Gaspé region."

"Oh, I've always wanted to go there! Percé Rock is supposed to be beautiful. But why do you want to travel all of a sudden?"

"I need to visit someone who lives there and tell him that the Hunter is retired."

"Okay, *Mist*-erious." She poked him in the chest with a grin. "You can explain what that's about on the way."

"You will come with me?"

She smiled. "Of course I will. You know I'll follow you anywhere. Even to the pits of Hell."

26

FLOWER POWER

THOUGH HE'D NEVER ADMIT IT, LILY KNEW MIST needed more time to rest after his ordeal. He certainly had a lot of healing to do, and while he did it remarkably fast, it still took its toll.

Shortly after their postcoital cuddling, he drifted off. She dozed with him for a while but soon found she was too hungry to sleep.

And she wanted to talk to her sister.

Iris had been equally exhausted and traumatized after they'd stepped through the gate and landed back in Mist's bedroom, and as far as Lily knew, she had used Belial's enormous shower and then fallen asleep on the sofa. Lily also knew there was a danger of Iris and Meph stabbing each other, so she figured it was a good idea to go check on her and make sure everything was okay.

Slipping out from under Mist's heavy arm, she dressed quickly and headed to the door, stopping to look back at the big demon sleeping peacefully. Her heart felt like it would burst, and she had to go back and kiss him before she could make herself leave.

After a quick trip to the bathroom to wash, she headed down the hall to find her sister.

Unsurprisingly, Belial was in the kitchen, stirring a big pot of something on the stove. He gave no greeting at her arrival, nor did his expression change in any way.

"Hi." She was pleased to hear her voice didn't squeak. Facing off against Paimon had strengthened her backbone, apparently. "That smells delicious."

"Your sister's still asleep."

"Oh. Um, thanks."

He glanced at her sidelong. "You're lucky Meph has been pulling his disappearing act lately. Don't think she likes him much."

"Sorry about that." She hated that her sister's acerbic personality might strain things with their hosts. Demons or not, they were gracious ones.

He shrugged. "I don't blame her. I don't like him either."

She smiled to herself but refrained from mentioning the note of affection in his voice that belied his words.

"Oh, wow, it's later than I thought." The clock over the stove said it was nearly midnight.

Crossing to and from Hell had messed with her perception of time. She couldn't even remember what time of day it had been when they'd left in the first place, let alone when she'd fallen asleep.

"Hungry?"

"I am, thank you."

She perched on one of the barstools across the island, and Belial served her a steaming bowl of soup. It was delicious, and she ate so quickly, her tongue was considerably burnt by the end. He served her a second and had one himself, and neither of them spoke the entire time.

When they finished, she washed their bowls and then set them in the dish drainer.

"Thank you," she said, turning to face the imposing demon now hunched over a recipe book.

He flicked his hand in a dismissive gesture, not looking away.

"Not just for the soup."

He pulled out an electric mixer from one cupboard and baking supplies from another. Then he uncovered a bowl of egg whites that appeared to have been sitting out for some time.

"I mean about making that deal with Murmur to get him to help us."

"Wasn't just for you." He started pouring sugar into a measuring cup. "Eva guilted me into it."

"Well, if it wasn't for Murmur—for you—there's no way we would have made it out of there. So thank you."

The sugar bag was set aside, and finally, he turned to face her. Their gazes met, and it felt like she was being electrocuted by his eyes. "You're welcome."

"How did you know to send him?" she dared to ask. "How did you know he would help us?"

He scowled and turned away like he didn't care for her line of questioning. "I have connections in Hell."

That explained absolutely nothing, but she knew better than to press him for more information. Everything in his body language told her to drop it, so she did. They were alive and safe, and that was all she really cared about in the end.

"Well, I'm glad." It felt like a lame thing to say, but she didn't know how else to respond to his obvious evasiveness.

His brow lifted like he thought the same, and the corner of his mouth quirked briefly. "You might want to wake up your sister now because I'm about to do it myself with the mixer."

"What are you making?"

"Macarons."

She blinked. Belial was an enigma, that was for sure. "I'll go talk to her." She smiled. "Thanks for the soup."

With a grunt, he turned back to his baking.

Lily hurried over to the sofa only to find Iris already sitting up, rubbing her eyes. She looked out the big windows at the night cityscape and frowned. "What time is it?"

"Almost midnight," Lily replied, sitting beside her.

"That's awful. Traveling to Hell is like the worst jet lag possible."

Lily snorted. "Fitting, really."

Iris looked at her. "How are you?"

"Good."

"How's Mist?"

"He's good too."

"How did he take . . . you know?" She glanced down at the brand on Lily's chest.

"He said he doesn't care. He—" Her breath hitched. "He said he likes that we're connected." She dragged her hands down her face. "How can he think that? I'm so guilty I feel sick."

Iris punched her arm. "Bitch, you literally saved him. Give yourself some credit."

"Ow!"

"I'm serious. You were straight badass. You saved your demon boyfriend from his evil mistress or whatever. You're a hero. Act like it."

"All I did was fall in a hole and—" She broke off.

Yeah, some of what happened had been accidental, but the fact remained that she had gone to Hell, faced off Paimon, and survived. She wasn't going to discredit that or talk down on herself.

She was done apologizing for her own existence. From now on, she was going to take up some damn space in the world, and she wasn't going to be sorry about it.

She nodded firmly. "I still wish I could've taken the brands away instead of keeping them in a different form. They're horrible, no matter who controls them."

"And you will. I have no doubt about that. Now that I've seen what you can do when you're properly motivated, I'll never doubt your ability to achieve anything again. And neither should you."

She leaned her head on her sister's shoulder. "Thanks."

"You shouldn't be thanking me. You should still be pissed at me."

"I told you I forgave you. And yeah, it might take me a while to rebuild the trust between us, but you're still my sister, and you still have my back. You proved it when you literally threw yourself in front of Paimon to save me. I know better than to doubt you."

"Thanks, Lil."

The mixer fired up in the kitchen.

Iris frowned. "What is that?"

"Belial's making macarons."

"Belial?" She rubbed her eyes. "That's so weird, honestly."

"I think it suits him. He looks like a chef."

"Yeah, and Mist looks like a cuddly puppy."

"You're right," Lily said with a smile, and Iris snorted.

"I need to get out of here. No offense to your new mates, Lil, but I think it'll be better if I try not to hang out with them much."

"Bel said Meph isn't here right now, so you don't need to worry."

Iris shrugged. "Dunno what you mean."

"Sure, sure."

"Are you coming? Do you want me to walk you home?"

"No. Mist is asleep, and I'm going to join him now that I've had some food. I'm still knackered."

"Me too, but I want to sleep in my own bed." Iris stood up and winced. "And I need to mix up a good healing draft."

"Are you okay?"

"Just sore, and I've got a killer headache. Call me to-morrow?"

Lily stood too. "I will."

"You sure you're okay, Lil? You wrestled with a demon queen, for fuck's sake."

"I'm fine. Promise." She was well aware she could have died falling into the Pit, or at least broken her spine, but she wasn't even bruised.

The sisters stared at each other for a moment, and then Iris snorted. "God, it feels weird leaving you in the company of a bunch of bloody demons and not being scared about it."

Lily grinned and snatched her twin up into a hug. "Thank you."

"Careful of the ribs!"

She leapt back. "Oh, sorry!"

"And what are you thanking me for anyway?"

"For being my sister."

Iris grumbled and looked away. "Whatever, cheeseball. Just be careful. They're still demons."

She rolled her eyes. "Sure. Okay. Let's meet up for brunch tomorrow at the diner by your place. I'll bring Mist and show him how to eat eggs Benedict." She grinned. "He's going to hate it."

"What? Why?"

"Because he'll have to eat with a knife and fork in front of a bunch of humans in human form. He'll be growling the whole time." She couldn't stop grinning at the thought.

"You have a weird sense of humor," Iris said approvingly. "Call me when you're up, and I'm there. Just don't bring any of the other demons. I'll make an exception for your guy, but I don't think I'm ready for anyone else yet." She cast a suspicious glance at the kitchen.

"Baby steps," Lily replied.

They embraced again, and Iris left shortly after. After bidding Belial goodnight as he sifted almond flour, Lily finally crawled back into bed beside Mist. Her hunter snuggled against her from behind, nuzzling her hair, and her whole body tingled with a sense of rightness. She fell asleep instantly.

A short time later, however, she jolted awake. Opening her eyes, she wondered what had woken her—

Oh. That was what.

"Lily?" Mist's deep voice rumbled beside her ear. Her sudden tension must have woken him too.

"It's okay. I'm just glowing again, and it startled me."

He smoothed a hand down her side. "I like it."

I think I do too. "Mist, I think it . . . When I fell into the Pit—"

His arm clenched around her. "I couldn't reach you in time. I saw you falling and—"

"It's okay." She stroked it to soothe him. "I'm okay. I'm completely okay. That's what I'm saying. I don't have a scratch on me."

"Maybe it's a shield, then. It protects you from harm."

"Yeah, I— I think it might." She shook her head. All the times she had panicked upon waking in the night to her glowing skin . . . only to discover now it was a gift meant to protect her. Something to be grateful for, not ashamed of.

Would she still continue to awaken in the night to random bouts of luminescence? Or, now that she understood the ability, would it only come when she needed it?

She wasn't in need of it now, though. She'd been sleeping deeply, not even caught in a nightmare, which was surprising after the horrors she had just faced in Hell.

So perhaps she would have to accept that she was a witch who occasionally glowed at random times. And in turn, when she needed protection, the strange ability would shield her. It was a compromise she could gladly make.

"I can't believe I hated it," she told Mist, "when all along I should have been grateful."

"We fear what we don't understand," he said. "But now you know. It's like a superpower."

A surprised laugh burst from her, and she rolled onto her back to look at him. "Where did you learn about superpowers?"

"In addition to romantic films, Eva showed me superheroes."

She tried to picture him watching the latest Marvel flick and laughed again. "Did you like them?"

"No. Humans would not manage well with such abilities. They are too lawless and impulsive. Beings of power need discipline."

"Still a stickler for the rules, then?"

"Only the ones worth following." He smiled, though his eyes were closed again. "A wise witch taught me that."

Lily chuckled. "She sounds amazing."

"She is."

He mumbled something else incoherent and pulled her closer, the sound of his deepening breath indicating he was lost to sleep once more. She turned on her side to face him and watched him sleep, totally and completely head over heels for him.

She was humbled by his trust in her. After everything he'd been through, that he would give her the gift of his love meant the world. She would guard it until her dying day—which might be a very long time from now if that silly prophecy was anything to go by.

She mentally scoffed. As if she was actually destined to be some legendary, immortal witch.

And then she stopped that train of thought in its tracks.

Timid, Self-Deprecating Lily was dead. She'd burned up somewhere in Hell.

Who said she wasn't a legendary, immortal witch? She'd already done a few things that were pretty damn legendary. As for immortal, well . . . time would tell.

But if she was what the prophecy proclaimed her to be, then she would begin her reign of power by finding a way to get rid of Mist's brands once and for all. And she would use her strength to protect the ones she loved, just as her parents had done for her.

With that conviction, she drifted back to sleep, safe in the arms of her demon.

MEPHILOGUE

V ALEFOR, DUKE OF HELL, SAT IN HIS STUDY, PORING over ancient texts in a rage. Paimon's territory had fallen, its queen with it. How had he not seen this coming?

"The prophecy said *King* of Hell, damn it!" He smashed a fist onto the desk, sending papers flying.

He'd been foolish to believe the humans' interpretation of the seer's words from centuries ago. He should have done his own analysis and translations. Maybe then he would have realized that since humankind had already mistaken Paimon for a King, it stood to reason they might make that same mistake elsewhere.

It was a minor miscalculation, but one with disastrous consequences. Because of that one mistake, he'd been looking in all the wrong places. All his careful plans were moot now, and it was too late to turn the situation to his advantage.

Like most powerful demons, Valefor had his own agenda. He hadn't cared about preventing Paimon's fall, but he had cared about taking her territory for himself and amassing enough power to hold it in the process. He'd cared very much indeed.

But thanks to the misinterpretation of the prophecy, he hadn't been in position to fight when Paimon had fallen. He

hadn't even had time to gather his legions. Worse, someone else had already claimed it, and he didn't have a clue who it was.

He'd sent spies to scout the territory, but whoever it was had already reinforced the boundary wards, and his minions had yet to successfully breach them. He had no doubt word would spread soon, but in Hell, it was always wise to be the first to know things.

"Cursed fucking witches!" He slammed his fist onto the desk again. This time it cracked in two and fell into his lap. The text he'd been looking through slid down and hit the floor, scattering half the pages in the process.

Valefor leapt to his feet and roared a mighty roar that shook the foundations of his lair. Collecting himself, he looked around the ruins of his office and sighed. He'd just had it reorganized after his last outburst, and now he'd have to do it again. Maybe he was overreacting a bit.

Or *maybe*, if life didn't keep fucking him over, he wouldn't be forced to react this way.

A summons request tugged at the corner of his consciousness, and he sneered. *Murmur.* As if he would leave his lair at the beck and call of that zombie-faced freak. If Murmur wanted to see him, he could damn well come himself.

He made the other demon aware of this by reversing the call of the summons. A battle of wills would ensue. Two rivals would not acquiesce to each other's will without a fight.

But, to his surprise, a wind picked up in the hellgate in the corner almost immediately.

It swirled with greater effect until the tall, looming figure of a demon with proud upward-pointing horns appeared in it. The souls of the damned sworn to Murmur's service swirled around his feet for dramatic effect, the vague outlines of their heads and shoulders just discernible.

Murmur stepped out of the sigil and approached gracefully.

With his dead eyes and deader complexion, the Necromancer had always creeped Valefor out, but he hid it well. He was not without his own power, after all, and they were considered equals. Two Dukes holding counsel.

"To what do I owe the displeasure of your company," Valefor drawled at his guest.

Murmur rested an idle hand on his sword hilt. Paying no mind to the destroyed table and scattered pages, he fixed his bloodshot eyes on Valefor.

"I have something you want."

"Indeed?" Valefor leaned back in his chair and crossed his arms. If Murmur wasn't going to acknowledge the broken table, he wasn't either. "And what is it you think I want?"

"You're obsessed with collecting artifacts of power because you want to become a King. And you want your favorite toy back under your control so you can do it. You know that without him, you're not strong enough to hold a larger territory."

Valefor kept his expression neutral. "I don't know what you're talking about. If I wanted more territory, I could have taken Paimon's."

Murmur smiled. "No, you couldn't have. Because *I* took it, and you wouldn't have stood a chance against me."

His shock got the better of him, and he stood abruptly. "*You* took Paimon's territory? How?"

"Careful preparation."

The corpse looked so damn smug, Valefor wanted to make him regret it. But even as violent thoughts arose, the souls churned around Murmur's feet, reminding him that at present, he wasn't equipped to face this foe.

But he could be. With the right weapon at his disposal, he could defeat anyone.

The bastard was right. Valefor needed his "toy" back.

He dropped back into his chair and steepled his fingers. "So tell me, Necromancer. How can you give me what I want?" That smirk never leaving his face, Murmur reached inside his coat and withdrew a vial full of red liquid, held carefully between his claws. "Allow me to explain exactly what happened to Paimon."

"I already know." Valefor waved a hand in impatience. "She was betrayed by the Hunter and defeated by the bloodborn twins."

"And then the Hunter went rogue." Murmur gave him a pointed look.

He straightened in his chair. "Rogue? Like . . . ?"

"Yes. In fact, Belial himself made a bargain with me to assist him and the witches in their escape and return to Earth."

"Belial?" This was . . . unexpected.

"And what does this vial have to do with anything, you might ask?" Murmur's smile returned. "The liquid within was charged with a simple siphoning spell. I hid it beside the hellgate the Hunter and the witches used to return to Earth. The gate was locked, and I didn't try to track them, as per my agreement. But this siphon . . ." He shook it lightly. "There is more than enough information here to trace the gate's path back to its precise location on Earth. I can't use it, as I vowed I would not . . . but someone else can."

Valefor had frozen, his gaze locked avariciously on the vial. "I have here a direct route to Belial and the other rogues. Tell me, what do you think that information might be worth to others? To Lucifer, for example?" One brow lifted. "And yet, I am here, talking to you."

"Why?" Valefor transferred his gaze to the Necromancer's.

There was no point pretending he didn't want the vial as badly as he did. Murmur knew how desperate he was to retrieve his former weapon and exact revenge. No one stole from him and lived to tell the tale. Nothing that was his was ever surrendered.

And Mephistopheles . . . terrifying, ungodly creature that he was . . . had always been his.

"Why you?" Murmur asked. "Because there is something I want—in addition to ample payment, of course. And you are going to get it for me."

Dear Reader,

IHOPE YOU LOVED MIST AND LILY'S STORY! MIST WAS SUCH A fun character to write with his primal possessiveness and slightly feral mannerisms, and I will always have a soft spot for him.

As you may have guessed already, next up is Meph's book. I'm so excited for this one. You'll finally get to learn about his "terrifying, ungodly" other half—and I don't mean his future heroine, though you could say that as well. We already know she's going to be a handful.

Most of the demons in the Hell Bent series are named after the evil spirits in the *Ars Goetia*, part of the *Lesser Key of Solomon*. (Belial, Paimon, Raum, etc.) There are many interpretations of those old occult texts, and mine is certainly not meant to be anything but an expression of my overactive imagination. Mephistopheles, however, is from the German legend of Faust, and Naiamah (more commonly spelled Naamah) originated from Jewish scriptural texts. Mishetsumephtai's tongue-twister name is entirely my own invention.

Thank you so much for following this series. I'm beyond grateful for your support. If you enjoyed the book, I hope you'll leave a review and/or reach out to me online. I love to keep in touch with my readers.

xx Aurora

P.S. Follow me on social media (@aurora.ascher.author) and join my mailing list so you don't miss out on my next release.

If you want to know what happens when Mist and Lily make that trip to the Gaspé to visit Eligos, check out my slice-of-life short story, *Mistified*. Or you can start from the beginning with Eligos & Natalie's novella, *My Demon Romance*. Both are free and exclusive to my newsletter subscribers.

You can find links to everything on my website.

www.auroraascher.com

Not ready to leave the underworld yet?

Join Aurora's Underworld Patreon to unlock exclusive art and short stories featuring your favorite characters. You'll get access to illustrations by me (some NSFW!) and cute, funny, and sexy tales to relieve your book hangover.

Join a passionate community of romance lovers, and be part of the adventure!

patreon.com/auroraascher

DEMON WITH BENEFITS

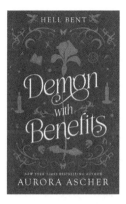

Don't miss Meph and Iris's story!

A hot-headed witch and a lovable bad-boy demon add up to a scorching enemies-to-lovers tale in the latest spicy paranormal romance from instant New York Times bestselling author Aurora Ascher.

They can run from their demons . . .

The jokester of the demon brothers, Meph wears his grin like armor and uses humor as a mask. But lately, his composure has been slipping, especially around her. Iris. The blue-haired witch with a vicious temperament. Something about her soothes the darkness within him . . . but he's not looking for a savior. There's no such thing for someone like him.

But they can't hide forever . . .

Bitter and haunted by her traumatic past, Iris Donovan isn't keen on welcoming demons into her life—even if they're her sister's friends. Especially not teasing, tattooed, Meph, with his red eyes and devilish smile. After a toxic relationship, she's sworn off commitment, and she's not looking for another Mr. Damaged. Yet she can't stop craving what she shouldn't want.

To conquer this monster . . . they must tame it together.

With the return of a deadly enemy, the pain they've been suppressing is exposed, and Meph and Iris can no longer deny their feelings. Before Meph is swallowed by his darkness, Iris must overcome her fears and embrace that terrible part of him . . .

Or lose him forever.

Excerpt from
DEMON WITH BENEFITS

THE DEMONS SOMEHOW TALKED POOR LILY INTO watching a horror movie.

Iris would have felt bad if she wasn't secretly relieved. She would rather watch zombies eat people than a rom-com any day.

The gore took on a whole new meaning in present company, however. In case Iris had forgotten they were demons, she was given a disturbing reminder every time one of them laughed when someone was eaten or disemboweled.

Belial, currently dwarfing the armchair he sat in, would scoff when he didn't find the violence believable, reminding her that he knew from experience.

Raum sat on the floor with his back against the couch arm, Faust cuddled in his lap, the little traitor apparently content to just lie there getting his ears scratched.

It wasn't fair. When the dog sat on Iris's lap, he would wiggle so much she could barely get a grip on him and bite anything he could get his mouth on.

As for the humans, Lily was cringing and hiding her face against Mist, Eva was doing the same on Ash's lap from the other chair, and Iris, who'd seen more than her fair share of horror films, wasn't paying attention at all.

She was more focused on the hard, hot body pressed against her left side.

"Nice," said Meph with a chuckle as a guy was savagely decapitated.

Yep, Meph had decided to show up for movie night.

He'd arrived late, letting himself into Lily's flat like he owned the place shortly after they'd started the movie. Worse, with all the people crammed into this tiny room, there was only one place left for him to sit—beside Iris.

He could have sat on the floor like Raum, but no. Without so much as a glance in her direction, he dropped into the sofa beside her, and the movie continued.

It was awkward and torturous—for Iris. Meph was still acting like she didn't exist.

To make matters worse, it felt like her body was burning up at every point of contact between them. And considering Lily's couch was tiny and Iris was already squished beside her and Mist, there were a lot of points of contact.

Meph's thigh was pressed into Iris's all the way up to the hip, and his shoulders were so wide, she had to lean way over to put a little space between them. Not that it worked.

He seemed oblivious to her struggles—to everything about her, really—while her heart had been racing since the moment he'd sat beside her with that ridiculous grin on his face.

To prove her point, he guffawed loudly as a zombie's head exploded, and Iris squirmed uncomfortably. She couldn't take this. How long was this damn movie? She was practically jumping out of her skin. It felt like hours had passed, but by her estimation they weren't even halfway through yet.

Just when she was thinking up excuses to flee, to her surprise, Meph stood abruptly. "Be right back."

"Want me to pause it?" Lily asked, peeking through the cracks between her fingers.

"Nah, I've seen this movie like ten times." He winked at Lily before stalking from the room, and Iris felt a sudden hot burning in her chest.

It was Lily, she reminded herself. It wasn't like he was flirting with her—

Oh god, was she jealous? The full weight of it hit her. She was jealous because he was turning his charms on someone, anyone, *everyone* else besides her. She got bland looks and blank stares or worse, was completely ignored.

Because that was what she'd asked for.

Suddenly, she couldn't stand it another second. She leapt up from the couch. "I'll be right back too."

"Do you want me to—"

"Nope, I'm good."

She didn't look back because she could feel the knowing looks burning into the back of her head as she disappeared down the hallway. She wasn't sure what her plan was beyond knowing she couldn't take another minute of sitting there pretending everything was fine.

Meph was in the kitchen, palms braced on either side of the sink, head down. He turned around when she came in, and his face darkened.

Iris shifted on her feet. "Just . . . grabbing a glass of water."

Water. Right. That was a good idea.

Trying to look casual, she went to the cupboard and grabbed a glass. By the time she turned around, Meph had slunk away from the sink to the far side of the room as if trying to escape without her noticing. As she filled the glass with tap water and he continued to edge toward the hallway, she realized he had no intention of sticking around.

"Wait," she said, before he could leave.

Iris Donovan, what the bloody fuck are you doing?

He stopped. "What."

Her head came back a little at his sharp tone. "Don't bite my head off." She'd never seen him get mad before. She didn't think she'd even heard him raise his voice.

His eyes narrowed, and he sure looked mad now. He took a step closer, looking primed for a fight. "Why are you always following me around?"

She sputtered. "I'm not—"

"You told me to leave you alone, and that's what I'm doing." He was careful to keep his voice low so the others wouldn't hear over the movie, but there was still plenty of anger expressed in that whisper.

"I don't—"

"What do you want, Iris? Because I'm sick of the mind games."

"I didn't—"

"You made it perfectly clear how you felt about me, so now let me make something else perfectly—"

"Will you let me speak?" she hissed, slamming her glass onto the counter so hard, water sloshed out. She ignored it and stepped closer to him. "I'm sorry, okay? I shouldn't have said that shit to you. It was a bitch move, and I didn't mean it."

His mouth snapped shut, and he looked momentarily stunned, like apologizing was the last thing he'd ever expected her to do. *You and me both.*

"You done?" he asked flatly, not acknowledging her surprise admission at all.

She nodded because she wasn't sure what else to do.

"As I was saying, you made it clear how you felt—"

"I just said I—"

"And *now*"—his glare warned her not to interrupt again—"it's my turn to make myself clear."

Her eyes narrowed, but she nodded again.

"I want to fuck you. I want to rip your clothes off and fuck you until you're screaming. And if you don't start leaving me the hell alone, I'm going to do it. I'm a demon, sweetheart, and I don't practice self-fucking-control. So I'm warning you now, stop following me around trying to make conversation and stop rubbing up against me on that goddamn sofa or you're going to end up on your back under me, got it?"

Her mouth opened and closed, fish-like. She couldn't make a single sound except a subtle choke as she tried to swallow and failed.

And then he spun around and stalked out of the room.

Taking two steps backward, she sagged against the countertop as all the air gusted out of her. Her skin was hot and her pulse was racing.

"Holy shit," she whispered to the empty kitchen.

I want to rip your clothes off and fuck you until you're screaming.

There was no way she was going to get that out of her head. Ever.

She'd known he was attracted to her. She'd known he knew she was attracted to him. The two of them had been dancing around each other for months, but she'd never expected him to just lay it all out there like that.

And damn if it wasn't the hottest thing he could have possibly done. And damn if she didn't want him even more now.

She took a big gulp of water, nearly choked on it, and then groaned at the thought of going back out there with the others. How was she supposed to sit through the rest of that damn movie now?

Look for DEMON WITH BENEFITS coming soon from Kensington Books!

About the Author

© Sergio Veranes

Aurora Ascher is a *New York Times* and *USA Today* best-selling fantasy and paranormal romance author. She loves misunderstood monsters, redeemable anti-heroes, and epic happily-ever-afters. A woman of many creative pursuits, Aurora is also a musician and visual artist. She is currently based between Montreal and British Columbia, Canada. Visit her online at auroraascher.com.